Little Black Everything

Little Black Everything

ALEX COLEMAN

POOLBEG

Published 2009
by Poolbeg Press Ltd.
123 Grange Hill, Baldoyle,
Dublin 13, Ireland
Email: poolbeg@poolbeg.com

13 5 7 9 10 8 6 4 2

A catalogue record for this book is available from the British Library.

ISBN 978-1-84223-353-5

Typeset by Patricia Hope in Sabon 11/15
Printed by
Litografia Rosés S.A., Spain

www.poolbeg.com

Note on the Author

Alex Coleman is married and lives in Dublin with the mandatory pair of writer's cats, who have asked not to be named.

Also by Alex Coleman

The Bright Side

Acknowledgements

First and foremost, I would like to acknowledge the love and support of my other half, who puts up with a hell of a lot and hardly ever threatens divorce.

I'm also grateful to Paula Campbell and everyone at Poolbeg for their guidance, and to Gaye Shortland for her excellent editorial advice.

Special thanks go to Emma Gillies, Linda Darby, Marie Owens, Eithne Howard and my agent, Faith O'Grady, to whom this book is dedicated.

Alex Coleman

To Faith

Chapter 1

Holly Christmas stared into her wardrobe and frowned. Then, as a sort of underline, she issued a deep sigh. The problem facing her was one of colour, or rather the lack of it. Looking into Holly's wardrobe was like looking down a well in the dead of night. She knew that. She'd known it long before the first of approximately four thousand friends, acquaintances and virtual strangers had noted her fondness for black. If any of them had been present at that moment and had spotted the sudden slackening of her features, they might have concluded that she had finally come around to their point of view, that the scales had fallen from her eyes and, at long last, she had realised that she couldn't go through life dressed like a ninja. They would have been wrong. Holly wasn't frowning because she had nothing cheery to wear. She was frowning because the light in her bedroom was poor and the wardrobe was very deep; it was hard to tell what was what in there. If time had been against her, she

1

would have grabbed a few things more or less at random and pulled them on as she hopped down the stairs, the theory being that Black Thing X couldn't possibly clash with Black Thing Y. It was a risky strategy; even with the issue of colour neatly bypassed, some things just didn't go together. There was one particular shirt and trouser combination that somehow managed to make her look both eight months pregnant *and* sixty-seven years of age.

In any event, time wasn't against her now. She had an hour, more, before she had to leave the house, so there was no excuse for not dressing with some degree of care. Moaning softly, she reached into the bowels of the wardrobe and plucked out a few hangers. It was bad enough to have to work at putting together an outfit – an activity that Holly ranked somewhere between weeding the garden and cutting her toenails – but to have to do it for *Kevin*. She threw the clothes on to the bed and rested her hands on her hips.

There was one positive note in all of this, she supposed. For the first time ever, she would be the one doing the dumping.

Almost as soon as the taxi driver moved off into traffic, Holly knew she had made a mistake. She'd noticed the smell the very second she'd opened the door – it was unavoidable, really – but two factors had convinced her to climb in anyway. The first was the nature of the odour. It wasn't quite a stink. There was chip fat in there for sure, together with a hint of body odour and something else, something medicinal; the words "Muscle

Pain" flashed in her mind. Although the combination certainly wasn't pleasant, it had seemed manageable. The second factor was personal. Holly had recently become concerned about the high percentage of her interactions with taxi drivers that ended in screaming matches and/or threats of litigation. If she told this one that she'd changed her mind, he might simply shrug and go on his merry way. On the other hand, like several of his colleagues before him, he might turn around and go for her. The upshot was that she'd taken a deep breath and climbed in. Now, mere seconds into the journey, she realised that the smell was one of those that worked its evil with a cunning subtlety. It wasn't a hammer to the head; it was a stiletto between the ribs. As she looked around, she half-suspected that she could actually see it – a faint yellow mist, creeping through the air.

"Jesus Christ," she said under her breath – but not quite as under her breath as she imagined.

The driver peered at her in the rear-view mirror. "Y'all right back there?"

Holly manufactured a small smile. "Yeah. Just . . . Traffic's mental, isn't it? Even at this time of night."

"Dublin's gone to hell," he sniffed. "Don't get me started."

"Wasn't trying to," Holly replied, meaning it with all her heart.

"You know what else gets on my nerves?" he said.

She dug her fingernails into her thighs and made a noncommittal noise. But he didn't get a chance to elaborate. His attention was diverted by his ringing mobile. He groped around on the passenger seat until he found it and then held it in mid-air just over the gear stick. It had multicoloured lights all around the case that were flashing in time with the ringtone – a giggling baby, speeded up. He didn't answer it; he just held it out there. The only explanation that Holly could come up with for this behaviour was that he was *showing* it to her. He was *proud* of it. Eventually, after what felt like several minutes, he jabbed at it with his thumb. "Yeah?" There was a long pause. Then: "I'm out working for a living, where do you think I am? What do you want? . . . Oh yeah? Go on then." He was one of those mobile phone users who apparently had very little faith in the technology and thought you had to help it along by shouting. There was another pause while the caller said his piece. Holly knew it was a man because he too was a shouter. The voice was muffled but indisputably male. After a few seconds, the taxi driver had a heart attack. At least, that was how it looked and sounded. He collapsed over the wheel, then threw his body back into his seat, then slowly fell forward again, all the while making a noise like a partially blocked drain. The effect on his ability to steer was substantial but short-lived. Holly barely had time to start regretting all the things she hadn't done with her life – would she really never see Rome? – before he regained control of the car. At that point, it became clear that he had been laughing, rather than dying.

"Brilliant!" he roared. "That's a classic . . .Yeah? Go on, so . . . ."

After a brief hiatus, he repeated the heart-attack

routine. This time it went on for a little longer; there were four cycles of the fall-forward/rock-back business. Apart from being annoying in itself, all that movement seemed to be stir up a lot of odour molecules. Holly was overwhelmed by the conviction that someone nearby was frying a sausage in a combination of human sweat and Deep Heat.

"All right," the driver said when he had regained equilibrium. "One more . . . "

This joke, apparently, was less hilarious than its predecessors. It prompted no rocking or wheezing, just a simple "Ha!"

Holly looked out the window at the pedestrians on the footpath. Despite the light rain that was drizzling down on them, they looked so happy, so carefree.

"You're an awful bastard," the driver said then. "But you're a funny one, I'll give you that. Right, I'm away. I'll see you later. Good luck." He hung up and placed his phone back on the passenger seat. "Jokes!" he said brightly to the rear-view mirror.

Holly nodded. "Yeah. So I gathered."

"Helen Keller."

"Excuse me?"

"Helen Keller. The jokes . . . Why was Helen Keller's leg all yellow? Because her dog was blind too."

He got the giggles again to such an extent that he didn't seem to notice Holly's silence. But he recovered soon enough. "How did Helen Keller's parents punish her for swearing? They washed her hands with soap." This time he registered her lack of response and shook his head. "Nah, I didn't really like that one either. Try this one: what was Helen Keller's favourite colour? Give up? D'ye give up? Corduroy."

She maintained her stony silence. He regarded her in the mirror for a moment, a puzzled expression troubling his doughy features. Holly considered her options. They weren't even a third of the way into town yet. And then there was that drizzle to consider . . . She decided not to go nuclear. The subtle approach, that was the way to go.

"Who's Helen Keller?" she asked sweetly.

"Oh! Right. I was wondering. She was this deaf, dumb and blind woman. American, I think she was. They made a movie about her. It was always one of me ma's favourites. All about how this other woman taught her to communicate. Imagine that. Deaf, dumb and blind. Makes you think, doesn't it?"

"God, yeah. Imagine that. Must have been terrible. And her dog was blind too, was that it?"

"Sorry?"

"Her dog? You said she had a blind dog?"

"No, that's the joke. Why was Helen Keller's leg all yellow? Because her dog was blind too."

"Right . . . "

"D'ye not get it?"

"Um . . . No. Not really."

"He pissed on it! The dog pissed on her leg!"

"Because he was *blind*?"

"Yes! He thought it was a tree or something."

"Oh! Right! Yeah!" The simplest course, she decided, was to simply copy what the driver had done. So she rocked back and forth for a while, cackling insanely. "Oh . . . my . . . God," she croaked then. "That's brilliant. A blind woman, sorry, a deaf, dumb *and* blind woman is funny enough on its own, but a blind dog too . . . It's nearly too much."

"Yeah," the driver said uncertainly.

"So the soap one? How does that work?"

Oops – had she gone too far? His suspicions were definitely aroused. He gave her a long look in the mirror, so long in fact that he almost rear-ended the van he was following.

"Shit!" he yelped, standing on the brakes.

"Careful," Holly muttered.

"What are you telling me? You don't get the soap one either?"

Holly looked down. "Sorry. I'm hopeless with jokes."

"Jesus, you sure are. Right, well you know that old thing of getting your mouth washed out with soap? When you said a bad word?"

"Yeah. But you said Helen Keller couldn't talk."

"I know, but sign language – "

Holly exploded. "Oh, I get it! I get it! They wash her *hands*, because, because . . ." She became hysterical. It was a tricky thing to judge, but she thought she pulled herself together again before it became too ridiculous. "Oh, that's great," she said, wiping away a non-existent tear. "That's some funny friend you've got there."

"Yeah. Now you get the other one, don't you? The corduroy one?"

"Wait, gimme a second."

She counted to twenty in her head, slowly. Before she had reached five, the driver had started to drum his fingers on the steering wheel. By ten, he was mumbling darkly to himself.

"Right," Holly said eventually. "She can't see, right? So she doesn't know what a colour is?"

"Exactly. Well done."

"So the joke is that corduroy's her favourite colour because . . . it makes a noise if you scrape it? No, wait, crap, that can't be it – she's deaf too. I give up."

"It's a braille thing, fucking *braille*. She feels it with her fingers."

Holly pulled a face. He had stopped looking at her in the mirror by now, but she thought it would help her stay in character. "Oh," she said in a disappointed tone. "Right. Sorry, I don't think that one's very funny."

He shook his head. "Whatever."

She leaned forward and put her head between the front seats. "It's weird, isn't it, humour? You thought the soap one was no good and I thought the corduroy one was no good."

"Yeah."

"Still, I think we can both agree that there's almost nothing as funny as profound physical disability. Right? Am I right?"

He made a noise, halfway between a snarl and a sigh, and she sat back again.

"I must tell wee Mrs Hickey the Helen Keller jokes," she said. "That's a neighbour of mine. She's in her eighties now but she still lives on her own, blind and all as she is.

She loves a laugh. And she always gets jokes, not like dopey old me."

At last, the driver snapped. "Are you taking the piss out of me?" he barked.

"God, no!" Holly squealed. "What makes you say that?"

He made the noise again; evidently, it was his fall-back in times of uncertainty. The rest of the journey passed in delicious silence. When they reached the pub, Holly thanked him again for the jokes and gave him a tip of six cents. He stared at her for some time. She stared back. Then she got out and he drove away at some speed. She couldn't help but be pleased with the way it had gone. There had been no screaming, at least.

The list of Kevin's habits that Holly found annoying was long and varied but two of the entries near the very top were *He has a fondness for humorous T-shirts* and *He's always calling me "You"*. When she took her seat beside him in the pub and noted the slogan *Also Available in Sober* emblazoned across his chest, her heart sank. When he leaned across, pecked her lips like a chicken who'd spotted a grain and intoned, "Hey, you, how's it going?", it sank a little further. Holly found her attitude to humorous T-shirts confusing. She liked humour as much as the next girl and had nothing specific against T-shirts (black ones, especially). And yet, somehow, the combination of the two made her want to scream. Kevin's were particularly annoying because almost all of them – and he seemed to have a significant collection – featured jokes about

9

alcohol. *If Found, Please Return to Pub. Everyone Needs to Believe in Something – I Believe I'll Have Another Beer. Take Me Drunk, I'm Home Again.* Maybe the effect wouldn't have been quite as grating if he had been a talented drinker, but he most certainly was not. Holly considered herself to be long past her prime, boozing-wise, but she could drink him under the table; had already done so, in fact, twice. On one of those occasions – their third date – his forlorn attempts to keep up had led to his being violently ill. She hadn't witnessed the event first-hand, but she had no doubt that it had happened. He'd excused himself "to take a quick slash" – his exact words – but a certain desperation in his gait as he stumbled, crab-like, towards the Gents had given the game away. Besides, there'd had been nothing "quick" about it; he was absent for almost fifteen minutes.

The second time Holly had comprehensively out-drunk him was just a few days previously, at his cousin's wedding in Offaly. Before they'd even left the church it had become apparent that they were both very nervous; they'd only been going out for three weeks and hadn't spent more than a few hours in each other's company. When the subject came up, Holly said it was good they were being honest about it and proposed the obvious solution. Sadly, Kevin took her excited whisper of "Let's get squiffy and see if we can't have a laugh" to mean "Let's get absolutely stupefied and fall asleep on a table by the dance floor before eight thirty". She found him in just that condition, face-down on his folded arms, when she came back from the loo. One of his shirtsleeves was

10

rolled all the way up to the elbow while the other was still buttoned at the cuff. Evidently he had lost consciousness while halfway through the process of relaxing his dress. She left him to it and headed straight upstairs to her room (they had separate quarters; early days). There, she had a long bath before climbing into a fluffy robe and installing herself in the welcoming folds of her foot-thick duvet. *Toy Story 2* was on TV and she let it wash over her in a warm wave. As sleep approached, she had a serious heart-to-heart with herself. The relationship had been doomed from the start, really. She'd only agreed to the first (blind) date with Kevin because she had recently started to panic. The turning point had been a questionnaire in a magazine; in response to the prompt *Describe your love life in one sentence*, Holly had scribbled *Long periods of loneliness punctuated by brief, usually joyless affairs that are invariably terminated by the other party*. On reflection, her relationship with Kevin had been less of a fling than a flail.

She woke up the next morning with her mind made up. Now, four days later, all that remained were the formalities.

"What'll I get you to drink?" Kevin asked as she wriggled out of her jacket.

"Gin, please. And tonic, I suppose."

He beckoned a passing member of the floor-staff and gave her the order.

"So!" he said then. "Did you have a good day?"

"Yeah. Not bad. Went into town, mooched around the shops a bit. Nothing too exciting. "

"Won't be long now."

"Sorry?"

"Until school starts. Back at it. You may make the most of it now."

"Yeah. What about you? Good day?"

"It was all right. Had the meeting from hell, though. Two and a half frigging hours."

Holly made fists. *Please don't tell me about it*, she thought. *Please. Please. Please.*

"There was only three of us," Kevin began, "so I thought it might be quick enough. You usually need a bit of a crowd in there before things get badly out of hand, y'know? But oh no, Pat had other ideas . . ."

Holly nodded and let his voice fade away into the background. She wasn't at all clear on the specifics, but she knew that Kevin worked as a software engineer; something to do with the banking industry. When he first told her about it, he'd said with an embarrassed smile that it was all profoundly boring, which was certainly true. Holly had never been able to understand why, if he knew full well that it was a tedious subject, he seemed to relish talking about it at such length. It was part of a pattern with him. More than once he had started a joke by saying, "This isn't funny, but I'll tell you anyway . . ." The meeting from hell, predictably enough, spawned the anecdote from hell. Holly tried to tune back in a few times, but every time she did, she caught a phrase – "standardised procedures", "client-centric approach" – that made her tune straight back out again. At one point, she caught herself wondering if it would be poor form to interrupt him mid-flow and give him the bad news slightly ahead of schedule. And then, at last, it was over.

"Sounds awful," she said, quite sincerely. She'd finished her drink and Kevin's pint had seen better days. "Same again?" she asked, pointing at his glass.

He made no reply. At first, she thought he hadn't caught what she'd said. She was about to repeat the question when he exhaled and said, "No. No, I won't. Listen . . . Holly . . . I'm not staying long."

Me neither, she thought. And then the penny dropped. It was written all over his face.

"You're joking me," she gasped.

"I'm sorry. I really am."

"I don't believe it . . ." She struggled for air. The room seemed to be tilting first one way and then the other.

"It's just not working out. But you're a great kid –"

"Kid! I'm twenty-eight! You're only a fucking year older than I am!"

"Don't get upset, please."

She took a calming breath. "I'm only upset," she said, "because I was planning on saying the same thing. Tonight."

Kevin's features rearranged themselves into a smirk. "Holly . . . come on."

She gritted her teeth. "It's the truth."

"All right, all right. If you say so."

"Don't give me that. Don't give me 'If you say so'."

The smirk intensified. "All right then," he said. "It seems that neither of us is happy with where this is going so why don't we just –"

"What's wrong with me?"

The words were out before she'd even realised that they were forming. She almost put her hand over her mouth like a child that had just heard herself swearing in front of Granny. Of all the terrible things that a person could possibly say while being dumped, she had somehow hit upon the very worst. Her mind reeled. If the look on his face was anything to go by, so did Kevin's. She knew she should say something quickly, something funny if possible, or at least cute. But she couldn't think of anything. It was as if the speech centre of her brain had decided to end its long and illustrious career with "What's wrong with me?"

"Okay," Kevin said and clasped his hands his hands together in front of him. "Let me see."

She gaped at him. He was actually going to give her an answer?

"I'm not sure how to put this," he said. "But you're just not like other women. You're so . . . sharp. And blunt."

Holly blinked at him. "Sharp *and* blunt? What the f–"

"Maybe it's your name," he went on. "I suppose it gave me ideas about you. Ideas that turned out not to be true. Not by a long way."

She found her voice again. "Ideas? Like what?"

He shrugged. "You know. 'Holly Christmas'. It sounds so jolly. When I first heard it from Mark, I got this picture in my head. Cheery, chirpy, festive. Happy-go-lucky. You're not . . . Well, you're not any of those things, are you?"

Mark was Holly's neighbour and a friend of a friend of Kevin's. He was the one who had set them up.

"I'm not trying to be mean," Kevin went on. "But you did ask."

Holly considered going for an ironic explanation of the term "rhetorical question" but feared that doing so might make her look like even more of a buffoon than she already did. Instead, she countered with, "You don't think I live up to my stupid bloody name? What kind of –"

"I'm just saying, that's all. I had different expectations. That's my own fault, fair enough. But it wouldn't make any difference what you were called, really."

"Right. If I was called Shitty McNasty, I wouldn't be able to live up to that, even."

He sighed long-sufferingly, in the manner of patient teacher who had been landed with a particularly dull child. "Look, forget about your name. It's not your name. It's your . . . it's your attitude. You seem kind of, I don't know, spiky or something. Always so sarcastic and smart-arsey. Like at the wedding."

"The wedding you fell unconscious at?"

He ignored that. "I just couldn't believe some of the stuff you were coming out with."

"Stuff? What stuff? Give me a for instance."

"Well, there was that business with the priest, for a start."

"The priest, Kevin, was a complete tool. It was supposed to be a celebration. He didn't have to start banging on about how they'd be there for each other when they were *dying*. And he certainly didn't have to go into detail. Beeping machines and nurses and tubes and God knows what. He was upsetting people. Your aunt was mortified. I saw her face."

"Maybe so, but you can't start booing in a church, Holly. It just isn't done."

"I didn't *boo* him, don't exaggerate. I may have made a small noise of protest."

"People were looking at you . . ."

"And smiling! And nodding! Everyone was thinking exactly the same thing, they were all talking about it afterwards!"

Kevin didn't look convinced. "What about the bride's mother? You had a go at her too."

"I didn't 'have a go at her', but she certainly deserved it. She was a snobby bitch. First thing she asked me was my name, second was where was I from and third was what did my father do. It was like something out of the nineteenth century. Nobody talks like that."

"'What does you father do?' 'Not a lot, he's dead.' Nobody talks like that, either."

"I do. To people like her."

"I meant nobody normal."

Holly almost choked. "Nobody *normal*? Now I'm fucking *abnormal*?"

"You swear a lot, too," Kevin added.

Holly sucked in a breath and slowly got to her feet. "But that's all, right? If you think of anything else I need to change, you'll be sure to let me know, won't you?"

Kevin sat back in his seat. "I'm sorry it didn't work

out with us. I really did fancy you, honestly, as soon as I laid eyes on you."

This, apparently, was his attempt to end on an amicable note. Holly wasn't having it.

"You must have been very torn," she said. "'She's sharp and blunt and abnormal and she swears a lot, but then again she's got nice tits.'"

Kevin shook his head. "You see? There it is again. Norm– . . . most women don't say that sort of thing."

There didn't seem to be much she could add. She grabbed her jacket and left.

Chapter 2

Holly's place in Portobello was technically a house, but square footage had not been among its selling (or rather renting) points. She lived there alone, having long since decided that cohabitation was not for her; the extra expense was worth it, she felt. When she arrived back, she saw that Mark and Lizzie next door were still up. She took a moment to get herself together – or at least, reasonably together – and rang their doorbell. As ever, Mark answered. They'd been neighbours for more than four years and in all that time, Holly had never known Lizzie to answer the door. She'd brought it up once, just out of curiosity. Lizzie said it was down to division of labour: Mark answered the door and she did everything else.

"Jesus!" Mark said when he caught sight of her. "Are you all right? You look like shite. Come in, come in."

"I won't," Holly said, doing her best to sound composed. "I just wanted to call and tell you that the great Fix-Me-Up experiment is over. We tried it and it didn't work, so let's just all move on. Never again."

Mark cocked his head. "What? Why, what happened?"

Lizzie appeared in the doorway alongside him then, causing further strain to Holly's neck. Mark was tall (and shaven-headed – he had kind of a Nosferatu thing going on), but Lizzie was taller still, six-two in her stockinged feet. Her hair was almost as short as his. People stared at them on the street.

"What is it?" she asked. "What's wrong?" Her voice was incongruously high-pitched. It lent even her most serious pronouncements a slightly comical edge.

"It's nothing," Holly said. "I just don't want to be fixed up again. Once was enough."

Lizzie issued a stagey gasp. "Did you get dumped?"

Like her husband – and Holly – she had a tendency to be blunt. Holly had often wondered about that. Had one of them changed to be a better fit with the other or had they both started out that way? Was a certain lack of subtlety one of the things that attracted them to each other in the first place? Couples were so mysterious; Mark and Lizzie doubly so.

"Yes. Yes, I did get dumped. Bastard. And just when I was about to dump *him*. My first ever dumping. And he ruined it on me."

Her neighbours exchanged a look. "I don't get it," Mark said. "What's the problem? I mean, if you were going to dump him anyway . . ."

Holly suddenly felt exhausted. "Never mind," she said feebly. "I'm going to bed."

"Nooo," Lizzie squeaked. "Come in, for God's sake. Tell us all. Spill. Unburden. You'll feel better. Or your money back." She stepped aside to clear a path. Mark followed suit.

"There's wine," he said, which was a largely redundant statement. At Mark and Lizzie's, there was always wine. And it was always good stuff. Holly felt her feet beginning to move.

Mark and Lizzie both worked from home, which was some feat given that their place was no bigger than Holly's. Lizzie made jewellery; Mark, who'd lived in France for several years, translated business documents. It was perfectly understandable, Holly thought, that the house should mean a lot to them. But it sometimes seemed that it meant a little too much. They were like a sovereign nation with a population of two, citizens, not of Ireland, but of 27 Hartely Road, Portobello. Holly didn't have a political bone in her body, but at any given moment, she would know, for example, who was Minister for Finance or Health or Education. Mark had once admitted (although that was the wrong word – it was more like a boast) that he didn't know which *party* was currently in. Lizzie was just the same. Holly asked her one day which side she had been on in the Saipan debacle, Roy Keane's or Mick McCarthy's. Lizzie's response was to look up from her newspaper and say, "What the hell's a side pan?" When they spoke about going out on even the simplest errands, they used words like "expedition" and "voyage". Although they were both fond of giving heartfelt speeches about the transforming power of the Internet, they seemed to admire it not because it made information freely available or because it allowed people to communicate across previously unbridgeable gulfs, but because it helped them to get stuff without leaving the house. Their world seemed very small to Holly, but she had to admit that it was filled with vibrant passions. Books were one, bonsai trees were another. Then there was the wine. Mark and Lizzie were the only people Holly had ever known who were actually interested in it, as opposed to being interested in getting drunk on it. They never had less than a couple of dozen bottles lined up in the kitchen and frequently had many more. The only serious criticism they ever levelled against their house was that it didn't have a cellar. They subscribed to several magazines, contributed to innumerable websites, and even, on admittedly rare occasions, ventured out for tastings. When they'd first become friends, as opposed to mere neighbours, Holly had tried to match their enthusiasm if not their expertise, raving goggle-eyed about wines that she might otherwise have described as "nice" and pouring hot scorn on those that, in other company, she would have labelled "not great". She soon gave it up, however. If they didn't agree with her assessment, her hosts would seem personally offended; there were many ugly silences. Generally speaking, Mark and Lizzie were laid-back, entirely affable people, always ready with a joke and a smile. But they had no sense of humour about wine. None. They had once given Holly a taste test, using a tea towel as a blindfold. Could she, after more than an hour's rigorous coaching, finally tell the difference between a Rioja and a Cabernet Sauvignon? "I'm pretty sure," she said, after taking several careful sips of Sample A, "that this is . . . red. Am I right? Red?" There was no response. She removed the tea towel and found them scowling at her, utterly unimpressed. No amount of back-pedalling could undo the damage. They refused to give her another, "proper" go and the evening quickly fizzled out. But those were the early days. Once she got a little experience under her belt, Holly soon realised that, provided you were careful to agree with everything they said and didn't try to belittle their obsession, a person could have a fine old time in Mark and Lizzie's. Better yet, as time wore on, they stopped trying to educate her on the subject of viniculture. They hadn't realised that it was impolite, she suspected – they'd simply concluded that there was no point.

"Go on then," Mark said when they had settled down in the front room. "Tell us."

Holly took a generous mouthful of the Zinfandel he had poured for her and bit down on the compliment that she thought it deserved. It didn't take her long to tell the story; there wasn't much to tell.

"Wow," Lizzie said when she had finished. "I've never come across that one before. 'What's wrong with me?' Jesus . . ."

"Pretty bad," her husband agreed. "What the hell were you thinking of?"

"Thank you, as ever," Holly said, "for your sensitivity. I wasn't thinking, was I? It just came out. I was in shock.

Just when I was about to launch into my little speech. *It's not you, it's me.* I had my lies all ready."

"Don't give up," Lizzie said. "I'm sure we can think of some–"

"Please don't."

Mark rubbed his chin. "I suppose I could give Tea-bag a shout. I think I still have his number, somewhere."

Lizzie almost choked. "Absolutely not. She's desperate, but she's not Tea-bag-desperate."

"Thanks," Holly said, raising her glass. "Who's Tea-bag?"

"You don't want to know," Lizzie assured her. "Mark knew him at university. He shows up every few years looking for a bed for the night."

"What's he like?"

"He's been in prison, Holly."

"Oh. Right. What for?"

Lizzie's mouth fell open, just a little. "What do you mean, 'what for'? Does the word 'prison' not put you off on its own?"

"Yeah," Holly admitted. "Maybe you're right. And anyway" – she shook her head, as if to clear it – "no more fix-ups. I'm serious. My mind's made up."

Lizzie nodded at Mark who hastily refilled their glasses

"Tea-bag's a bad idea anyway," he said. "Even leaving the prison thing aside. I could tell you why he's called Tea-bag and that would put him out of the running on its own."

Lizzie raised a hand to her brow. "Please don't tell her

23

why he's called Tea-bag. It reflects badly on you for knowing him and it reflects badly on me for marrying you. Just drop it."

There was a silent interlude, during which Holly noticed for the first time that music was playing. This was another of Mark and Lizzie's little quirks. They liked only the very quietest of musical acts – Cowboy Junkies, Mazzy Star, Damien Rice – and even those they listened to at almost undetectable volumes. Holly sometimes theorised that it was a way of letting in the outside world on their own terms. If they ever succumbed and finally bought a TV, she liked to imagine that they would cover the screen with gauze.

"You could take lessons of some kind," Mark said.

Holly felt her brow crease to the point of cramp. "Lessons? You think I need How-To-Get-A-Boyfriend lessons?"

"No, no, no, like, I dunno, dance lessons. Ballroom dancing or, what do you call it, the sexy one . . . salsa. Meet new people, all that shite."

"I hate dancing," Holly said with what she hoped was some degree of finality.

"It doesn't have to be dance lessons," Mark replied. "You could take up the guitar or something. Learn a language. Painting. There's loads –"

"This is a crappy idea," Lizzie interjected. "Holly can't do lessons! She's not exactly a joiner-inner, is she? She's more of a standing-at-the-edge-taking-the-piss type."

"Well, that's true," Mark admitted, "but sometimes sacrifices have to be made."

Lizzie still wasn't buying it. "Come on. Can you see her in a painting class? She'd just do angry clowns all the time. And they criticise each other's work in those things! She'd have them all in tears."

Holly noisily cleared her throat. "Hello? I'm still here, you know."

"Sorry," Mark and Lizzie said together. They took simultaneous sips of their wine.

"Listen," Holly said then. "I want to ask you something. That stuff Kevin came out with. About me being sharp and blunt and all that. Not like 'other women', whoever they are. I've heard that sort of thing before. Several times."

"No shit," Mark snorted.

Holly bristled. "From men, I mean. While they were . . . dumping me. You don't think it's anything to worry about, do you? You don't think maybe this is the reason why I'm always . . . why I can't . . . keep a . . ." Her voice trailed off. The thought was too depressing to complete.

There was a horrifying pause. "You're just unusually honest," Lizzie said then.

"You call a spade a spade," Mark added brightly.

"You don't suffer fools gladly."

"You don't suffer them at all, in fact."

They smiled briefly at each other, evidently pleased with their joint performance.

Holly waited for them to say that these were admirable traits and nothing to worry about. After a minute or two, Lizzie broke into a smile and said, "I love this song." She reached out and tickled the back of Mark's hand.

"Yeah," he said. "Lovely."

Holly strained to hear what they were hearing, but she couldn't make it out. It occurred to her that this might be a useful metaphor for something, but she didn't want to think about it too hard.

"I think it's time I went home," she said.

When she opened her front door and stepped inside, Holly found Claude sitting perfectly upright in the centre of the hall. She knew it was silly to attribute human emotions to a mere pet, but she sometimes found it hard to avoid. In this instance, for example, everything about his posture seemed to say, *And what time do you call this?* All he was missing was a wristwatch that he could tap accusingly.

"What's new pussy-cat?" she said as she closed the door behind her.

Claude didn't react. Even when she hunkered down beside him and gave him a tickle behind his left ear (a notorious hot spot of his), he stared straight ahead, utterly immobile.

"Come on. Don't give me a hard time. I'm here now."

He kept up the cold-shoulder act for another few seconds and then finally melted, turning slightly to rub his cheek along the backs of her fingers.

"That's my boy," she whispered. "I knew you'd come round. You like me just the way I am, don't you?"

He looked up at her and issued one of his silent miaows, a sure sign that he needed – or rather wanted – to be fed. Holly went down the hall and into the kitchen.

Claude followed, jogging along by her ankle, already purring. She grabbed a pouch from under the sink and squeezed its contents into his bowl, grimacing slightly at the smell. He got tucked in straight away, pushing his head so far into his supper that he seemed to be in imminent danger of suffocating.

"You're welcome," Holly said. "Seriously – don't mention it."

Claude munched on, oblivious. Now that she had satisfied his desire for food, she knew that he would more or less forget that she existed until some other urge presented itself. That was fine by Holly. It was one of the things she loved about him and cats in general – you always knew were you stood. She left him to it and went back into the living room where she flopped down on the sofa and tucked her legs up underneath her.

There wouldn't be anything worth watching on TV. She knew that, but she grabbed the remote from behind a cushion and switched it on anyway. It took her about thirty seconds to click through every channel and confirm that her original assessment had been correct. "Shite . . . Shite . . . Shite . . . "

Once upon a time, she would have left it on MTV and turned her attention to something else, safe in the knowledge that sooner or later they were bound to play a song she liked. But MTV didn't do music videos any more. Somewhere around the turn of the century, its executives seemed to have decided that people were no longer interested in that sort of thing. What people wanted now was something called "reality" which, as

27

far as Holly could see, involved little else but rich, obnoxious teenagers getting drunk, feeling each other up and declaring things to be either "awesome" or "gay". Holly had always known that one day MTV would make her feel out of touch. But she'd always thought it would do it by featuring music and haircuts and clothes that, try as she might, she just didn't get. She greatly resented being made to feel out of touch because she couldn't understand why a channel called Music Television could get away with showing no obvious interest in music. That seemed unfair, somehow – a moving of the goalposts.

She peered at the shelf suspended underneath the coffee table and saw that it was home to a grand total of one magazine. It proved to be a two month-old copy of *Hello*. A few minutes later, she had flipped through it in much the same way that she'd flipped through the TV channels; it now lay splayed on the floor, where she had dropped it in disgust. She knew that she must have read it before at least once, yet none of the stories that she'd sped past had seemed familiar. What was the point, she asked herself plaintively, of an experience that left no lasting impression on your consciousness and wasn't even fun at the time? And how *could* it be fun? How were pictures of Anthea Turner "relaxing at home" supposed to enrich her life? Why was she supposed to care that Baron so-and-so, eighteenth in line to the Danish throne, had a "lovely new bride"?

Just as she was vowing never to buy the bloody thing again, Claude padded into the room and hopped up

28

beside her. He licked his chops, looking very satisfied with life, and then head-butted her hand to indicate that he was ready for his petting now. Holly absent-mindedly obliged, running her fingers around his neck and periodically tickling him under his chin. After a couple of minutes, he lay down on her feet and fell instantly asleep. She kept petting anyway. As she did so, her mood darkened further still.

She saw herself as if from the other side of the room, a single woman, living alone with a cat, complaining. Maybe this was how it started – the long, slow, slide. Next thing you knew, you were deciding that your cat might be lonely and you should probably get him a little friend. The two of them turned out to be so cute together that you went ahead and got a third. On those rare occasions when you brought boyfriends home, they poked fun and you laughed along. It was no big deal and you knew the cats would be there long after the boyfriends had gone. Meanwhile, you got more and more angry about the crap they printed in magazines and the crap they showed on television and the crap they talked on the radio and the crap they sold in the shops. Everything was going to pot – how come you were the only one who could see it? You got the blues for quite a while at one point – doctors were involved – but you cheered yourself up by getting another cat. Number four seemed to add a certain something. Two little couples, you told yourself – like Abba. One day you found yourself writing to an editor because you liked a laugh as much as the next person, but something-or-other had gone too far. Your letter didn't get published, but you felt better because you had taken a stand; you had called a spade a spade. Somebody had to and it sure as hell wasn't going to be this generation coming up, was it? They didn't give a damn about anything, just standing around, laughing at nothing, calling you names when you went past. When you were their age, people had a little thing called respect . . . You had five cats by now. They took a lot of looking after, but they were worth it, weren't they? They were good company, especially at night.

And then one day you realised that you hadn't been on a date for a long, long time. And you looked in the mirror and you could see why. And you weren't twenty-eight any more, you were forty-eight. You were a forty-eight-year-old woman who lived alone with a bunch of cats and you spent your life giving out. Holly dabbed a tear from her cheek and looked at Claude with a sense of terror.

Back to school on Monday.

Chapter 3

When people who had just met Holly learned that she was a teacher, they didn't bat an eyelid. If they stuck around and got to know her, however, sooner or later they would give her a curious look and ask her to explain why. The question was always delivered in the same way, in a tone of incredulity. They weren't looking for a run-down of the attractions and benefits of the teaching life; they were wondering why she personally would do it. The words "don't seem the type" were invariably added somewhere. Holly had a stock answer: she was sick of being surrounded by morons and teaching seemed to be the simplest way to do something about it. This usually raised a laugh and, as often as not, a sigh of relief; suddenly, everything made sense again. Holly had given the stock answer so many times over the years that she could no longer remember if it was a joke or not.

When she first started teaching at St Brendan's in Harold's Cross, she was delighted with it. The students

– the majority at least – were pleasant and had a passing interest in learning. Her colleagues were like people anywhere. Most of them were perfectly nice and a handful were insufferable. The principal was a friendly, slightly manic creature named Ursula McCarthy. It didn't take Holly very long to discover that she was top dog in name only. The real centre of gravity for the teaching staff was a woman named Eleanor Duffy. Eleanor was primarily an English teacher, although she dabbled (as she invariably put it) in geography and history. She was in her late forties, a little on the short side, a little on the tubby side, and forever smiling. She'd been at St Brendan's for her entire career and knew it inside out. Everyone liked Eleanor, which was perfectly understandable; she was easy to like. Holly thought of her as the sort of person who made you try a little harder in everything you did – the way you carried yourself, the way you did your job, the way you stirred your coffee. You wanted her to notice you and you wanted her to be impressed by what she saw. But life around Eleanor wasn't all roses. By the end of her first month, Holly had formed a theory; the more she looked for evidence, the more evidence she found. The bottom line was that her colleagues – not all of them, but most of them – had a label. The label was first applied, and then repeatedly reinforced until it stuck, by Eleanor. The thing about Peter Fogarty was he did magic. The thing about Greg Tynan was he used to live beside Colin Farrell. The thing about Ursula McCarthy was she couldn't boil an egg. The thing about Louise Dillon was she was always moving house. The thing about Larry Martin was he knew a lot about old movies. The thing about Enda Clerkin was he collected antiques. As soon as the truth dawned, Holly began to worry about her own fate. Would she be getting a label of her own? And if so, what would it be? *The thing about Holly Christmas* . . . Her initial assumption was that Eleanor would go with the obvious: the thing about Holly Christmas was that she was called Holly bloody Christmas. And, of course, comments were made, jokes were cracked, questions were asked, some of them by Eleanor. Holly did her best to respond pleasantly – initially, at least – and concluded that it could be worse. But then she noticed to her surprise that the subject of her name was more or less dropped (by the teachers, at least; the students never quite got over it). It got an airing again in December, naturally enough, but no more than she would have expected. By the time school broke up for her namesake holiday, Holly was beginning to think that maybe she would be one of the lucky ones and would remain unlabelled. It was a pleasing thought, one that soothed her just a little through the ragged torment of the yuletide season.

Then, one morning in the first week of the new year of 2006, a little amber light appeared on the dashboard of her car. She consulted the owner's manual and discovered that it related to the Engine Management System. Somehow, this news filled her with her horror. She hadn't expected good news – it was hardly going to turn out to be the *Everything's Okay* indicator – but still, the word "Management" sounded terribly ominous.

Holly had never been particularly car-proud and had cheerfully ignored many a knock and rattle in the past, but she lost no time in getting the battered Micra round to the nearest garage.

And that was where she met Dan.

It was one of those modern, family-friendly establishments with a waiting area that featured a coffee dock, a selection of comfortable chairs and a kids' toy box. Dan was a sort of receptionist. He sympathised with her recent difficulties and seemed genuinely tickled by her fear that the car was about to blow up.

"An explosion is unlikely," he told her. "But I couldn't rule out an implosion. Worst case scenario is the formation of a black hole that consumes the Earth, then the nearest planets and finally the sun itself. This is an urgent case if ever I saw one. I'll get someone on it right away."

Holly liked that. And she liked his face too. It was the face of a man who knew how things worked – things both mechanical and physiological. They chatted for a few minutes and might have chatted for a few hours if a queue hadn't started to form. She reluctantly stepped aside and took the seat with the best view of the reception desk. When her car had been seen to – his promise of prompt attention had not been an idle one – she took the keys from him and made sure their fingers touched. He smiled. She smiled back. They were having a moment, she was sure of it, but she didn't know what to do next. Eventually, she concluded that just standing there smiling was making her look like a mental patient, so she reluctantly said goodbye and slipped away to collect the car, which was now parked round the side. She had just got herself settled down in it – hadn't even turned the key in the ignition – when her mobile rang. It was Dan.

"I got your number from the form," he said. "Look – a braver man than me might have said this to your face, but there were too many people around and I didn't want anyone to see me crying if it didn't go well. Would you like to go out for dinner some time? Some time like tonight, maybe?"

Holly held the phone away from her face and issued a muted squeal of delight. "Well," she said, "my schedule's pretty packed. But I'm sure I could make room."

He named a time and a place and she said she'd be there. Then his voice dipped low. "There's one other thing," he said. "When I was getting your number, I couldn't help but notice your surname. I'm sure you're sick to death of talking about it. I just want you to know that I won't bring it up over dinner tonight or over any other dinner we might have in the future."

A vivid thought flashed in Holly's mind. It was not like any regular thought. It seemed to have colour and fragrance and, somehow, texture. The thought was this: *I am falling in love.* It took a while, maybe a couple of weeks, before she stopped worrying that she might be imagining things. Dan, apparently, was a mind-reader. At every turn, he knew exactly what to do and say to make her fall a little bit further, a little bit harder. He pulled her chair back in restaurants but took it for granted that she knew how to change a plug. He complimented her on her eyes and, once in a while, on her ass. He asked her opinion on things and when he thought she was talking rubbish, he told her so – then seemed to greatly enjoy her fighting back. He sent her sexy text messages late in the evening when he was sober but not in the middle of the night when he was drunk. He gently mocked the limitations of her wardrobe but said it wasn't a big deal because no one could wear black like she could. When he didn't want to see her, he told her so; he didn't show up under duress and then sigh and fidget all night long, looking at his watch. He made her laugh, which was good, and *she* made *him* laugh, which was better. In marked contrast to everyone else she'd ever gone out with, he seemed to get a real kick out of her rants about the endless torrent of mouth-breathing nitwits with whom she was obliged to share a planet.

Orla and Aisling, her oldest and closest friends, had always been harsh judges of her romantic choices (few and far between as they were), but they liked Dan right from the start. Aisling liked him a little too much, in fact. She rang Holly at seven o'clock one Saturday evening, already cocktail-tipsy.

"There's something bugging me," she said, "and I want to get it out in the open."

"Go on," Holly said, intrigued.

"Okay. Okay. Okay, the thing is, I seem to have developed a bit of a thing for Dan. There have been . . . dreams. And daydreams. I'm not doing it on purpose. But I feel like shite about it and I want to get it out in the open."

Aisling had been mistaken for Jessica Biel on at least two occasions that Holly knew of and had no trouble garnering male attention. As a result, she had very high standards indeed. Holly took this drunken confession as a serious stamp of approval and tried to keep the smile out of her voice as she graciously accepted it. Apart from Orla and Aisling, there was only one other person whose opinion really counted, and that was Holly's mum. Mrs Christmas lived in permanent fear that her daughter would wind up on the loftiest and hardest to reach of all shelves and as a consequence had standards every bit as lax as Aisling's were strict. Even so, Holly was amazed by her mother's reaction to Dan. At the end of their first meeting, she hugged him for what seemed like half an hour and then called him "son" – twice. Holly spent the journey back to hers feverishly vowing to Dan that her mum used that word all the time and hadn't meant anything by it.

"I mean, you don't have to worry. We won't have to get married this weekend or anything! Ha! Ha!"

Dan grazed her thigh with the tips of his fingers. "Just as well," he said. "I have things to do around the house at the weekend. I'm free next weekend, though."

Holly almost crashed into a skip.

Only once before in her entire life had she found herself going out with someone on Valentine's Day. It was at university. His name was Paul. He didn't bother calling around (or ringing or texting) on the fourteenth but showed up the next day with a card, inside which he had written his name in block capitals with a red pen. There was no message. It didn't even say, "*From PAUL*", much less "*Love, PAUL*". It just said, "*PAUL*". She hadn't minded particularly, because she hated the concept of Valentine's Day. It was so tacky, so unspeakably vulgar. She had said as much to Dan and he'd agreed, just as she'd expected he would. When the day dawned and she saw that her only post was a gas bill, she genuinely didn't mind. She left for work feeling free and easy. Her colleagues knew she had a boyfriend, of course; she could barely get through a sentence without mentioning him. They were also aware that she was almost always single and that her six weeks with Dan constituted her longest ever relationship.

She wasn't surprised, then, when the questions started as soon as she arrived at school. What, no card, no flowers? Surely Superboyfriend couldn't forget, could he? Holly flapped them away.

"I've discussed this with Dan," she said, "and we are of one mind on the subject. Valentine's Day is for suckers, and tasteless ones at that."

By the time she arrived home again, however, she was beginning to wonder; it was a little odd that Dan hadn't called at all, if only to join her in laughing at the idiots who at that very moment were jammed shoulder-to-shoulder into terrible Tex-Mex restaurants, faking smiles as they exchanged cards on which fluffy teddy bears proclaimed their wuv. Then again, she hadn't just casually pooh-poohed the idea of Valentine's Day, she had torn it apart and set fire to the pieces. The phrase she'd used to describe those who found it amusing, or worse romantic, was "emotionally retarded". Why on earth would Dan so much as dip his toe in it after hearing that sort of thing? He'd have to be nuts. She was being silly. Shaking her head and sighing, she got a bottle of wine from the kitchen and poured herself a half-glass. Claude appeared just as she finished it, and presented himself for petting. He'd been out and about, judging by the coldness of his paws. Holly hoped he hadn't brought home any little presents. She got the impression that he wasn't much of a hunter – he had trouble cornering cotton balls on the bedroom floor – but once in a while she went into the kitchen and found a dead mouse by the catflap. That, she could do without. The phone rang at about half past ten.

"Listen," Dan said. "We have to talk. I've met someone else. I didn't mean to. I didn't go looking for her. But now that I've got to know her a bit, I can see that you're . . . well, you're all wrong for me. I need someone a bit more . . . I don't know, bubbly. Someone not quite as prickly. It's over with us. I'm sorry. I hope there'll be no hard feelings."

The whole thing took about three minutes. For more than an hour after she hung up, Holly just sat there, frowning and blinking, blinking and frowning. The only sound was Claude's purring and the occasional hum of a passing car. Eventually, she managed to move but only as much as was necessary to pour a fresh glass of wine, a full one this time – full to the point of overflowing. She called in sick the next day and the day after that. When she did return to work, she was determined that she would not shirk the issue. If someone mentioned Dan, she would tell them the truth. She'd been dumped again. Turned out he'd been steadily going off her and she hadn't noticed. No big deal. Someone did mention Dan. It was Eleanor Duffy. She mentioned him as soon as Holly walked into the staff room.

"Well," she cooed, "did he come up with the goods for Valentine's Day? Or did he take you at your word and avoid the whole thing?"

Holly hadn't even taken her coat off yet. She cleared her throat and started to explain the situation. But she didn't get very far. The tears began to flow almost immediately. Eleanor stepped forward and took Holly's hand in both of hers. She wore a peculiar expression on her face. There was sympathy in there – lots of it – but there was something else too. And just like that, Holly knew. It would be a while before it was confirmed, but she knew right there and then. She had her label: the thing about Holly Christmas was she had terrible trouble with men.

Chapter 4

On Saturday afternoon while she was on her hands and knees tidying up under the kitchen sink, Holly received a phone call. It was Orla.

"Is this a good time?" she asked. "I don't want to be getting in the way if you're still upset. Are you? Are you still upset?"

Orla had one of those husky Kathleen Turner-esque voices. It didn't lend itself easily to sympathy, but she was doing her best. She knew about Kevin, of course. Holly had texted her and Aisling that morning but had added (melodramatically, in retrospect) that she wanted to be left alone for a while. She wasn't surprised to find that her instruction had been ignored.

"No," Holly whimpered. "I can barely function. I don't what I'm going to do."

There was a long pause. "Are you taking the piss?"

"I can't eat. I can't sleep. I'm a wreck. What's to become of me? Help me, Orla! Help me! Pluck me from this sea of pain!"

"Right. So you're fine. I get it."

In truth, Holly was far from fine, but she was determined not to show it. "You wouldn't believe how many different Stain Devils I have."

"What?"

"Sorry, I'm tidying under the sink. I have about twenty different Stain Devils. I'm just looking at them here. Every couple of weeks I get a stain on something and I buy one and I find it doesn't work and I throw it under the sink. And Mr Muscles. I have one, two, three, four different Mr Muscles. Two jumbo bottles of bleach. *Jumbo*, mark you."

"Holly, are you bored?"

"I'm distracting myself, that's all."

"From what?"

"School, for one thing. Back on Monday."

"Jesus. You sound more like a pupil than a teacher."

"It's going to be terrible. They'll drive me nuts inside an hour. Eleanor Duffy will make sure of it. 'Still single, are you? Aw!'."

"It'll be grand."

"It'll be terrible."

"Grand."

"Terrible."

"Grand."

"Terrible."

"Are we going out tonight or what?"

Holly and Orla had an unspoken agreement that, whenever possible, it should always be one of them who organised social forays. Aisling simply couldn't be trusted on that score. On those occasions when she was first on the phone making suggestions, the three of them invariably found themselves in a restaurant where you had to cook your own food or a pub that served only blue drinks. Aisling was a slave to fashion not just in the strictly sartorial sense – although she was certainly that – but in all things. If a venue was even vaguely trendy, that was good enough for her. No concept was too ridiculous, no cover charge too exorbitant. A single mention in a weekend supplement was enough to get her squealing, pleading and using phrases like "anybody who's anybody". The best approach, Orla had once explained to Holly, was to speak to her as if she'd been saying all week that she didn't want to go out, but you weren't going to take no for an answer. You'd chosen a venue and that was that. No ifs, no buts, none of her nonsense. Wouldn't be the same without her, and so on. If you did it just right, she went all gooey and said she wouldn't miss it for the world. On this occasion, Orla had told Aisling that the night, nay, the whole weekend would be ruined for herself and Holly if she didn't join them in Outer Mongolia on Dawson Street at eight. Aisling had agreed immediately and promised that she would do her very best to be on time. She wasn't, of course, but she was only fifteen minutes late, which was good going by her standards. Holly and Orla had shared a taxi and, because they knew that Aisling's promises weren't worth a damn, had been in no particular rush themselves. In the end, they met at the doorway right under the bouncer's nose. Aisling and Orla claimed that this was "a good sign" that augured well for the night ahead. Holly was quick to pour cold water on this idiocy – signs, indeed – and got two dirty looks for her trouble.

Without exception, all of Holly's previous visits to Outer Mongolia had involved a great deal of standing around. It was one of those places that had space for three hundred people and seating for thirty-five. It was more of a shock than a surprise when, within seconds of their arrival, a booth emptied right in front of them.

"Lookit!" Orla screamed, elbowing Holly so hard that the wind was forced out of her. "They're leaving! They're leaving!"

"I can see that," Holly replied. "Unfortunately, I have to go to the hospital now because I've got three cracked ribs."

"What?"

"Nothing."

They maneuvered themselves into position so aggressively that they more or less limbo-danced underneath the people who were getting up to go. There was competition for the seats from several sources but none of their rivals had enjoyed their positional head start.

"I don't believe it," Aisling said when they had established territorial dominance. "This is a first. I've never seen the place from this angle."

"Right," Holly said. "Who's going to the bar? And what are we drinking?"

"I'll go," Orla replied. "And vodka."

"Vodka," Aisling agreed. "But I'm not really drinking tonight."

Holly experienced a brief rush, somewhere between excitement and fear. It was going to be a vodka night. She made a mental note to drink two pints of water as soon as she got home, knowing full well that she would forget. The Stoli went down surprisingly well and before long they were on the far side of giddy, laughing too loud, all jabbering at once, covering at least two subjects at any given moment. Although the music, as usual, was playing at a volume that made you think they didn't want you there, Holly was surprised to find that she not only recognised but actually liked quite a lot of it.

They did their usual catching up. Aisling reported that she had made good on her long-standing threat to take up yoga. Every time she'd mentioned it in the past, and that had been almost weekly, she'd spoken loftily about her desire to improve her muscle tone or, if she was feeling especially pretentious, get in touch with her body. It now emerged that a large part of her motivation, somewhere in the region of ninety-five per cent, had been of a more social nature. But it seemed that she had been sold a pup. Over and over again, she had read that yoga was seriously popular among men. Well, not the class she'd joined. There was precisely one man, and he was a dead ringer for Christopher Biggins. He'd approached her after their first session and informed her, as he wiped the sweat from his face, that she had a really nice arse on her. In his opinion, it was the second best in the whole class.

Orla had troubles of her own. Her parents had been on bad terms for almost a fortnight and the past couple of days had seen a dramatic escalation in hostilities; now, in their thirty-fifth year of marriage, they were sleeping in separate bedrooms. Holly and Aisling found this hard to believe and pressed for details. At heart, the dispute was financial in nature, although Orla's mother believed that money was only part of it. What had really upset her was the deception, the betrayal of marital trust. The bottom line was that a husband who would secretly spend two thousand euros on a fancy new computer just so he could pretend to be a fighter pilot might be capable of almost anything.

Holly limited herself to bitching about the horrors that awaited her in the school, or rather in the staff room. Aisling and Orla did their best to be sympathetic at first but soon lost patience. They had heard these complaints after every school break for the past several years and they were all out of things to say.

As ever, there was plenty of work talk. Aisling worked as a PA to the Creative Director of an advertising agency on Fitzwilliam Square. Orla was the deputy financial controller of a small haulage company in Clondalkin. Each of them seemed to think she had the worst job in Ireland and regularly tried to outdo the other with tales of office horror. Although she would never have said as much, Holly was firmly of the opinion that Orla had more to complain about than Aisling. They were some monsters in Aisling's company by all accounts, but at least they were young and trendy monsters. On top of the everyday trials of working life, Orla had to put up with a boss who owned three cassette tapes – two Roger Whittakers and a Nana Mouskouri – which she had been playing one after the other in their shared office every day for four years. This time they got into a discussion about which one of them did the most overtime. At first, it was competitive but friendly. Points were conceded. Jokes were cracked. After a few minutes, however, the tone abruptly changed. Orla was the one who changed it. For no apparent reason, her comments and glances suddenly acquired an edge. Aisling didn't seem to notice at first, but she cottoned on eventually and immediately hardened her own responses. Twice, Holly felt the need to step in with a gag before one of them said something she would regret. Just when she was beginning to worry that they were headed for a real argument, the subject changed (to the Eurovision Song Contest, admittedly, but that was still an improvement as far as Holly was concerned).

And then it was Aisling's turn to go to the bar. She'd been gone for about twenty minutes when Holly and Orla started to wonder. She wasn't in the loo, they were sure, because she'd just been. And there was no way it could have taken her this long to get served; they knew from their own rounds that the bartenders were all male. Aisling could stand around all night waiting for female staff to notice her, but when there were men involved, even at the most crowded of bars, her waiting time could usually be measured in seconds.

Orla had a vivid imagination when it came to potential trouble. Before long she was gripping Holly's forearm and painting a luridly bloodstained picture.

Holly didn't get quite as carried away. They probably shouldn't have started talking about abduction and murder, she pointed out, until they'd at least got up off their arses and looked around a bit. Then again, that would mean giving up their seats, almost certainly for nothing. This part didn't go down well. For all they knew, Orla sniffed, Aisling was currently waking up in the boot of some lunatic's car and all Holly cared about was their *seats*? Holly started to argue, then paused. Suppose Aisling did end the night in more than one piece? Bad enough to be left with a solitary best friend instead of two but to have that best friend saying, "I told you so" for the rest of your life . . . She gave in. No sooner had she done so than Aisling appeared, bearing drinks and looking entirely unharmed. Orla looked relieved for all of two seconds. Then she looked angry.

"Where the hell where you?" she asked, shouting even more loudly than was necessary to make herself heard.

Aisling shrugged. "Nowhere."

"Did it ever occur to you that we might be sitting here worrying?"

"No. Not really."

Orla stared at her, nostrils flaring. "Brilliant. Just brilliant. Won't bother wondering next time, so. You can go and get yourself killed, if that's what you want."

"She's been running *The Silence of the Lambs* in her head," Holly explained, hoping to lighten the tone. It didn't work.

There was something of a Mexican stand-off for a

couple of seconds. Then Aisling retook her seat and distributed the drinks. Holly could tell by the expression on her face that she had been chatted up. She could easily picture the scene – the hair-flips, the giggles, the back-arches, the sly smiles.

"I got talking to these two boys," she said. They were always "boys", Holly had often noticed, whether they nineteen or thirty-seven. "I just couldn't get away from them, honestly."

"Yeah, I bet you tried really hard," Orla said. "We all know how you hate that kind of thing. *Oh no! Boys! Run!*"

Holly froze, once again surprised not so much by the words but by the viciousness with which they were delivered. What was wrong with her? Was she trying to start a row? Aisling's latest drink was halfway to her lips. She left it there and turned to check if Orla was joking. Orla glanced away immediately. Then Aisling turned to Holly and raised both eyebrows.

Holly did her best to mouth the words "*She was worried*" but wasn't at all sure that she got the message across. "Were they lookers?" she asked in an attempt to move things on quickly.

"Actually, yes. One more than the other, granted. But even number two wasn't bad. Anyway, they're not hanging around for long. They're going on to a party. Wanted to know if we're interested."

"Oh yeah? What kind of a party?"

"Birthday," Aisling replied. "Johnny's sister. He's the better-looking one."

"Is it somewhere out of the way?"

"Not really. Ballsbridge."

"Ooh," Holly said. "Sounds all right to me. And it's a girl's party so it shouldn't be too disgusting." She had no interest whatsoever in attending the event in question. But she was afraid that if they stayed put, things would fizzle out, or worse, go on fire. A change of venue might be just the ticket. She leaned across Aisling and tried to involve Orla, who'd been making a point of staring straight ahead, pretending not to be listening any more. "What do you think, Orla? Party in Ballsbridge? There'll be at least two men, one of whom is good-looking and one of whom isn't bad, which is probably code for Herman Munster, but still?"

Orla responded with a one-shoulder shrug.

Undeterred, Holly tried again. "Come on! A party! Who doesn't like a good party?"

"You don't, for one," Orla pointed out. "You hate them. I've never been to a party with you where you didn't end up standing in the corner with your arms folded, giving out shite about the music or the people or the carpet or the –"

"This one will be different!" Holly countered. "Come on. Whaddayasay?"

There was a brief pause, just long enough for them to overhear a passing hipster scream, apparently at no one, that he was going to get all fucked up and dance, dance, dance.

Then Orla said, "You two go if you like. I'm gonna head on home." There was no anger in her voice. But neither was there any indication that she was merely tired. The tone was entirely flat.

"Ah, Orla, come on," Holly said. "Don't be like that."

A second or two went by before Aisling added, "Yeah, we're only getting started."

"No, honestly." The monotone persisted. "I'm off. You two go to the party. I'm sure you'll have fun."

She didn't add the words "without me" but they seemed to hang in the air regardless. Holly heard Aisling clear her throat with a spiky little cough and guessed that trouble was coming. She got in quickly.

"Well, if you're sure. You're not sick or anything, are you?"

This was a sort of invitation. It was supposed to afford Orla an opportunity to clear the air. She could say something along the lines of "Don't mind me, I'm in a funny humour" and leave on a reasonably pleasant note while Holly and Aisling cocked their heads to one side and made sympathetic noises.

Orla declined the invitation. She shook her head and said, "No. I'm not sick. I'm just going, that's all."

"Oh," Holly said. "All right then." Now that it had no tactical value, the party had lost all appeal. She turned to Aisling. "Maybe it's not such a great idea for any of us."

"Aw!" Aisling complained. "But I was just starting to get –"

"Don't bother, Holly," Orla said as she got to her feet. "You're wasting your time. She has the scent now."

Aisling glared up at her. "Scent? What scent? What are you talking about?"

Orla leaned down and more or less spat her next sentence: "The scent of men."

"What the hell d–"

"We all learned a long time ago, Aisling, that if there are men around, it's a bad idea to stand in front of you. A person could get trampled on."

This got on Holly's nerves more than anything that had preceded it. The word "we" suggested that this was something that she and Orla had discussed before. Worse still, it *was* something that she and Orla had discussed before – but only in jest. She braced herself, feeling certain that Aisling was about to turn on her. That didn't happen. Aisling was entirely focussed on Orla. For a moment, it seemed certain that things were going to deteriorate still further. Then Orla gave a small nod, as if she had received some instructions on a hidden earpiece. She grabbed her bag and took off without another word. As soon as she was out of sight, Holly and Aisling turned towards each other and pulled identical faces.

"What the fuck?" Holly said.

"What the fuck *indeed*," Aisling agreed. Her strange emphasis on the last word had made her sound like a Jane Austen character, albeit a foul-mouthed one. "She's been poking at me all night, don't say you didn't notice. And that wasn't the first time lately."

Holly was reluctant to take sides. "There was tension. I saw that all right. But I couldn't tell you who started it."

"She did!"

"All right, maybe she did." Holly thought for a moment. "Aisling, listen. This is the kind of thing that will fester. You have to go after her."

Aisling shot her a look. "I'm not going anywhere. You go after her if you want."

"What's the point in that?" Holly asked. "It's you she seems to have a problem with."

Aisling fumed for a few seconds. "So, let me get this straight: even though she insulted me –"

"Hurry up," Holly pleaded. "She could be in a taxi by now."

In truth, Holly had simply been chancing her arm. She was really quite surprised when Aisling got to her feet and made off in the direction of the door. Her surprise deepened when there was no immediate return trip. Fifteen minutes slipped by. It was entirely possible, of course, that they were simply arguing on the street, but Holly doubted that they'd be able to keep it up for so long; one of them was bound to have stormed off by now. She sipped her drink and waited. Then Aisling emerged from the crowd and slumped into her seat again.

"Well?" Holly said.

Aisling took a hefty drink. "She's depressed."

"What?"

"Depressed. And she used that word – 'depressed'. People never say they're depressed. They say they're feeling down or they're under the weather or they've got the blues or something. You always know what they mean, but still – to come right out and say it. I took that to be a bad sign."

"What's she depressed about? Is it something specific?"

"Yeah. It's boyfriends. The lack of them."

"Oh."

"Yeah. Oh."

Orla's almost total lack of experience with men was a subject that came up every so often between Holly and Aisling. They never got very far with it. Their pet theory was that she'd been scarred by the experience of losing her virginity in an alley behind a chipper at the age of fifteen and had been put off men for life. The obvious flaw with this idea was that her subsequent celibacy was completely involuntary.

"What did she say specifically?"

"She said it had been on her mind for a long time – in a serious way, I mean – and that she was finding it hard to be around . . . uh . . . me."

"Because you're so gorgeous and all the fellas –"

"Because I . . . don't have any trouble on that score. Now, let's skip that bit. I feel like a complete wagon as it is."

"Huh. So she has no problem being around me."

"For fuck's sake, Holly!"

"Sorry, sorry. You're right. This isn't about me."

"Correct. It isn't. The point is, what can we do?"

"Exactly."

"Yeah."

"Exactly . . . "

"Hmmm."

They fell silent.

"We've had this conversation before, of course," Aisling said eventually.

"We sure have."

"'You've got so much going for you.' All that rubbish."

"Yup. We've done that. Didn't work."

"No."

There was another silence. This one was longer and deeper than its predecessor.

"All right," Holly said when she finally grew tired of it. "There's something that needs to be said here. And I'm going to say it."

Aisling gulped. "OK."

Holly guessed that she knew what was coming and that spurred her on. "I'll put it as kindly as I can . . . Orla has . . . let herself go."

"Yes."

The response came so quickly and was so emphatic that Holly was further emboldened. "I don't mean that in a nasty way."

"No. Of course you don't."

"And God knows, I'm no Christy Turlington myself."

"But it has to be said . . ."

"It has to be said . . . she's not making the most of what's she got."

"You're right, Holly. You're so right. It was the first thing that came to my mind too. It's all well and good to go 'Boo-hoo-hoo, I never get a second look' but, for the love of God, lose the baggy jumpers and the grotty runners."

"Get your hair cut by someone who's done it before."

"Put on some make-up once in a while."

"Cut down on the chip butties."

"Holly!"

"What? I thought we were agreeing."

"We are, I suppose, but I was going to leave it at clothes and make-up, not . . . y'know."

"She's piling it on, Aisling. You know it as well as I do."

"Well . . . "

"Let's drop the sisterhood crap. Tough love, that's what's needed here."

"OK. You go first. This is right up your alley."

Holly felt her shoulders tense up. "Meaning what?"

"Giving out. You're an expert."

"Excuse me. I don't spend my whole life moaning and sniping, y'know."

"Yes, you do."

She delivered the line with such simplicity and innocence Holly had no doubt that she wasn't trying to be funny.

"Anyway," Aisling went on, "we can talk about this later. Now, you want to go to this party or not?"

"No. I really, really don't."

"Let's get another drink then."

Holly's eyes flitted around for a moment. "I think maybe we should call it quits. I'm not in the mood any more. Let's just give her a chance to get away and then go ourselves."

"She's gone now," Aisling said. "I saw her into a taxi."

"All right, then," Holly said. "Let's go."

Aisling responded with a frown and a slow, sad shake of her head. Then she grabbed her jacket from the back of their seat and groped around under the table for her bag. Holly did likewise. They adjusted straps and buckles and headed for the exit.

Chapter 5

On the first morning of the new school year, Holly was alarmed to find herself briefly paralysed from the waist down. The problem arose when she was leaning against the kitchen counter, draining a glass of orange juice. Claude had just come through his catflap and was diligently washing himself in a patch of sunlight on the floor. Even though she was already late – the getting out of bed process hadn't gone particularly well – she allowed herself to be mesmerised by him. He looked so calm and untroubled. Ignoring the fact that he almost always looked calm and untroubled, she couldn't help but draw an unpleasant comparison with her own state of mind. It was eight twenty. Forty minutes. She had forty minutes left in which to be merely single, as opposed to pathetically, tragically, irrevocably single. Five more minutes went by as she watched Claude make a little washcloth of his right paw before applying it liberally to his face. Then he suddenly stopped what he was doing and gazed up at her. *Look at the time – I'd get a move on if I were you.* She sighed, swore under her breath and placed her glass on the counter.

It was then that she found that her legs no longer worked. They weren't numb. They weren't disembodied. They just wouldn't carry her in the direction of school, that was all. The effect was more interesting than alarming; she imagined that it must be the same sort of feeling that stage hypnotists induce. She pondered her predicament for a little while and then began to feel deeply silly. "Come on," she said, peering downwards. "You have to . . ." She paused. Talking to yourself was bad. Talking to your legs specifically was much worse. The distraction of realising this did the trick, at least. Her brain re-established relations with the lower half of her body and suddenly she was in motion. The best approach, she quickly decided, was to keep going and not look back. She went straight past Claude, not even pausing to give him a little stroke, grabbed her jacket from the back of a chair and sped off down the hall. Her car keys were in a wooden bowl on a console table by the door. She grabbed them, undid the latch and more or less threw herself out in one fluid movement. Within seconds she was in the car and pulling out of her parking space in a manner that owed more than a little to *Starsky and Hutch*. It wasn't until she was a couple of minutes away from the house that she did a scan of her body and found that every single muscle was clenched tight. She made a conscious effort to relax and smiled with relief as the tension eased. Then she remembered why she'd been tense in the first place. Her muscles re-clenched, her smile disappeared and she slowed to twenty kilometres an hour.

The main building of St Brendan's secondary school was a large, two-story C-shaped affair, set far back from the main road and partially obscured by a line of stubby trees. The relative abundance of greenery on the site and the long, snaking avenue that bisected it combined to give a false impression of wealth and privilege, Holly had often thought. A first-time visitor could be forgiven for thinking that they were entering an establishment where the pupils wore blazers, owned horses and had neat partings in their hair. That, of course, was very far from the truth. The mistaken visitor would begin to realise as much when they got closer to the main building and noted its many cracks and blemishes. A quick glance through a classroom window would shatter the illusion forever.

There was a small car park on the left at the end of the avenue. Holly slotted into the one remaining space and killed the engine. A peculiar aspect of school life that the teachers often discussed amongst themselves was the phenomenon of car-park abuse. Classroom abuse was really quite rare, despite what the newspapers said, but for some reason the students seemed to think that anything went in the car park. It might not have been so remarkable if the same had been true of the playing fields or the courtyards or any of the other outdoor areas that counted as school property. But it wasn't. The most popular theory among the teachers was that the area represented a sort of no-man's land between school life and civilian life. It was nothing to do with indoors versus outdoors. A teacher who was getting into or out of his car wasn't *quite* at work and had no real right to complain when someone popped up and called them an arsehole. There were rules, of course. Only in extreme cases – the legendarily nasty Seán Cooper came to mind – would the abuse be a face-to-face affair. Usually, it was more akin to having your pocket picked; you'd realise you'd been hit and would spin around looking for the source, but they'd already have melted away into the crowd. Holly counted herself as one of the lucky ones in this regard. Her name was such an obvious gift that there was no need for anyone to get any more personal. They sang carols at her. They threw tinsel at her. They Ho-Ho-Ho-ed as she went by. Understandably, this last was far and away the most popular. Singing carols took a certain amount of gumption and throwing anything, even tinsel, was a little too close to violence for most. Any fool could Ho-Ho-Ho. And they did. On this particular morning, she had only just emerged from the car – hadn't even locked it yet – before the first volley sounded. Holly spun to her left and saw immediately who the culprit was – a boy called Fintan Scully. She'd taught him for the previous two years. He wasn't difficult to spot. For one thing, he had made a real mess of melting away into the crowd, largely because it was still early and there was no real crowd to melt into. He was standing completely exposed with two smaller boys, both of whom were in hysterics, more at his incompetence than his nerve, Holly suspected. There was another factor that made him stand out. He had raised his hands to his mouth for amplification purposes and, worse, said mouth was wide open. Apparently, he had been drawing breath for another Ho-Ho-Ho and when Holly turned to face him, he had simply frozen. It wasn't until she stepped towards him that he finally dropped his arms to his sides and allowed his gob to close.

"Hello there, Mister Scully," she said.

He shifted his weight from foot to foot. His two associates took a couple of steps back, as if he was in danger of combusting and taking them with him. "Miss."

"You do know that you don't start until tomorrow, don't you? Just first years today."

"Yes, miss. Me ma wanted me to see him to the door." He pointed to his right with his head. "That's my wee brother. Starting today."

"Which one of you is the brother?" Holly asked. One of them raised his hand. "And what's your name?" she asked.

"Cillian. Miss."

She returned her attention to Fintan. "Did you have a nice summer?"

He nodded. "Miss."

"What did you get up to, then?"

"Nothing much, Miss. Football, Miss. Hung around. Xbox. That sort of thing."

"Sounds good to me."

"Yes, Miss. I suppose it was."

"So. Junior Cert this year. I'd say you're really excited about it."

He shrugged. "Not really, Miss. No."

"You look a bit discombobulated, Fintan. Is something up?"

He frowned and gave "discombobulated" a bit of thought. "No, Miss."

"You're not mad at me, are you?"

"Mad . . . at you? No, Miss. Why, Miss?"

"Ah, you know. You were in the middle of a big 'Ho-Ho-Ho' there and I turned around and ruined it on you."

The smaller boys went rigid. Fintan screwed his face up into what he presumably thought was an expression of puzzled innocence; in reality, he looked as if he'd swallowed a bee.

"Miss?"

"I'd hate you to get your year off to a bad start, Fintan, and you not even in uniform yet. Why don't you give it a lash now?"

"Miss, I wasn't –"

"Go on. You'll feel better."

"You want me to . . . What do you want me to do?"

"The old 'Ho-Ho-Ho'. Go on. Let 'er rip."

He swallowed. "I don't think I will."

"No? You sure? This is your last chance, you know, Fintan. If I hear a single 'Ho-Ho-Ho' out of you for the rest of the year, you'll be in detention until you're forty. But if you don't want to take me up on the offer . . ."

"No, thanks. You're all right."

"Fine," she said. "It's up to you. But remember, Mister – *until you're forty*."

He nodded, looking deeply unhappy with the way his life was turning out.

"Go on then," she said. "On your way."

They scarpered.

It was remarkable, Holly thought, as she made her way to the front door, how quickly she had slipped back into teacher mode. As soon as the chance arose, it was "Mister Scully" this and "discombobulated" that. She had used the latter word perhaps ten times in her life and all of them had been attempts to wrongfoot a student. In her own schooldays she had often wondered why teachers spoke and acted the way they did. It wasn't just that they were adults; they seemed to be a particular species unto themselves. Where did the schools find them, all these weirdly different creatures? Now she knew the answer. They weren't different – they just felt compelled to act that way as soon as they got on school premises. It was all but unavoidable.

"Hello there!"

It was Eleanor Duffy. Of course. She was waving for all she was worth as she approached from the top of the avenue, as if Holly was a barely visible figure in the hazy distance.

"What's the problem?" she asked when she caught up. "Are we not friends any more?"

"Sorry," Holly muttered. "I was miles away."

"Not there now. At the entrance. You drove right past me. You nearly drove *over* me, actually."

"Did I? Sorry. I didn't see you. I was –"

"Miles away? Looked that way, all right."

"Why are you on foot? Health kick?"

"God, no. Car's on the blink. Timing belt, whatever that is. I should have it back tomorrow. I had to get the bus across and that took a lot longer than I allowed for and . . . Anyway, never mind that, how was your summer?"

She started walking and didn't pause, apparently assuming that Holly would trot after her. Holly did so.

"Grand. It was grand. How was yours?"

"Great. We had a couple of weeks in France, which was lovely. Mind you, my youngest got a terrible stomach bug as soon as we got back, which kinda took the good out of it, you know?"

"Yeah."

"So! Tell me. How's the love life?"

Holly very nearly stumbled. Then she very nearly screamed. Then she very nearly turned for home. She'd known it was going to be bad but . . . she hadn't even made it *inside* yet.

"Not bad," she squeaked for the want of something better to squeak.

"Oh? Brilliant! What's his name?"

"Robbie," Holly said. It just slipped out. As her eyes widened and her tongue flapped around in her treacherous mouth, these were the words that filled her mind. *It just slipped out.* She'd heard a Robbie Williams song on the radio on the way over. That, presumably, explained where the name had come from. The general concept of inventing a boyfriend where none existed remained thoroughly unexplained. They reached the main door then. Eleanor held it open and ushered Holly through.

"Where's he from? What does he do? Details, woman, details!"

Holly swallowed. "He's a . . . musician. Robbie's a musician. From . . . he's from . . . Galway, originally, but he lives here now. In Dublin. Here in Dublin."

"Ooh, a *musician*," Eleanor cooed. "What does he play?"

"He plays bass guitar." This lie came quickly and sported none of the hesitation and false starts that had accompanied its predecessor.

"In a proper band?"

"Uh . . . yeah."

"And what are they called? I'll have to look out for them."

"They're called The Puny Humans." Again, the lie came easily to her lips. The Puny Humans was a band that Mark had briefly drummed for in his college days. They'd lasted for a couple of months and had eventually split over musical differences: the lead guitarist could play his instrument and the others could not. Lizzie brought out the photos once in a while when she felt like a giggle. To Holly's relief, her answer seemed to pour cold water on Eleanor's enthusiasm for the musical line of questioning. Unfortunately, she simply changed tack.

"How long have you been together, then?"

Holly tried to give this one a little thought. She felt sure that one particular lie might do more damage than another, but she couldn't work out which was which. They'd taken a few steps in silence when Eleanor glanced across to make sure that Holly hadn't gone deaf.

"I said, how –"

"About a month."

This seemed like a reasonable compromise.

"Oh, you're getting close to your record!" Eleanor said. "Well, I'm delighted for you. Only *delighted*. I hope he works out. God knows, you deserve it after the luck you've had. What does he look like? Sorry, that's very rude. But still – what does he look like?"

The expression on her face was a combination of cheek and mild embarrassment. Holly guessed that Eleanor fancied herself to be getting too old for what-does-he-look-like conversations and was greatly enjoying the novelty.

"He looks a bit like . . . um . . . "

Faces flashed through her head. None of them seemed suitable. They were at the staff room door now. Voices and laughter came from within. Holly had a moment of clarity. The lie was unsustainable. She couldn't keep this Robbie character around indefinitely, which meant that sooner or later there would have to be a break-up, at which point her reputation as love's greatest loser would only be enhanced. In the meantime, even if Eleanor didn't tell any of the others – which was tremendously unlikely – she would still have to be conned on a daily basis herself. No, there was nothing for it. Holly stopped walking. Eleanor carried on for a couple of steps, then came back.

"Are you all right?"

"Listen, Eleanor. Listen. I've got something to tell you."

"Oh?"

She sucked in some air. "There is no Robbie, Okay?"

"Excuse me?"

"I made him up. Just now."

The news took a second to sink in. "You made him *up*?" Eleanor rested her hand on her forehead where it gently trembled. "Oh, Holly . . . you poor thing. I knew things were bad, but I never dreamed they were *this* bad."

"Well, things aren't all that bad, it's just –"

"You know, I was thinking about you on my walk in. I had my fingers crossed for you. Honest to God, I did." She shook her head. "*Inventing* boyfriends. I don't know what to say. How long has this been going on for?"

"What? About a minute."

"Holly . . . come on. You can tell me. I won't judge."

"Honestly! About a minute! I just panicked a bit when you asked me. I panicked and I made someone up."

Even before she spoke, Holly could tell that Eleanor hadn't taken this in.

"Friends, family, God knows who else . . . you must be in a terrible mess."

"Eleanor. Pay attention. There are no friends involved, no family, no God knows who else. Just you. Got it?"

The last couple of words came out with a degree of venom that she hadn't meant to inject. Although this was a phenomenon with which Holly was intimately acquainted, it still rankled. She was about to apologise but didn't get a chance.

"Why me?" Eleanor asked. She looked a little spooked now. "I mean . . . what have you got against me?"

"I haven't got anything against you, Eleanor. It's just. . ." She failed to complete the sentence. They stared at each other for a moment. Then Eleanor shook her head and opened the staff room door.

"After you," she said.

Holly squeezed through. When she turned back, she saw that Eleanor was moving away from her as quickly as she could, given the crowded conditions. "Hello"s and "How are you?"s came from every direction (more were aimed at Eleanor than herself, Holly noted). She gave a general wave to the assembly and tried her best to smile. Then she became aware of a presence by her right shoulder. It was Peter Fogarty. As was his wont, he seemed to have simply materialised beside her.

"I really think this might be my last year," he said, as he did every September. "What's the point in having loads of time off if you want to kill yourself when it ends? I'd rather have normal holidays. No highs, no lows, just a nice smooth ride."

"Yeah," Holly said. "Hello to you too."

"Computers," Peter continued. "I like computers. I could start again, get a new degree or qualification of some kind, anyway. 'Systems Analyst'. I've always liked the sound of 'Systems Analyst'. It has a ring to it, doesn't it?"

"Yeah."

"I don't know what it means, mind you. Something to do with analysing systems, I suppose. They say –"

The door swung open then and in swept Ursula McCarthy. Almost immediately, the noise in the room fell away to nothing. Holly wondered if Ursula ever tired of it happening every time she appeared.

"Hello, everyone," Ursula said, and without even waiting for reciprocation, launched into her Welcome Back address. She expressed her hope that everyone was well-rested and made a couple of limp gags about the disappointing nature of the recent meteorological conditions. With the preliminaries out of the way, she moved on to speaking loftily, yet hopelessly vaguely of the challenges that lay ahead.

As ever, her performance was stupefyingly dull. This was

a phenomenon that Holly had never been able to understand. Up close and personal, Ursula was bright, chatty, friendly, sometimes even funny. She smiled almost as much as Eleanor and was one of those people who are given to sudden, frantic gesticulation. Provided she didn't knock the coffee mug from your hand or poke you in the eye – both fairly regular occurrences – her flailings about could be quite endearing. Put her in front of a crowd, however, and she was immediately bleached of all personality. It was like staring at a shop-front mannequin while listening to a recording of the shipping forecast, played at the wrong speed.

After about five minutes of horrendous tedium, Ursula raised a finger and said, "Oh, as you have no doubt noticed, Louise Dillon isn't here today."

All around the room, heads swivelled. Holly hadn't noticed, actually, and took the swivelling to mean that nobody else had either.

Ursula made another attempt at humour. "What are you all looking around for? Do you not believe me or something?"

Everyone looked in her direction again.

"There's some bad news, actually," she went on. "Some of you may know that Louise was a keen mountain-biker."

"Oh no!" someone cried.

From her unfortunate position, wedged in against a wall behind Peter, Holly couldn't make out who it was.

Ursula frowned in confusion and then realised what she'd said. "Sorry, sorry – *is* a keen mountain-biker."

There was general tittering, followed by some embarrassed coughs as people reminded themselves that this was no laughing matter.

"I got a call from Louise's husband late last week, informing me that she'd come off her bike while going very fast down a very steep hill somewhere in, uh, Wicklow, I think he said it was."

Someone said, "Oh no!" again. It was an exact replica of the first "Oh no!" Holly wasn't sure if it was the same person but it didn't really matter; the comic effect was too much for her. She barked out a guffaw, catching it at the source with her cupped right hand. A few of her colleagues in the immediate vicinity heard her aborted outburst and half-turned in her direction. She stared straight ahead.

"I'm sorry to say," Ursula went on, oblivious, "that she did a fair bit of damage. A minor skull fracture and a broken collarbone, amongst other things. A broken wrist, for one."

Gasps were issued. Holly braced herself for another "Oh no!" but none was issued. She breathed a sigh of relief. There was no way she would have been able to hold it together.

"Yeah," Ursula said. "Pretty horrific. Needless to say, Louise won't be teaching for quite a while. By the sounds of things, she won't be doing *anything* for quite a while. I've organised a sub. He should be here any minute."

Holly rolled her eyes. She wasn't a fan of subs; they had it easy. Because they knew that they didn't have to hang around for the long haul, they had the luxury of choosing the persona that they would present to the pupils. If they felt like being Mr or Mrs Cool, they could project that image in the short-term, knowing they'd be long gone before they were unmasked. If they wanted to act like a strict, no-nonsense hard case, they could do so and, chances were, no one would ever discover them crying in their car one lonely Tuesday lunchtime. Just then, a firm knock rat-tat-tatted on the door. Ursula pulled a face and opened it.

A strange man stepped into the room. The sub, Holly presumed. Her first thought on seeing him was that he appeared to be utterly calm. If he was experiencing any new-guy nerves, he was doing a great job of hiding them. He wasn't smiling exactly, but he looked as if he had only recently stopped and would probably start again any second now. The second thing that struck her was that he was wearing a suit. There was a teachers' dress code at St Brendan's but Holly doubted that anyone, not even Ursula, could quote it to any great extent. It boiled down to "No Jeans, No Trainers". The men, in particular, seemed to find this directive a little vague and often had trouble finding the right tone, clothes-wise. None of them ever wore a full suit; there was an unspoken consensus that suits were overkill. They were, however, given to showing up in jackets and ties, often of dubious pedigree. It was only a short step from there to the fabled elbow patches and this, astonishingly, was a mistake that one or two of them had made. Not only was the newcomer wearing an entire suit, it looked seriously expensive. His tie hadn't come from Dunnes Stores either, by the look of it.

"Talk about timing!" Ursula cooed. "My last words were 'He should be here any minute'."

The sub nodded. "I was listening through the keyhole. Just wanted to make a big entrance."

Judging by the expression on her face, Ursula seemed to be on the point of taking this literally. Then she smiled and turned back towards her colleagues.

"I'd like to introduce James Bond," she said when she was sure that all eyes had turned in her direction. This, Holly presumed, was an attempt at humour that was possibly going to be followed by some gentle ribbing of the school's normal sartorial standards. It earned a couple of chuckles.

"I know," the newcomer said. "It's ridiculous, isn't it?" He did a little *What-are-you-gonna-do?* shrug.

There was a pause and then a collective gasp as the penny dropped. It wasn't a joke. He really was called James Bond.

"Wait a minute," Larry Martin said. "That's your real name?"

"That's right."

"Your *real*, real name?"

"Yes."

"James Bond?"

"*Yes*," Eleanor Duffy said. "How many times do you want him to say it?" She stepped forward and extended her hand. "You're very welcome, James. I'm Eleanor."

He took her hand and shook. "Hi, Eleanor. Nice to meet you."

"Short notice, eh?"

"Yeah. But that's what it's all about, isn't it, subbing? I'm glad to be here. There's only so much *Dr Phil* a guy can watch. 'How's that workin' out for yeeewww?'"

This last line was delivered in a reasonably good Texan accent. No one seemed to understand that it was an impression of said Doctor. Holly felt sorry for the guy, although he didn't seem to be at all embarrassed by the ensuing silence.

"You'll be glad to hear," Eleanor said then, "that you won't be alone on the unusual name front."

Holly's toes curled.

"Is that so?"

"It is. Believe it or not, we have a Holly Christmas."

Peter nudged her in the back, as if she hadn't recognised her own name. Although she didn't particularly feel like doing so, she thought she'd better step forward and say hello.

"Hiya," she said. "Holly."

"James. Nice to meet you." They shook hands.

"You know what you should say," Mike Hennessy said, standing on his toes to make himself more visible from his position at the back. "You should say, 'Bond – James Bond'." This drew a few moans. Mike swiftly backtracked. "Sorry. You probably get that all the time."

"Well, I can't say that was the first time," James said

75

cheerfully. "But don't worry about it. If you're going to have a name like mine, you can't expect people not to crack jokes. You must get something similar, Holly."

"Yeah. But I'm not as nice about it. I usually stab them with whatever's handy at the time." She gave him a smile and retreated to her original position.

With the introductions out of the way, Ursula went back to the important business of droning. When she eventually ran out of things to say, those teachers who were taking the first classes of the day took final sips of coffee and brushed past her into the corridor. Holly was one of them. She hadn't gone very far before she heard rapid footsteps behind her. They belonged to Peter.

"James Bond!" he said as he caught up. "Imagine that. And I thought your name was bad. I mean . . . I didn't mean *bad*, I meant –"

"I know what you meant, Peter," she said.

"It's crazy, isn't it?"

"What is?"

"James Bond! Imagine going through life being called James Bond! I can't decide if I'm jealous or not."

"Let me clear that one up for you right now. You're not jealous. Or at least you shouldn't be. I know he lets on that he doesn't mind the jokes, but I bet you any money he's slammed a lot of doors in his time."

"Maybe . . . Right, this is me." He stopped by his classroom door and peered through the little window. "So peaceful," he said. "So quiet. And half an hour from now . . . "

"You'll be grand," Holly assured him. "Good luck."

"Yeah. You too."

The plan, as ever, was that the first years would gather in the assembly hall where they would be addressed and assigned to their classes by Ursula, the vice-principal Greg Tynan and a small sample of the less intimidating-looking staff. Meanwhile, teachers who were due to take the first classes of the day, like Holly and Peter, would prepare for the onslaught. Holly had done everything she needed to do inside five minutes and spent the rest of the time pacing up and down the aisles. It seemed fairly obvious that James Bond's arrival would have repercussions for her, but she wasn't sure whether they would be positive or negative. On the one hand, it was possible that there was only so much name-related hilarity to go around. If so, he would surely be the target for most of it; "James Bond" was undoubtedly a richer source of material than "Holly Christmas". On the other hand, the presence of another person with a stupid name might merely serve to increase general consciousness that there was such a thing. If she wasn't careful, she could take a lot of collateral damage.

Her class was due to start at ten thirty, which she took to mean eleven. It was something of a surprise then, when she heard activity in the corridor outside at ten thirty-five. She answered the knock at the door and found Greg standing at the head of what seemed like an endless line of boys.

"Miss Christmas," he said in a voice that bore no relation to the one he used every day. "I have a special delivery for you."

Holly made a concerted effort to make her own voice sound bright and friendly. "Great, where do I sign?"

She stepped aside, as did Greg. The boys trooped in and took seats. She kept up a steady stream of "Hello"s and "Nice to see you"s as they filed past. It was amazing, she thought, as she did every year, how much you could tell about them just by the way they entered the classroom. A few sauntered in as if they owned the place. Most came in sheepishly, staring at their feet. One or two almost had to be pushed in by the boy coming along behind them. None of them looked directly at her unless she spoke to them. Even then, they took only the briefest of glances.

"I'll leave you to it," Greg said when everyone was inside.

"Thanks," Holly said. "I'll talk to you later."

When the door closed, she turned to her new class. The majority were settled in but a few were still squabbling over the seating arrangements.

"The chairs are all the same," she said. "There's nothing special about any of them, so you might as well just sit down in the nearest one. We did have some magic chairs that were worth fighting over, but we got rid of them a couple of years back."

She immediately regretted this small joke. No one laughed or even smiled and, judging by his dropped jaw, one little boy in the front row seemed to take her seriously (she made a mental note to keep an eye on his academic progress).

"Okay then," she said when at last everyone was seated. "My name is Miss Christmas" – cue giggles – "and I'll be your science teacher –"

A hand shot up. It belonged to a mono-browed lump of a lad who looked at least sixteen.

"Yes?"

"Seriously?"

"Seriously. I know an awful lot about science. Go on – ask me anything."

He frowned. "No, I mean, seriously, is your name really Christmas?"

"It's really *Miss* Christmas, yes."

"And is it true that your first name is Holly?"

For a moment, she considered denying it. "Yeah. It is."

"No way."

"Do you think I'm making it up?"

"No. Suppose not. Do you like Christmas or is just a name?"

There was no real logic to that, but she decided to answer as if there was. "Of course I like Christmas," she lied.

Another hand went up. This one belonged to a red-haired, freckle-faced boy who looked, she couldn't help but think, slightly coked-up. His eyes were wild and his fingers didn't seem to be under his conscious control.

"Do people make jokes about it all the time?"

"Well, not all the time, no, they –"

"Are we allowed to make jokes about it?"

There was something about the way he said it that immediately endeared him to her. Where his predecessor had sneered, this one twinkled.

"No," she said. "You're not allowed to make jokes about it. But thank you for asking. Now, that's enough about my name, we're not going to get very far if I don't know what you lot are called. Here's what we're going to do. I want you all –"

"My name's Mickey Hallowe'en."

This was Mono-brow again. He got a big laugh.

"Okay," Holly sighed. "Thing one: when you want to say something, raise your hand first. If I'm interested in hearing what it is, I'll let you know. Thing two: your joke doesn't really work. My name is absolutely *hilarious* because 'Holly' and 'Christmas' go together. 'Mickey' and 'Hallowe'en' don't go together. Or am I missing something? Maybe you could you tell us what the connection is?"

Mono-brow glared at her.

"No? Okay then. So we're agreed: your joke didn't work and you should never, ever try to be funny again. Now, as I was saying – I want you all to split up into pairs. I'm going to give you a few minutes to have a chat and then you're going to tell us all about each other."

This was something she did with every new class and it never ceased to amaze her how unpopular it was.

"I hear a lot of moaning," she said, raising her voice. "But it's either this or you stand up and tell us all about *yourself* – in the form of a poem." The moaning doubled in volume. "I thought so. Okay, then, off you go."

The room descended into chaos immediately.

"You don't have to shout your entire life story!" she called out. "You can just whisper the important bits. All we're looking for here is your neighbour's name, what school he was at before now, what his hobbies are, is he married or single, that sort of thing."

At last, she raised a laugh. She gave them five minutes and then called on the first student, who seemed to get to his feet in slow motion.

"Don't be nervous," she said. "We're all friends here."

He was a slight boy with a bad haircut and a hangdog look. Holly would have put money on him having bullying problems somewhere down the line. She mentally crossed her fingers, hoping he wouldn't have a lisp or a stutter. He didn't.

"This is Dylan Lawlor," he said, pointing a thumb at his neighbour, who looked absolutely delighted with his fifteen seconds of fame. "His last school was St Mary's. He's from Rathmines. He's into football and swimming . . . uh . . . What was the other thing?"

"Cars," said Dylan.

"Yeah. Cars."

"Well done," Holly said as the boy collapsed gratefully onto his chair again. "Now, Dylan. Your turn."

Dylan got to his feet. As he did so, Holly couldn't

help but glance at her watch. Ten minutes gone. Nine months to go.

The staff room was always hectic at lunchtimes, but on the first day of a new term it was almost unbearable. Everyone talked at once, each firmly convinced that he or she had the killer anecdote of the morning. The physical and aural chaos was amplified by the endless toing and froing that went on between the tiny kitchen area and the table where lunches were consumed. This combination of excited chatter and frantic face-stuffing always put Holly in mind of a student house on the morning after a party. If there had been a few sleeping bags on the floor and a home-made bong lying discarded in the corner, the illusion would have been complete.

By all accounts, it had been a perfectly run-of-the-mill start to the term. Greg Tynan had a puker. Eleanor Duffy had a crier. Mike Hennessy had an uncontrollable giggler. Almost everyone had identified an obvious troublemaker (or two, or three). Some had picked out favourites too, kids for whom they had already developed soft spots, based on almost nothing but the look in their eyes or the way they said their name. Nuala Fanning, in particular, seemed to be besotted with a lad in her class simply because he'd just had braces put on his teeth and seemed to be constantly on the verge of choking to death ("It was just so cute!" she marvelled).

James Bond hadn't shown up at the eleven o'clock break, but that was not unusual; the time allotted was so short that lots of teachers used it as an opportunity to grab some fresh air or, conversely, a cigarette, rather than race to the staff room to throw back a cup of bad coffee. Holly had cut short her own visit when Larry Martin started to tell her all about his summer trip to Medugorje. James also failed to show up at lunchtime, however, and that did not go unnoticed. Around the table, a number of theories were put forward to explain his absence. He'd been captured by SPECTRE. He was in bed with a Russian agent. He was getting a briefing from M. As soon as the first of these feeble jokes had been cracked, the situation had been wrung dry of potential humour, Holly thought. She wasn't surprised to find that no one else shared her opinion. The gags just kept on coming, each delivered with a little more desperation than its predecessor. He was flirting with Moneypenny. He was getting a new gadget from Q. He was fighting with Jaws. He was scraping gold paint off his girlfriend. He was strapped to a table with a laser pointing at his goolies. There was only so much of it that Holly could listen to. She was on the point of leaving when the door opened and in he walked.

Enda Clerkin spotted him first and, being the social H-bomb that he was, quieted the table with a "Shush!" that was considerably louder than any of their speaking voices. The subsequent silence seemed to go on forever.

"Hello, everyone," James said as he got his lunch from the fridge. They responded with wildly over-enthusiastic greetings. He approached the table slowly, as if awaiting permission to sit down.

"Sit, sit," Eleanor Duffy said, pushing her own chair aside to make room. "Did you have a good morning?"

"Not bad. They started cracking jokes as soon as they heard 'Bond'. You can imagine the reaction when I told them about the 'James' bit."

"You told them your first name?" Eleanor asked. "Is that not asking for trouble?"

"They always find out eventually anyway," James said. "Might as well get it over with. And some of their jokes weren't bad, I must say."

Holly was sitting almost directly opposite him. She took a good, long look across the table at him as he sat down, all the while pretending, of course, to be thoroughly absorbed in her sandwich. He was still wearing that same expression, the is-it-or-isn't-it-a-smile. What was he so pleased about?

"You poor thing," Eleanor said. "You must be sick to death of it."

He shook his head and then, at last, broke into a genuine grin. TV teeth, Holly noticed. And TV hair, too. Factor in the nice suit and there was something of the anchorman about him.

"Not at all. As I said earlier, you have to expect a few comments. Especially from kids. And they're really good about it, usually. I'm sure I have ten different nicknames already but that's fine by me, so long as they're not nasty. And they never are. It usually settles down to '007' sooner or later."

There was widespread nodding.

"I have to ask," Mike Hennessy said then. "Now, you can tell me to mind my own if you want to –"

"What the hell were my parents thinking?"

Mike nodded. "Well . . . yeah."

"I wonder that myself sometimes. But it's pretty simple, really. My grandfather – my mother's father – was called James. She was very close to him, my mum. He died when she was a teenager and she swore that if she ever had a son of her own, she would call him James. The way she tells it, it was one of those graveside promises, you know, in the middle of a storm. All *Wuthering Heights*. She didn't know then, of course, that she would end up married to a man called Bond. Anyone with a bit of sense would have changed their mind, obviously. Not my mum. 'Stubborn' isn't the word for it. I've got three sisters, all older than me. My dad knew about this dopey promise and I think he was kind of relieved that he was getting away with it. And then they had one of those little forty-something surprises. He tried to talk her out of it, but she wasn't having it. They still argue about it to this day, thirty years later. Damn, now I've given away my age . . . "

"You don't look a day over twenty-five," Nuala Fanning said and then blushed as she realised that the line had come out with a lot more sauce on it than she'd intended.

James gave her an *aw-shucks* sort of look and began work on his lunch.

"I'd say you had an awful hard time of it at school,"

Larry Martin said. "You must have had the shite kicked out of you every day of the week."

"Language, Larry!" Eleanor said with a sideways glance at James.

He seemed to be on the point of reminding her that they were none of them children when James dabbed his mouth with a napkin that – Holly couldn't help but notice – he'd apparently brought with him. He seemed to have brought his own disposable cutlery too.

"Nope. Never once. Just the opposite. It made me kind of . . . popular. I don't mean that as a boast, I just mean that people liked my silly name. It made them smile. I'm sure you get the same sort of thing, Holly."

He looked at her over the top of a plastic forkful of mixed leaves.

"Me?" she said and felt immediately ridiculous.

He munched and swallowed. "People must love that, surely? 'Holly Christmas'? How could you not *love* that?"

"Holly seems to manage all right," Larry said. "She fucking hates it, in fact."

Eleanor rolled her eyes. She seemed to realise, as Holly did, that this particular swear-word had been inserted for purely mischievous purposes.

"I don't hate it," she said somewhat weakly. There was general murmuring and snorting. Larry issued a cackle. "Well, you do a very good impression of someone who hates it."

"And," Enda Clerkin said, "you're always in filthy humour around Christmas."

"More than usual, even," Mike Hennessy said. That got a laugh.

Holly felt her cheeks begin to burn. "What is this?" she said, trying to keep her tone light. "Kick Holly Day?"

"I'm sorry," James said. "I didn't mean to start anything."

She sighed. "To answer your question: yes. People like it. They certainly mention it, anyway."

"I bet. And – if you don't mind my asking – what's the story behind yours? Is there one? Were you born at Christmas?"

"Nope," Holly said. "No story. Sorry. Christmas. Holly. Holly Christmas."

"Cool," James said. "Then again, I love anything to do with Christmas."

"Really."

"God, yeah. Love it. Love it. What's not to love?"

"How long have you got?"

"You really don't like it?"

"No. I don't. I really, really don't."

"I presume that's because you get more comments on your name at that –"

"I don't think so. I mean, that doesn't help. But I think I'd still hate Christmas if I was called Mary Smith."

He nodded but not in agreement. "Carols? Turkey and roasties? Giving and getting presents? Seeing friends and family you haven't seen in ages?"

Holly felt her cheeks flush. "Look, I don't want to get

into it. But it's not the specifics. It's *this*. It's exactly this, now. You're not allowed to say anything bad about Christmas. No criticism allowed. I read a quote somewhere: it's like living in some brutal dictatorship where you have to smile on the leader's birthday or they take you out and shoot you."

Larry Martin made one of his infamous nose-noises. Those who had sandwiches on the way to their mouths put thoughts of eating aside for the time being. "Scrooge," he said when the echo had faded.

"Also," Holly noted, "you get called Scrooge a lot by morons." Eyes widened. Gasps were emitted. "Just kidding. Larry knows I love him dearly."

"I love you too, sweetie," Larry said.

Holly was impressed, despite herself. He had managed to inject a level of sarcasm that made her own seem positively anaemic.

"If you don't like your name," James began, "why –"

"I didn't say I didn't like my name," Holly interrupted. "I said I don't like Christmas."

"Yeah, but your name is *Holly Christmas*. It's bound to remind you of . . . well, Christmas."

He didn't add "Checkmate", but he might as well have done. "If you don't like it, why don't you change it?"

Holly looked right at him. He didn't seem to be mocking her. His tone had been merely inquisitive.

"I have thought about it," she said. "But it would annoy my mother. A lot."

"What about your dad? Maybe he –"

"He died before I was born."

"Oh. I'm sorry to hear that," James said. For the first time, Holly thought she saw some self-doubt on his face. But it didn't last very long. No more than a couple of seconds had gone by before he returned to his default setting, the half-smile.

"One of my best friends is called John Lennon," he said then. There was a chorus of "No way"s and "You're joking"s, which he seemed to greatly enjoy. "Honestly. John Lennon."

"That's some coincidence," Mike Hennessy said.

"To be fair," James replied, "it wasn't really a coincidence. He was a friend of a friend – actually, a friend of a friend of a friend – and they put a lot of effort into getting us both to the same party, just so one of them could say, 'James Bond, I'd like you to meet John Lennon'. Which I thought was kind of admirable. The effort, I mean. They didn't know we were going to hit it off and become proper friends. That must have seemed like a bit of a bonus."

"We'll have to get the three of you together," Nuala Fanning said. "James Bond and John Lennon and Holly Christmas." She frowned and bit her lip. "Although that doesn't really work. James Bond and John Lennon are famous names. Holly Christmas is just weird."

"God, I apologise," Holly said. "'Just weird'. How disappointing for you. Maybe I could change it to Marilyn Monroe, would that help?"

"This John Lennon character," Larry said. "Is he a fan of John Lennon? *John Lennon* John Lennon?"

James chased some errant morsel with his fork. He seemed at first to be ignoring the question, but it soon became apparent by the slow shaking of his head that he was thinking something through. After he had cornered and eaten his quarry, he turned the shake into a nod and said, "What the hell. None of you are ever going to meet him. So I suppose I can tell you his deep, dark secret. He's a Beatles *nut*. He lets on he can't stand them. Says if you put a gun to his head, he'd admit that McCartney knows a melody when he hears one. Truth is, he's obsessed with them, like, to the point of madness. And he's into Lennon's solo stuff too. He would absolutely kill me if he knew I was telling anybody that. No one can ever know, you know? He's so embarrassed about it. He was only called John in the first place because his parents were shocking hippies, his dad especially, and, obviously, serious Beatles freaks. You know those old guys you see walking around with a ponytail halfway down their back and three wispy wee hairs on top? That's John's dad. He spent the sixties and seventies wishing he was called John and not Frank and, much like my own mother, I suppose, he did the old solemn vow business. 'If I ever have a son . . . ' She's not far behind him. Valerie. Lovely people and all, just lovely, don't get me wrong. But it's one of those leave-your-shoes-at-the-door, don't-hit-your-head-off-the-dream-catcher sort of houses. John pretends he only likes music that was made last week because they'd be unbearable if they knew his secret passion. They're more or less unbearable as it is."

"That's so sad," Eleanor said, staring into the middle of the table. "Not to get along with your parents like that."

James was quick to correct her. "No, no. They get on great. It's just the music thing. And it's not just them. He doesn't want anybody to know. And I can see his point. Wouldn't it be odd if I'd showed up today saying, 'My name's James Bond and the big thing about me is, I'm really into James Bond'?"

"Yeah," Larry agreed. "That'd be like Holly Christmas saying she was feeling jolly. It'd be all wrong. You'd think the world had gone mad."

There was a ripple of muted giggling. Holly's right foot started to tap on the floor.

"Tell me, James," Eleanor said, somewhat over-formally. "What do you think of the movies? Or the books? Have you read the books?"

"I read one, ages ago," he said. "*Diamonds are Forever*. Didn't care for it. Really racist and sexist. You wouldn't believe some of the stuff he comes out with – Fleming. I do like the movies, though."

"Who's your f –"

"The new guy. Sorry, Eleanor. I should have let you finish your question."

"That's all right," she smiled. "You guessed correctly."

"Yeah, Daniel Craig is my favourite. He seems closest to the original character who is, let's face it, a sociopath.

Next is Sean Connery. Pierce Brosnan was pretty good, I thought, but the films themselves were terrible. That one with the media mogul, what was it called, *Tomorrow Never Dies*? Brutal. Absolutely brutal. Roger Moore started out OK, but he did it for far too long. He was getting really creaky by the end there. Plus, he got the worst scripts of any of them. People always have a go at him for playing the thing for laughs, but he's just an actor. He can only read the lines they give him. And they gave him some awful toss."

Holly looked around the table. He wasn't saying anything particularly clever or insightful, but they were hanging on his every word.

"I thought Timothy Dalton was the best of all," Mike Hennessy said then, in a small, uncertain voice. He sounded like a man declaring a fondness for crystal meth. Sure enough, he was immediately set upon. As the slurs and counter-slurs were traded, Holly pushed back her chair and went to get some more water. James followed her immediately.

"Listen," he said. "I hope you weren't too hacked off with all the name talk."

"Nah," she said. "And it was hardly your fault anyway."

"If you're sure." He put the back of his wrist to his forehead and bent his knees. "I know your pain."

"Liar."

He was surprised by this; so was she.

"Well –"

"I'm sorry. I didn't mean that in a nasty way. I just

meant that you seem so cool." She gulped. And then smiled, too quickly. "About the name thing, I mean. You'll have to let me in on your secret."

"I don't think I have one. But if anything comes to me, I'll let you know."

His half-smile turned into a whole smile. He had a pretty good one, Holly found herself thinking.

"OK then," she replied. "You know what, I think I'll go and get some air."

"Okay."

She nodded. He nodded. She left.

Chapter 6

Mrs Christmas poured herself another cup of tea and snapped the edge off a Rich Tea biscuit. She popped the nibble into her mouth and shook her head almost imperceptibly. These moves were entirely typical, Holly thought. Her mother was not a showy person. She loved Rich Tea biscuits with a deep, persistent passion, but she ate them slowly and deliberately, as if each one was the last she would be getting her hands on for a long while. Not for her the frantic dunking and slurping that her daughter, for example, employed when dealing with Chocolate HobNobs. By the same token, when Mrs Christmas was upset or annoyed, she eschewed flailing about and roaring in favour of occasional sighs and tiny head shakes. On this occasion, there had already been several sighs. Now, here was the head shake.

"It's no big deal," Holly said. "He was a gobshite anyway."

"You seem to be surrounded by them," her mother replied. "And morons. And cretins. They all seem to be different in your head, but I've never worked out how."

"Believe me," Holly said, "you wouldn't have liked him." She paused briefly, then decided to push it. "That was one of the reasons why I got rid of him, actually. I asked myself, *Would Mum like this guy?* And I decided that no, you wouldn't."

Holly had given her break-up with Kevin a lot of thought in advance of this visit home. If she told the truth she would certainly receive a lot of sympathy, but she would also see a certain look on her mother's face, a look that said, *What did you do to annoy this one?* There would be nothing nasty behind it, but still. It would get on her nerves. Pretending that she was the one who had broken it off would make her seem proactive, at least.

Nothing else was said for a while. Mrs Christmas traced a finger around on the table while Holly pretended to be suddenly fascinated by the arrangement of her cup and saucer (her mother was a cup and saucer woman, always; her oft-stated position on mugs was that they were "impolite"). As the seconds ticked by, Holly began to get nervous. She knew that her failure to acquire a boyfriend whose tenure could be measured in months was a source of constant worry to her mum and that, once in a while, even though it went against her nature, she would feel the need to "say something". It had happened no more than a handful of times, but it was always unpleasant for both parties. One of those conversations – it was a couple of years ago now – had featured the word "spinster". It had been hastily retracted but still. The longer the silence went on, the more certain Holly became that she was in for another gentle, circuitous but nonetheless infuriating grilling. She probably shouldn't have said anything, she thought; her mother had already seemed preoccupied when she arrived.

"I went to see Lillian the other day."

"Oh? How is she?" Holly asked.

She was delighted by the appearance of this fresh topic and tried not to read too much into her mother's expression, which had suddenly made the small leap from preoccupied to troubled. Lillian was an elderly lady who lived two doors up. She had no family apart from a greasy nephew who showed up once in a while to check if she had died yet. In Holly's mind, she had always been old but, weirdly, never seemed to get any older. It was if she had reached a certain age and decided that it suited her. Mrs Christmas had been calling in on her, doing odd jobs, and generally making sure that she *didn't* die for as long as Holly could remember.

"She's fine. Much better now that the new hip has settled in. She's still very slow, God love her, but she's not in as much pain."

"Good, I'm glad," Holly said and drank some tea. She held the cup to her mouth for much longer than was necessary. The truth was she wanted something to hide behind. She hadn't known that Lillian was having an operation – she hadn't even known she had a dodgy hip – and she was afraid that her expression might give the game away.

"I went over at lunchtime," her mother continued. "I don't stay long, usually. I just tidy up a bit and make sure she's got all the essentials, you know, maybe run to the chemist or the post office for her. But the other day I stayed for ages. We got talking. I mean, we talk all the time, but it's just chit-chat, you know, complaining about the racket the bin men make or going over what happened in *Coronation Street*, you know?"

"Yeah. Small talk."

"I don't know how it got started or who . . . No, that's not true. I do know how it got started. I started it." She looked up as if asking for permission to proceed.

"Started what?" Holly asked nervously.

Mrs Christmas drew in a long, slow breath. "Talking about . . . partners."

"Partners," Holly repeated. The word didn't sound quite right coming from her mum. "You mean, like, husbands and wives, boyfriends and girlfriends . . . "

"Yes. They call them partners now, don't they?"

"Sometimes, yes. What about them?"

"Well . . . Lillian lost her husband at an early age, like me. She wasn't anything like as young as I was, mind you, but still. She was only about fifty, I think. You wouldn't remember him, of course – you weren't even born. Barney he was called. Big, tall, strong-looking man. Very quiet. Very shy. One morning, he just didn't wake up. Heart attack in his sleep. We hadn't been living here very long, so we didn't get too involved, but I remember it well. All the people coming and going, everyone saying she was going to wind up in a mental hospital, she was that devastated. I remember thinking how terrible it would be to be left on your own like that, just out of the blue. One minute, he's there by your side and the next, boom. Your whole world's upside down and inside out. If I'd known then that I was going to be in the same boat inside a couple of years, I'd have lost my mind."

"Right," Holly said. It was all she could come up with.

Her mother talked about her husband all the time, of course, but almost always in an attempt to give Holly a sense of what he had been like. Despite everything, those conversations tended to be light-hearted. They usually centred around three different types of anecdotes. In the first kind, her father was a Frank Spencer-ish sort of figure, enduring appalling physical calamities but emerging on the other side with his sense of humour still very much intact. In the second, he was frankly Christ-like, forever turning the other cheek and forgiving those who knew not what they did. In the third, he was more like Dirty Harry, steely in his resolve and admirably unbound by petty regulations. As far as Holly could recall, the number of occasions on which her mother had spoken of him in terms of something she personally had lost could be counted on the fingers of one hand.

"Anyway," Mrs Christmas went on. "We got talking about how years ago, in your grandparents' time, say, when a woman was widowed, or a man for that matter, well, that was that. Not all the time, but usually. The idea that you should go off looking for someone else wouldn't have entered their heads. Not in a million years. It just wasn't done."

Holly gulped. "Suppose not."

"But by the time Barney died and your father died, things had already changed a lot. And sure these days, people would think you were weird if you didn't try to find someone else. Isn't that right?"

An awkward moment passed before Holly realised that this was not a rhetorical question. "I wouldn't go that far," she said cautiously. "But yeah, lots of widowed people find new . . . partners." She gulped again. "Mum, what are you try–"

"So I kind of lost the run of myself and I asked Lillian why she'd never done it. Not recently, obviously – when she was younger. And she said it was never an option to her, and it was nothing to do with the times. Nineteen-seventies, nineteen-eighties, nineteen-forties, it made no odds. No way, no how, absolutely not. She was Barney's wife and that was the end of it. Didn't matter if he was alive or dead, she was still his wife. What do you make of that, Holly? Never mind what's normal now and what wasn't normal years ago, what do you think?"

"I think . . ." Holly began and then realised that she couldn't answer without knowing all the facts. "Mum, what's going on here?" she asked. "Are we just talking in general or are you . . . I mean . . . are you thinking of joining some dating agency or something?"

She thought there was a good chance that her mother would explode into laughter at this ridiculous misunderstanding. But she didn't. Instead, she kept her gaze fixed on Holly and said, "No. I'm not thinking of joining a dating agency. I would just like to hear your opinion."

There didn't seem to be any alternative but to provide a straight answer. "I think that if a person is single, whether it's because they're divorced or widowed or were never married in the first place, and that person meets another person who is also single, and the two of them are interested in each other, then there's no good reason why they shouldn't pursue it." She frowned. Her response had sounded cold and mildly legalistic.

"OK," Mrs Christmas said. "That's what I thought you'd say."

"Mum, what is this –"

She stopped short because her mother had raised her hand, palm outward, like a traffic cop. Holly's temperature rose. The game-playing was becoming tiresome. But then something told her to hold off on the huffing and puffing that she'd been preparing to do. It was more like an atmospheric change than anything else. She held her breath, waiting for something to happen. It took a while. Mrs Christmas poured herself a third cup of tea and stared at it for a few seconds before taking the tiniest of sips. Then she did some more staring, took another sip and finally brought her hands together on the table as if she was about to launch into a prayer.

"About a month ago," she said, "I came back from the shops and I saw this man at the front gate, looking up at the house. Just standing there with his arms folded, looking all over, as if he was thinking of buying it or something. I didn't know what to do. Was I supposed to ask him what he was at or was I supposed to just brush past him? In the end, I kind of split the difference. I walked past him, but I gave him a good look as I was doing it, you know?"

Holly nodded. "Go on."

"Well, I caught his eye and I soon as I did, this big grin came over his face and he started staring at me the way he'd been staring at the house. I swear to God, Holly, I was about to run. I thought he was some sort of a nut-job. And then he said, 'You don't recognise me.' Even at that stage, I was half-thinking of running. Because, I don't know, maybe that's the sort of trick nut-jobs use to get your defences down. They say, 'You don't remember me' and you step closer to get a better look and they hit you over the head with a blunt whatchamacallit. Instrument."

"Right," Holly said.

"Tell you the truth, I think I took a step *back*. And maybe the light changed or maybe his voice just sank in or maybe it was something else, but I suddenly had him. It was Charlie Fallon."

She bit her bottom lip and looked to Holly for a response.

But Holly had nothing to say. She'd never heard of Charlie Fallon. "You've lost me," she said. "Who's he?"

Her mum raised her chin a fraction. "Hm. I was wondering if I'd ever mentioned him. Obviously not. Charlie was my first proper boyfriend. We were an item for a good few months, almost a year, in fact. This was long before I met your father. I was twenty, twenty-one, he was a bit older. He had a bit of a reputation, early on. You know. A bad boy."

She smiled weakly and Holly tried to smile back. But it wasn't easy. Her heart was going wild and her stomach seemed to be slowly rotating. There was no doubt about where this was going. Her mother – her mother! – had a new boyfriend. A new old boyfriend, at that.

"You know what you're like at that age. I thought the sun shone out of him. Granny wasn't too chuffed about it but she was sure it would blow over. Your Granda nearly lost his life, though. All he knew about Charlie was that he used to break a lot of windows. I tried telling him that he'd changed, but he wouldn't listen. There were rows, slammed doors. And he didn't calm down as time went on, Daddy, he got worse and worse. By the time it all ended, me and him were hardly speaking."

"And how did it end?" Holly asked.

"Suddenly, that's how it ended. I was thinking marriage, Holly, I don't mind admitting it. Looking back now, I don't know if that was just youth talking or what, but that's where we were heading, to me anyway. Then one day, Charlie asked me to go for a walk and just like that, he told me he was off. New York. He had relations in Brooklyn and there was nothing around here for him, work-wise. So he was going. And did I want to go with him?"

This detail startled Holly more than anything that had gone before. The idea that her mother had once been a teenager with a dodgy boyfriend whom her father despised seemed faintly absurd, but it was graspable. Somehow, it was much harder to picture her contemplating emigration. Delia Christmas, or Delia Byrne, rather, on the streets of New York . . . Try as she might, Holly couldn't make the image stick.

"You said no, obviously."

"I thought about it. I thought hard about it, for days and days. You know why I didn't go?"

Holly shook her head. "Tell me."

"Well, for one thing, I plain old didn't want to. Some people heard 'New York' and got all excited – I got scared. All those strange, angry people. Skyscrapers and endless traffic. Guns and drugs and God knows what else. But that wasn't the main reason. The main reason was that he didn't try to talk me into it. It took me a couple of days to notice that. He just asked the question and then left it hanging. And it's not like we didn't see each other. We met up as often as ever and I'd squirm and fidget and worry and Charlie'd carry on as if nothing was up. His attitude was he was definitely going and he had no real objection if I tagged along. It wasn't exactly romantic."

"No. Suppose not. So you split up."

"So we split up. My father was delighted. So was my mother, but she tried not to let it show. I cried for a month."

"And you hadn't heard from him since? Until just now?"

"Nope. Well, he used to write, at first, but he stopped after a while. Actually, I think I probably stopped before he did. What was the point? And he's been back and forth, of course, plenty of times. He just never looked me up."

"All right, so he's standing outside the house and you suddenly recognise him . . . "

"Yes. And it's all hugs and I-can't-believe-its and you-look-greats. I asked him in for a cup of tea, of course, and we did all the catching up, all thirty-odd years worth of it. He was here for hours."

"What's he doing home?"

"He's back for good. He's retired – from a very successful business, by all accounts. Catering equipment. Restaurants, hotels, all that. He's been back for months, has a house here and everything. Out in Dundrum somewhere. Supposed to be massive."

"How the hell did he find you?"

"He looked up an old pal of his, Bernie Maguire. I haven't laid eyes on Bernie in twenty years but he knew I'd married a man called Christmas. And there aren't too many Christmases in the phone book, so . . . "

Holly tried to phrase her next question carefully. "Is Charlie's wife with him?" she asked.

"Nope. There is no Charlie's wife. He never married."

"Right. Annnd . . . "

Holly's mother stared across the table at her. Now that the moment was here, she seemed incapable of taking the final step. She swallowed a few times and shifted her position in her chair a few more, but she couldn't summon any words.

"Mum," Holly said. "I'm just going to come out and ask you. Are you and Charlie an item now? Is that what you're trying to tell me?"

She shook her head, paused, and then shook it again.

"Oh," Holly said. "What was all the 'partner' business about then? I thought –"

"He wants . . . that. Charlie does."

This, apparently, had taken a lot of effort to say. Mrs Christmas slumped slightly in her seat and rubbed the back of her neck as if she'd just finished a long session stooped over a difficult maths problem.

"And what do you want?" Holly asked.

This time, the reply came immediately. "I don't know. I really don't. It's affecting my health, I'm a mess here."

"So you've seen him again since that first day?"

"Yes. I have. Five or six times."

At this point, Holly's mind was flooded with so many questions that she experienced a brief drowning sensation. "What have you been doing?" was the first one that found its way out.

"Eating out, mostly. Charlie's a serious, what's the word, foodie these days. We went to a Thai place one night. Have you ever had Thai food?"

"Yeah. I have."

"It's nice, isn't it?"

"Eh . . . yes. It is."

"We went to see a film too. I hadn't been to the cinema in years. A French thing with subtitles. It was . . . . good. I wasn't sure what everyone else was laughing at half the time, but I still enjoyed it."

"So you've been out together a few times. Quite a few times."

"Yes."

"But just as . . . what? Friends?"

"I don't know what we are. But there have been no shenanigans."

"No *what?*"

"You know what I mean."

"Okay."

They looked at each other. Holly was waiting to see what her mother was going to say next. Several seconds went by before she realised that her mother was waiting to see what she would say next.

"Am I supposed to be talking now?" Holly asked. "Because if I am, I honestly don't know what I'm supposed to be saying. Are you asking me if I think it's all right for you to have a partner? I think I've already answered that one. Yes. Yes, it is all right. I mean, it'll take me a while to get used to the idea, but if you really –"

"That's not what I'm asking."

"Oh? What then?"

"Well, that's part of it – should I? Have . . . one."

"And what's the other part?"

Mrs Christmas took a moment. The subtle movement of her lips told Holly that words were being carefully chosen. "The other part is should I have this particular one?"

Holly stared at her. "Sorry? You're asking me if I think you should go out with this Charlie guy specifically?"

"Basically, yes."

"But I've never met him!"

"I know. I want you to. I can set it up."

Holly leaned on the table and rubbed her temples. "You want me to meet him and tell you if I think you should let him be your boyfriend?"

Her mother smiled and nodded vigorously in a way that, somewhere at the back of her brain, reminded Holly of Harpo Marx.

"This is starting to feel like a really weird dream," Holly said. "What am I supposed to do, hold up cards with scores on them? Do you want to give him a questionnaire to fill in? Should I ask him where he sees himself in five years time?"

"Don't be sarcastic," Mrs Christmas said.

Once, long ago, she had said that she was going to give up telling her daughter not to be sarcastic because she was wasting her breath. It was the first time Holly had heard the words in quite a while. She was surprised to find that they had an effect.

"Sorry," she mumbled, feeling very small. "But still. Tell me how you see this going. I'm all ears."

"Well, now that you're asking me, I'm not sure how to put words on it. I suppose I just want a second opinion really." She paused, then her face lit up. "It's like if you were buying a car and you didn't know anything about cars, you might bring along someone who knew more than you did. Right? Someone who knew what questions to ask so you didn't get ripped off." The smile that had blossomed on her face slowly died. "Okay, so it's not exactly like buying a car."

"Not 'exactly'? Mum! It's nothing like buying a car."

"All right, all right, let me try again. I'm fifty-four years of age, Holly. I've been on my own since I was twenty-six. If I ever did know anything about men, and that's debatable, I've long since forgotten it."

"I'm not exactly an expert myself."

"I know. But you're all I've got."

"Jesus. Cheers."

"Sorry. That came out wrong too. But, come on, you know what I mean."

Now it was Holly's turn to choose her words carefully. "Maybe I'm missing something, but isn't this just as simple as . . . do you like him?"

"Maybe. But I don't know for sure that I like him. I mean, I like him, but I don't know if I *like him* like him. It'd be such a huge step."

"Yeah, but if –"

"Holly. Please. I'm asking you for a favour. Will you

meet Charlie and tell me what you think? That's all I'm asking. Meet the chap and tell me what you think."

Put that way, it seemed like a sensible request. Holly was sure there was a good reason why she shouldn't, but she was damned if she could think of what it was.

"All right. If that's what you want. I'll meet the guy."

Her mother nodded solemnly. Holly nodded back, fully expecting to wake up any minute.

Chapter 7

The rest of the first week back at school slipped by relatively quietly. Classroom crises were few and far between and, among the teaching staff, the only real drama occurred on Wednesday when Julie Sullivan and Barry Dwyer, the school's resident couple, had a falling-out. Nuala Fanning overheard them arguing in what they had mistakenly presumed to be an out-of-the-way corner and lost no time in expressing her concerns to her colleagues. Although she didn't know what the problem was, she was firm in her conviction that they'd been going at it "like a couple of cats". Holly wasn't surprised to find that Eleanor Duffy was sent into a tailspin by this intelligence, but she was really taken aback by the reaction of her other colleagues, who were almost universally horrified. Was this a mere tiff or something more serious? Would it blow over or get completely out of hand? Surely the relationship wasn't in any real jeopardy? All day long, they stopped each other in corridors to report in hushed tones on the latest sightings of the unhappy couple (Barry looked "drained"; Julie sounded "tense"; Barry sounded "angry"; Julie looked "emotional"). The drama – or rather the speculation – continued all day long but ended abruptly at four o'clock when Mike Hennessy strode into the staff room and announced that he's just seen Julie and Barry giggling and cooing at each other in the car park "like a couple of cats". Holly was intrigued. He'd used exactly the same words that Nuala had employed to describe the opposite scenario, but no one else seemed to notice. They waved her away when she mentioned it and flatly ignored her when she pointed out that "like a couple of cats" wasn't even an idiom. Her repeated attempts to get someone, anyone, to agree that this was at very least a strange linguistic phenomenon eventually resulted in Greg Tynan telling her to stop complaining and just be happy that everything had turned out all right. Holly protested that she hadn't been "complaining" but no one wanted to listen.

Thursday morning was strange. It started out well – Julie and Barry's reunion had raised the collective spirits – but went rapidly downhill when Larry Martin raised the subject of pyjamas. He had called in to his corner shop on the way home the previous day and had been appalled to see not one but two women shopping in their nightwear, fluffy slippers and all. This, according to Larry, was a slap in the face of all that was good and decent. It was slovenly. It was disgusting. It was disgraceful. The end of the world was surely at hand. When he'd finished his

111

broadside – it was a couple of minutes long – the room fell silent. Holly assumed that this was because no one wanted to be seen to agree with the old fart. She was genuinely astonished when Ursula McCarthy spoke up and said she didn't see what the big deal was. So what if they weren't dressed by five in the afternoon? It was nobody's business but theirs. And pyjamas were clothes of a sort. It wasn't like they were going to the shops in the nip. These statements were greeted with a small chorus of agreement, at which point Holly almost had a stroke. Before she knew what she was doing, she had embarked on a scalding rant that made Larry sound undecided on the subject. It built to a storming climax in which she heard herself howling that women who went to the shops in their pyjamas had no right to complain about muggers and burglars and junkies because they themselves were playing an important part in society's gradual breakdown. It was about standards; either you had them or you didn't. When she'd finished howling, she tried not to mind that everyone was staring at her, open-mouthed.

Then Enda Clerkin nudged James Bond and said something that sounded a lot like "I told you".

Holly suddenly saw herself not as a righteous crusader for decency and common-sense – the image she'd been working with up to that point – but as a sour little curmudgeon who took her lead on social issues from Larry bloody Martin, a man who was widely known to be in favour of homosexuals getting an island of their own. She was too shocked and panicked to have a go at Enda. Instead, she tried to make herself as small as possible and waited for someone to change the subject (Larry obliged; he changed it to *National Service – Worth a Go?*).

At lunchtime that day, Holly arrived in the staff room to find a small crowd gathered around James Bond. This was not unusual in itself. Holly had yet to see him sitting or standing alone. And it wasn't just the teachers who seemed drawn to him; she had even heard a couple of the kids using the word "cool" in the same sentence as his name without the traditional accompaniment of "thinks he's so . . ." . It soon emerged that James's car – everyone except Holly called it the Aston Martin; it was a pale blue Mazda 3 – had been vandalised. Someone had drawn a large rectangle on its roof and inside that rectangle, just for clarity, had scrawled the words *Ejector Seat*. At first, Holly was sympathetic. Over the years, she'd suffered a variety of vehicular embellishments – the addition of blow-up Santas, fake snow, and so on – but they'd all been easily removed. The vandal in this case had used permanent marker and it was proving difficult to shift. Her sympathy wavered, however, when she realised that James was not just sanguine about his misfortune, but positively tickled. It was a new one on him, he said, and he was impressed by the inventiveness behind it. He even praised the vandal's draughtsmanship – the rectangle had been carefully measured and drawn in perfectly straight lines with gently rounded corners. The other teachers seemed to find his response delightful – Eleanor Duffy used the word "inspirational" – but

Holly felt dizzy and confused. When she offered her take on the situation, namely that there was nothing funny about vandalism and that the little hood responsible should be found and suspended from school if not from a tree, she was treated to several groans and a couple of expletives. Then Mike Hennessy said that she and Larry Martin should form a posse. When they found the vandal, they could give him the birch and then send him off to national service. That got a big laugh.

When Holly arrived home on Thursday evening, she found Lizzie scrubbing the outside of her front-room window. She was completely absorbed in the task and performing it with such vigour that her right arm was just a blur. Holly sneaked up behind her and whispered in her ear.

"Hello."

Lizzie leaped a clear inch off the ground before spinning around. "Hmph. And to think I was looking forward to you coming home."

"Yeah? Why's that then?"

"Some little toe-rags threw an egg at the window. I was in there, I saw them legging it down the street. Couldn't have been more than ten."

"Tossers. What's it got to do with me?"

"I want someone to bitch with. Someone who's really good at it."

"Oh. Okay. Kids, eh?"

Lizzie frowned. "That's it? 'Kids, eh?' Jesus, Holly, I could have come up with that myself. Where's the bile? Where's the scorn?"

"Sorry?"

"Are you all right? You look a bit . . . I dunno . . . peaky."

"I'm fine."

"First-week blues?"

Holly shrugged. "Maybe. Probably. Yeah . . . So, wait a minute, you think I'm good at bitching, is that what you're saying?"

"Not just good, Holly, world-class. You know that."

"But is that how you think of me . . . all the time? I mean, when you hear my name, is that what comes to mind? *Really good at bitching?*"

Lizzie stepped closer. "Are you sure you're okay? What's wrong?"

"Nothing," Holly said, regaining the composure that had been rapidly deserting her. "I'm grand. First-week blues, like you said. I'll leave you to it. If I think of any good lines about today's youth, I'll let you know."

With that, she turned and made the journey of a few feet across to her own front door. It seemed to take her several minutes to find her keys in her bag. Although she didn't look back, she was acutely aware as she fumbled through the tissues and mints that Lizzie had yet to return to her scrubbing and was staring at her intently.

Holly had been home for half an hour or so when the phone rang. It was her mother. She ran through some preliminary pleasantries before announcing that she had some news. Holly almost bit clean through her tongue. This was going to be about Charlie Fallon. She had yet to assimilate the fact that he a) existed and b) required her personal evaluation, but here it was, news of their first meeting.

"Go on," she said, her voice a tremulous little warble.

"I've had a letter," her mother said. "From England. Did you get one?"

"A letter? No. Who from?"

"It's from a man named Simon. Simon Christmas."

Holly did a quick memory-scan. She had no relatives of that name, as far she knew. "Who's he then?"

"We don't know him. He must have got my address on the Internet."

As ever, there was fear and caution in her voice as she said the word "Internet".

"And, what, does he think we're related?"

"Why don't I just read it out to you?"

"Go on then."

"Right. It starts out with *Greetings* in huge letters with one, two, three, four, five, six exclamation marks."

"Nice," Holly said. "If you're going to use multiple exclamation marks, six is a good number. Five's not enough, but seven would just look silly."

"It goes on '*I am writing to you today to bring you news of of*' – two 'ofs' there, that's a mistake – '*an exciting event that is upcoming*'. That's a stupid way to put it, isn't it? An event that is upcoming? Would you not just say '*an upcoming event*' and have done with it?"

"Yup."

"Anyway: '*My name is Simon Christmas and I am the founder and I am also the president of the Christmas Society, which is a society for people like yourself who*" *have the best surname in the world, which is, of course, Christmas, as you know.'* It's really badly written, isn't it?"

"Yes," Holly sighed. "It is. Go on."

She didn't need her to go on, of course; she'd already guessed that this was some sort of clan-gathering. The very idea made her intestines shiver.

"*'As you may know or may not know, we Christmases have found a home in every corner of the glob.'* I presume he means *globe*."

"One would imagine."

"*'I have done my best to compile a list of international Christmases, to "coin a phrase".'* He has '*coin a phrase*' in quote marks, for some reason. *'These letters are going out to England, Scotland, Wales, Ireland, America, Canada, Australia and Canada, to "name but a few".'* That last bit's in quote marks too. And he said Canada twice."

"Mum, you don't have to correct the whole thing as you go. Just read it out."

"All right, all right. *'It has been a great pleasure to me to compile the list and I hope you are happy to receive the letter. To cut a long story short, my first act as the founder and also the president of the Christmas Society is to formally invite you all to a family gathering of sorts which will take place on a date yet to be decided in a location that is also yet to be decided. Although they have yet to be decided, I have decided that the best location would be some hotel in Southampton, which is where I currently lay my head, and the best time would* definitely be what else can you guess but Christmas or shortly before it, rather.' I know that doesn't sound right, but that's what it says here. 'The actual venue will depend on how many of you decide to come. I hope all of you' – three exclamation marks. 'Such a gathering will be an opportunity for us to get to know each other and do a bit of research about our histories and of course share some of our experiences of having such a brilliant name. I don't know about you but I thank God every day for having such a brilliant name. It is always an ice-breaker at parties' – three exclamation marks. 'I conclude now by hoping that this letter finds you well and also by hoping that you will respond with a big yes' – four exclamation marks. 'Thank you. Yours Christmasly, Simon Christmas.'"

Holly gasped. "It doesn't actually say that . . . "

"Say what?"

"Yours Christmasly?'"

"No, it does."

"Jesus."

"So. What do you think?"

"I think he sounds certifiable."

"Holly."

"Really. Maybe he's been locked up already. Is the letter typed or did he do it on toilet roll with a crayon?"

"My funny, funny daughter . . . I wonder if Aidan and Alice got one?"

Aidan and Alice were Holly's uncle and aunt. They'd been living in the middle of nowhere in Kerry since the sixties and were rarely heard from. Holly had only met them a handful of times and had come to share her mother's opinion that they were several different kinds of weird.

"Who knows? I doubt they'd be interested. I doubt anybody with a functioning brain would be."

"Am I to take all this sarcasm as a no, then?"

Holly pulled a face. And then she realised that when her mother said "What do you think?" she wasn't asking her to judge the letter writer's sanity or lack thereof. She was asking her what she thought of his *idea*.

"Holy crap," she wheezed. "You're not really giving it serious thought, are you? You are!"

"Well . . ."

"No! I thought you were just telling me for a laugh! You were mocking his exclama–"

"So? That's beside –"

"Mum!"

"What? It might be nice to meet new people. Some of them are bound to turn out to be related, even if it's only distantly."

"Mum. Listen to me. I would rather die than go to a Christmas gathering of Christmases. Okay?"

"*Holly*. Don't ever say you would rather die than do something. You're tempting fa–"

"Fine. I would rather scoop my eyes out with a spoon. I would rather chew glass. I would rather be locked in a dark room with ten thousand Daddy Long-Legses."

She hoped this last one would carry some sway. Her mother was well aware of how she felt about those particular insects. Mrs Christmas exhaled with some force, sending a wintry crackle down the phone line. "Fine. Have it your way. I just thought it might be . . . I don't know . . ."

A few choice phrases suggested themselves to Holly. They seemed to queue up behind her lips, each jostling to be the first one out. *Excruciatingly boring? Life-threateningly irritating? Heart-squeezingly stupid?* She waited for them to be still.

"Okay then," Mrs Christmas said after an edgy pause. "Things to do, better get going. I'm sorry to have bothered you with the dopey letter."

"You didn't *bother* me with it," Holly said weakly. "I just don't –"

"Okay, then. Bye bye."

The line went dead. It was such a surprising development that Holly sat with the phone pressed to her ear for a few seconds, listening to the hum. Her mother had never even come close to hanging up like that before. Normally, she had just the opposite problem when it came to terminating phone calls. She was the sort of person, Holly had once told her, who would respond to "I have to go now, there's a burglar coming through the window" with a long review of an article she'd recently seen in which the writer gave tips on securing your house against burglars.

Holly scratched the back of her head and sighed. She had been a little harsh, possibly. But the Christmas Convention of Christmases was the sort of idea that had to be nipped in the bud, trampled underfoot and then thrown off a cliff. Better to be harsh now and get it over with rather than to fake interest for weeks only to arrive at the same result in the end. And, of course, she had said yes to meeting Charlie Fallon, so she was still a net contributor to her mother's happiness. It probably wasn't healthy, she realised, to be so calculating about these matters. But such was life.

On Friday morning, Holly woke up feeling hot and dizzy. Her head ached and there was a maddening itch deep in her throat. She contemplated taking the day off but decided, after a lengthy bout of gland-feeling and tongue-examining, that there was no need. Her primary motivation was to avoid something that she thought of as Greg Tynan Syndrome. It was a condition that to the inexperienced eye could easily be confused for common-or-garden hypochondria, but the two were not quite synonymous. Regular hypochondriacs were convinced that multiple illnesses existed were there was none. GTS sufferers, on the other hand, suffered from a single, highly specific delusion: they were forever coming down with "the flu". In Greg's particular case, Holly had lost count of the number of times he had shown up coughing and spluttering after a single day's absence and attributed it to those three little letters. Each and every time, Holly told him that, no, he hadn't been suffering from "the flu". He'd had a cold. They were different. A person with a cold felt a bit bunged up and out of sorts. A person with the flu was bedridden for a fortnight and contemplated suicide for every miserable minute of that time. There was simply no mistaking the two. Greg invariably cast his eyes to heaven and moved away, muttering under his breath. Some time later, he would show up sucking a Locket and ask if he'd missed any scandal the previous day, when he was out with the flu. Over the years, Greg and his fellow sufferers had driven Holly to such rage and despair that she had become their polar opposite, refusing not just to confuse a cold with the flu but to countenance the idea of illness in general. In all of her time at St Brendan's, she had taken only three sick days, all of which had involved gastrointestinal problems that required unencumbered access to toilet facilities. On this occasion, she concluded that while she had felt better, she was certainly fit for duty.

Her opening class of the day was science, with first-year students. It featured a long discussion on the characteristics of living organisms. This wasn't a bad thing in itself but unfortunately, it necessitated her use of the word "reproduction". As a result, the experience turned out to be something of a trial. She went out of her way to use the unsexiest examples she could think of, namely amoebae and chestnut trees, but that made little difference. As she saw the ripple go through the room like a shock wave from a nuclear blast, she realised that she might as well have mentioned Angelina Jolie and Jessica Alba. It wasn't as if everybody started openly giggling, although one or two of the stupider boys were unable to help themselves. It was more like a change in atmosphere, a sudden thickening of the air itself. Nods were nodded and winks were winked. *There was a woman in the room and she was talking about reproduction.* If that could happen, they seemed to think, then who knew what else was around the corner? One of the things that was around the corner, of course, was a series of classes on honest-to-God human sex. At this point, it was still a long way off, but that was of little comfort to Holly. The best she could hope for was that by the time she was obliged to say "vagina" with a straight face, they would be ready for it. Over the years, Holly had learned that reproduction should be the last characteristic of living organisms to get an airing because once the word was out there, the class was effectively over – or at least she thought she had learned that. In this case, for some unfathomable reason, she had mentioned it first. The thirty minutes between her dropping the R-bomb and the bell for the end of the lesson dragged by with glacial slowness. She might as well not have been there, she felt, for all the attention that was paid.

If anything, her second class of the day was worse. This time, she was teaching physics to third years – or at least she was trying to. She knew that something was up from the moment they trooped in and she soon found out what that something was. In the first class of the day, Larry Martin had called one of their number "a little bollocks"; now, revolution was in the air. Holly couldn't quite tell if the anger on show was genuine or had been manufactured in the interests of wasting time, but it hardly mattered. No one wanted to hear about Newton's Laws of Motion. They wanted to talk politics. It wasn't right, they yelped – in fact, it was a form of abuse. This sort of thing could be psychologically damaging. There could be a law suit here. The Department of Education should be informed. Holly allowed them to vent for a little while, hoping that the subject could then be put behind them. This proved to be a mistake. They took it as a sign that she sympathised with their cause and moved from issuing their own complaints to trying to get her to admit that Larry had stepped out of line. It was a tricky scenario. She certainly didn't want to condone what the old goat had done. But she didn't want to align herself with the mini-Spartacuses either. The water was further muddied by the fact that the boy at the centre of the drama was Owen Quigley; "little bollocks" wasn't far off the mark. The end result was that almost half of the class was taken up with diplomatic wrangling. By the time she finally lost her temper and told them that she didn't want to hear another word on the subject, she had lost the will to teach. She did her best but was glad that there were no inspectors around for the second half of the lesson. It was not her best work.

The third period of the morning was a maths class with fifth years. Holly gave such a lacklustre performance and was in such patently bad form that she thought she saw genuine concern on some of the boys' faces. She couldn't wait for the bell to ring and more or less ran to the staff room when it did. There, she made herself a cup of strong coffee and found a quiet corner in which to sip it. She sincerely hoped that no one would bother her for the duration of the break but in this she was disappointed. Peter Fogarty joined her almost as soon as she was in position and spotted immediately that she was not in stellar form.

"Not in the mood for talking, eh?" he observed.

Holly shook her head. "No."

"Why? What's the problem?"

"I've had a brutal morning, Peter. I don't feel well. And I had three shitty classes in a row."

"Why? What was so shitty?"

She gazed up at him. "The words 'not in the mood for talking' have literally no meaning for you, do they?"

"Oh dear. You are grumpy, aren't you?"

Just then, James Bond appeared at Peter's shoulder. Holly hadn't even noticed him approaching.

"Morning," he said. "Gorgeous day, isn't it?"

Peter put his finger to his lips. "Shhh. Holly's in a bad mood. Even by her standards."

"You know what?" she snapped. "I'm getting pretty sick of this Holly-and-her-moods rubbish."

"She's not feeling well," Peter whispered.

James nodded. "Is that right? What's the problem? Flu?"

She put her coffee cup to her mouth and bit down on its rim for a moment to stop herself saying something unpleasant. In truth, she felt pretty awful. She would have given a finger – one of the useful ones – for a lie-down in a nice quiet room.

"It's nothing," she said then. "Just a bit of a headache. That and the fact that I'm a crap teacher."

"Well, I know that's not true," James said. "I've heard just the opposite."

"Really? Someone said that? Who?" As soon as the words were out, she wanted nothing more from life than to have them back. Could she possibly have sounded any more needy and pathetic? It didn't seem likely.

"That would be telling," James said. "Everyone has the odd bad class now and again, don't they? I know I sure as hell do."

"Me too," Peter agreed. "Definitely."

Holly didn't doubt for a moment that Peter had made some howlers in the past but somehow she got the impression that James was merely being polite. Nevertheless, she found that she appreciated the effort.

"I have one more class before lunchtime," she said. "If I can get through that in one piece, I'm sure I'll be fine for the afternoon."

"You know what you need?" James said. "You need soup."

She thought she'd misheard him. "Sorry, did you say 'soup'?"

He nodded. "Never underestimate the power of a good soup. Nothing like it. Comforting, delicious, satisfying. Have you ever been to Souperior?"

This was a new café in Rathgar. Some of the teachers raved about it but Holly had never been.

"No. Never."

"Right. We'll go at lunchtime, the three of us. We'll have to hurry, but it's doable."

"I've got a sandwich with me," Peter said sorrowfully.

"So? Have it tomorrow. It'll keep."

Holly had been about to raise the same objection but now realised that it sounded deeply silly.

"All right then," Peter said. "I'm in."

They both looked at Holly. "Okay," she said. "Let's go wild. Soup it is."

Souperior turned out to be one of those places that had a couple of tables at the back for show but was really more of a corridor than a café. The queue for take-out ran all the way out the front door and on to the pavement. Holly despaired when she saw it but James insisted that it would move quickly. Irritatingly, he was correct. As they approached the checkout, he further opined that he had a feeling they would even get a table (he felt it in his bones, apparently). Sure enough, just as Peter paid for his Tomato and Basil, a couple of suits got up to leave. They pounced. It was the Outer Mongolian booth all over again. Holly hoped this excursion would have a more upbeat ending.

She had plumped for Mexican Bean and found that it was everything James had said it would be. It not only tasted divine but seemed to have genuine medicinal qualities; before she was even halfway done her headache began to lift. The combination of improving health and a sense of having actually taught something – her pre-lunch class had gone quite well – was having a considerable effect on her mental state.

And then James said something that put a genuine smile on her face. On the way over in Peter's car, they'd been listening to a phone-in on the radio. The subject under discussion was shyness. They'd passed a few comments but hadn't really paid much attention. Now that lunch was behind them, however, they'd fallen into the topic again. Peter said he knew for a fact that shyness wasn't necessarily a permanent condition. Growing up, his little sister Cathy had lacked confidence to such an extent that she would physically squirm if someone outside of her immediately family so much as spoke to her. Somewhere along the way, however, she'd simply grown out of it. These days, she was the life and soul of every event she attended and seemed to have a couple of dozen "very best friends". James shook his head sadly. His pal John Lennon had shyness issues too, but he very much doubted that the guy would ever leave them behind him. Peter probed for details. It wasn't as if John was a recluse or anything, James explained. He just had trouble talking to women. It was starting to get him down. This was the moment when Holly broke into a smile.

"Wow," James said. "You look pretty chuffed to hear that. I didn't know you were a sadist."

"I'm not pleased to hear that he's unhappy," Holly said. "But I have a friend in the same sort of boat. Trouble meeting men, I mean. I'm just wondering if maybe . . . you know."

"What? Get 'em together?"

"Yeah. Why not?"

"I don't know, Holly. What's your friend like?"

"You go first. What's John Lennon like?"

James hesitated. She noticed.

"Ah, shite," she said.

"What?"

"You paused. There's something wrong with him. What is it?"

James looked offended. It was a look that Holly hadn't seen on his face before. "There's nothing wrong with him," he said. "I wouldn't be friends with him, would I, if there was something *wrong* with him?"

"Except . . . ?"

James looked briefly to Peter as if asking for fraternal support. "Well. He's a bit sensitive about his, uh . . . weight."

"I see," Holly said. "What are we talking about here? Bit on the plump side or carrying a bottle of oxygen?"

"Oh, plump," James assured her. "At worst. It's all in his head, really."

"And around his waist, presumably."

"He could stand to lose a few pounds," James said with an air of finality. "It's no big deal. Honestly. What about yours?"

"Orla," Holly said. "Her name's Orla. I've known her since primary school. She's lovely. Very kind. Soft-hearted. And she's got one of those voices, those husky ones that men seem to love."

"Oooh, Kathleen Turner," Peter said. He looked very pleased to have been able to make a contribution.

"Yeah," Holly said. "Exactly. That's what everyone says . . ."

"That sounds good," James said. "So, what are you not telling me?"

"Nothing. Orla's great."

"And yet she has trouble meeting men. Come on, I told you about John's . . . extra . . . I told you about John."

129

Holly chewed it over for a moment. There was no need for details. "It's just my opinion," she said slowly, "but if I was her . . . I'd give my wardrobe a rethink."

She had chosen this as the least horrible of the options available to her. But now that she'd said it, she was filled with such a profound sense of guilt that she began to feel unwell all over again.

"Oh," James said. "Bad taste in duds? That's not so terrible."

"This is good coming from you," Peter said to Holly. And then his eyes turned to saucers. "Wait . . . Wait . . . There's a joke in there somewhere. Pot, kettle, *black* . . . Hang on, give me a minute."

Holly puffed out some air. "We haven't got time for your tiny mind to cobble together a feeble crack, Peter, thank you very much." She returned her attention to James. "You're right. It's not so bad. If Orla had someone else doing her clothes shopping for her, she'd be beating them back with a stick, lemme tell you."

"Okay. I believe you."

"Good."

"Now – what are we going to do? I don't think John would go for the whole blind date thing. He'd be too nervous."

"No. Neither would Orla. And besides, I wouldn't like her to think that I was intervening. She has her pride."

"So has John," James said.

"Jesus, look at the time," Peter said. "We have to go. You can work this out later."

Holly and James looked at each other. Simultaneously, they squinted with concentration. Apparently, neither wanted to get up from the table before a plan had been formed. Holly joined her hands together and rested her chin on them. James followed suit and added a raised eyebrow to the mix.

"We could just get them to the same place at the same time," he said slowly. "Introduce them and see what happens. I'll bring him, you bring her."

"We just bump into each other accidentally . . ."

"Yeah."

"Okay. Somewhere informal. Relaxed."

"Exactly."

"Low pressure."

"They mustn't suspect a thing."

"I'm off now," Peter said, getting up. "If you want a lift, I'd suggest –"

"Cinema?" James ventured. "We all go to the same flick and afterwards just happen to meet up in –"

"Nah. They could just wander off. We have to meet at the *start* of whatever it is."

"Dinner, then? Join tables?"

"Maybe . . . "

"Pub?"

"I don't know. Seating arrangements could be tricky. They might never even talk to each other. We need something active, something fun, something where we're bustling around each other, y'know, interacting. Plus, if it's a bit different we can use that as a selling-point. Not just the same old pub and restaurant shite."

"Yeah, that's true. What about bowling? John *loves* bowling."

"Bowling," Holly said, trying the word out. "Bowling. Bowling."

"Bowling it is!" Peter said and walked off, his patience finally gone.

Holly and James gave each other one last squint.

"Bowling," they said together.

Chapter 8

Holly was surprised – stunned, really – by Aisling's response to the blind-date plan. She had expected her to argue with it for no better reason than she hadn't thought of it herself. But no.

"Fucking deadly," she said when Holly rang her from home. "And bowling's perfect. Orla loved it when we went on my birthday. She laughed her ass off the whole way through. And ate three or four hot dogs."

This was a habit of Aisling's that Holly had never quite got used to – referring to events in the distant past as if they had only just happened (and displaying a quite freakish ability to recall the details). They had indeed gone bowling together, just once. Holly guessed that this was in 1994, maybe 1995. Her own memories of it were somewhat hazy. She seemed to recall a lot of noise and heat and a general sense of being out of her natural environment.

"Right."

"So, what's the story? Are you being all self-sacrificing now?"

"Sorry?"

"Bowling. You hate bowling."

Holly frowned down the line. "Do I?"

"Well, you certainly hated it that time. You gave out shite for about a week afterwards."

"Did I?"

"Jesus, Holly, are you losing track of all the things you can't stand? It can't be easy, right enough. Maybe you should keep a journal of some kind. Or do up a spreadsheet."

"Piss off."

"I'm telling you – you *hated* it. A lot. Even by your standards. I can't believe you don't remember this. You had an argument with the people in the next row or strip or whatever they're –"

"Lane."

"Lane. You had an argument with the people in the next lane because they were making animal noises. We presumed they were high? One of them threw a can of Fanta at your head?"

Suddenly, there it was, the whole scene. "That's *right*," Holly marvelled. "It's coming back to me. They were doing cows and monkeys . . ."

"That was them. Even apart from the Fanta-throwing and all, though, you were miserable. Complained all night long. I gave out yards to you about ruining my birthday."

"Yeah, that rings another bell."

"But you might be thinking of another time I gave out to you for ruining my birthday by complaining all night."

"Har-de-har."

"Right, so you're not being all self-sacrificing. You just *forgot* that you hate bowling."

"Hm. Anyway. It's still a good plan. Tomorrow night then?"

"I'll be there. Can't wait to get a look at this Bond . . . *James* Bond. See if he's as good-looking as you say."

"Hang on, I didn't say he was good-looking. I said he looked like an anchorman."

"Yeah, and they tend to be good-looking. Is he much of a bowler?"

"Couldn't tell you. He seems to breeze through everything, that one, so he'll probably turn out to be brilliant at it."

"Yeah. And he might be a good bowler too. Wa-hey!"

"Christ. It's like being friends with Julian Clary."

"Thanks!"

"That wasn't a compliment, Aisling."

Holly took a few minutes to gather her thoughts before making her next call. She made herself some tea and tried to interest Claude in a toy she'd bought on a whim a few weeks previously. It was something akin to a thin plastic fishing rod with a bell and ball combination instead of a hook. He ignored it completely when she dangled it in front of his face and trailed it along the ground around him. She did manage to get a reaction when she bounced the ball on top of his head but it was hardly the one she'd been hoping for. Rather than seizing it with his mighty jaws or even giving it a playful swipe, he simply got up off his hunkers and moved a foot to one side, all the while staring at her with an expression of deep disappointment. Holly gave up at that point and returned to the sofa, phone in hand.

Okay, she told herself. *Nice and easy. Casual. Cool as a breeze. Like Saturday night never happened.* She dialled.

"Hiya. It's me."

"Well. What's up?"

"Not much. Listen: I was wondering if you fancied doing something tomorrow night. Something different."

"Yeah? Like what?"

"I was thinking maybe, I don't know . . . bowling?"

There was a pause.

"*Bowling?* You hate bowling. We tried it once, didn't we? Ages ago?"

"I don't know, I think –"

"No, wait, we *did*. Definitely. You hated it."

"Well, you know me, Orla. I'm not one to hold grudges. I'm willing to give it another try, if it'll have me."

"I don't get it. What brought this on?"

Holly had an answer all ready for that one. "I'm just sick of pubs and restaurants. Aren't you sick of pubs and restaurants? Same old thing, every weekend. I just thought we should branch out, you know? It was either bowling or Go-Karting."

Orla made an alarming noise. For a moment, Holly was sure she was choking on something. Then she realised that the raspy gurgle had not been prompted by a wayward peanut but by simple excitement.

"Ooh! Go-Karting! To hell with bowling! Let's do that! That's a brilliant idea!"

"Uh –"

"You know *Top Gear*? They do that celebrity time trial thing? Every time I see Gloria Hunniford or someone pootling around at fifteen miles an hour, I get a serious urge –"

"One thing at a time, Orla, one thing at a time. Let's give plain old bowling a shot and if we like that, maybe we'll try something with crash helmets."

"Have you ever been Go-Karting?"

Holly silently cursed herself for her choice of fictional alternative activity. She should have said Pitch'n'Putt, she now realised. Orla's hatred for golf was a matter of public record and presumably applied to the sport's little brother too. "No, Orla, I've never been Go-Karting."

"Well, then. Who knows? You might love it. And we know for a fact that you hate bowling. Doesn't it make sense to at least give ourselves a chance of all having a good time?"

"Yeah, but –"

"Let me put it another way," Orla continued. "I quite like the idea of bowling. But I'm not going with *you*. Sorry. I just don't want to listen to all the bitching."

Holly's mind raced ahead. Could she rearrange the whole thing and have James show up at a Go-Karting track somewhere? She supposed she could; she had his number. But what would be the point? John and Orla weren't going to get to know each other while whizzing about at speed. And besides, for all she knew, James had already made his call. How would it look if he had to ring again to tell his friend that his sudden, irresistible urge to roll a heavy ball along the floor had changed into a sudden, irresistible urge to drive a glorified lawn-mower around in a circle? No – there was nothing for it. She would have to somehow talk Orla into bowling without making it sound like too much of a big deal.

"What if I promise not to bitch?" she asked tentatively.

"No offence," Orla began. "But when it comes to bitching, your promises aren't worth –"

"All right, all right. Jesus. I don't know why it popped into my head. It just suddenly seemed like a really good idea."

"It isn't. *Go-Karting* is a really good idea."

Holly saw that she had no chance of getting anywhere while this was a choice between bowling and the thing Orla actually wanted to do. Her only chance was to make it a choice between bowling and nothing. "Well," she sighed, doing her best to sound genuinely saddened, "it looks like we're out of runway. Because I, for one, am definitely not getting into a Go-Kart. That ain't happening."

"Okay. Back to the pub or restaurant, so."

"Looks that way."

"Sure does."

"Oh well."

"What are you gonna do?"

"Pity. Aisling will be disappointed too. I just called her and she was very keen."

"So? Maybe if I called her and suggested Go-Karting she'd be very keen on that too."

"That's a laugh. Aisling would never put on a helmet of any kind. Think of the havoc it would wreak with her hair."

At that point, Orla suddenly opted out of the jokey back-and-forth routine they'd got going. "What's going on here, Holly?" she asked. "You sound weird. This is all very suspicious."

"What? I don't know –"

"Is this something to do with a man?"

Holly's heart-rate doubled. "What? What makes you say that?"

"It is, isn't it? You've met some bloke who works in a bowling alley and you're trying to drag us along while you scope him out."

"Oh! No. God, no. Honestly, Orla. No. Nothing to do with men. It'll be a laugh. Come on. Please."

Orla didn't reply immediately but Holly could hear her breathing down the line. Cogs were definitely turning.

"If you do any complaining," Orla said then, "about the noise or the morons in the next lane over or the rules of the game or the taste of the munchies or *anything* – I'm leaving right away. Got it?"

"Right. Got it."

"Sure?"

"Yes. Cross my heart."

"All right then. Where and what time?"

The plan that Holly and James had concocted between them via text message was a simple one. The girls would arrive at the MegaBowl in Blanchardstown at eight; the boys would follow at eight thirty. James would spot Holly (or vice versa) and suggest that they make one party. This was the tricky bit. There was every chance that Orla or John – or both – would be unhappy with this arrangement and cut their evening short. But that was an unavoidable risk; they would just have to keep their fingers crossed.

Holly and Orla shared a taxi while Aisling made her own arrangements. There was almost no chance that the latter would be on time, Holly had assumed. But she was wrong. As they pulled up at the MegaBowl, she glanced out of the window and saw that Aisling was standing by the entrance tapping her watch.

"What time do you call this?" she said when they approached.

"I call it five to eight," Holly replied. "Let me guess – you got the time mixed up."

Aisling didn't even bother to deny it. "Yeah . . . I thought we said seven."

"And what time did you get here?"

"Seven thirty. I remembered as soon as I arrived. I've been standing here like an eejit for half an hour."

"Twenty-five minutes," Holly corrected. "*We're* early – as opposed to wrong. Okay then. Shall we?"

"We shall."

They trooped inside where they met a quartet of teenage boys coming in the opposite direction. One of their number – he couldn't have been more than sixteen – stopped dead and looked Aisling over from head to toe, pausing along the way at the more obvious landmarks. "Now we're talking," he said. "Just the way I like 'em." He swivelled as she passed and gave her another once-over, this time from the rear. "Front *and* back," he said approvingly. "What's your name, darlin'? Aw, don't run off, don't be shy."

His mates cracked up as only teenage boys can, falling over each other and cackling like wild dogs. Holly slowed, stopped, then turned to face him.

"Wow," she said. "So it's true . . . excessive masturbation *does* cause spots. I always thought that was just a myth."

The boy's hand went reflexively to the crusty landscape of his forehead. As soon as he became conscious of the move, he pretended that he was merely running his hand through his hair. This made him look even more ridiculous and he seemed to realise as much. His friends did their best to show some solidarity by putting a lid on their laughter, but it proved too much for them; almost immediately they collapsed into even greater hysteria. As she turned away from them again, Holly felt a heavy wave of satisfaction roll over her. Aisling and Orla hadn't so much as broken stride and she had to break into a trot to catch up with them. Neither of them mentioned the teenagers. Holly didn't either. Par for the course.

"Quiet, isn't it?" Aisling said. "I would have thought it would be busier on a Saturday night."

"I would have thought just the opposite," Orla said. "People have better things to do. Like Go-Karting"

Holly pretended not to have noticed this response. She'd heard several swipes in the car on the way over. They were playful, she'd assumed, rather than malicious and would probably taper off if ignored.

"All the better if it's quiet," she said. "There'll be plenty of –"

The word "lanes" died on her lips. James Bond and another man – John Lennon, presumably – were coming through the door.

"What's wrong?" Orla said.

Earlier in the day, Holly had given a lot of thought to the moment when she would have to fake surprise at bumping into a colleague; she'd even practised a little, staring wide-eyed into the bathroom mirror. Now she realised that she needn't have bothered. She was genuinely startled. And judging by the expression on his face – he had spotted her right away – so was James.

"Nothing. Just, that's, eh . . . that guy over there is the new sub. At school."

Orla spun around, as did Aisling. James had already started towards them, one hand raised in greeting. John Lennon stayed put, just inside the front door.

"Hi, James," Holly said when he arrived. "Small world."

"It sure is," he said. Then he smiled too broadly and for too long. Holly tried to communicate with her eyes that *she* had come at the right time and that *he* was early. She wasn't at all sure that the message got through.

"Oh, these are my friends," she said then, "Aisling and Orla."

"Hello, Aisling," he said extending a hand and giving two brisk shakes. "I'm James Bond." The name had barely left his lips before he rolled his eyes and said, "If you have any jokes on the subject, feel free. I won't mind. If you have something original, I might even laugh."

"James Bond?" Aisling said. "Really? Wow. But there'll be no jokes. Holly has us well-trained on that score. Name jokes are a no-no around here."

James twinkled at her. She flipped her hair.

"Hi," Orla said as he turned and took her hand. "Orla."

Holly's toes clenched. Was it her imagination or had there been a certain stiffness about this opener? No comment on his name, even?

"Hi, Orla," James said. "Nice to meet you."

"So, are you a big bowling fan?" Holly asked him as innocently as she could.

"Not really," he said. "We were just bored, so we thought we'd give it a go. You get sick of doing the same old thing every weekend, don't you? Pubs and restaurants, that's all we ever seem to do."

Orla went up on her toes. "Wow, that's weird. That's what Holly said. I mean, that's *exactly* what Holly said."

"There you go," James said. "Great minds and all that."

"Who's your friend?" Aisling asked. "Isn't he going to come over?"

Holly was impressed with the acting, if not the material. John was already looking a little forlorn and out of place; Aisling's intervention had only served to draw attention to that fact. James glanced behind him, then waved.

"John's a little shy," he said.

Again, Holly was both impressed and irritated. He'd sounded perfectly natural, but why bother pointing out that the guy was shy? Wasn't that obvious? Even if it hadn't been clear from the way he'd hung back by the doorway, there was no mistaking his disposition as he approached. He had the look of a man who was on his way to the dentist at best or the gallows at worst. That was besides the point, though. The most noteworthy thing about him, Holly thought, was that he wasn't ugly. The notion occurred to her in exactly those words: *he isn't ugly*. She felt thoroughly ashamed of herself for making such a superficial judgement but immediately forgot her scruples and moved on to considering his weight. Again, the news was pretty good. He was never going to have a career as a ballet dancer but the ground wasn't shaking underfoot either. James started speaking to him while he was still several metres away; Holly guessed that he was trying to give him a soft landing.

"John, this is Holly. She's a teacher at the school I just started in. And these are her friends, Aisling and Orla."

Holly and Aisling said hello; Orla merely stared though narrowed eyes. Her mouth had set into a hard, straight line. Holly tried to pretend that she hadn't noticed these details. John nodded, paused, and nodded again. Then he shifted from one foot to the other. Then he scratched the tip of his nose. Then he put his hands into the pockets of his jacket and took them out again. Finally, he said, "Hello. There. Hello there."

His voice was surprisingly soft, Holly thought, like that of a late-night DJ. It was the first quality of his about which she had felt positive, as opposed to merely not negative, and she clung to it for a moment. The best word for it was "soothing", she supposed, but in the right circumstances, she could even imagine that it would be quite sexy. She wondered if Orla was thinking the same thing but didn't dare to glance in her direction.

"You probably thought it was a serious treat meeting James Bond," James Bond said. "Well, get ready for a bonus. This isn't any old John we have here – this is John Lennon."

"You're kidding me!" Aisling cried. For the third time, Holly felt conflicted. Aisling's delivery of the line was perfectly believable, but she'd screwed up the timing; James had barely got the words out before she'd reacted.

"Nope. Honest to God."

"John Lennon and James Bond! And you're actually *friends*?"

"As opposed to what?" Holly said. "Strangers who hang around together to give everyone something to talk about?"

Aisling supplied a dirty look. Holly couldn't tell if it was genuine or part of the act.

"Well, I consider John to be a good pal of *mine*," James said. "I don't know if he feels the same way."

Everyone looked at John. He looked at his feet.

"Clearly not," James said in a mock-wounded tone.

Everyone kept looking at John. He kept looking at his feet. Holly found herself getting angry. There was shy around women and then there was just plain rude.

"How in the name of God did two people called John Lennon and James Bond get to be friends?" Aisling asked then, putting the awkward moment out of its misery.

"Were you both part of a support group or something?"

"Support group?" James asked. "Why would we be in a support group?"

Aisling shrugged. "For people with . . . unusual names. No offence."

"James doesn't mind his name," Holly explained. "He likes it, as far as I can see. Correct?"

"I do," he said, nodding and smiling.

Holly turned to John. "Where do you stand on all this? Would you rather be a John Smith? Or a David Lennon?"

A direct question was bound to get a direct response, she reasoned. At first, it seemed that this was not necessarily true. John's chin remained anchored to his chest and, while his eyes did rise to meet hers, he didn't appear to be all that keen on producing actual words. Holly's teeth ground together.

She was on the point of asking him if he'd heard her talking to him when he said, "I'm not crazy about it. Sometimes I think it's kind of funny, I suppose. And sometimes I'm a jealous guy. Jealous of all the normal names, I mean. Jealous . . . guy."

He smiled a strange little smile. Holly was genuinely frightened for a moment; he looked frankly creepy, smiling at nothing. And then she cottoned on to the joke.

"Oh, *Jealous Guy*!" she said. "I get it. Very good." She turned to Aisling and Orla, both of whom looked bewildered and slightly alarmed. "The song," she explained.

"Ohhh," Aisling said. "Nice one."

Again, Orla merely nodded.

It was a poor joke, Holly thought. In fact, it didn't even qualify as a joke; it was just a pun. And he'd delivered it badly. Still, he'd made an effort, that was the main thing. It had clearly taken a lot out of him too – he seemed to be breathing a little more heavily, as if he'd just jogged up a flight of stairs.

"To answer your question," James said to Aisling, "I knew someone who knew someone who knew John. They thought it'd be hilarious if we met. Simple as that."

"I see," Orla said. "So you were set up – like a blind date sort of thing?"

Holly's joints stiffened.

"I suppose so," James said. "But it's not the way I'd choose to think about it, personally."

"So!" Aisling said then. "Are we going bowling or what?"

"Yeah," Holly said. "Let's get started. Those pins aren't going to knock themselves down."

"Okay then," James said.

"Righty-o," Aisling said.

"Grand," Holly said.

They stood there in silence for a few excruciating seconds. Holly caught James's eye. She didn't trust herself to hold his gaze for more than a micro-second but she hoped it would do the trick. It did.

"Hey," he said. "Why don't we all hook up? Might be better crack with a bigger group."

Orla clapped her hands together so loudly that everyone else jumped a little. "*What* a good idea!" she cried. Her face was blank. "Let's do that."

147

She turned and marched off in the direction of the shoe desk. Holly and James exchanged another glance, a longer one this time. He looked the way she felt – slightly nauseous. It seemed perfectly possible – likely, even – that Orla, at least, had cottoned on. But there was no backing out now. Holly did her best to smile.

"Shall we?" she said.

Chapter 9

There was a moment, perhaps five minutes after they started their game, when Holly seriously considered simply walking out. It would be an unpopular move, for sure, but at the time it seemed like her only option. She would be apologetic, she decided, but also firm. The gist of it would be that she'd made a mistake, pure and simple. When she'd promised not to complain, she had done so in good faith. But it had turned out, to her genuine surprise and disappointment, that she'd promised more than she was able to deliver.

Her difficulties had begun before she'd even taken her seat. There were two couples at the next lane. Only the men were bowling; the women just sat there chatting, or rather booming at the top of their voices. The ambient noise was shocking (Holly was fully aware of that), but these two were drastically over-compensating. If they'd been telling the greatest jokes ever told, it would have still have been annoying. But they weren't telling jokes, great or otherwise.

They were talking about astrology. When Aisling first overheard them – like everyone else within a thirty feet radius, she had no choice in the matter – she spun around in Holly's direction and wagged a finger, as if to say, *Now, now – don't let this get you going*. Holly nodded back and stiffened her spine. Then one of the loud women expressed the hope that if she ever had a baby, it would be a Virgo because she always got on well with Virgos. For a few seconds, Holly thought she might scream or cry or simply faint with irritation, but she did some diaphragmatic breathing and was able to regain her composure.

Then, after they'd entered their names into the computer – a process that seemed to have been deliberately designed to make a person feel stupid and clumsy – Holly learned to her horror that she was first up. James and Aisling offered some cheerful encouragement; John and Orla stayed mute. She selected the lightest ball she could find, trotted towards the line and released her missile in an action that was more hurl than bowl. It bounced twice and meandered into the gutter about a quarter of the way down the lane. Her next effort fared marginally better, making it almost halfway to the pins before it too fell by the wayside. As she turned to her companions and shrugged a tiny shrug, Holly realised that whatever fun bowling had to offer, she'd just had it. As the night wore on, she would probably get better and would knock down an occasional pin or maybe even several. But the fundamental experience would be the same. You picked up a ball and rolled it towards some objects, hoping to hit them – The End.

James went next. While he wasn't quite as useless as she was, Holly was shocked to discover that he was pretty awful. His first effort missed entirely and his second clipped a lone pin at the edge of the pack. It wobbled briefly, as if trying to make up its mind whether to fall over or not, and then settled on its base again. This news might have cheered her up a little if it hadn't been for James's reaction. He couldn't have been more pleased with himself if he'd knocked every last one of the things clean through the back wall. It was hardly a surprise, she supposed, that he was one of those it's-not-the-winning-it's-the-taking-part types, but still – she felt even more ashamed of her own performance, which had ended with her pulling a face and flopping down on her seat like a four-year-old denied access to chocolate.

Orla went after James. Her first attempt took down six pins and her second took two more. By the standards thus far, it was a remarkable achievement. But Orla didn't seem particularly pleased. She completely ignored the quick congratulations that Aisling offered as she stepped forward and returned to the pillar she'd been leaning against, where she folded her arms and scowled venomously. She was standing about as far away from the others as it was possible to stand and still be considered a member of the same group. Holly was now seriously worried that she'd guessed what was going on. She frowned, sank still further into her seat and watched Aisling emulate her own score of precisely zero.

Just then, a passing male pointed a finger-gun and told her, without slowing down, that she should cheer up because it might never happen. He was gone before she had even opened her mouth to issue a violent rebuke. Holly had been on the receiving end of this saying so many times in her life that she'd thought it had long since lost its power to upset her. Apparently not. What was wrong with people? Didn't they realise that "Cheer up, it might never happen" was an insult? That you might as well mumble "Miserable bitch" and be done with it? This was the point at which she considered making an exit. The goal of the exercise had been to get Orla and John in the same place at the same time. They'd already achieved that and may well have been caught doing so. What difference would it make, really, if she upped and left? There'd be harsh words and dirty looks, granted, but she was well-used to harsh words and dirty looks. A few more of each would hardly kill her.

She was chewing on her lip, weighing the pros and cons, when James sat down beside her and said, "That was so *rude*. Your man."

She turned to face him so suddenly that a small muscle in the middle of her back made a squeak of protest. "Yes! It was, wasn't it? Gobshite."

James nodded. "He hasn't got a clue what's going on in your life."

"Exactly."

"For all he knows, you've just lost your job or you're worried about your health or something."

"That's so weird – that's *just* what I always think. Who is he to make assumptions?"

"And even if he did know the truth, the fact that you're crap at bowling is none of his damn business."

Holly was only just able to stop herself from agreeing. "I see," she said then. "We have a comedian on our hands."

"If you thought it might help," James replied, all wide-eyed innocence, "I could give you a few pointers."

She gestured up at the scoreboard. "If you look carefully, Mr Bond, I think you'll find that you're in no position to offer advice."

He shook his head. "That sentence sounded like something Blofeld would come out with. And, might I remind you, *I* made a pin wobble about a bit, which is a lot more than you achieved."

"Oh, sorry, I forgot about that. Yeah, you're quite the expert."

He bowed. "I try."

"Yup. You're trying all right."

He smiled. "It's your turn again, Holly."

As she got to her feet, two thoughts occurred to her. The first was that she was suddenly determined not only to stay but to do well. The second was that she really liked the way James Bond said her name.

She did get better as the evening progressed, but even her relative successes – one of her shots knocked down seven whole pins – felt like nothing more than statistical inevitabilities. Regardless of her approach or aim (she tried a multitude of techniques), the ball went where it felt like going – sooner or later, it was bound to go down the middle. James improved too, as did Aisling. John had no need to. He'd started out well enough but by the time he'd "got his wrist in", as he put it – Holly had to bite her tongue – he was in a different league to the others. Orla, by contrast, got progressively worse as time went by. She started out steadily enough, but her play quickly became erratic, then poor and finally embarrassing to behold. Her bowling ability was not the only thing to plummet; her mood went from bad to much, much worse. There was no way for Holly and Aisling to discuss it properly without being obvious, so they were reduced to pulling occasional faces at each other.

They'd been bowling for about three-quarters of an hour before Holly summoned up the courage to make an overture.

"Are you OK, Orla?" she whispered, having sidled up towards her like a pickpocket. "You look a bit glum."

Orla stared straight ahead. "I'm not fucking stupid," she said.

Holly feigned surprise. "What? What does that mean? Who said you were stupid?"

"You're in enough trouble as it is, Holly. Don't add to it by letting on you don't know what I'm talking about."

In for a penny, Holly thought. "But I don't know what you're talking about! What is it? Is it something *I* did?"

"The two of you. Her too." She jerked her head in Aisling's direction. Aisling was looking at the scoreboard and didn't notice.

"Maybe I'm being thick," Holly began but Orla cut her off before she could get any deeper into the lie.

"Oh, fuck off!" she spat. "Aisling told you I was

lonely and you put the feelers out and your good buddy James fucking Bond said, 'Tell you what, I've got a fat friend too – they're bound to get on. They can be fucking *jolly* together!'."

That was a lot of swearing for Orla, Holly realised. She was seriously mad.

"Look –"

"Don't bother, Holly. Just. Don't. Bother. This whole thing is a set-up, a blindingly *obvious* set-up and I'm not fucking having it. I knew this was suspicious, I fucking *knew* it. 'Oh, please come bowling, Orla. I know we never, ever go and none of us are remotely interested in it and it's completely out of the blue but it'll be something different. Hey, look – there's some men I know and you don't arriving at exactly the same time! What a pleasant coincidence!'"

Holly went up on her toes and stayed there, chewing her lip, lost in embarrassment and alarm until, at last, it was her turn to bowl. It was a wait of no more than thirty seconds but it felt like a month. When she returned from duty, she made a point of standing off to the side, alone. She desperately wanted to talk tactics with Aisling but it was impossible. James soon came to join her.

"Not my finest hour," he said.

"Sorry?"

"What, you weren't watching? I was under the impression that you studying my every move, hoping to glean even the tiniest –"

"Nope."

"Oh."

"This is a frigging disaster," Holly said through her teeth then. "Orla's twigged. And she's raging."

"Ah. I was wondering. She looks ready to do murder."

"Yeah. And it's me and Aisling she's going to do it to."

"Well, we can't have that. How about I have a word with her – tell her the whole thing was my idea?"

Holly found this oddly touching. She felt her cheeks glow. "That's a nice offer. But I don't think it would help. She'd still want –"

She broke off because Orla, on returning from her latest go, had made a beeline for John. It was the first time she'd even acknowledged his existence, let alone addressed him directly, since they'd started the game. James noticed too. He briefly grabbed Holly's forearm. She flinched and then did it again deliberately in some semi-conscious attempt to look as if she was just flinching a lot today and he shouldn't read anything into it.

"Progress," James whispered.

"I really doubt it," Holly replied.

"Now, now. Let's just wait and . . . Oh."

Orla had already finished saying whatever it was she'd had to say to John and was now storming – that was the only word for it – towards the exit. Aisling had been bowling during the brief *tête à tête* and only caught the storm-off.

"Where's she going?" she asked in a manner that made Holly think she'd guessed exactly where Orla was going.

"She's going home," John Lennon said, stepping forward rather dramatically. "She's really upset."

"What about?" Aisling said meekly.

John folded his arms. "She said she wanted me to know that this whole thing was a set-up to get me and her together. Is that right? James? Is it?"

James scratched the tip of his nose. "Well . . . a little bit, yeah."

A small smile grew on John's face. "Aw. Cheers."

"Oh. Right. Don't mention it."

"Wait a minute," Holly gasped. "You're pleased?"

He shrugged. "Why wouldn't I be?"

"That's so cute," Aisling said and gave his shoulder a little pat.

He recoiled as if she'd punched him and then stared at his feet, obviously trying not to smile. It was, Holly had to admit, quite an endearing sight. Then he suddenly looked up again.

"I'll tell you something I'm not that chuffed about though. And I want an honest answer. She said you only thought we'd be a good couple because we're both . . . y'know . . . a wee bit . . . plump."

"What?" Holly and Aisling cried together.

"That's ridiculous," Holly added.

"Mental," Aisling agreed.

"Look," James said. "Here's the truth: we just got to talking the other day, me and Holly, about our friends and what-not, and we realised we both knew someone who was single and looking. So we decided that maybe we could try to get them together. That's all there is to it."

John gave this some thought, but not a lot of it. "Fair enough," he said then.

Aisling and Holly turned to face each other. "Sometimes, I wish I was a man," Aisling sighed.

Holly nodded. "That's just what I was thinking. Look how simple it is! And look at the nightmare we're facing."

"I tried to tell her she isn't plump," John said. "But she wouldn't listen."

"She isn't," James agreed.

"I can't believe she said that to you," Holly tutted. "Ridiculous."

"Shocking," Aisling nodded. "And not true."

"Yeah," John began and then paused for a deep breath. "Tell you the truth, I think . . . I think she's kind of cute."

The other three exchanged little glances.

"Well, you're pretty cute yourself," Aisling told him.

This time her intervention seemed to make him positively faint. He rocked back and forth on his heels for a moment and seemed to be on the point of reaching out for physical support. Holly couldn't help but wonder if he'd have reacted in the same way if the compliment had come from her. Almost certainly not, she concluded.

"So," she said. "What are we going to do now?"

"Well," Aisling said, "it's not going to be easy, but if we can get Orla to just –"

"Not about that," Holly snapped. She gave Aisling a serious glare. John had, in fairness to him, been reasonably subtle in putting down his marker. Despite the evening's shortcomings, he was interested. They could have all just left it at that. It would have been nice and neat. Now it was anything but. "I mean, what are we going to do right now?"

"Oh."

"No reason why we shouldn't keep bowling, I suppose," James said.

Holly looked around. The place seemed to change right before her eyes. Now it looked just as it did when she first arrived – crowded, dirty and entirely without appeal. The two women in the next lane were bellowing more loudly than ever. The carpet was sticky under her feet. The air was stale. The game itself was pointless. Whatever changes James had wrought in her attitude, it seemed that they had been temporary.

"Or we could say to hell with bowling and go for drinks," she said.

James tapped on his chin. "Drinks, you say. I've heard good things about drinks." He raised an eyebrow in John's direction. "What do you think?"

John pursed his lips. "I dunno . . . "

"Oh, go on," Aisling said, leaning in towards him. "It'll be a laugh."

She had barely finished speaking before he started nodding. "All right then," he said. "Why not?"

Chapter 10

On Sunday mornings Holly usually had what she like to call a cub – a "little lie-in". Nothing serious – she was invariably up and about by ten thirty, even when she'd had more to drink the previous night than was strictly necessary. This particular Sunday was different. When she finally opened one eye and used it to peer at the alarm clock by her bed, she saw that it was just after one thirty in the afternoon. A second realisation quickly followed: her knees were killing her. Holly put these facts together and concluded that she had – or rather would shortly have – a hangover. Most people, she understood, knew they had a hangover as soon as they awoke. Hers tended to sneak up on her. She could be fine all day long and then, *wham*, at four or five or six o'clock some invisible someone would tiptoe up behind her and hit her over the head with a lead pipe. Over the years, she had learned to look for signs that her day was doomed and she shouldn't make any serious plans. Weirdly, the most reliable indicator of trouble brewing was sore knees. Why exactly an excess of alcohol should make her knees hurt, she had no idea, but as a clue, it had never let her down. She had even honoured it with a little mnemonic: *Sore knees in the morning: hangover warning; sore knees at night: doesn't really mean anything.*

She rubbed her eyes and set about reconstructing her movements. They had gone from the bowling alley into the bar right next-door. It was a horrible pseudo-American sports joint whose name she hadn't even bothered to register. And there, sitting at a small table all alone, they had found Orla. Apparently, she had intended to spend the rest of the evening at home with at least one bottle of wine but was in such a bad way that she had required a quick vodka to give her the strength to find a taxi.

It was a disaster at first, of course. Orla made to bolt when she saw the others arriving and, for a moment at least, had to be physically surrounded. Since there was no way they could pretend that they didn't all know exactly where they stood, things came to a head immediately (James and John stole away to the bar, giving the girls room to fight). There were ugly accusations and heartfelt pleas for reason. There was finger-pointing and ego-stroking. Claim and counter-claim. Tears and taunts and threats. Sighs and snorts and sneers. Orla made to leave on several more occasions but always thought of one more thing she wanted to get off her chest first.

Gradually, however – it took quite a while – the tone softened and the volume decreased. There was no dramatic breakthrough, no turning of a corner, no moment of joy and reconciliation. Instead, a sort of exhaustion seemed to settle over the three of them. Things weren't great, but given that Orla's storm-out had happened less than twenty minutes previously, they didn't seem hopeless either. Holly distinctly recalled thinking that at least they could now part on semi-reasonable terms.

What she could not recall, distinctly or otherwise, was how they wound up looking for a table that could accommodate all five of them. One of their number had suggested it, presumably, but she had no idea which one had done it and what form of words had been used. In any event, they found a table easily enough and took their seats gingerly, each wearing a pale imitation of a smile. What happened next was entirely predictable. They were uncomfortable, they were Irish, and they had easy access to alcohol. There could only ever be one outcome. Even so, the speed with which their collective condition degenerated had been remarkable. Usually when Holly performed this sort of postmortem, she could look back at a part of the evening when she could and should have drawn the line; she thought of it as "pleasantly sloshed". In this case, there seemed to have been no such period. Apparently, she'd gone straight from stone-cold sober to rubber-legged pissed and skipped everything in between, like someone who'd managed to drive from Canada to Mexico without visiting America.

The words "Hard Rock Café" flashed in her mind. She rubbed her right temple and frowned, wondering why that was. Then it came to her and her hand moved from her temple to her mouth. The pub – "sports bar", rather – was one of the worst she'd ever been in and she'd said so. Everything about it was not only fake but not worth copying in the first place. And it was all wrong for Dublin. There were *baseball bats* on the walls, for God's sake. Themes were just plain wrong in her book and anything that employed one – a pub, a restaurant, a party – was doomed to failure. James disagreed with considerable enthusiasm. This specific pub was fairly awful, he admitted, citing in particular the fact that there was a blaring TV stuck to every surface – but what about the Hard Rock Café? Had she ever been in one? They were terrific! Holly's memories of the subsequent exchange were reasonably vivid. She remembered assuming that he was joking and taking some convincing that he was not. She also remembered the sense of ambush that swept over her when Aisling piped up to counsel James that there was no point in trying to argue the point. Themed bars and restaurants were on Holly's list, and that was that. Once a concept made the list, it stayed put. James was intrigued. What else was on this list? Aisling was quick to fill him in. Well, there was astrology, obviously, as he may have noticed earlier. Reality TV. Mothers who have their baby's ears pierced. Organised religion in all forms. The phrases "At the end of the day", "If you ask me", "This isn't rocket science", "Very unique", "Your call is important to us" and many, many others. Waiters who keep asking if everything's all right. People who emphasise their sneezes . . . At some point, Orla joined in, quietly at first but with ever-increasing zeal. What about creationists, she said? And psychics. That man with the ghost show on Channel Four. Products that are as individual as you are. Drivers who take up two parking spaces. Nicotine beard stains. Tiny hotel kettles. Cyclists on footpaths. People who whistle tunes that they just made up . . .

Holly did her best to smile throughout all of this but eventually decided that enough was enough and spoke up in her own defence. They were making it sound as if she hated everything and everyone, she said to James (who regarded her with a sly smile), but that wasn't true. The only difference between her and everyone else was that she was comfortable talking about the things that annoyed her while everyone else bottled it all up. She recalled ending this observation with an unconvincing grin. It had felt silly at the time and felt doubly so now. James had responded by saying that she didn't have to defend herself to him and that, somehow, had made her grin all the harder. Looking back now, she couldn't remember how the conversation had moved on but she had a terrible suspicion that she had maintained the ridiculous leer for quite some time.

Her next semi-clear memories were of the moment when she realised that their physical arrangements had settled down. As the night wore on and they made their multiple trips to the bar and the loos, they had shifted and rotated into a wide variety of seating plans. Eventually, however, they'd become a table of two halves. On one half, Holly and Aisling faced each other with James, perched at the end on a low stool that made him look faintly preposterous, forming the apex of their triangle. The other half was Orla and John's. There was no obvious physical divide between the two groups. A passer-by would have called it a table of five. But the separation was very real. Holly's half of the table never got the chance to discuss this remarkable development, but she recalled a great many raised eyebrows and head-points. When she tuned in to Orla and John's conversation, as she regularly did, she found it to be polite and safe and friendly – work this, family that. Nevertheless, the fact that they were having what amounted to a private chat had seemed remarkable. As far as memories went, that was almost it. The rest was a series of blurs of varying hues and intensity. She could glimpse images – John spilling a drink, Aisling having a fit of the giggles – but could form no cohesive narratives. There was something in there about a taxi too, but it was vague in the extreme. Yup, that was almost it. Almost. She did seem to recall something about deciding that James Bond was the man for her.

It was nothing specific, nothing that she could put her finger on at any rate. In retrospect, it seemed as if the feeling had just crept over her. She'd arrived in the sports bar thinking he was a nice guy and she'd left it thinking he was a nice guy that she wanted all to herself. He hadn't said or done anything in particular. It was just his . . . She pulled the duvet up to her nose and struggled to find words other than

ALEX COLEMAN

"essence" or "spirit" – words that wouldn't make her feel like a fourteen year-old drawing love hearts on the back of her geography book. It was his . . . himness? His himissitude? She sighed. It was just *him*. The way he was. The way he acted, the way he spoke. She'd met happy-go-lucky people before and she'd always hated them with a sizzling passion. They were always so insufferably twee, bouncing around in their pastels, humming stupid songs and babbling about upside-down frowns. And that wasn't all. She'd never met one who hadn't wanted her to be just like them, either by "cheering up" in the short-term or completely transforming her life in the long-term. James was different on both counts. Somehow, he managed to be positive and upbeat without being insufferable. And he didn't seem to give a damn if she – or anyone else, for that matter – followed suit. It was a combination that she found . . . tantalising.

She lay there for another hour, staring at the ceiling, feeling tantalised.

It was almost four o'clock when the phone call came. Holly had emerged from a hot bath and was curled up at one end of the sofa half-watching an old movie in which Cary Grant was getting himself all worked up about Katherine Hepburn. Claude was at her feet dreaming vividly; his little paws were twitching so much he seemed to be receiving mild electrical shocks. As predicted, her head had started to pound and her stomach was churning ominously.

"Hello," she sighed into the phone, not bothering to make an attempt at sounding pleasant.

"Hello, Holly," her mother said. "You don't sound very pleased to hear from me."

"Mum. Sorry. It's just . . ." She paused. No reasonable excuse presented itself. "Well, I overdid it a bit last night, that's all. Feeling a bit delicate."

"Oh dear. You don't need alcohol to have a good time, you know."

This was all Mrs Christmas ever had to say on the subject of booze. This was perhaps the five hundredth time Holly had heard her say it.

"Yeah. You're right. I know."

"So . . . what does 'delicate' mean? Are you bedridden?"

"God, no," Holly replied and then immediately regretted it. She had been trying to portray herself as someone who'd had two glasses of wine instead of her usual one, rather than someone who could scarcely remember how she'd made it home. But she hadn't considered the possibility that her mother wanted her to go somewhere or do something. Now she had painted herself into a corner.

"Good," her mother said. "Because tonight's the night. For meeting Charlie, I mean. Obviously."

Several of Holly's organs seemed to swap places. The possibility hadn't even occurred to her. It seemed too soon. "You're joking me."

"No. Why would I be joking?"

"It's not much notice, is it?"

"Sure what do you need notice for? And besides, I didn't get any notice myself. He's only after ringing me. He's talking about dinner in town."

"And what did you say? 'Can my daughter come too and do you mind if she brings a notebook?'"

There was a small chuckle on the other end. "I did very well, Holly. Do you know what I said to him? I said I already had plans to meet you and you were really looking forward to it and all – but I supposed we could join the two things together."

There was a pause during which Holly slowly came to understand that she was supposed to be issuing congratulations. "Well done," she said through her teeth.

Another chuckle. "I know, I was all pleased with myself. So – what do you say?"

"Where does he want to go?"

"Why? What does that matter? Are you not coming if it's not swanky enough?"

"Mum . . ."

"It's called The Green Panda. Chinese. South William Street. Great reviews in the papers, so he says. Have you heard of it?"

"Yes."

"And what have you heard?"

"Yeah. It's supposed to be lovely."

"Oh good! Chineses don't always agree with me, as you know, but Charlie says this is nothing like a take-away down the road."

"Hm. What time? This is a school night, you know, so I can't –"

"Seven thirty. Nice and early. You'll be home again before you know it. So you'll be there?"

Holly had immediately regretted the schoolnight remark. She'd agreed to this, after all. There was no point in complaining now. She closed her eyes and gave the heartiest "Of course!" that she could muster.

When it came time to leave the house, Holly realised that she was facing something of a dilemma: should she drive or take a taxi? In other words, should she leave open the alcohol option? Her hangover had developed rapidly. Mercifully, it had stopped getting worse at around six but had not yet started getting better. All things being equal, she couldn't see herself having another drink for the remainder of the decade. Then again, what if all things turned out to be unequal? What if she found herself gagging for a softener and unable to do anything about it? She thought about it long and hard as she oscillated between bedroom and bathroom and ultimately came down on the side of driving herself. Even if the meal was a disaster, she could hardly sit there and get plastered. Why go to all that hassle *and* run the risk of having Bernard Manning for a driver just so she could have what undoubtedly would amount to no more than a tipple?

The trip into town took longer than she'd allowed for and she found it necessary to speed-walk the short distance from the car park to the restaurant. This unexpected spurt of physical activity had two unfortunate consequences. Firstly, it made her head throb a little harder. And secondly, it covered her in a thin film of what Aisling called "dew" and everyone else called "sweat". When she finally arrived, she discovered that the interior of The Green Panda was much more spacious than the exterior promised. At first glance, nothing about it said *Chinese*. There wasn't a dragon or a fan to be seen. It was decorated in muted pastel tones and delicately lit. The owners seemed to have gone out of their way to make sure that every edge was straight and every angle a right one. The lampshades and candle-holders were cuboid. The picture frames and menus were square. Holly decided at once that she liked it. There was a pleasant hum of activity and the air itself seemed tasty. She was greeted by a startlingly beautiful Chinese woman who wondered if she had a reservation. Holly was tempted to say that she wasn't happy about the whole Tibet situation but decided that the joke was too obscure and would probably earn her nothing more than a squint and an *"Excuse me?"*.

"No," she said, still struggling to catch her breath. "I'm meeting . . . oh, it's a couple, a middle-aged couple. I think the reservation is in the man's name, but I can't seem to remember . . . Uh. His first name's definitely Charlie. And the woman's name is Delia Christmas, if that's any help. She's my mother."

All of this had tumbled out of her in a sort of heap that now seemed to lie between them on the floor. Too late, Holly realised that she might as well have drawn a picture. *My mother's out on the town with some man who isn't my father*. A second dragged by.

"Christmas?" the woman said then. "Really?"

"Yes," Holly said and before she knew she was doing it, added, "Don't start."

The woman flinched. "Well. Let me see here . . . Seven thirty, is it?"

"Yes."

"Charlie . . . Ah. I have a Charles Fallon by three?"

"That's him."

"Okay. This way, please. May I take your jacket?"

Holly shimmied out of the garment in question, which was immediately palmed off on an underling who seemed to appear out of nowhere and then disappear again with equal stealth. The table she was led towards was right at the end of the restaurant which, apart from the odd nook and spur, was broadly L-shaped. Right up until the moment when her host came to a stop, Holly had been unable to see which one they were heading for. She didn't know what Charlie – or "Charles" – Fallon looked like, of course, but she'd expected to recognise her own mother.

"Mum!" she wheezed when it became clear that she had failed to do so. "Look at you! You look great!"

"Have a nice evening," the Chinese lady said and crept away.

"Oh, thank you," Mrs Christmas said. "So do you."

"But I *mean* it," Holly said. It was the truth. Although her mother had done nothing else but spend some time

171

on her notoriously unruly hair and apply a little make-up, the effect was startling. "You look like someone from an *After* picture," Holly marvelled. "I mean, as opposed to a *Before*. That came out wrong. But you know what I mean."

This drew a small chuckle from Charlie and gave Holly an excuse to look at him properly. "I'm sorry," she said. "You must be Charlie. I'm Holly. I'm sorry I'm late."

"Not at all," he said and got to his feet.

He extended his hand and when she took it, drew her towards him. Before she knew what was what, he had deposited a small kiss on her cheek and basically *pushed* her back to her original position. It was more wrestling move than greeting. Holly made a conscious effort not to mind. *Early days*, she thought as she took her seat. She had somehow assumed that he would be a large, leather-skinned sort of creature with brilliant white teeth and a thick head of silver hair; something like a movie mafia Don. Where she had acquired this image, she had no idea. She guessed that she had just heard the words "New York" and let her imagination run away with itself. Given her expectations – silly though they were – she couldn't help but feel a little disappointed by the figure sitting opposite her now. Charlie looked like a retired jockey. He was short and slightly built. His salt'n'pepper hair was not so much receding from his forehead as energetically fleeing it. The little that remained had been coerced into forming an ill-advised miniature quiff. His skin had a blue-ish tinge and seemed to have been borrowed from a much larger man.

"I've never been here before," Holly said. "It looks really lovely."

"Oh yes," her mum said. "All . . . modern."

Charlie wobbled his head. "But you can't tell, can you? That's the kicker. I've been in some beautiful places where the food was no better than mediocre and, obtusely, I've been in some real dives where they served nothing less than heaven on a plate."

Holly winced. She wondered if she should correct him. Her mother either didn't notice his mistake or – this was more likely – didn't care.

"Charlie's quite the *gourmand*," she said with what sounded like a degree of pride.

"No, no, Delia," Charlie said, patting her wrist. "A *gourmand* is just someone who likes eating. I'm a *gourmet*. That's someone who knows what they're talking about. Big difference."

"Oh," Mrs Christmas said. "Sorry."

Holly chewed on the tip of her right index finger for a moment. She had no idea if he was right about the *gourmand/gourmet* thing but that was hardly the point. For a man who said "obtusely" when he meant "conversely", he was awfully quick to correct other people.

"So," she said when her fingertip began to hurt. "Mum tells me you've been living in New York?"

"That's right. Thirty-odd years. Greatest city on Earth. Capital of the world. You ever been, Holly?"

"Once, yeah, a few years back. Just for a long weekend."

He spluttered. "A weekend? But that's no good. You couldn't even scratch the surface in a weekend, long or not."

"Well, we did know that at the time," Holly said, doing her best to smile. "It's not like we thought we were going to turn into Woody Allen after three days."

She picked up her menu, hoping the move would instigate a change of subject. It didn't.

"What did you do and see while you were there? Tourist crap, I suppose?"

Holly's sole companion on the trip had been Aisling. Orla had planned to go too but had been laid low at the last minute by an unspeakably nasty throat infection. The upshot was that Holly had spent the majority of her time on Fifth Avenue standing outside changing rooms while Aisling tried on the shop's entire stock. The remainder had indeed been devoted to tourist crap.

"We saw the sights," she said from behind her menu, "if that's what you mean. What else are you supposed to do on your first trip?"

"Get off the beaten track!" Charlie said. "First trip or not. Strike out! Explore! See the *real* New York!"

His accent up to now had been just what Holly had imagined it would be – ninety per cent Dub with a sprinkling of American on top. His delivery of his adopted city's name, however, was pure parody: *Noo Yawk*. She found herself holding this detail against him.

"I'm sure Holly will be more adventurous next time," Mrs Christmas said, perhaps sensing trouble. "Now – what are we going to eat? We've been putting off choosing until you got here."

"Yeah, let's get to it," Holly said quickly. "Everything looks great."

They perused in silence for a moment. Then Mrs Christmas said, "It's all a bit confusing to the likes of me." She leaned over the table and dropped her voice as if she was divulging a great secret. "They don't seem to have chicken balls and tubs of curry sauce, which is what I normally go for."

Holly gave her a wink. Charlie gave her another pat on the wrist.

"Leave it to me, Delia," he crooned. "I'll order for you."

"Oh, I'm sure that won't be necessary," Holly said through gritted teeth.

"I really don't mind," Charlie said, as if that was the issue. "It would be my pleasure. Holly, would you like me to order for you too? Maybe –"

"No, thank you," Holly said, returning her gaze to the menu for fear that it might betray her. "I can order for myself. Maybe you could cut things up for me, though. I'm not great with a knife and fork."

Charlie tut-tutted. "Surely you won't be using a knife and fork?"

"As opposed to what?" Mrs Christmas said.

"He means chopsticks," Holly replied.

Her mother flinched. "Oh no, I don't think –"

"No problem, Mum. Look, they leave knives and forks on the table for a reason. Don't worry about it."

"But it's so easy!" Charlie squeaked. "Look . . . " He broke his chopsticks open and used them to snatch at the thin air like the little old man in *The Karate Kid* trying to catch a fly. "You see, Delia? See how they pivot? See? Open . . . closed . . . open . . . closed . . . open . . . closed."

Holly stomach gurgled. She wasn't sure if the cause was hunger, her hangover or simple annoyance.

"Well, I'll give it a go," Mrs Christmas said. She opened her own chopsticks and ever so carefully attempted to copy Charlie's movements.

Holly tried not to watch. She looked like someone who was learning to use a hand they'd just acquired from a donor.

"Not bad for a beginner," Charlie said. "But you're gripping the top one like a pen – that's all wrong. More like this, look. See? Open . . . closed . . . open . . . closed."

The worst part about all of this, Holly thought, was the expression on her mother's face. She looked embarrassed – not by Charlie's attitude but rather by her own shortcomings. And she seemed so keen to learn, so keen to please him. The lesson went on for a couple of minutes. Holly realised that she might as well not have been there and eventually started scanning the room for an available waiter. She soon caught one's eye and was greatly relieved when he approached and asked if they were ready to order.

"Yes," she said firmly. "I am, anyway."

Charlie seemed a little disappointed by this interruption to chopstick class. He picked up his menu and said, "Yes. I'll be ordering for myself and the lady beside me."

The waiter shifted from foot to foot. "Certainly."

"But first," Charlie said, "I have some questions regarding the wine list . . ."

An hour and a half later, as she examined the dessert menu, Holly found herself wondering about her hangover. It should have been on the way out by now, but it was still firmly in its plateau phase. Although there were any number of factors that she could have held responsible – Chinese food was hardly a good idea, for a start – she decided that the number one reason why she was still feeling unwell was because she'd spent the evening listening to Charlie frigging Fallon. In fact, she was quite sure that if she'd arrived feeling on top of the world, he would have *given* her a headache and an upset stomach. Although it seemed unfair to dwell on just one of his many transgressions against common taste and decency, the moment when he expressed his "pity" for the friends he'd left behind in Dublin had been a real low. They'd been talking about the émigré life in New York – a subject that occupied them for about three-quarters of the meal – when he dropped that particular bomb. Holly had allowed him to twitter on for a while about the experiences they'd missed out on and the bitterness they must harbour towards the likes of him before she pointed out that her mother was one of those "sad cases", as he'd called them. She'd imagined that he would hastily backtrack and looked forward to seeing him squirm a little. But he didn't backtrack, much less squirm. He smiled and said that "obviously" he'd been talking about men. It was different for women. They had "their own role in life". Holly would have liked nothing better than to explore this topic a little further and to ultimately leave him curled up in the corner, weeping and promising to never express an opinion about anything ever again. But she'd kept her mouth shut. It was already becoming clear to her even then that, somehow or other, her mother actually liked this tool – or, at least, was impressed by him. Again and again she had displayed the same attitude that she'd adopted during the chopstick lesson: Charlie was a knowledgeable and sophisticated man of the world and she should count herself lucky that he was showing an interest in a timid little ignoramus like herself. Holly would have found it thoroughly inexplicable if it hadn't been for those occasional moments when Mr Start-Spreadin'-the-News paid her mother a compliment. They were small asides, all of them – she had a wonderful laugh, her perfume was refreshingly subtle, she had the delicate fingers of a concert pianist – but the effect they had was considerable. Her mum positively swooned each time and then broke into a giggle that she found hard to control. Once she even slapped him playfully on the bicep. That constituted Voluntary Physical Contact and VPC, Holly had read somewhere, was one of the seven signs of something or other. Holly spent an alarming portion of the meal wondering about Charlie's bladder capacity and hoping it was significant. The last thing she wanted was for him to go to the Gents, leaving her alone with her mum. She was bound to ask her what she thought of him – that was the point of the whole exercise, after all – and Holly felt that she needed time, possibly several weeks' worth of it, in which to choose her words.

"So," Charlie said after they'd spent a silent minute with the dessert menu. "Anyone tempted?"

"I don't know," Holly said.

"Neither do I," her mother agreed. "I won't get through the door when I get home."

Charlie shook his head emphatically. "Nonsense! You're as slender as a reed."

Cue swoon. Cue giggling fit. They went back and forth on the subject for a minute or two before all three ultimately succumbed.

As the waiter made off with their order, Charlie joined his hands in front of him, looked at Holly and said, "Science, huh?"

She didn't even know what he was talking about at first. And then she realised that he was referring to her teaching career. He had asked about her job way back during the starters but had offered no follow-up questions when she gave him the headlines; instead, he had embarked on a long review of Frank McCourt's book about teaching in New York.

"Yup," Holly nodded. "Science. And maths."

"Hmmm. Gets us into a lot of trouble, doesn't it? The old science lab."

Holly took a deep breath. "Oh? What do you mean by that?" She knew fine well what he meant by that; she was merely buying time for more deep breathing. Her instincts told her she was going to need it.

"You know," he said. "Weapons. And fiddling with genetics – making mice with ears growing on their backs. All that."

She forced herself to finish her breathing exercise before replying. "Really? That's what you think of when you think of science? Weapons and mice with ears on their backs?"

"Oh, I know what you're going to say."

"Do you?"

"You're going to say, 'What about curing diseases?', 'What about inventing useful things like airplanes and television?'"

"I have to admit, you got me. So – what about curing diseases? What about inventing useful things like airplanes and television?"

"Those are good," he said. "I'm not saying they aren't."

"Phew."

"I'm just saying, we have to have a little perspective. Science gave us penicillin, sure, but it gave us the bomb too."

"Science is just a method, Charlie," she said as evenly as she could. "It's just a way of finding out about the world. It's up to us how we use it. If we use it to invent nuclear weapons or poisonous gases or whatever else you care to name, that's our fault. Not science's."

"And what about the genetic end of things? Do you approve of that?"

Holly took a sip of coffee. "I don't think it matters one way or the other if I approve. It's not as if the world's geneticists are sitting around waiting for me to –"

"You're avoiding the question." He said this in a sing-song voice with a playful shake of his index finger, as if trying to emphasise that they were just talking, not arguing.

"I wouldn't like to be that mouse with the ear on its back," Holly said, "if that's what you're asking me. Then again, I wouldn't particularly like to be a mouse, full stop. Not a big cheese fan."

"Once again, you're av–"

"Broadly speaking, I think that fiddling with genetics, as you call it, is a very exciting prospect. Anything that can help us cure horrible diseases and, you know, *save people's lives*, I'm all for."

Charlie shook his head sadly. "And what about God?"

"What about Her?"

"Don't you think that tinkering about with life is God's domain and not ours?"

Mrs Christmas cleared her throat. "Charlie . . . has strong religious views," she said.

Holly nodded and considered her options. She considered them for so long that Charlie eventually prompted her with an urgent "Well?"

"We'll have to agree to disagree on this one," she said carefully. This was the only one of the options she'd considered that did not include shouting and creative swearing. She felt oddly pleased by her self-restraint. And there was no doubt that she had done the right thing. The look on her mother's face – it was if she'd just been told that a relative had survived delicate surgery.

"A conversation for another time, perhaps," Charlie said.

Yeah, Holly thought. *Behind the bicycle sheds after school. Bring an ice-pack.* "Perhaps."

Their desserts arrived shortly afterwards. Like their main and starter predecessors, they were universally declared to be delicious. Holly thought she might have enjoyed her cheesecake even more if she hadn't – twice – caught Charlie stealing a peek at her boobs. Mark from next-door had once explained to her that a woman should never be offended when she caught a man's eyes going south because they genuinely couldn't help themselves. It was a reflex. Built-in. Hard-wired. They no more decided to do it than they decided to jerk their leg when the doctor hit their knee with the little rubber hammer. Still, given their relationship – she was Charlie's potential girlfriend's *daughter*, for Christ's sake – she was more than a little horrified. Once again, she thought of several interesting spears she could throw at his head and once again, she decided against all of them. Perhaps realising the effect they were having, he had increased the flow of his compliments to her mother – she could really tell a story, her watch was a thing of rare beauty – and this alone stayed Holly's tongue.

When the bill arrived, Charlie was horrified by her offer to split it. She assumed that his dismissal would quickly segue into a lecture about the "man's role" but, to be fair to him, he made no such error.

"Well then," Holly said when the moment came, "I suppose I'd better get going. School in the morning . . ."

She stood up and pushed her chair in. Neither of the other two budged. She had assumed that they would all leave together, but apparently she had been mistaken. What was that all about? Were they relocating to a wine bar somewhere? Going for a game of pool? Heading – dear God – back to his place? The cold reality washed over her. This could turn out to be a genuine *thing*.

"Thanks for coming," her mother said. Her expression said that this was no platitude; she really meant it.

"Yes," Charlie nodded. "It was great to meet you. I'm sure you and I are going to have a lot of, uh, interesting discussions."

This sentence, it seemed to Holly, was crying out for another clause. When were they going to have these discussions? When he finally pulled her mother?

"I'll look forward to it," she said. "It was lovely to meet you too."

She went around to the side of the table and kissed her mum goodbye. Charlie got to his feet and gave a repeat performance of his initial greeting, once again leaving her rocking on her heels.

"Okay then," she said. "Be good."

She turned and strode away, feeling fairly sure that Charlie was checking out her ass. *Be good*, she said to herself with a shudder. What the fuck was that supposed to mean? Suddenly, she felt lost and alone and deeply, deeply confused. Her overriding thought as she waited for her coat was that she wished she could talk it all over with someone cool-headed and sensible. James, for example.

Claude seemed unusually pleased to see her when she got home. He trotted around after her as she got into her pyjamas and made herself a cup of tea, then followed her to the sofa and nestled on her slippered feet as she drank it. Her hangover had finally begun to fade; there was nothing to it now but a mild feeling of nausea and that, she suspected, had more to do with indigestion than the previous night's exertions. She turned on the TV and then proceeded to pay it no attention whatsoever. Her mobile phone, she couldn't help but notice, had found its way to the arm of the sofa. She picked it up and flipped through its various menus, not looking for anything in particular. Calendar, Games, To Do; so many functions that she would never use . . . Before long, she found herself browsing through her phone book. It had twenty-seven entries. She wondered if that was a little or a lot. It sounded like a little. And she didn't even know who some of the twenty-seven were. Sheila P? She couldn't remember having ever met such a character, let alone taken her number. What was the point of having an unknown person's phone number? With a small shake of her head, she deleted it. She scrolled on, up and down, down and up . . . Lizzie, Ursula, Kevin – *Kevin*! How could she have forgotten to erase his presence? It was unlike her. Ex-boyfriends usually went through a process that she called "scrubbing", the first and simplest part of which was the removal of their phone number. She did it now, pressing the buttons with a great deal more force than was necessary. Going through the list again – for no real reason, it was just for something to do – she saw that a disturbing proportion of the remaining twenty-five weren't social contacts. They were doctors and dentists and plumbers and taxi firms. This seemed like a bad sign, but she supposed that she could be reading too much into it. She made a mental note to look through Aisling and Orla's phone next time she got a chance, just for the sake of comparison.

James B. There he was. She'd never actually dialled his number. Her only phone contact had been via text messages and, if his early arrival at the MegaBowl was any indicator, he hadn't paid very much attention to those. Even as her thumb hovered over the little green button, she told herself that she wasn't going to actually *call* him. God, no. She was merely pondering the prospect. Toying with it.

He answered on the first ring.

"Holly Christmas," he said. "Good evening."

She could actually hear his half-smile. "Hi. Hi there. Uh . . . how are you?"

"Grand. To what do I owe the pleasure? Postmortem on last night?"

"Well, that and . . . yes, that."

"Oh? There's something else?"

"No, no, I . . . It was an interesting evening, huh?"

"It sure was. Have you spoken to Orla today?"

"No. What about John?"

"Not today, no, but he did a lot of rambling in the taxi last night."

This small piece of information unlocked a few more memories for Holly. Yes: James and John had shared a taxi, as had she and Aisling. Orla had left a little earlier, citing profound drunkenness. Aisling had seen her into the car and had been chatted up twice on the way back.

"Yeah? What sort of rambling? The good sort?"

"Wouldn't you like to know . . ."

"Yes. I would. That's why I'm asking." Her brow furrowed. Had that come out playfully sarcastic or nastily sarcastic?

"Well, then," James said. "I suppose I'd better tell you. It was the good sort. Very good, actually. He's quite taken with her. More than taken. I'd go so far as to call him 'smitten'."

"Smitten, you say?"

"Smitten."

"That's great. I'll have to have a word with herself but from what I saw last night – the bits that I can remember, anyway – I wouldn't be surprised to find out that it's mutual."

"Great. I'm quite chuffed with myself, are you?"

"Oh yeah. Definitely. Victory from the jaws of defeat and what have you."

There was a brief silence. Holly could hear music in the background on his end. She found herself desperately wanting to know what it was, but she couldn't make it out. Something with a lot of guitars anyway.

"So . . ." he said then. "What was the other thing?"

She played dumb. "What other thing?"

"You sounded like you had something else to say. A minute ago."

"Oh. Yeah. Kind of. Nothing important."

"Go on."

"I dunno, I just wanted some . . . advice, I suppose."

"You've come to the right man. I've had a lot of compliments on my advising."

"Okay. Good. It's about my mother . . ."

She talked for five minutes without pause and said far more than she meant to. Her intention had been to give him the bare bones and then ask what he would do if he were in her shoes. This would mean providing a little background, obviously, but nothing too elaborate. She was surprised when she went into some detail about how her mother had been widowed before she'd given birth to her first child and hadn't so much as looked at another man in all the intervening years. But this surprise was as nothing compared to the deep shock she felt when she heard herself discussing her own private theory about her name. It was a topic that she had broached only a handful of times with her nearest and dearest, let alone someone she barely knew. James seemed to sense this. Up until that point, he'd supplied an occasional "Hmm" or "I see", just to prove he was still there, she guessed. But he was utterly silent as she explained that, in her opinion, the ridiculous joining of "Holly" and "Christmas" had been her distraught mother's attempt to be, well, cheery; that it was nothing more than over-compensation in the face of horrific grief; that she probably now regretted it almost as much as Holly did. By the time she finally got around to describing her evening out with Charlie, she felt exhausted and ran through it at speed. The bottom line, she said, was that, okay, the guy wasn't exactly evil, but he certainly wasn't ideal either. And now she had to give him a review. What the hell was she supposed to say? She still hadn't posed this question to Aisling and Orla. Part of the reason was that she knew their responses would be more long-winded than helpful. *On the one hand this, but on the other hand that. You have to do X, but you mustn't do Y.* There was nothing long-winded about James's reply. She had no choice, he said; she had to say she approved. It wasn't as if her mother was contemplating marriage here. She was having an occasional dinner and night out at the cinema with this man. If Holly reported that she didn't like him, there were only two possible outcomes. Either her mother would continue to see him anyway and there would be horrible tension between them all, or she would put a stop to it and hold a grudge against her daughter for ruining it. But if Holly told her to go for it, then she could more or less wash her hands of the whole thing. Her mother was a grown woman. Anything else that arose between her and this Charlie character was her own business. He delivered this assessment with a frankness that bordered on the blunt but was simultaneously measured and kind-hearted. Holly found it deliciously refreshing.

"Don't hold back," she said when he had finished. "Tell me what you really think."

"Sorry, I just –"

"No, I'm joking, I'm joking. Nice to get clear advice for once. We girls don't really do clear. We like to cover all bases."

"Really? When I talk to my pals about this kind of stuff, I'm lucky to get *one* base covered."

"Heh. Yeah. Yeah. "

"You sound . . . hesitant."

"Um."

"Holly?"

"It's just . . . You're saying I should lie?"

"I wouldn't put it like that. I'm saying there are times in life when you shouldn't necessarily give your real opinion and this, if you ask me, is one of them."

"Hmmm. I'm not really known for my ability to hold back my opinion."

"So I've gathered. But maybe you should give it a go. You might be surprised at the results."

Holly didn't reply straight away. The words "So I've gathered" had set her teeth on edge and her heart pounding.

But her initial anger faded away with an ease and speed that pleasantly surprised her. Coming from James, the sentiment sounded different, somehow.

"Maybe you're right," she heard herself saying. "OK, then. See you tomorrow, I suppose."

"That you will. Anything else I can help you with?"

"No, James. That's it for tonight."

"OK. Goodnight, so."

"Goodnight. And thanks."

"You're more than welcome. See ya."

"Bye."

She hung up. A huge smile had installed itself on her face. She felt faintly ridiculous and tried to wipe it away, but it wouldn't budge.

"Hey, Claudio," she cooed, reaching out for him. "What a handsome man you are!"

Claude allowed himself to be picked up but wriggled away, wide-eyed and mewling, when she hugged him close to her chest with more enthusiasm than he was used to.

Chapter 11

Monday morning was a breeze. Holly felt like a teacher in a Hollywood movie, the sort who instilled a sense of wonder in her charges and kick-started a life-long love affair with learning. She was patience personified, offering an encouraging word here, a gentle reminder there. Concepts that had eluded all but the brightest students suddenly became clear to all. Not even Malachy Murphy (a vicious little thug who wouldn't have been out of place in a Roald Dahl story) could derail her Education Express, and he really, really tried. When lunchtime came, she set off for the staff room with a spring in her step and a song on her lips. Along the way, she bumped into Eleanor Duffy, who was heading in the opposite direction.

"Not coming in for lunch?" Holly asked.

Eleanor shook her head. "Not today. I'm going to pop out and get the car taxed."

"You can do that online, you know."

191

"So I believe. You're the third person to tell me that today. But I don't know, I don't like paying for anything on the World Wide Web. I don't trust it."

Eleanor always called it that, dragging the individual words out as if she wasn't quite sure she was pronouncing them correctly – *Worrrrld Wiiide Webbb*.

"You should get together with my mother," Holly said. "She is afraid of the Internet too."

"It's an age thing. Anyway, listen, *listen*: I believe you were out socialising at the weekend with a certain Mr Bond?"

Holly's smile slid off her face. "What? Who told you that?"

If Eleanor noticed the change of expression, she didn't let it show. "He did. Why? Are you mad?"

It was a good question. Holly gave it some thought. "Well, I'm . . . What did he say?"

"It wasn't exactly a long conversation, Holly. I was only asking him what he got up to at the weekend and he said he'd been out with you, a whole gang of you, all together. Bowling. And you know what else?"

She stepped a little closer and checked for eavesdroppers, which was ridiculous; they were standing like rocks in a fast-running river of noisy boys. She could have roared out that she was a closet lesbian and no one would have heard a word.

"What?"

"He got all . . . smiley . . . when he talked about it."

Holly froze and then rapidly melted. "Smiley?"

"Yup."

"What do you mean, smiley?"

"I mean, *smiley*. He was smiling."

A couple of seconds floated past before Holly cobbled together a response. "Well, he probably enjoyed it, that's all. The bowling."

"No, no, no," Eleanor spluttered. "I know my smiles, Holly Christmas, and this was one of *those*."

"Nah," Holly said. "Nah. And anyway, sure he's always smiling."

"I'm telling you."

"Nahhh."

"Yup. It's a bit of a puzzler, granted . . ."

"Excuse me?"

Eleanor covered her mouth and giggled. "Sorry, I didn't mean that the way it came out. I just mean, I wouldn't have put the two of you together in my head. He's so easy-going and laid-back about everything, isn't he, and you're . . . the way you are. Mind you, they do say that opposites attract."

Holly felt her face contort. "Why –"

"Anyway," Eleanor said. "The point is, what are you going to do about it?"

"Nothing," Holly shrugged. "I mean – even if he was interested, what makes you think I am?"

"Ha! Because you just did it too. The smile. And I know my smiles. I have to go."

She patted Holly's arm and took her leave, evidently quite pleased with her parting words. They weren't bad, Holly had to admit.

James was in the staff room when she arrived. He'd

already eaten his lunch, apparently, and was now having a coffee. Barry Dwyer and Julie Sullivan were there, as was Mike Hennessy. The thing about Mike Hennessy (as Eleanor would have said), was that he was always trying to prove how cool he was. This was embarrassing enough when he did it front of the kids, asking what they thought of the new Arctic Monkeys album and complaining that *Battlestar Galactica* had gone downhill, but it was many times worse when he did it in the staff room. Even before she got within earshot, Holly could have guessed that he was embarrassing himself again; his companions were all slightly slumped in their seats and none of them was looking directly at him. Sure enough, as she took her seat beside them, Mike was in full flow.

"I mean, it's pretty dark stuff, I'm not denying that. But you can't say he isn't funny. If you ask me, he's a riot."

"Who's this?" Holly asked, as she dealt with the Cellophane on her sandwich (bog-standard cheese and tomato).

"Eminem," James told her. "Mike's a big fan."

She tried to look at him without making it obvious. Yup – the half-smile was there, as usual. But was that being "all smiley"? She couldn't tell, largely because she wasn't sure what she was looking for. "Oh yeah?"

"Yeah," Mike said. "He's a bit of a hero of mine, actually."

This was a peculiar quirk of his. The man was up to his armpits in heroes. Or at least, he claimed to be. They were all suspiciously edgy and dangerous – Sean Penn, Quentin Tarantino, the guy who wrote *Fight Club*, and now Eminem. Mike could have been the world's most devoted admirer of, say, Bill Cosby, Holly had often thought, but none of them would ever hear about it.

"Hero?" she said. "Really? Why so? Doesn't he just shout abuse about niggas and bitches?"

Mike did a pretend faint, then recovered. "I can't believe my ears," he said. "He shouts *abuse*? What's the matter with you? It's poetry! Just because it's poetry accompanied by some fat beats, there's no need to get all snooty about it."

"I'm sorry," Holly said, "did you just use the term 'fat beats'?"

"Laugh all you want. But our kids are going to be asking us what it was like to be around when Eminem first broke out. Another couple of decades time, he'll be up there with Dylan and Bowie and all the biggest hitters. You mark my words."

Holly had taken a mouthful of cheese and tomato. She worked on it for a moment and then gulped it down. "I apologise, Mike. If any child of mine ever asks me what it was like when Eminem first broke out, I'll be sure to tell them that it was always kickin' and occasionally even dope. And I'll make damn sure they know all about the fat beats. Back in those days, I'll tell them – sorry, back in *the* day – back in the day, you could hardly spin around on your head without bumping into a fat beat. They were *everywhere*."

"You think you're funny," Mike said. "But you're just . . . not."

195

Holly whistled. "Ouch. Nice comeback."

Mike shook his head and pushed his chair back from the table. "All right, I have to go. James, Julie, Barry, I'll see you later. Holly – go fuck yourself."

He gathered the remains of his lunch together and left them to it.

"Wow," James said when he was out of earshot. "That was a bit . . . wasn't it?"

"What?" Holly, Barry and Julie said as one.

James used his thumb to point at the chair that Mike had just vacated. "'Go *fuck* yourself'?"

"I don't think he was entirely serious," Holly said. "And even if he was, I'm sure he'll get over it."

"Holly's well used to this sort of thing," Barry added. "She gets told to go fuck herself or get fucked or just plain fuck off on a fairly regular basis."

Julie nodded in agreement. "I think I've told you to eff off a few times myself, haven't I, Holly?"

"Probably," Holly shrugged. "I'm effed if I can remember."

James didn't respond but his expression clouded.

"What?" Holly said.

"Nothing."

"You . . . have a look."

"Well . . . "

She felt something wobble deep within her. "Yeah?"

"You can't be happy with that, surely? Being told to fuck off or whatever? I mean . . . repeatedly."

"She's well used to it at this point," Barry said.

"Water off a duck's back," Julie added.

They both looked to Holly then, waiting (she presumed) for her to say something similar. She tried to comply but the words stuck in her throat.

"Not much I can do about it," she croaked eventually.

James popped his shoulders. "I wouldn't say that. You could always try not being so . . . y'know . . . sarcastic."

Julie and Barry guffawed in unison.

"Yeah, right," Julie said.

"And you," Barry said, looking very pleased with himself, "could try not being tall."

This raised a chuckle. Holly joined in with a small smile of her own and made a point of catching James's eye as she did so. He held her gaze for as long as she offered it. As she returned her attention to her sandwich, she became aware that no one had said anything for a few seconds. The silence deepened and became embarrassing. *Please*, she thought. *Please, someone say something. Anyone. Anything.* She looked up then and, for the first time ever, was delighted to see Larry Martin approaching.

"Jesus Christ," he said as he collapsed on to a seat. "Keep it down, you lot. People are complaining about the noise."

"We're just comfortable in each other's company," James told him sweetly.

"Either that," Larry said, "or you're all having a day like mine."

To Holly's great relief, he embarked on a story about the hellish time he'd had with his second years. When she had finished her lunch, she crept away as quietly as she could and took a walk down the road to kill the rest of the free time. Teaching-wise, her afternoon wasn't exactly a disaster but it fell a long way short of the morning's high. She tried to console herself with the notion that it wasn't her fault.

Her mind was elsewhere.

"Go on then," Mark said that evening as he poured her a second glass of wine. It was an Argentinian Malbec. He had characterised it as "provocative"; Lizzie, by contrast, had complained that it was "imprecise".

"Go on what?" Holly said and then immediately wished that she hadn't. It had been quite obvious from the moment that she'd shown up on the doorstep that she wanted to give something an airing.

"Please," Mark said. "Look at you, you're itching to go. What happened? Did a Jehovah's Witness call? Did you see someone with a Bluetooth headset? Did you accidentally catch a bit of *Hollyoaks*?"

Holly took a drink. She couldn't see how a person could call it either "provocative" or "imprecise". It was wine, end of.

"All right," she said. "Remember when I was in here the other day bitching about Kevin and the way he talked about me? That I was all smart-arsey and not like other women and –"

"Yes," Mark said. "We're not senile. We remember."

"Shut up, you," Lizzie said and shot him a look. "Let her talk."

"Right," Holly went on. "Well, I've been thinking about that – a lot. The way things are going. With me. And men. I mean, I don't want to wind up one of those crazy old cat ladies, do I?"

Mark screwed up his face in puzzlement. Lizzie nodded for her to continue, which she did.

"So, anyway, there's this new guy at school. James B– . . . James. Subbing, just for a while. I didn't think all that much of him one way or the other at first, but we wound up seeing a bit of each other over the last few days and I started to . . . y'know. He, uh . . . this is going to sound really corny, but he *intrigues* me. Nothing seems to bug him. Everything's great all the time. I've never heard him say a bad word about anyone or anything. He's so . . . nice."

"Opposites attract," Lizzie said.

Holly wrinkled her nose. "Jesus! I wish people would stop saying that! I do have feelings, you know! And it's bullshit anyway. It's just one of those things that sounds like it might be true because it's a neat phrase. But it's clearly a load of shite. All right, you might be able to name an occasional time when it's worked out with opposites, but to go from that to a blanket rule of 'opposites attract' is like saying cigarettes must be good for you because there's a guy down the road who smoked like a train and lived to be a hundred and eight. Look at you two. You're like peas in a frigging pod. So are most couples."

"Yeah, all right," Lizzie conceded.

"The point. . ." Holly sighed. She felt exhausted all of

a sudden. "The point is, he's said a couple of things. One about how I shouldn't always say what I think and one about my . . . sarcastic . . . tendencies."

"Tendencies?" Mark laughed. Lizzie threw a cushion at him. Holly threw a look at him.

"Today. At lunchtime. He said maybe I could, y'know . . . tone it down a bit."

"And what did you say?" Lizzie asked after a brief silence.

"I didn't say anything. But I was thinking. You don't suppose maybe he was . . . hinting? That he might be, you know, interested. If only I was a bit less . . . me?"

Lizzie and Mark exchanged a curious half-glance. Then Mark said, "Well, I don't know about this guy in particular, but you did have that conversation with Kevin. And it wasn't the first of its kind – you said so yourself. There was Dan, for one."

For a moment, Holly was sure she had misheard him. It was a sort of unwritten rule between them that Dan's name was never to be mentioned.

"Dan? I'm sorry? *Dan?*"

"You were nuts about him and he dumped you for not being frothy enough."

Lizzie rolled her eyes and flopped back into her armchair. "For fuck's sake, Mark."

"What? He did. He told her she –"

"Listen, Holly," Lizzie said, cutting him off. "Listen. Listen. All right . . . to tell you the truth, we did a bit of talking about you behind your back after you left the other night."

Holly drained her wine. "Oh yeah?"

"And . . . I don't know if you've just forgotten this or blocked it out of your mind or what. But, yeah, Dan did say all of those sorts of things to you too."

"I haven't forgotten it *or* blocked it out," Holly said.

Lizzie looked to Mark who folded his arms as if to say, *Leave me out of this.* She frowned and scratched the top of her head. Holly heard the noise the gesture produced and thought of sandpaper.

"I'm trying to think of the right way to put it," Lizzie said.

"Just put it," Holly told her. "What am I gonna do, thump you?"

"I dunno, you might. All right, lookit. You've asked the question – twice now, really. And the fact is, you do get this 'lighten up' stuff from men. If you're waiting for someone to tell you it's your imagination, you're out of luck. Sometimes you get it from men like Kevin, fair enough. But sometimes you get it from men you're completely in love with."

"One man," Holly argued. "Dan was a lot of things but he was *singular*."

Lizzie went on as if she hadn't spoken. "And now you're getting it from a man you find 'intriguing'. The point is, what are you going to do about it? I'm not trying to be harsh, Holly. I love you to bits, I think you're great. But if everyone you meet keeps telling you your breath stinks, then maybe it's time for some TicTacs."

"Holy shit!" Mark said. "*I* would have put it better than that!"

201

Lizzie looked suitably forlorn. "Sorry, Holly, that was . . . I could have . . . sorry. But you know what I mean. Maybe this James guy *is* hinting. And maybe it wouldn't kill you to dial it down a bit, with him at least. See how it goes. You love your science – you could think of it as an interesting little experiment."

Holly made a conscious effort to calm down. There was no poing in getting all maudlin about Dan. She had asked, and they had answered. Full stop.

"Okay," she said. "Okay. That's what I've been thinking too. But how do I go about it? I mean, I've seen a lot of shitty movies that start out this way. How would I get started on this transformation – with a frigging montage?"

"You'll be fine," Lizzie replied. "Do a little tongue-biting. If you can't say something nice, don't say anything at all. That sort of thing. Just keep your eye on the prize and go with the flow."

Mark said nothing for a moment. Then he showed the palms of his hands and said, "Yeah. Flow-go."

There was a certain weariness in his voice. His patience with this line of conversation had clearly expired already. It didn't matter, Holly thought. She had what she came for.

"Okay," she said. "Thanks."

It was nine thirty when Holly returned from Mark and Lizzie's. She checked the phone and saw that her mother still hadn't called to get the verdict on Charlie Fallon. That was no surprise. Mrs Christmas wasn't a particularly patient woman – in all likelihood, she was going up the walls – but she would always choose suffering in silence over entertaining even the remotest possibility that she might make a nuisance of herself. As she hit the speed dial, Holly felt a strong pang of guilt for having left it this long to make the call. Best thing for it, obviously, was to concoct a series of lies.

"Mum?"

"Oh, hello there. How are you? Having a quiet night?"

Her voice was muted, faux-casual. Holly lost no time in launching Operation Fib. "Yeah. I didn't feel great this afternoon when I got in and I went for a wee nap. I was going to stay in bed for an hour or so and call you then. I don't know, maybe there's some sort of a bug working on me or something, but I've only just woken up."

"Aw, are you all right? Sure you could have called me any time. There was no rush."

"No, no. I was dying to get you, honestly. Sure we have to have our chat about himself."

"Well, that's true. I suppose we do."

"So!"

"So . . . "

Holly straightened her spine. "I really liked him, Mum. I thought he was great."

A long pause. "Did you?"

"Yeah, I did."

"Are you sure?"

"Yes! He was very, uh, chatty. Sociable, I mean."

"He's that all right, yeah."

"And he's so . . . " The words stuck in her throat. She gagged for a moment and then forced them out in a sort of linguistic Heimlich maneuver. "So sophisticated. He's a real . . . man of the world."

"Oh! I'm surprised to hear you say that, Holly. I really am. I got the impression you thought he was a bit of a gasbag. About his travels."

He hasn't travelled, Holly thought. *He made it as far as New York and stayed there for thirty years. That's not travelling. That's moving house.*

"God, no. What gave you that idea?" She realised that her mother was about to answer and moved hastily along. "And I'll tell you my favourite thing about him – he wasn't shy about paying you compliments. He was at it all night, wasn't he? Lovely this and delightful that." She exhaled. It was a relief to have said something that had some grounding in fact.

"He wasn't doing that to impress you," Mrs Christmas said quickly. "He's been like that every time I've met him."

"I'm sure. And you were loving it, don't deny it. I could tell."

"I've no intention of denying it. Who doesn't like compliments? It's just been so long since I've had any from a, you know . . . man. It feels funny."

"I can imagine."

"Holly, are you sure you're not just trying to be nice?"

"Of course I'm sure."

"You really liked him?"

"Yes. I did."

There was a long silence. "Well, I'm really . . . I'm stunned, that's what I am. I would have bet my left leg you were going to lay into him today. All that stuff about science and God and all that, I know that's one of your subjects."

Holly's teeth ground together. Aisling and Orla talked about her "list". Her mum talked about her "subjects". She wondered if anyone else had a pet name for her various anti-passions. She put considerable effort into making her next contribution sound casual.

"So we disagree on a few things! We're both adults, Mother, we're allowed to have our own opinions. Doesn't mean we can't like each other."

"I suppose. And he did like you, by the way."

"Oh yeah?"

"Yeah. He said you were very 'feisty'."

Once again, Holly's jaw clamped shut. This time it wasn't so easy to pry it open. "Feisty", indeed. That was the word choice of a sexist. It meant that she was a woman who didn't know her place and would probably have to be reminded of it once in a while. If she'd been black, no doubt he would have called her "uppity".

"Okay," she said through her teeth.

"And pretty! He said you were very pretty. But that only led him on to buttering *me* up a bit more. Her mother's daughter and all that."

What about my tits? Holly thought. *Did he say he liked my tits? Because he certainly seemed to be giving them a lot of thought.*

"What did you get up to after I left?" she said. "Crap, that came out wrong. I mean, did you go on somewhere or –"

"No, no. We just sat there chatting for a wee while – a good while actually, they started giving us dirty looks – and then he put me in a cab. There was no, you know . . . no, uh . . . I just went home."

"Okay. So. Are you going to see him again?"

"He wants to."

"Do you?"

Mrs Christmas exhaled at length. "You really liked him, Holly? I know this must be very strange for you, God knows. But . . . you really liked him?"

"Yeah. Of course I did."

Another exhalation. "Well then," her mother said. "I think I'll . . . just . . . play it by ear."

"Okay," Holly gulped. *Play it by ear.* She'd never heard it called that before.

Chapter 12

On Tuesday morning, Holly sprang from her bed as if stuck with a pin. Usually this sort of thing only happened when she'd been long-fingering some tedious chore. Tired of the endless procrastination, her subconscious would stage a mini-coup, giving her a shot of adrenaline and kicking her out of bed. Not until the room was half-painted or the lawn half-mown would she regain full control of her faculties. On this occasion, she had showered, dressed and eaten and was bouncing from foot to foot like a boxer waiting for the bell before it occurred to her that there was no domestic task awaiting her attention. Still only half-awake, she had to give the matter quite a bit of thought before she remembered that this was the first day of her experiment with James. Disappointingly, however, he was nowhere to be seen when she got to school. He did show up at the mid-morning break but just stuck his head into the staff room, called out a general hello, and then disappeared again. Holly was only just able to stop herself from getting up and following him. She started in her seat and wasn't all surprised, when she turned her head, to see that Eleanor Duffy had noticed. Lunchtime, she told herself, as she tried to erase the image of Eleanor's half-suppressed giggle; it wouldn't be long until lunchtime. Once again, however, her luck was out. She was making her way to the staff room when her mobile buzzed in the pocket of her jeans. The caller was Aisling. She sounded glum.

"What's wrong?" Holly asked, tucking herself into a relatively quiet corner. There was no reply. "Aisling? Are you there? Are you all right?"

"Yeah, yeah." Her voice turned to a whisper. "I think . . . I think I've got a stalker."

The steel claws that had taken Holly by the shoulders released their grip at once. This was not the first time that Aisling had claimed stalkee status. It was not even the second. By Holly's estimate, it was the seventh or eighth. Nothing much ever came of these dramatic declarations; sometimes they were never even mentioned again. In her darker moments, Holly suspected that they were simply Aisling's way of pointing out that there was a downside to being unnecessarily attractive.

"Oh."

"'Oh'? Frigging 'Oh'? Is that all you have to say?

"Sorry. Go on."

The stalker, Aisling revealed after a short period of fuming silence, was a copywriter at work – Kieran. He had asked her out to dinner a few weeks previously and had not taken it all well when she shot him down ("He's got one of those little Satan beards," Aisling reported by way of explanation for her decision). Apparently, his bottom lip had trembled and it taken him a full thirty seconds to turn and walk away. In the days that followed, he had gone to some lengths to avoid her, and when avoiding her was impossible, to stare hard into the middle distance. None of this was particularly surprising and Aisling had assumed that he would soon get over his embarrassment. Then one day, he emailed her a picture of Brad Pitt along with the message "I suppose this is the sort of thing you'd prefer." Aisling replied that she wouldn't say no, if it could be arranged, and tried to tell herself that his tone had been light and breezey, even though he had employed none of the symbols that people usually included when they wanted to imply levity – no smileys or exclamation marks, nothing of that nature (she'd gone for two of each herself). A couple of days passed. Then he sent her a picture of George Clooney accompanied by the line "What about him?" Alarm bells rang at that point and Aisling made no reply, jokey or otherwise. A mere twenty-four hours later, a third picture arrived. This one featured Ricky Martin. Holly gasped at this point in the story. Aisling agreed that yes, indeed, this was the moment when she became truly frightened. It was one thing to receive unwelcome attention from a man. It was quite another to receive unwelcome attention from a man who was under the impression that women lusted after Ricky bloody Martin. She wouldn't have been any more disturbed, she said, if he'd sent her a photo of himself posing with the mummified remains of his dead mother. From past experience, she knew that these things had to be stopped early and invited him to have a word in private. They convened in an unused meeting room and Aisling told him that she didn't know what he was trying to achieve but the emails had to stop. As she'd expected he would, he claimed the whole thing had been a joke and said he was sorry that she didn't have a sense of humour. If he'd known that this was the case, he added, he would never have asked her out in the first place. This withdrawal of the original offer, Aisling informed Holly, was textbook behaviour. She'd once had a guy claim with a straight face that she had *misheard* him; he hadn't said, "Would you like to go for a drink sometime?" but "Would you agree that drinking is sublime?" She'd resisted the urge to mock Kieran and said she hoped they could leave it at that. For a while, it seemed to have worked. And then, this morning, she'd opened the top drawer of her desk and found a page torn from a magazine.

"What kind of magazine?" Holly asked.

"*Take a Break*," Aisling said. "The puzzle page."

"Really?"

"No! Of fucking course not! Porn, Holly, porn! Some young one on all fours with three guys – *three* of them – all waving their d–"

"All right, all right. You don't have to go into details. Jesus, that's . . . Ugh. And you're sure it's from your man? Kieran?"

"Well, who else would have put it there? One of the cleaners? Jenny the receptionist?"

This was a fair point. "I suppose you're right."

"So what am I going to do? I'm at my wit's end here."

"What do you mean? You're going to tell someone, naturally. You going to tell someone and you're going to get the little prick fired."

"But I haven't got any proof."

"You've got the emails, haven't you? In fact, never mind the emails at first, just show the porn thing to your boss. He'll ask questions, have you any idea who could be behind it and so on, and then you drop the emails bit. They're not exactly proof of anything, but they paint a bit of a picture, don't they?"

"Maybe," Aisling said.

"There's no maybe about it. I don't see what's difficult about this."

Aisling didn't respond. "Unless, of course," Holly added with a sigh, "there's something you're not telling me."

"I just wish," Aisling said in the pained tone that she reserved for her most melodramatic pronouncements, "that Eamonn was still my boss."

"I thought he was."

The pained tone was dropped in favour of something a little sharper. "You never listen, Holly, that's your trouble. Eamonn left months ago, nearly a year ago, actually. Moved to London. Big job opportunity, blah, blah. I told you all about it."

"All right, so who is it now then?"

"Justin! Justin! I've described him to you in detail about a dozen times!"

"So why can't you tell Justin?"

A long sigh. "He has . . . a bit of a . . . thing for me."

Holly issued a sigh of her own. "Has he now."

"Yes. And before you say anything, I'm not imagining it. That night out we had for the company's tenth anniversary? He got drunk and gave me the whole my-wife-doesn't-understand-me bit, like, with no irony whatsoever. Kept saying how great we'd be together if only he was twenty years younger. Yeah, like *that's* all that's stopping me. And he stands too close to me all the time. *Much* too close. He tells me filthy jokes too, that's another dead giveaway. Double entendres all day long . . . So no, no way. No way am I going to go to him with a dirty picture in my hand. I can just see him now, leering at me –"

"Okay, fair enough. What about *his* boss then? Or does he fancy you too?"

"She. Carmel. And no, she doesn't fancy me, she hates my guts for some reason . . . frumpy old cow."

Holly understood at once the significance of these last three words. They were meant to indicate in a relatively subtle way that this Carmel character was simply jealous.

"I don't know what to tell you, Aisling. This creep has to go. I don't see how you have any choice. You have to tell someone and your boss, even if he is a complete arsehole himself, is the obvious choice. You'll just have to swallow it."

"That's *exactly* the sort of thing he says to me all the time."

"Ew."

"Don't get me started."

Holly looked at her watch. She was supposed to be in the staff room, being herself. But Aisling had found her second wind now and launched into a breathless diatribe about the many other ways in which Justin made her skin crawl (and stomach turn, and toes curl). She didn't mention Kieran at all during this outburst. Holly let it go on for several minutes before she felt obliged to drop his name herself. Aisling seemed positively irritated by the intervention. As she returned to complaining about Justin, adding an occasional dig at Carmel, Holly felt her mood darken. She really wanted to be sympathetic – for once, Aisling did seem to have a genuine grievance. But these sub-plots – this one clearly fancied her, that one was clearly jealous of her – gave Holly the impression that she was the only one taking the real problem seriously and that, sure enough, the main point of this call was to complain about how hard it was to be beautiful. Her suspicions were not allayed in the least when Aisling eventually ran out of steam and sighed, "Anyway, enough of that – have you spoken to Orla about the other night?"

It wasn't exactly a gentle segue from one topic to the other; it was more like a handbrake turn.

"Oh. So, what, are we all done with the stalkin' talkin'?"

"Yeah, well, let's just see how it pans out."

"Right. Okay. And the answer is no, I haven't spoken to Orla. Have you?"

"Yeah. Last night."

Holly looked at her watch again. "And?"

"She definitely fancied him. John. She didn't say it in so many words but it was still pretty obvious. And, better yet, you and I are in the good books. Or at least, we're not in the bad books."

"Mission accomplished then."

"Well, no, not yet. They didn't even exchange phone numbers or anything. I asked. She pretended she found the idea only *hilarious,* but I could tell that she was sorry they hadn't."

"I see."

"Yeah. I was thinking – maybe we could do a repeat performance, the whole gang of us. No pressure. I mean, we'd all know why we were there, really – it'd be like an open secret. One more push over the cliff, like. This weekend, if we can arrange something. Sooner the better, I think, for Orla's sanity."

Holly was struck by two emotions at once. The first was guilt for having thought badly of Aisling for much of the conversation thus far. She really was a kind and thoughtful person. The second was excitement. From a purely selfish point of view, a repeat performance would be just the job. She'd be going into it with a new-found sense of perspective regarding James and would be able to . . . concentrate.

"Sounds good," she said, trying hard not to make her enthusiasm obvious. "I'll have a word with James."

"Ah, yes, Bond, James Bond. I thought he was lovely, Holly. Such a sweetheart, so good-natured. Anything on the horizon there? He seemed to be smiling at you at lot, I noticed."

"I don't know if he was smiling at me or laughing at me," Holly said quickly. She'd meant it as a joke but as soon as she'd said it, a little shiver ran along her arms. "And that just the way he is, anyway. He's never done smiling."

"Maybe so," Aisling replied. "Then again, you never know."

Holly paused for a moment, then took the plunge. "Can't really see the two of us together though, can you? We're not exactly cut from the same cloth."

"That's true," Aisling said. "Then again, they do say that opposi–"

"Don't even finish that sentence," Holly said. "I'm warning you. Not another word."

"Okay. Jesus."

Holly feared that she'd gone too far. "Not that I would be interested, mind you. I'm not."

"If you say so. Anyway, I meant to ask – how's your mum these days?"

Holly looked at her watch for a third time. A big chunk of the lunch break was already gone. But she had to tell her friends about Charlie Fallon sooner or later. She might as well start now.

"Actually, there's a bit of news there these days . . ."

It didn't take long to tell. She skipped over the details and didn't mention her own involvement in the vetting process; she started to do so but felt immediately ridiculous and retraced her steps. Aisling had plenty of questions, however, most of which had follow-ups. By the time they had exhausted the subject and said goodbye, Holly only had time to run to the staffroom and cram a sandwich into her face before the afternoon classes began. She missed James; he'd just left, according to Larry Martin. It made no difference, really, Holly concluded. They would only have had time for a quick hello and she really wanted a good long run at being the new her all over him. Even if she didn't get prolonged face time at school, with any luck, she would get plenty at the weekend.

Blind Date Take Two was going to be interesting.

Holly got a chance to broach the subject with James first thing the next morning. He was getting out of his car as she parked and hung back to walk in with her.

"Good morning," he said as she approached. "Another lovely day."

Holly cast her eyes upwards. There were patches of blue up there, she was willing to admit, but they were almost lost among the broad expanses of pale grey dullness. It was not, by any stretch of the imagination, a lovely day. Mark and Lizzie popped up in her mind like disapproving meerkats.

"Yes," she said. "Yes. It is. A lovely day."

"Did you get up to much last night?" he asked.

"Sat in and petted the cat in front of the TV. Tuesday night is usually movie premiere night, so it made a nice change."

"I know what you mean. It gets tiresome, doesn't it? 'Come on, hurry up, the private jet's waiting.' I mean, gimme a chance to get my suit on. Giorgio's still fiddling with it."

216

There was no doubt about it, Holly thought – this was banter. Banter!

"I don't suppose you've spoken to John since the weekend?" she asked then.

"Nope. Why?"

"I had a chat with Aisling yesterday and she told me that Orla definitely seems, well . . . not uninterested."

"Really? Great. Like I said on Sunday, I'm sure it's entirely mutual – this lack of apathy."

Now he was gently mocking her. That was a good sign too, surely?

"Mind you," James went on, "I wouldn't put any money on him actually doing anything about it."

Holly nodded. "Well, this is just what we were talking about. Orla's not exactly Samantha Jones herself."

"Who?"

"*Sex and the City.*"

"Ah."

"So maybe it wouldn't hurt if we did a repeat performance of the whole thing, the five of us. Not bowling, if it's up to me, but something. What do you think?"

They had reached the entrance now. James skipped forward and held it open for her. "Sure. Sounds good. I'll have a word with himself. What, are we just letting on that we had such a great time on Saturday that we're going for a re-run?"

She squeezed past him. "Yup. Nothing needs to be said out loud."

"But it'll be an open secret sort of thing?"

"Yeah. That's exactly what Aisling said."

He stepped inside behind her. "So we're all on the same page. Now if you can just remember to show up at the agreed time for a change, we're on easy street."

Holly laughed, suddenly and loudly. It wasn't that she found his gag particularly hilarious. Humour had almost nothing to do with it, in fact. It was the laugh of someone who was suddenly having a good day.

No firm plans were made until Thursday evening. Holly had just arrived home when Aisling rang to say that, through work, she could get her hands on five tickets for a play that was running in town. The tickets were for Saturday night, which was perfect. Holly was not immediately overcome with joy, however; she was not a fan of the theatre. There was something about having live actors in front of her that always made her nervous. She could never shake the feeling that one or more of them was bound to screw up their lines or bump into a colleague or plain old fall off the edge to the embarrassment of all. Orla, on the other hand, would watch almost anyone do almost anything on a stage. In her time, she had paid actual money to see a *ventriloquist*, which was something that Holly found genuinely unfathomable. It was with a profound sense of valiant self-sacrifice (was that a bugle she heard in the distance?) that she told Aisling to go ahead and snap them up. She called Orla as soon as she'd hung up and, sure enough, the proposition was warmly embraced. It made a pleasant change for Aisling to have access to so many tickets, Holly said casually. These things usually came in one and twos. It seemed a shame to let the extra ones go to waste – why didn't they ask James and John to come along too? Orla did a good job of making her reply – "It's up to you" – sound equally casual.

There was one more call to make and Holly made it eagerly. *The theatre?* James cooed with predictable enthusiasm. A fantastic idea. He *loved* the theatre. He'd never heard John expressing an opinion one way or the other but no matter – he'd make damn sure he came along too. Just before they ended the call, he told Holly that he was getting a warm glow all over, like the *Ready Brek* kid. Her heart stopped for a couple of seconds. Really? Yeah, he said. They were doing a good thing, the three of them, helping their pals out like this.

Oh, yes, Holly agreed. She had a glow too. For the same reason.

Chapter 13

The play, which was called *The Tyrant*, was running in a city-centre theatre called The Black Box. The venue was new, small and out-of-the-way. Holly was first to arrive in its lobby and was joined shortly afterwards by Orla. The latter was wearing a shapeless pair of brown trousers and a too-tight mustard shirt that she had owned, by Holly's reckoning, for at least five years. It was a warm evening, so she was carrying rather than wearing the cheap grey hoodie that was her near-constant companion. Her shoes were black and bulbous. They too had seen better days, although it was hard to believe that they had been much to write home about even when new. Holly felt terrible for noticing these details – especially with her record, fashion-wise – but her guilt was run neck-and-neck by her irritation. What was wrong with her? Had she failed to understand – the presence of three other people notwithstanding – that this was a date?

Neither of them said much about their previous meeting, beyond acknowledging that it had happened. They spent a couple of minutes on work-related chat before Holly decided to seize the opportunity and give Orla the gist of her mother's news. The version of events that she supplied was even more truncated than the one she had given Aisling. It was perhaps for this reason – although it may well have been plain shock – that Orla didn't seem to have much to say on the subject. She wished the potential couple well; that was the extent of it.

James and John arrived next. They gave a repeat performance of their arrival at the MegaBowl. James chatted away, declaring his enthusiasm for (amongst other things) going to plays, early autumn evenings, fun-size Milky Ways and jeans that fit just right. John, meanwhile, looked at his feet and occasionally cleared his throat. His attitude reminded Holly of something or someone. When she figured out what it was, she was so pleased with herself that she almost told everyone: he was like a child who'd been dragged out shopping by his mother and just when he thought the ordeal couldn't get any worse, his mother had bumped into a friend. It wouldn't have looked out of place, Holly thought, if he'd taken James by the hand and tried, uselessly, to haul him off in the direction of home.

When it became obvious that they were in danger of missing the start of the play, talk turned to Aisling's tardiness problem and its possible psychological underpinnings. They had just decided to go in without her – they were the only ones left in the lobby – when she appeared. Holly could see at a glance why she was late this time. Her hair and make-up were perfect and she was dressed for somewhere a lot classier than a tiny theatre at the end of an alley in Temple Bar. The word for it, Holly supposed, was "co-ordinated". She was wearing a cream-coloured trouser suit and was carrying a tiny metallic-looking purse that shimmered so vibrantly Holly half-expected to see a power cord trailing behind it. Her jewellery – small pearl ear-rings and a slender silver necklace – seemed to have been designed with this particular outfit, and possibly this particular lighting in mind. Even by her own lofty standards, she looked sensational. Despite her best intentions – she consciously reminded herself that she didn't care about clothes – Holly felt herself shrink a little.

After greetings were exchanged and Aisling had made a vague swipe at blaming traffic for her late arrival, they presented their tickets and took their seats. This process was not as simple as it should have been. It didn't occur to Holly until it was almost too late that Orla and John should be sitting next to each other. They wouldn't be able to have much of a chat, granted, but that wasn't the point. The physical proximity could do wonders for their boldness. Unfortunately, Orla was at the head of the little train they made as they went down the theatre aisle, while John trailed at the very back. Holly was directly behind Orla. Thinking quickly, she paused by the entrance to their row, ostensibly to switch her phone off (as if that couldn't be done from her seat). Aisling was coming along behind her but she completely missed the point. Seeing no other alternative, Holly felt it necessary to give her a swift kick on the ankle as she passed. There was no power behind it, but the fright caused Aisling to issue a high-pitched "Jesus!". Some of their fellow audience members had been tut-tutting and dirty-looking their late arrival as it was. Now there was a more general mumbling of discontent. It was only when Holly widened her eyes and jerked her head that Aisling cottoned on. Even then, she merely retreated back to Holly's position where she stood stiffly with her arms by her side, looking slightly lost. Holly tried to rescue the situation by pretending that she was asking advice on how to deactivate her phone but this, she suspected, only served to make her look mentally defective. James, at least, twigged what was going on and made a slightly better fist of swapping places with John. But he was hardly subtle about it. He simply stopped dead in the hope that his friend would step past him. John drew level but then he stopped too, as if that was what was expected of him. At that point, James placed his hand in the small of his back and shoved him forward with such force that he very nearly lost his footing. He scampered into the row and took his seat beside Orla with some speed, fearing, Holly suspected, that further violence might be visited upon him if he didn't. Aisling followed, as Holly had hoped she would. This meant that she and James were together. There was a pleasing symmetry to it, she thought – two potential couples on either side of a neutral observer. As they settled in, Holly realised that this was the closest she had ever been to James. She found herself angling her head towards him and taking a slow, subtle noseful of the air. This wasn't something she was in the habit of doing; in fact, she couldn't recall ever having done it before. He smelled like warm linen. She had no idea what she had expected, but somehow, this discovery delighted her. As the house lights went down, she thought, *I'm sniffing around like a barnyard animal. What's next? Marking territory?* There was no doubt about it. She was losing the run of herself. Seconds later a man unicycled on to the stage carrying a Rubik's Cube. And so began the worst entertainment-related evening of Holly's entire existence.

The best thing that could be said about the play was that it was short, but even that had its downside; there was no time for an intermission and Holly, for one, could have really used the break. By the time it was all over and they spilled out on to the street, she felt quite faint with anger and irritation. It was difficult to believe that someone had written such a thing, that other someones had agreed to act in it and that still others had paid to see it. Expletives tumbled around in her mind like socks in a drier but they refused to come together in anything resembling a coherent thought.

"Well," James said cautiously, "That was . . . interesting. I think it was about how difficult modern life can be. Trying to be different things to different people, you know."

"No doubt," Aisling said. "But it was really more like a circus than a play. And there was way too much –"

"Juggling," Orla agreed. "I know. Fair enough, she

could juggle for Ireland, your one. But she sure as hell couldn't rap. I'm almost afraid to ask but what did you think, Holly?"

Aisling giggled and ducked, her hands clamped across her ears. Holly fully intended to say something positive; this was a great chance to show what she could do. But when she moved her lips, the only sound that emerged was a small squeak.

"Ah, look," Orla said nodding at Holly. "She's been struck dumb."

"I've seen this before," Aisling noted. "We'd better get her into a pub. Gin and tonic, 'stat'."

They hurried into the first joint they passed and got themselves seated with little ceremony. Orla and John sat next to each other, Holly noted. They had no sooner given their order to a passing floor girl than the dissection proper began. A consensus quickly emerged: the play had been a bit of a mess but was not without its charms. The performances had been pretty good overall and there had been one or two thought-provoking moments. As she might have guessed, Holly was alone in believing that the thing had been irredeemably awful, soup to nuts. Naturally, she said no such thing and limited her contributions to occasionally nodding when someone else said something reasonably complimentary. Try as she might, she still couldn't come up with a full-throated pleasantry of her own. It was beyond her.

Conversation soon turned to the character of Frederick. He was the one who had unicycled onto the stage with a Rubik's Cube. While everyone had experienced problems juggling their various responsibilities (and in some cases with *literally* juggling), Frederick was the one who seemed to have the most going on. At various points throughout the evening, he had been obliged to hop around on one leg while balancing a teddy bear on his head, to roller-skate backwards in circles while speaking in backwards sentences, to build a house of cards on a lop-sided table while saying a decade of the rosary – the list went on and on (and on and on and on). Frederick was even more annoying than his colleagues, Holly thought, because the actor who played him had a horrible voice. Why, she wondered helplessly, would someone who made a noise like a faulty oboe get involved in acting in the first place? Hadn't anyone ever pointed out to him that it was a bad idea? Did he have a cross-eyed sister who was determined to be a model? And there was no way that he'd put it on for the role. No one was that good, least of all this guy (he'd quite obviously forgotten his lines on at least two occasions). It was almost more than Holly could bear when James and the others described the character as "possibly overcooked". A feeble whimper escaped her as – for want of something else to praise – they admired the actor's haircut. Next, they turned to the play's theme. Orla said she supposed it was all about how difficult it is to do more than one thing at once. Holly squirmed in her seat. *It's difficult to do more than one thing at once* was something that *toddlers* knew. It was hardly the stuff of great art. What was next? *Some days it's cold and some days it's warm?* As the others chipped in with their forced, desperate compliments and feather-light quibbles, Holly finally centred herself and sat up straight.

"It wasn't a bad premise," she said, choking on every syllable. All eyes turned to her. She realised that this was the first full sentence she had issued since they arrived. Delivering it had made her feel instantly exhausted.

"You're back!" Aisling cried and raised her glass. "I was beginning to think you'd gone for good this time. Remember *Runaway Bride*, Orla? She didn't speak for a full two hours after it. Go on then, Holly. Hit us."

"It wasn't a bad premise," Holly said again.

Aisling's nose twitched "What, that's it? That's all you have to say?"

Holly nodded and hid behind her drink. Everyone stared, even John who up to that point had been gazing at his own lap.

"Are you all right?" Orla asked.

Holly glanced up, but where she expected to see a cheeky grin, there was only a look of genuine concern. "I'm fine," she said.

Orla nodded. "Okay. And you thought the play had . . . a decent premise?" She screwed her face up as she said it, as if the words themselves had a peculiar taste.

"Yes," Holly said. "It wasn't a bad premise." *Stop saying that!* a voice in her head screamed. She hid behind her drink again. No one spoke for a moment. Then James said, "Let's face it, the play wasn't the best any of us has ever seen. But all experience is good, eh? What doesn't kill you makes you stronger."

"Huh," Holly said. "Try telling that to someone who

lost a leg in a car accident." There were audible gasps all round. She shrank a little, cursing herself to Hell. "I mean . . . I just hate that saying, that's all."

"One more for the list, so," James said.

"Sorry?"

"Your list. Of things you hate. I'm saying, new addition. Do we ring a bell or something?"

He wasn't trying to be nasty, Holly told herself. Not in the least. There was no need to get all upset.

"No, there's no bell," Aisling giggled. "But it's a neat idea. We could all get little flags too. Ring a bell, wave a flag. Add a little festivity to the thing."

"They'll have to be small flags and bells," Orla added. "Otherwise I can see us getting very tired."

"Good one!" Holly said, trying to undo the damage. "That's me told!"

Even she could tell that her voice sounded brittle and hollow. Orla's look of concern returned. No one spoke. Time seemed to slow down.

"I've never seen a Shakespeare play," John remarked after a few excruciating seconds had ticked by. "I mean, I had to read a couple at school like everyone else, but I've actually seen one performed." Holly felt pathetically grateful to him for ending the silence. Then he added, "Have you, Orla?" and she realised that he hadn't been trying to do her a favour; he was merely trying to get a conversation going with her friend. It worked too. Orla turned to face him properly, putting her shoulder to the group. Holly, James and Aisling took the hint and sent small looks to each other. Just as they had done the previous week, they had now effectively split into two factions.

Holly sipped on her drink, feeling quite sure that she had made no progress whatsoever. On her side of the divide, none of them seemed to have any stomach for continued discussion of the theatre – John and Orla had no such qualms – but no other topic presented itself. They busied themselves for a few moments with smiling inanely and trying to look like they weren't eavesdropping on the other pair.

Then Aisling half-choked on her drink. "There's Ronan," she said, wiping her chin. "Isn't it? It is. Oi! Ronan! Ronan!" She got to her feet and started waving so frantically that her hip jarred Orla, who spilled a fair portion of her wine all over John's lap, much to their mutual horror.

The man Aisling was waving at was Ronan O'Dowd, an ex-boyfriend. Aisling's relationships hardly ever ended well – she seemed to go out of her way to make sure that they didn't – but her break-up with Ronan had been a rare exception. Not only was the actual split relatively civil, they had remained quite friendly. This made him utterly unique. He and Aisling weren't exactly close, but they got together once in a while, usually (as far as Holly could tell) when one of them had something new in their lives that they wanted to boast about. Aisling hadn't mentioned him for some time, which seemed to indicate that their semi-friendship was, at long last, petering out. Holly and Orla had certainly hoped so; they'd always hated his guts. Tonight, Ronan had a female in tow. She was tall – much taller than Ronan, who had the approximate dimensions of a fridge – and irritatingly pretty. Not as pretty as Aisling, Holly noted, but still way out of this clown's league (*How does he do it?* she wondered absently). They approached slowly for extra drama, or rather Ronan did and she followed suit. To her credit, she had an impatient look on her face and seemed to be on the point of prodding him in the back and telling him to get a move on.

"Well, well, well, look who it isn't," Ronan said as he arrived. "It's Charlie's Angels."

He'd always called them that when he and Aisling were together. It made Holly want to go for his throat with her teeth.

"Where have you been hiding?" Aisling said, leaning across the table to give him a peck on the cheek.

"I've been around and about," Ronan said. "You know me, Aisling. Never stand still, that's my motto."

"Never trust a person who has a motto," Holly said. "That's my motto." Everyone looked at her. She'd done it again. In her mind's eye, she gave herself a good slap. *If you can't say something nice,* she reminded herself.

He gazed right through her. "Hello. On your way back from another funeral, I see." His companion gave him a not-very-inconspicuous elbow in the ribs. "I'm only joking," he explained. "She has a thing for black. It goes with her soul." He laughed at his own joke. He didn't just smile or giggle; he laughed.

"I'm Michelle, by the way," the mystery woman said. The girls nodded and said their names. Aisling gestured to James and John and supplied theirs too.

"Michelle is my special lady," Ronan purred. He was obviously being ironic but it didn't sit well with him, Holly thought. It was like watching George Bush pretending to make a gaffe.

"And how long has this been going on?" Aisling asked. She waggled her finger between them, her tone mock-disapproving.

"Just a few weeks," Ronan said. "We met at the gym."

A wide variety of slurs jockeyed for position in Holly's mind. With a tremendous effort of will, she pushed them all aside.

"Good for you," Aisling said. "And how is he treating you, Michelle?"

"Not as well as he should," she said with a smile that was perfectly judged; it probably looked real enough to Ronan, but a woman would know that it had undertones. Holly decided that she liked her.

"What about you?" he said to Aisling. "Anything wild or wonderful?"

"Not a thing. Same old same old."

Ronan nodded. Aisling nodded back. There was silence – lots of it.

Then Ronan beamed. "Have a guess," he said to Michelle, "what Holly's second name is?"

"Good God . . ." Holly said and took a gulp of her drink.

"I wouldn't have a clue," Michelle said. She was clearly embarrassed.

"Go on. Guess."

"I don't *know*."

"Yeah, but just g–"

"Smith."

"Christmas!" he boomed. "Holly . . . Christmas. Isn't that wild? It drives her nuts. Doesn't it, Holly?"

"Things could be worse," she said with a small shrug. "As I'm sure Michelle would agree."

This little barb was quite justified, she felt; she was merely defending herself. Ronan tried to smile but didn't quite pull it off. Michelle fared much better with her effort. Holly's opinion of her rose still further. She sincerely hoped that she would do better for herself, and soon.

"Holly Christmas," Ronan repeated. "I'll never get over it."

"My second name is Bond," James said brightly. "What do you make of that? You know – James Bond, the celebrated spy. I'm sure you've heard the name before."

Ronan peered at him. Holly knew that like all humourless people, he lived in fear of ridicule. She greatly enjoyed watching his eyebrows fall and rise as his tiny brain tried to work out whether or not he was being mocked.

"Funny," he said, somewhat uncertainly.

"I'm not joking," James assured him. "Would you like to see some ID?"

Ronan shook his head.

"I love having an unusual name," James went on in the same breezey tone. "I think it's a hoot. Holly does too, mind you. She just doesn't like to admit it." He shot a quick look in John Lennon's direction. Holly understood this to mean: *Would you like to join in?*. John gave his head the tiniest of shakes. This was probably for the best, Holly decided. It would be over-egging the pudding. James immediately returned his attention to Ronan. "What's your own surname, by the way?"

Ronan swallowed. "O'Dowd."

James smiled. "Ronan . . . O'Dowd." Holly wasn't quite sure how he did it, but he managed to make it sound pathetic. "Well . . . that's nice too."

"Yeah," Ronan said, recovering just a little of his swagger. "I get by. Anyway, listen – we have to get going. We're meeting some people and we're late as it is."

Aisling went in for another cheek-peck. "It was great to see you," she said, unconvincingly.

"You too," Ronan said.

"Nice to have met you all," Michelle said and – somewhat unnecessarily, because she hadn't moved an inch – waved from the elbow.

"Yeah, see you, Michelle," Holly added before giving her boyfriend the briefest of glances. "Ronan."

The others raised hands and mumbled farewells. Ronan made one more attempt at a grin, then turned on his heels and left much more quickly than he'd arrived. Michelle walked behind him – quite a bit behind, Holly was pleased to notice.

"Christ, that was a bit awkward," Aisling said as soon as they were gone.

"Well, what the hell did you call him over for?" Holly

snapped and then immediately softened her tone. "They were on their way out. They would have just wafted on by."

"I dunno," Aisling shrugged. "I just got the feeling that he'd been ignoring me lately. He hasn't called in ages."

"Had you called him?"

"No."

"Well, then. You don't really want to be friends with him. It's just a bit of a novelty, having an ex-boyfriend who doesn't wish you dead because you handed his heart to him in a little bag."

"Ah," James said. "An ex. I was wondering."

"In fairness to her," Holly went on, "not all of her exes are as obnoxious as he is."

"Ronan isn't obnoxious," Aisling countered. "He's just a bit . . . "

". . . of a tool?" said Holly.

"I was going to say 'insecure'."

"Anyway," Holly said quickly – the tool comment had just slipped out – "thank you, James, for leaping to my defence." Her fingers clenched. Now she was sounding impossibly wet. Had she no control of herself whatsoever? "On the name thing. He takes the piss every time we meet."

James nodded, then caught John's attention by throwing a beer-mat at him. "Wouldn't have killed you to back me up there, Mr Walrus," he said.

John made a gesture of indifference.

"While you've got your shining armour on," Aisling

said, "maybe you could pop over to my office and sort something out for me."

"Oops," Holly muttered. "Forgot to ask. How's that going?"

Aisling gave her a look. "Yeah, cheers. I could be spending my fifth night tied to an altar in his secret lair for all the attention you've paid."

"What's this all about?" James asked.

Aisling told him all about Kieran, making an extra-special effort (it seemed to Holly) not to sound conceited and irrational. Orla only paid attention up to the point where the word "stalker" was mentioned; thereafter, she re-engaged John in their private *tête-à-tête*. James, on the other hand, listened carefully. His eyes grew ever wider as the story progressed and when she came to the revelation about her desk-drawer discovery, seemed to take over the top half of his face.

"Wow," he said. "That's not good."

She shook her head. "Nope. Tell you the truth, James, I've been a bit upset about it."

"So what's the latest?" Holly asked.

"Nothing's happened since," Aisling said. Somehow, she managed to deliver this piece of non-news as if it was the climax of a spooky story.

Holly drained her drink. "Grand, so."

Aisling shook her head and gave James a sad little glance as if to say, *You see what I have to put up with*.

"I'd hardly call it 'grand'," he said. "This sounds serious to me. You've told your boss, I presume, Aisling?"

Her head drooped. "No. I don't know, I just . . . I

235

suppose I'm kind of embarrassed. I'm afraid of sounding paranoid."

Holly waited to see if she would add anything else. Double entendres? Wife doesn't understand him? She didn't.

"That's understandable," James said. "But still. You can't let him get away with that sort of carry-on."

Holly looked around for someone to order more drinks from but there was no one. "I'm going to the bar," she announced. "Same again all round?"

Aisling and James nodded. Holly practically had to wave her arms about to get Orla and John's attention. They seemed to have made a lot of progress very quickly. Both wore dopey grins as they agreed that, yes indeed, fresh drinks would be a fine thing. It seemed that on this score at least, the night was going to be a success. While she was waiting to be served at the bar, Holly took stock. It was beginning to dawn on her that she'd spent too much time concentrating on being pleasant – a task at which she had almost entirely failed, in any case – and nothing like enough on actual flirting. It was time to buckle down and get to it. Now, flirting – how did that go again? She bit her lip and frowned. She'd read countless magazine articles on the subject over the years, of course, but because she'd always thought that they were written by morons for morons, she'd never really paid much attention. Physical contact was an obvious one, but that wasn't going to happen. She'd trailed behind as they'd taken their seats and, despite her frantic jostling, had wound up on the opposite side of the table to James. There was no way she could casually brush his wrist, say, without first getting to her feet and reaching across like a drowning victim going for a rope. She'd had as much physical contact as she was going to get in the theatre, she feared, and that hadn't amounted to much (once or twice, while rubbing her forehead in an attempt to ease the tension, she had poked him in the arm with her elbow). Eye contact was another good bet, but that was not without its problems either. She'd been trying to maintain same all night and had discovered that it wasn't easy. James was the eye-contact type to begin with. Any attempt to match him eyeball for eyeball soon began to feel less like a sexy dalliance than a staring contest. Get touchy-feely, make eye contact . . . There was a third big one, she was sure of it, but she couldn't remember what it was.

She glanced back at the table – and froze. The sensation that swept over her (from the ground up, it seemed) was both confusing and disturbing. She felt a deep conviction that something was wrong, but it was not immediately obvious what it was. Her eyelids slowly closed and opened, closed and opened. There was nothing unusual about the scene. It was just as she'd left it. Orla and John. James and Aisling. And then it hit her. They looked like two couples. She could put it no other way. It was more a gut feeling than a coherent thought. Was it the way they were sitting? The angle of their heads? The gestures they were using? Their expressions? She couldn't put her finger on it. But she couldn't help but see a two-word phrase flashing in her head: *Double*

Date. Over her shoulder, a barman gruffly asked if she was just standing there for the hell of it or did she want a drink or what. She turned and gave him the order in a slow monotone, dimly aware that in any other circumstances she would be eviscerating him for his rudeness. She took a deep breath and leaned against the bar for support. What was going on here? Why did she feel so upset? So what if James and Aisling looked like a couple? Big deal. They weren't. And then her conscious mind reached the conclusion that her subconscious had apparently already embraced. They looked like a couple because, just like Orla and John, they were on their way to being one. She risked another glance at the table. As if on cue, James said something and shook his head in disbelief. Aisling threw her head back and laughed, then rocked forward again. As she did so, she grabbed his forearm, patted it once, twice, three times – *Stop it, you're killing me* – and then withdrew her hand. Holly's knees wobbled. The barman returned with the drinks. She paid him and made a triangle of the glasses between her hands. The walk back seemed to take several minutes. James jumped up from his seat as she approached and took the drinks from her. She went back to the bar to get the other two and her change.

"Cheer up," the barman said as he slapped the coins into a beer puddle by her outstretched hand. "It might never happen."

This snapped her out of her funk. "Get yourself some deodorant," she said as she made a big deal of picking up the money. "You smell like a chimp's crotch."

She turned on her heels and went back to the table.

"I've been doing my damsel-in-distress bit," Aisling informed Holly as she gave Orla and John their drinks (they barely looked up).

"Is that right?" Holly said. As if things weren't bad enough already, she misjudged the height of her seat; it was more of a falling-down than a sitting-down.

"Yeah. About Kieran. James is up for bumping into him in a dark alley somewhere. He's such a sweetheart."

Holly raised an eyebrow at him. "Really? I'm surprised. I didn't have you down as the physical type."

He frowned, or at least pretended to. "I never said anything about a dark alley, to be fair. I just said that someone should have a word with this guy. Actually, now that I think about it, I didn't even say it should be me."

Aisling reacted to this as if was some devastating Wildean quip. She roared with laughter and although she didn't go for a forearm pat this time, she did shake her head and say, "James, James, James, you're gas."

Say their name as often as possible, Holly fumed to herself. That was the third one. Get touchy-feely, make eye contact and say their name as often as possible. She didn't want to look directly at Aisling, but she was sorely tempted to tell her that she'd forgotten to add her trademark hair-flip. And this "sweetheart" business . . . She'd called him that during their phone conversation the other day too. The one in which she'd asked Holly if there was anything on the horizon between herself and James; the one in which Holly had said no – she wasn't interested.

"Are you all right, Holly?" James asked. "You look a bit miserable."

"But then again, don't I always?" she said with a little exhalation that even she recognised as sickeningly self-pitying.

"No. Of course you don't. Did something happen at the bar?"

She leaped at this unexpected opportunity. "Yeah. Well, sort of. Barman was a bit of a cretin, that's all."

For half a second, she allowed herself to hope that James might offer to "have a word" with him too. He didn't.

"Holly has the worst luck with cretins," Aisling said. "Service industry cretins, especially. She made a waiter quit on the spot once. Made him cry too."

"That's a total exaggeration," Holly said.

The incident in question had taken place a few years previously. They'd been out for a cheap and cheerful Friday-night pizza, just the two of them. Their waiter cocked up both starters *and* both mains, then began rolling his eyes and mumbling obscenities when they politely pointed out the mistakes. The final straw came with the bill. It seemed suspiciously heavy and, upon closer inspection, turned out to include the sum of thirty-odd euros for a bottle of sparkling water. Holly's recollection was that Aisling had been just as angry as she was and hence just as responsible for the waiter's sudden, tearful, furious and tremendously loud exit. Not that either of them was fully to blame, really. An apologetic manager had come over to explain that the guy had recently broken up with his girlfriend and had been showing up to work either late or drunk for a week. If he hadn't walked out, there was little doubt that he would shortly have been escorted out. The way Holly remembered it, she and Aisling had felt bad about their role in the end of his waiting career and had asked the manager to give the guy another chance if he ever showed up again. In the version of events that Aisling presented to James, however, the waiter had "been under a bit of stress", admittedly, but regardless of his mental state could not possibly have been expected to survive the "torrent of abuse" that Holly – acting alone, apparently – had heaped upon him.

When it became clear that she was getting turned over, Holly decided not to interrupt. She would keep her powder dry and issue a firm rebuttal when it was all over. But as the story dragged on, she decided that she couldn't be bothered. What was the point? What good would it do her in the long run? When Aisling decided to give a man a shot at the title, there was only ever one outcome. So it was already too late. In fairness to him, James didn't seem to think of it as a story about Holly at all. He was more interested in the poor waiter and his tragic romance. It was a response that just half an hour previously would have had Holly swooning. Now it made her feel even worse. She looked to her right and saw that Orla and John both had their phones out. They were swapping numbers. She looked back at Aisling and James. They were leaning towards each other now, gazes locked. A sense of panic swept over her. What was she supposed to do, just sit there and watch them edging ever closer together, pausing occasionally to give her a dirty look or, worse, a moment or two of pity attention? *Four's company*, she thought, *five's a crowd*.

"Listen," she said, so loudly that all four of them jerked their heads in her direction. "I'm getting a splitting headache. I think I'll just put myself in a taxi and head on home."

There was some perfunctory interrogation. Was she sure? This was very sudden. Would she be all right on her own? Had she any tablets in her bag? Then the questions just stopped coming. Before she had time to second-guess her hasty decision, she was waving goodbye over her shoulder.

Chapter 14

Holly spent a good portion of Sunday morning in a bath that she saturated with every oil and salt in her possession. Her intention was to create a sense of luxury and bliss, to give herself a pampering of such profound opulence that it alone would lift her mood. In reality, her only achievement was to render the air so sickly sweet that it was all but unbreathable. She had to open the window, in fact, to stave off suffocation, which meant subjecting the parts of her that were resting above the waterline to a stiff breeze. *It's never like this in the ads,* she thought as she lay there, choking and shivering.

Lunch was no great success either. She splashed out on a "Luxury Gourmet Salad" from a tremendously expensive deli down the road and was greatly excited to find out what was so different about it. Not a single thing, it turned out, unless you counted the exotic dressing, which tasted like vinegar cut with Fairy Liquid and came in a long pink sachet that bore a passing resemblance to an unrolled condom.

There was an old western on BBC2 in the afternoon and she watched a bit of that, marvelling in an absent sort of way that audiences were once willing to believe in cowboys with dazzling white teeth and crisp yellow neckerchiefs. Somewhere towards tea-time, she dragged herself into the kitchen and slurped her way through a bowl of Crunchy Nut Cornflakes. It had only just gone seven thirty when she first started to seriously contemplate going to bed. She felt silly for doing so and forced herself to sit through yet another documentary about sharks. Shortly after it ended, she received a text message from Aisling. It read "**Success!**". Holly's first reaction was to drop her arm limply by her side and wait to be swept away by some sort of breakdown. But then she realised that the message almost certainly related to Orla and John. Aisling was not in the habit of advertising her "hook-ups", as she called them, and even if she was, it seemed unlikely that she would describe the event as a "success". Successes were for people who had been working hard at something and were relieved that it had all come good. Aisling never had to work at hook-ups. As Holly was painfully aware, they just seemed to happen. She stared at her phone for a while (as if that would provide some mystical insight), then decided that she might as well put herself out of her misery. There was no way she could face ringing Aisling – *You and James? Well, I never! Good for you* – so she called Orla instead.

As conversations went, it was a little one-sided. Orla was sorry not to have made enquiries herself at some point during the day – Holly had almost forgotten about her headache claim – but she hadn't had the chance: John had only just left. She tried to say this casually, as if she had yet to decide if she was pleased about it, but her voice gave her away. Holly asked for particulars. Orla provided them, slowly at first but with ever-increasing gusto. Before long, she dropped the pretence entirely and allowed herself free license to froth and foam about John's many qualities. He was such a sensitive soul. He was an old-school gent. He did a mean Bertie Ahern. He made a lovely cup of tea. He knew a lot about history. He knew a lot about computers. He knew an *awful* lot about The Beatles. They hadn't gone "the whole hog", as she insisted on putting it, but they had slept in the same bed and had done a significant amount of "kissing and cuddling". The details just kept on coming. Holly felt like someone who'd asked for a sip of water only to be swept away down the street by a water cannon.

"So," she said at what seemed like an appropriate juncture, "what about Aisling? Did she get home safely?"

"Couldn't tell you," Orla replied. "She was still there when we left. Her and James. They seemed pretty drunk, the pair of them."

Holly's foot started to tap. "Is that right?"

"Yeah. She was worse than he was . . . Oh God, no!"

"What? What is it?"

"Oh, *shit*."

"Orla, what –"

"I think I made a joke about a dry martini, shaken not stirred."

"Oh. Right."

"Jesus."

"Don't worry about it. He probably didn't even notice, he's that used to it."

"*You* always notice when people –"

"So what? We're . . . different. Apparently."

This was not a topic that Holly was keen to explore. She steered the conversation back to John, to Orla's barely concealed delight. When the phone call finally ended – it took a while – she went straight to bed and pulled the duvet right over her head.

The following week was a deeply frustrating one. Holly cornered James at the first opportunity on Monday, but all he talked about was John. The two of them had met in town the previous day for a coffee and a bit of post-match analysis. According to James, John was a changed man; he actually *looked* different. Even if his relationship with Orla went nowhere in the long run, it had already been worth it. The very fact that there was at least one woman on the planet who found him attractive had transformed him, literally overnight. It was a marvel. Holly reported that Orla was similarly impressed with life and the two of them congratulated each other again on the great thing they had done for their friends. James asked about Holly's headache then and she told him it had cleared up quickly enough. Thereafter, the conversation simply ran into a wall.

Holly bounced up and down on her toes, trying desperately not to just grab him the shoulders and screech, "*Did you go home with Aisling?*" She was relieved when Eleanor Duffy joined them and started small-talking (even if Eleanor did keep catching her eye while raising her eyebrow a fraction in James's direction). Eventually, Holly had to leave for class. She didn't see James for the rest of the day. Tuesday and Wednesday were no improvement. She didn't get so much as five seconds on her own with him and, worse, was twice asked how they were "getting on" by Eleanor. Thursday was marginally better, in as far as she had James all to herself for three minutes in the corridor outside the art room. But no clues were dropped. There was no longer any doubt in her mind; she'd made a huge mistake in leaving the pub early. Staying put could well have turned out to be a horribly painful experience, but at least she would have known for sure. Anything would have been an improvement on the terrible limbo she found herself in now.

The week's final window of opportunity opened right at the last moment. Holly saw James getting into car when she emerged from the front door at the end of the day and jogged across the tarmac towards him, hoping that there were no students still hanging around who might see her and draw the correct conclusion. She couldn't help but hear Malachy Murphy's voice in her head as she went along: "*You'll never guess what I saw on Friday, lads – Ho Ho Christmas running after 007 like a bitch in heat!*"

James started to reverse out of his parking space as she approached, so she slowed down into what she hoped would look like a casual dawdle when he spotted it in his rear-view mirror. To her relief, he didn't drive off with a wave when he saw her coming but rather stopped and wound down his window.

"Another day, another dollar," Holly said breathlessly. She almost looked around to see who had spoken. It was one of the sayings on her list. *Don't overdo it*, she scolded her unconscious mind.

"Yup," James said. "Any big plans for the weekend?"

A sarcastic (albeit benign) response occurred to her at once. She swatted it away. "Not much, alas. Grocery shopping will be about as exciting as it gets."

"Yeah. Can't say I'll be getting up to very much either. I see a *Sopranos* box-set marathon in my future."

Holly was only just able to keep a smile from forming. She had given him a golden opportunity to say he was meeting her friend, actually, just the two of them, and he hadn't taken it. That had to be good.

"We're quite the pair."

"Ah well. You can't be wild your whole life."

"Oh? Are you saying you had a wild past?"

He winked, sneered and stuck his nose into the air. Just when Holly was beginning to panic, he hung his head and shook it. "No. I've always been more of a box-set kind of guy."

Holly felt her knees buckle a little – in a nice way.

"Okay," she said. "See you on Monday then. Say hi to the mobsters for me."

"Will do. Say hi to the frozen food section for me."

He drove off, waving all the while. It was some consolation, she supposed, that she managed to stop herself chasing after him again.

That night, shortly after she had polished off the Lamb Bhuna that she'd had delivered as a small treat, Holly decided that enough was enough. She was a grown woman, for God's sake, and she'd known Aisling for twenty years. It was about time she called her up on the damn phone and just flat-out *asked* her. Her new-found confidence survived the first part of the test – she did indeed call her up on the damn phone. But it melted away into a little puddle at the second. They talked about Orla and John, naturally, and did a little reminiscing about the play. When it became clear that the information she wanted was not about to be volunteered, Holly asked if Aisling had experienced any difficulty getting home.

"No," Aisling told her. "Of course not. Why would I?"

"No reason," Holly spluttered. "Just asking. You didn't go on anywhere or anything?"

"Nah. We stayed put. It was comfy enough in there, especially after a few voddies."

This was the moment when Holly's confidence failed her. She could hear the question in her head, clear as a bell: "*Did anything happen with you and James?*" She just couldn't make it come out of her mouth. She let the silence hang between them, hoping that Aisling would volunteer anything there was to be volunteered. But she didn't.

"Anything wild at work?" Holly asked eventually.

"Not much. Oh, one of the account manager's revealed that he's gay. It's sickening."

"Aisling!"

"No, I mean it's sickening the way everyone's carrying on around him. They're all falling over themselves to be his friend now, just to prove that they're not bigots. I don't get it. He was a prick before and now he's a gay prick. The key word is 'prick', not 'gay'. I said as much and they all turned on me. I thought of you, actually. It's not easy telling it like it is."

Holly didn't know whether to feel insulted or proud. "What about your stalker?"

"Meh. Haven't heard from him since, so I'm just going to pretend it never happened."

"Fair enough. So! What are you, uh, what are you getting up to at the weekend?"

"Not much. It's my cousin's birthday, Christina, the loud one, so I'm going out in an hour or so for that. But I'm not staying long. The rest of the weekend, I'm spending in my pyjamas. Yourself?"

"Much the same, without the drink with a loud cousin."

"All righty then. I'll have to run on. Talk to you soon, yeah?"

"Good enough. See ya."

Two out of two, Holly thought, after they'd hung up. So Aisling and James weren't meeting this weekend, at least. It didn't prove much in itself, but it was better news than the alternative. She went into the kitchen for a bottle of wine, then parked herself in front of the box. For the first time in a week, she felt relaxed.

Chapter 15

Holly was up and running early on Saturday morning. She gave the house a good working-over, even going so far as to change the bedclothes in the spare room – she couldn't recall the last time anyone had stood in there, let alone slept there – and then set out for the supermarket. Holly had often thought of grocery shopping as a sort of sport. Some days you played well and some days you simply weren't on form, retracing your steps in pursuit of forgotten items, realising at the checkout that you hadn't weighed your vegetables, and so on. Today, she played a blinder. She felt like some sort of shopping genius as she swept along the aisles, hardly ever consulting her list and barely slowing down as she plucked her items from the shelves and dropped them into just the right slot in her trolley. Barely an hour after she left the house, she was back in the kitchen, putting everything away while humming (for reasons that escaped her) the theme from *Home and Away*. When that task was behind her, she found that she still had energy to burn. A number of potential activities occurred to her. The one that she finally settled on was paying a surprise visit to her mother.

On the drive home – she still called it that – Holly started to panic that she might find her mum and Charlie Fallon lounging around in dressing gowns, feeding each other grapes. The thought was almost enough to make her turn back, or at least phone ahead. But she decided to press on. If she did find them in compromising circumstances, it would at least make up for the time more than a decade previously when her mother walked in on her and Vinny Simmons (who took an unfortunate couple of seconds to remove his hand from under her jumper after the living-room light snapped on).

As it turned out, she arrived at the house to find her mother slumped in a chair, sound asleep. Evidently she'd been doing a jigsaw and had nodded off. The half-completed puzzle was arranged on a fold-away board of some kind that was perched on the arms of her chair. It seemed borderline miraculous that she hadn't upset it in her sleep. Holly approached and gave her shoulder a little shake. Her eyes flew open and with impressive speed, she sat upright.

"What?" she said. "What time is it? Hello. Hello. Oh . . . Holly."

As her senses powered up, she blinked and looked around the room like someone who'd never seen it before.

"Hiya," Holly said. "Having a wee nap?"

Her mother rubbed a hand across her face and nodded. "I didn't mean to. Must have dozed off."

She looked slightly trapped underneath her jigsaw board. Holly wondered if she should offer to move it but supposed that her input wasn't necessary; it wouldn't be much of a product if its users needed external assistance to get out from under it.

"You mustn't have been out too long. I'm sure you would have sent this yoke flying sooner rather than later."

"I don't know," her mum replied. "It's pretty sturdy." She gave it an experimental wobble with her knees.

"How long have you had this? Where did you get it? Since when were you into jigsaws?"

Holly realised a fraction of a second too late that asking three questions in quick succession like this made her sound disapproving and even a little panicked. The truth was, she did disapprove and she was ever so slightly panicking. Jigsaws? Lunchtime naps? These were old-people activities. It was only a short step from lunchtime naps to little comfy boots with zips up the front.

"I sent away for it," Mrs Christmas said. "A few weeks ago. Saw an ad in the back of one of the Sunday supplements."

This was no solace to Holly. In her mind's eye, she saw the large-type ad, tucked away between promos for stair-lifts and expandable-waistline slacks.

"Oh. Right. And jigsaws in general . . ." She tried hard to keep the concern out of her voice but she knew even before her mother's expression darkened that she had failed.

"You look worried, Holly. What, do you think I'm losing my marbles?"

"Of course not!" She attempted a smile and found that it sat so weirdly on her face that she quickly dismantled it. "I just wondered, that's all."

Mrs Christmas looked at her daughter for a long moment and then looked down at the jigsaw. "They pass the time," she said. Her voice sounded as if it was coming from the end of a long hallway.

"Sure," Holly said, too quickly and too loudly. "Why not? What's it a picture of?" She looked around for the box.

"The Taj Mahal," her mother said without looking up.

Holly was stumped for a follow-up. "Nice," she said after a thick pause. "So . . . are we having a cup of tea or what?"

Mrs Christmas snapped out of it. She looked up and nodded. "Yes. I don't see why not. Stick the kettle on like a good girl."

Holly turned in the direction of the kitchen. She couldn't help but glance back over her shoulder as she left the front room and saw that although it was perfectly possible for a person to escape from under a jigsaw board on their own, it wasn't something that could be done with a great deal of dignity.

In the kitchen, they chatted about school. Holly provided the headlines of the term to date but didn't so much as reveal James Bond's very existence. She surprised herself with how upbeat her summary sounded, featuring as it did a mere trio of angry rants. When that subject had been

254

exhausted – it didn't take long – Holly took some heavily disguised deep breaths and said, "So, listen . . ."

Her mother eyed her with sudden suspicion. "What?"

"I was just –"

"What is it? You're making a face."

"I am not."

"Yes, you are. What's going on? Are you pregnant?"

"Mum!"

"Are you?"

"No! And, by the way, when you ask your unmarried, unattached daughter if she's pregnant, you're not supposed to have that hopeful look in your eyes."

"Ah, g'way. You're imagining things, Holly."

"Hm. Anyway. I was about to say . . ."

"Yes?"

"I was wondering about your . . . I was wondering about Charlie."

"Oh."

"Yeah. I haven't heard from you in a while and I didn't like to ring you up and badger you about it." When her mother didn't make any reply, she added, "So, what's the story? How's it going?"

It took a little while, but this time she responded. "It's not. Going. I haven't seen him since that night we had dinner with you."

"You haven't? How come? Did you fall out?"

"No."

"What, then?"

Mrs Christmas sighed so deeply that she seemed to physically deflate. "I don't know."

"Mum. Come on. Tell me."

A long pause. Then: "I just can't . . . I just can't take . . . the next step. We haven't so much as held hands. I'm terrified of the whole thing."

Obviously, this was territory in which Holly felt distinctly uncomfortable. The only thing that stopped her running out the door was the certain knowledge that it must be ten times worse for her mum. "That's only natural," she said, hoping she sounded wise and not patronising. "It'd be weird if you felt any other way, I think."

"Maybe."

"No, not maybe – definitely. I mean, you do want to . . . take some sort of a step? Don't you?"

"Maybe. I think so. I don't know. What do you think?"

"Mum! You're going to have to stop asking me what I think about all this. It doesn't matter what I think, it matters what *you* think."

"I said, I don't *know* what I think!"

It wasn't so much the volume of this line that shocked Holly – although that was certainly remarkable – it was the tone. There was a degree of anger in there and a great deal of confusion, but the thing that really stood out was the marked note of sadness. Mrs Christmas slumped still further into her seat. Holly's mind turned once again to the aging process. It seemed to be speeding up right before her eyes.

"Would I be right in guessing that this has less to do with Charlie than it has to do with Dad?"

Mrs Christmas tilted her head to one side and exhaled.

Holly took that as a yes. "Do you want to talk about it?"

"Not really."

"Try."

There was no reply at first. Holly put her elbows on the table and settled her chin on her fists. She hoped the gesture would communicate the idea that she was willing to wait for as long as it took.

Before long, her mother swept some imaginary crumbs from the table into her cupped hand and then deposited them in her saucer. "I feel . . . I feel like it's a no-going-back sort of scenario. You know? If I cross that line, then that's it, it can't be undone."

"Like losing your virginity," Holly said. She was trying to be helpful. But if the sudden corrugation of her brow was anything to go by, her mother didn't see it that way. "You know what I mean," Holly said before any complaints could be filed. "Go on."

It took her mother a moment to recover from the interruption. "Your father's been gone for twenty-eight years," she said then. "Suppose I do . . . suppose Charlie and me wind up . . . more than friends. And it only lasts a fortnight. I'd feel like my . . . Ah, never mind, it's silly."

"Come on, Mum. Just say it."

The response came shockingly quickly: "I'd feel like my good record had been broken. For nothing."

"There's nothing silly about that! Anyone would feel the same way. It'd be like if you hadn't had a cigarette in twenty-eight years, then you had one, decided you hated it and went back to being a non-smoker. If anyone asked, you wouldn't be able to say you hadn't had a fag in all that time. You'd have to have, like, in brackets, apart from that *one* time."

Holly seemed to hear herself saying all of this only after she had finished speaking, as if she was getting it via satellite. She braced herself for unpleasantness. If her mother had objected to the virginity analogy, then she sure as hell wasn't going to take kindly to this one, in which her marriage was likened to a nasty habit that she'd managed to kick.

"Well, exactly," Mrs Christmas said.

Holly tried not to look surprised. "Yeah. I understand completely, Mum. I really do."

"And I never had any plans on that front. It's not like I've been sitting around waiting for some man to show up."

"Of course not."

"Charlie's just . . . caught me at a bad time, that's all."

She said this casually, almost jovially, but Holly thought the words had a shadow behind them. After letting them dangle for a moment, she said, "What do you mean by that?"

"Ah, you know . . . "

"No. I don't. Tell me."

Mrs Christmas swept up more crumbs that weren't there. "It's no big deal. I've just, lately I've just . . . y'know. Been feeling a wee bit . . . lonely."

Holly couldn't really say that she was surprised to hear this. If anything, she was surprised that she hadn't heard it before. Her mum had one brother, who lived in Toronto, and one sister, who lived in Perth. She had never gone out of her way to make friends with the predictable consequence that she didn't seem to have any. While she was on good terms with most of the neighbours, these were hardly deep relationships. Holly had long since assumed that she was her mother's only regular visitor. Fearing a turn for the morbid, she decided to make a small joke.

"This would explain the Christmas Convention of Christmases," she said with a twinkle.

"Sorry?"

"There's no way you would have considered that for half a second if you hadn't been desperate for some sort of social outlet."

"I still say it might be fun. He wrote again, I meant to say. Your man. Simon Christmas. He's set a date. The twenty-ninth of November."

"Wow. The Christmas Convention of Christmases isn't even going to be in December. It just gets better and better."

"He found a hotel he really likes. That was the only date they had. Got a big response, he said. People are coming from all over."

"Well, they're not coming from Dublin," Holly snapped. She was sorry she'd brought it up. And sorrier still that she'd snapped. "Getting back to Charlie: you must have at least spoken to him since dinner, surely?"

"Yeah. A few times. He rings me up suggesting things to do. I tell him I don't feel well, or I've got something else on. Anything to get him off the phone. And then I kick myself for being such a coward. He rang again last night, but I didn't even answer it. I saw his number come up and I just let it ring like some mopey teenager having a row with her friend. It's pathetic, that's what it is."

Holly chose her next words carefully. What she really wanted to say was, *He's not going to hang around forever.* In the end, she came up with, "This must be confusing for him."

"I know, I know. Next thing you know, he'll give up altogether. Maybe that's what I want, underneath it all. I want the decision taken out of my hands. That's why I keep asking you to get involved too. I'm not stupid, Holly, I know how ridiculous that is."

Holly was pleased to hear that she wouldn't have to point out the obvious but alarmed by the new tremble in her mother's voice. She was getting upset. It was time to take the situation by the scruff of the neck. "It's not ridiculous, Mum," she said. "Come on. This is all a bit strange to you, that's all. It's no wonder you need a bit of a nudge. So what was last night's message?"

"Art."

"Who?"

"The National Gallery. He wants to go for a wander around it."

"Oh. But that sounds lovely."

"Holly, I don't know the first thing about art. I'd only make an eejit out of myself."

260

"You don't have to *know* anything about art to go to a gallery, Mum. Have you never been to one?"

"Never."

"But when you look at a painting or a sculpture, you know whether you like it or not, don't you?"

"I suppose."

"Well, then. That's all there is to it. You have a walk around – and it's a lovely building – and you look at the art. You like it or you don't. You move on. It's not an exam. No one's going to tap you on the shoulder and ask if you know a Monet from a Manet."

"Good, because I don't."

"Neither do I. But I still love the National Gallery."

"Since when?"

"Excuse me, I'll have you know I'm a regular patron. Have been for a while."

She hoped there would be no follow-up questions. Her patronage of the National Gallery had consisted, to date, of precisely two visits. Her companion and guide on both occasions was Dan, who was a genuine art fan. This pleasing incongruity – he seemed to know as much about Caravaggio as he did about car engines – was one of the things she had loved about him. It wasn't even in the top ten, but it was on the list somewhere. She hadn't contributed much to their tours herself, apart from making occasional efforts to start caption competitions. But her central point still stood: taking a walk round a gallery was a pleasant way to spend an afternoon.

"I didn't know that."

"Well, there you are. That's me – hidden depths. Why

don't you give him a shout and tell him you'd love to go?" There was no immediate refusal. Holly was encouraged enough to add a sweetener. "Did he have a time in mind? Because I could stick around for a while, give you a hand getting yourself ready and all, and then drop you into town." Still no refusal. She pressed ahead further still. "I've nothing else to do and it'd be fun. We could have a girly giggle and –"

"All right, Holly, don't lose the run of yourself. You've never had a girly giggle in your life and I'm fully capable of dressing myself. But I will take the lift, thank you."

Holly was so taken aback by the speed with which her mother relented that she fell momentarily silent.

"Oh! So you're going?" she said then.

"I . . . Yes."

"To the gallery? This afternoon?"

"Yes."

"And you're calling him now to tell him as much?"

"*Yes*."

"OK. Good. Off you go, then."

Mrs Christmas rose from the kitchen table, gathered her threadbare cardigan around herself, and hobbled off in the direction of the phone.

"You're limping," Holly said. "Have you got a sore hip or something?"

"No. Me foot's asleep."

Holly was relieved but, still, the image of her mum limping about didn't sit well with the nap and jigsaw images that were already swirling around in her mind.

She felt as if she was getting an unwelcome sneak preview of days to come. Seconds later, she heard a muted voice from the livingroom. It was enough to snap her out of her daydream. No; her mother wasn't some wizened old dear with one foot in the proverbial. She was a sprightly fifty-something who, even now, was setting up a hot date. A couple of minutes later, she returned, looking much brighter than she had when she left.

"I can tell already that you feel better," Holly said.

"I hate to admit it. But you're right. He was delighted I rang. Said he was getting worried about me."

"And?"

"Three o'clock at the main entrance."

"There you go. So, what are you going to w–"

"He wants you to come too."

Holly was sure she'd misheard. "I'm sorry?"

"I told him you were giving me a lift there and he insisted."

"What? What the hell would he want me there for?"

"He's just trying to get you on his good side, I think."

"Thanks, but –"

"Please, Holly."

Cogs turned. "Hang on a minute. Are you sure it's Charlie that wants me to go?"

Her mother smacked her lips. "Well, all right, it might have been my suggestion. But he didn't object."

"Mum!"

"Please. As a favour. It'll be less weird for me if you're there."

"It'll be *less* weird if I'm there? Fuck me."

"Don't swear. Just go for a while, at least. Holly –"

"All right, all right, Christ."

For the first time since she'd arrived, her mother smiled properly. "Give me twenty minutes."

Their arrival at the gallery was a masterpiece of timing. Holly peeked at her watch as they went through the main entrance and saw that it was twenty seconds past three. Charlie was leaning against a wall on the far side of the lobby. He was wearing a blue shirt and blue chinos. A luridly red sweater was draped around his shoulders, its sleeves casually knotted on his chest. At first glance, Holly thought he'd come dressed as Superman. When he caught sight of them he sprang forward to meet them, issuing hellos and great-to-see-yous and then abruptly stopped as if he wasn't quite sure what to do next. After a moment's pause, he lurched forward and gave Mrs Christmas a tiny kiss on the cheek before turning to Holly and doing his wrestling move.

"Well, isn't this great," he said, clapping his hands together. "An afternoon of culture! What could be better?"

"I don't know anything about art," Holly's mum said apologetically, as if this was something that needed to be cleared up right at the outset.

Charlie patted her shoulder. "Don't worry about that, Delia," he said. "I know more than enough for both of us."

A cold hand gripped the back of Holly's neck. This didn't sound good.

"Now," Charlie continued. "Shall we? I took the liberty of getting the tickets."

264

Holly wasn't sure that she'd ever heard anyone actually using the phrase "took the liberty" in a non-ironic way outside of a black and white movie. It was quite charming, she supposed. She looked at her mother and saw that she, for one, was chuffed.

The three of them walked across the lobby, presented their tickets and made their way up the main staircase. Within fifteen minutes, Holly had fallen a few paces behind them and was seriously contemplating trying to lose them entirely. There were two problems. Firstly, she had gravely underestimated how much this trip to the gallery would remind her of Dan. She'd known that he would pop into her head – how could he not? – but she hadn't realised that he would pull up a chair in there and make himself comfy. It was like being haunted. She kept imagining that she could see him everywhere in her peripheral vision, but when she turned, there was usually no one there. The sole exception was the case of a Japanese tourist who cleared ground when she did a sudden one-eighty to glare in his direction.

The second problem was even more predictable. On both of their visits together, Holly and Dan had wandered around at a reasonable pace, not rushing by any means, but not dawdling either. When something caught their eye, they stopped and had a closer look. As soon as they ran out of things to say, they moved on. Charlie took a different approach. He stopped at the first painting they came to and simply started talking. The piece in question was of a type that Holly had no time for – a depiction of rural life from a bygone era.

There was a barn. There were some chickens. There was a horse. There was a woman carrying a bucket. Holly wouldn't even have slowed down, let alone stopped by it; she wasn't sure that she would even have consciously *noticed* it. She gave Charlie the benefit of the doubt for about a minute and then concluded that, no, her first impression had been correct: he really was just describing the scene, as if they she and her mother were on the other end of a phone line. "Here we have a woman carrying a bucket," he said. "Here we have a chicken." It went on for several minutes. Holly noticed that her mother nodded occasionally as Charlie waffled, as if she was grateful for his insight (*Good God, you're right! It* is *a horse!*). When they eventually moved on, Holly almost broke into a jog. She had gone quite a way, skipping several paintings, when she realised that she was alone. Looking back, she saw that Charlie and her mother – in other words, Charlie – had stopped at the second painting. She moped back towards them. Painting number two was, to Holly's eye, practically indistinguishable from painting number one. It was a little darker, sure, and a little more wintry, but it was basically the same sort of thing. Charlie seemed to have even more to say about it than he had about its neighbour. After he'd described it for them (*"Here we have a farmer"*, *"Here we have a hedge"*), he moved on to a discussion of the artist's technique. "Note the use of reds and browns," he intoned, pointing to a patch of the canvas that was indeed red and brown. "These are rusty colours. Rusty? Rustic? Coincidence? Hmmm?" They spent at least as long on the second painting as they had on the first. Painting number three featured another farmer. This one was in bed, breathing his last. His family were gathered around him, all looking understandably upset, except for one plump daughter who was bent double, staring at the floor in the manner of someone who had just lost a contact lens. Holly let Charlie run through his routine again (*"Look – brush-strokes"*), but when they started off for the next painting, she spoke up.

"Personally," she said, "I'd like nothing better than to spend an hour in front of every single painting, but time is against us. Maybe it'd be better if we picked up the pace a little and stopped at the highlights only?"

This was a long way from the phrasing that had sprung to mind naturally. Her delight at having restrained herself was short-lived, however.

"That's the problem with your generation," Charlie said. "No attention span. You want culture – if you can be said to want it at all – delivered in handy, bite-sized chunks. If it can't be swallowed whole in one gulp, you don't wanna know."

He said all of this with the slight smile that she recalled from the Chinese restaurant: *I know it sounds like I'm having a go at you, but we're just having a laugh, really, like old pals.* Holly tried valiantly to come up with a gentle reply but she drew a blank. After staring mutely at him for a few seconds, she felt she had no choice but to say what she really thought.

"And the problem with *your* generation is that you can't tell the time very well. There are more than eleven thousand pieces of art in this gallery. So far we've spent five minutes on every one we've passed. The doors are closing at five thirty. Can you see the problem or should I get a calculator out?"

She mirrored his insincere smile.

"Maybe Holly has a point," Mrs Christmas soothed.

"Humph," said Charlie, somehow managing to make it sound like an excellent debating point.

Thereafter, they moved through the gallery like normal people, going through each individual room in no particular order, criss-crossing the floor and doubling back on themselves as they saw fit. They had been a rigid trio up to this point, but now Holly made a point of being a sort of satellite around the couple, travelling around in a loose orbit but never quite floating away entirely. For one thing, she felt like a total gooseberry, and a gooseberry to her *mother* at that; it was surreal. And for another, it was nice to periodically get out of earshot of Charlie. He was a little quieter for a while after they decided to speed up, but it didn't last. Before long, he was holding forth with as much gusto and as little intelligence as ever. Despite her best efforts, Holly inevitably caught some of it.

She couldn't help but compare Charlie's musings with Dan's. The latter had always supplied hard facts, putting the paintings and sculpture in historical or social context and, where available, sharing juicy gossip about the artist (this one died of syphilis, that one murdered her husband). He was never boring, quite the contrary – he made everything funny, even the syphilis and murder.

And yet he never sounded like he was showing off. In much the same way that she had never come to share Mark and Lizzie's deep love of wine, Holly never even got close to Dan's level of passion for art. But she appreciated his attempts to drag her up behind him. Charlie, by contrast, was starting to remind her of a psychiatric patient being presented with Rorschach inkblots – *Tell me what you see here*. Worse still, he was obviously convinced that he was a great expert. His chin rose and his chest expanded as he made some of his more grandiose exclamations ("This cloud looming in the distance is, of course, a reminder of our mortality").

One of the last paintings they came to was Caravaggio's *The Taking of Christ*. It was the only piece in the entire gallery that Holly knew by name. She wasn't sure if she had always known what it was called – it was, after all, probably the most famous painting in Ireland – or if she had learned its name from Dan, who'd had something of a mini-obsession with it. In fairness to him, it was an astonishing thing to look at. Its recreation of the moment when Judas Iscariot betrayed Jesus in the garden at Gethsemane seemed to owe more to photography than it did to painting. On this, her third viewing, Holly found that she was incapable as ever of articulating exactly what it was that made it so hypnotic. *The light*, she thought. *It's the way the light . . . the . . . the light's . . . really . . . nice.*

Charlie too knew it by name; for the first time, he didn't consult the little information card by the frame before he began pontificating (they didn't have audio guides – he had decreed them "unnecessary"). As ever, his analysis was strictly descriptive, but this time Holly was able to correct him when he got even that much wrong.

"Flanking Jesus, Judas and the Roman soldiers on the left and right," he droned, "are two mysterious figures. Who are they? What is their role in this terrible drama? We will never know."

"The one on the left is the disciple John," Holly said cheerfully. "The one on the right is generally believed to be a self-portrait of the artist himself."

Charlie seized upon her last few words as if they were the only ones she had spoken. "A self-portrait of the artist himself?" he sneered through downturned lips. "And who else would he do a self-portrait of?"

He turned to Holly's mother, apparently expecting that she would be highly amused by his skewering of her daughter's regrettable phrase. But Mrs Christmas looked back at him without expression. He gave up almost immediately and returned his gaze to the painting. Holly understood that he was embarrassed because she had chopped him off at the knees and she accepted that. Still – she thought she had glimpsed a side of him that was not merely buffoonish but downright unpleasant.

Her opinion of him didn't improve any when he said, "I wonder, Holly, if it has escaped your attention that a great many of the beautiful works we've seen here today were religiously inspired?"

She discarded the first response that came to mind, which was "*Oh, fuck off*", in favour of something a little more diplomatic. After a moment's thought she said, "Then again, most of these pictures are very old. I don't think modern artists are all that bothered about God."

In all modesty, she was extremely pleased with this reply. It was aimed at getting him off the subject of religion and back onto modern art. They'd already exchanged a few words on that topic. Charlie had tried his best to bullshit about the cubes and lines as much as he had about the horses and farmers but it had been obvious that his heart wasn't in it. There were a couple of occasions when he seemed to come perilously close to saying, "I could have done that!", which, Dan had advised her, was the stupidest thing a person could say in a gallery. Personally, Holly preferred the modern stuff. When confronted with a traditional figurative painting, she found it hard to judge it on any criteria other than how much it looked like the thing it was supposed to be. This was not a sophisticated attitude, she knew, but that was how she felt. Quite a lot of modern art, on the other hand, wasn't supposed to look like anything. This seemed to free her up, somehow, to consider it as an entity unto itself. She had started to say as much to Charlie about half an hour previously but had stopped out of fear that she would sound like one of those tedious clowns on *Latenight Review*.

"You're quite probably right," Charlie said. "These modern guys were probably Godless to the core. Which is why they end up *doodling* while the old school, the ones who knew the Power and the Glory, were able to create the likes of this."

"Hm," Holly said and strolled away, chewing her

tongue like it was a nice piece of steak. It did the trick. When Charlie and her mother caught up with her a couple of minutes later, there was no discernible tension.

They wandered through another couple of rooms and then agreed to call it a day.

"There's a café," Holly said when they reached the lobby again. "Cup of tea and a bun, maybe?"

Charlie rose on his toes. "Actually . . ." He pivoted to face Mrs Christmas. "I was thinking maybe we could go for something a little more substantial. Dinner for two?"

Holly took the brick-like hint and got in before her mother could reply. "Even better. The two of you toddle off and get something proper. I have loads to do at home anyway." She nipped forward and kissed her mother's cheek. "Did you enjoy yourself?"

Her mother blinked and blinked again. She had the look of a woman who'd just realised that she'd had her purse snatched. "Uh, yes. It was lovely."

"Great. Okay then. See ya later. Charlie." She extended her hand. He did what he always did. When she had regained her balance, she gave them a smile and a nod. Then she turned around and left them to it, telling herself that the nasty feeling in the pit of her stomach was hunger. She had only taken a few steps in the direction of the door when she stopped dead. Dan was standing on the street outside, talking on the phone. He was on his way into the gallery; he had to be. She refused to believe her eyes at first. This was bad luck of such colossal proportions that it seemed impossible. Predictably enough, he looked great. In fact, he looked exactly the same. It might have been the day after she had last seen him, not a few years later. She stared for a moment in shock and hastened back to her mum and Charlie.

"Hi again," she said.

"Did you forget something?" Mrs Christmas asked.

Holly slightly adjusted the angle of her stance to ensure that her back was as square to the entrance as possible. She also did her best to block the view of her mother, whom Dan might well have recognised. "Just wanted to recommend somewhere for dinner."

"Oh. Okay. Go on."

Holly drew a blank. At that precise moment, she couldn't recall the name of a single restaurant in the city, let alone a good one that was nearby. She decided to opt for the ridiculous.

"It's called . . . Plate," she said, picking the first food-related word that came to mind.

"Is it within walking distance?" Charlie asked.

"No. It's in, uh, Arklow. But you'd be there within an hour, if the traffic wasn't too bad."

There was a terrible pause during which she was sure that they were not only going to like the sound of this fictitious restaurant but also to be in the mood for a drive.

"That seems like a bit of a trek," her mother said finally.

"And besides," Charlie added. "I don't like the sound of it. *Plate*. I can't stand these pretentious one-word names. All style and no substance, no doubt."

Just then, Holly saw Dan out of the corner of her eye.

He was in a world of his own and sailed right past them. Mission accomplished.

"Fine," Holly said. "Just thought I'd mention it. See ya."

She made her second exit, already marvelling that her close encounter with Dan, hairy as it was, hadn't reduced her to a jibbering wreck. Its main effect, apparently, had been to fill her mind still further with thoughts of James.

Chapter 16

Holly overslept on the following Monday morning and arrived at school with just a few minutes to spare before her first class was due to start. She said as much to Eleanor Duffy when she stopped her in the corridor, but Eleanor didn't seem to care.

"Good weekend?" she asked, leaning against a wall and getting comfy.

"It was okay. You?"

"Never mind me. What did you get up to? Did you make any . . . progress?"

"Eleanor, I'm late, I –"

"You're not late yet, you've still got a couple of minutes. Come on. Tell."

There was no point, Holly supposed, in pretending that she didn't know what Eleanor was talking about. "There's nothing to tell," she sighed. "Honestly. I didn't see him this weekend. And to tell you the truth, I don't think I'm ever going to see him again, socially." The reason she had overslept, in fact, was that she was up half the night strategising. The way forward, she'd decided, was to pretend that her cowardly retreat from the pub had never happened and, henceforth, adopt a more proactive approach. She was going to see James again socially if it killed her.

"That's defeatist talk," Eleanor said, wagging a finger. "And I won't have it. You can't just sit around waiting for him to do all the work, you know. You have to take steps! You have to make moves!"

Holly shook her head sadly, even though these were exactly the sorts of phrases she'd drilling into her own head just a few hours previously. "I dunno. Let's just see how it goes."

Eleanor slid down the wall a little. "Nooo, no, *no*. Let's not just see how it goes. Lookit, none of my business and all, but you were making up boyfriends a few weeks ago. If I was in your shoes, I wouldn't be passing up opportunities. And he likes you, I know he does."

Holly's lungs briefly collapsed. "What? How do you know?"

"Well, I don't *know*, exactly, it's just a feeling. But it's a pretty definite feeling!"

"I have to go now, Eleanor."

"Okay, okay. But think about what I said."

"Which bit? The bit where you reminded me that I'm desperate? The bit where you told me about your 'feeling'?"

Eleanor was not in the least deflected by this. "The bit where I told you to get off your arse and make it happen."

Holly nodded and went about her business. Happily, her first opportunity to take a step and make a move came that same lunchtime. She managed to get James to herself for a while by dawdling at the staff room sink at the appropriate moment and, thinking quickly, suggested a walk. James, just as she might had hoped, thought this was a great idea. He needed razor blades anyway. They could go as far as the chemist and back. And so they set off.

For the first few minutes, their conversation never rose above the level of small talk. James confirmed that his weekend had indeed been "a wasteland", *Sopranos* box-set notwithstanding. Apparently, he had barely left the house at all, let alone left it to have wild, uncontrollable sex with Aisling. Holly hadn't even been aware that she was still worried about that possibility, but she presumed that she must have been; the feeling of relief that washed through her when he described his boredom told its own story. She told him that she was still following his advice regarding her mother and Charlie. He assured her once again that she was doing the right thing. Any other path could only lead to guilt and regret. And even if it all went wrong, her mum would still thank her one day. Life was all about taking risks and grabbing opportunities when they presented themselves. This last part had a whiff of Hollywood about it. If they had been sitting down together in some secluded corner, Holly felt sure that she would have been unable to help herself and would have kissed him there and then. Even here, on a cracked and gum-spotted pavement, with buses and trucks whizzing past, she was sorely tempted. But the moment passed. She did her best to be positive and upbeat as they strolled along, but the raw materials just weren't there ("Nice birdie!" she noted as a tattered city pigeon limped by on the footpath; "Cool car!" she gasped at a vehicle that, on closer inspection, turned out to be bog-standard '98 Golf). Next thing she knew, they had arrived at the chemist and her time alone with James was half over. The shop was cramped and poorly lit. Holly hadn't been in there for a long time and while she seemed to recall that it had never been a model of tidiness, it was beyond a joke now. Every inch of shelf space (and quite a lot of the floor) was taken up by merchandise, some of which was jammed together so tightly that the packaging had buckled and burst. As far as she could tell, about three quarters of the items on sale seemed to be related to haircare. Some of them were so dusty she could have written her name on them with her finger. In one corner of the ceiling, a huge cobweb had broken free of its moorings and was wafting about forlornly. There was one customer, a tiny old lady who was dressed for the Antarctic.

"Are you all right?" James asked Holly in a low voice. "You look a bit . . . concerned."

She nodded up at the ceiling. "I'm just getting myself ready," she murmured. "I might have to do a runner."

He looked up. "Wow. That's impressive all right. Still, I wouldn't have had you down as the scared-of-spiders type."

"I'm not scared of *everyday* spiders, James. But that web's like something out of an Indiana Jones movie. The fella that made it, I would guess, would be about the size of your fist. If he puts in an appearance, I'm not even opening that door, I'm going straight through it."

"Fair enough."

"What type did you have me down as, might I ask?"

He didn't hesitate. "The scared-of-nothing type."

"Ah. Sorry to disappoint." When he turned away again, she allowed a puzzled frown to form. What the hell did that mean? Was it a compliment? Or did he mean that he saw her as a tough old boot? Either way, she supposed, the exchange had been mildly flirtatious. *More of this*, she told herself.

"I'm scared of being buried alive too."

He faced her again. "Yeah?"

"I don't see it happening though. Seems highly unlikely, anyway." She swallowed hard. Had she gone too far? Burial alive, on mature reflection, didn't seem like a fit subject for flirting.

"Which sort of being buried alive?" James asked, to her immediate relief. "The put-in-a-coffin-by-mistake sort or the building's-after-collapsing-on-you sort?"

"I wouldn't be crazy about either. But if you're given me a choice, I'd be less bothered by the collapsed building. At least people would be looking for you."

"You'd be comfier in a coffin, though. Bit more wriggle-room. I mean, if you were going to die either way, you'd rather have a bit of space than be lying under a ton of rubble."

"Nah. I'll take the building. Some chance is better than none."

"The eternal optimist."

No one had ever called Holly an optimist before. For a moment, she was quite choked. Then she realised that he was probably joking – wasn't he? By now it was becoming obvious that the little old lady at the counter wasn't in any kind of hurry to leave. She had completed her transaction, that much was clear; she was clutching one of the shop's paper bags in her left hand. Holly tuned in to hear what was taking so long. As she might have guessed, it was nothing important. The customer was outlining her opposition to the theory that the Earth was heating up. Her central argument seemed to be that this could not possibly be the case because she personally was always freezing. The man serving her – the owner, Holly guessed – was no spring chicken himself. He seemed to have as little interest in getting on with his day as she had. Holly tried not to care.

"Starved of attention," James whispered after a minute or so, nodding at the old lady.

"Not really. But thanks for asking."

This drew a smile. Holly experienced a brief glow of satisfaction. Just then, conversation at the counter died down. This was the owner's chance. But he didn't take it. Instead of ushering the old lady gently to the side or at least looking over her head to his next customer, he simply stood there, waiting for her to say something else. Before long, she did.

"My son's coming back from London for a visit, did I tell you that?"

The owner seemed delighted that the awkward

silence was over. "No, Mrs Fitzgerald, you didn't. That'll be nice for you."

"It will and it won't. *She's* coming with him and we don't see eye to eye."

"Oh dear."

"Ah, she's all right, I shouldn't be talking. I just wish he'd found himself an Irishwoman, God knows, there's enough of them over there."

"True, true."

"And they won't even have the kids with them – not that they're kids any more, mind you, the pair of them are at university now. French, Michael's doing, the youngest one. French! His sister's going on for to be a solicitor. Susie. That much I can understand. People will always need solicitors. But what the hell's your man going to do with a whaddayacallit, qualification, in French? Sure he could have done medicine or engineering or something sensible and picked up the French at an evening class or somewhere if he really had to."

The shop doorbell tinkled then and a young woman entered, almost coughing up a lung as she did so. She took her place behind Holly and James, wheezing gently. Her arrival, Holly thought, was bound to move things along. She and James had been standing around chatting and had not projected any particular sense of urgency; the newcomer, on the other hand, was clearly in need of immediate medication. Her difficulties went unnoticed, however. When she fell into a fresh series of hacks and splutters, the chemist looked up for a moment, but then immediately returned to sympathising with Mrs

Fitzgerald about the many failings of her extended family. Holly's foot started to tap; in an attempt to calm it down, she clenched her toes to the point of cramp. Mrs Fitzgerald chose this moment to strike a more cheerful note, moving on from complaining about her family to praising the craftsmanship and attention to detail of the father and son team who'd just redone her patio.

"Lovely, they were," she chirped. "And such hard workers! You could hardly get them to stop and have a cup of tea."

The chemist seemed to find this subject fascinating. Where had she found them – in the book? How long did it take them to get the job done? Not to stick his nose in, but were they dear? Mrs Fitzgerald provided long and rambling answers to these and other questions, then moved on to tell the tale of a bad-mannered plumber she'd had in once. The doorbell tinkled once again and another customer entered. This one, a young mother – she looked all of fifteen – had a baby in a pushchair. Space was so short now that Holly and James had to move towards the counter. They shuffled forward in tiny steps, like prisoners shackled together at the ankles. The woman with the cough did likewise, closing the gap to Holly to such an extent that the volume of her wheezes seemed to increase dramatically. Holly's shoulders tensed still further. James seemed to notice, somehow.

"Shouldn't be long now," he said.

For the next couple of minutes, she stood there with her eyes closed, imagining herself to be standing at the summit of a glorious mountain, gorging herself on the stunning view as crisp, fresh air blew through her hair. It was reasonably distracting at first, but the effect was somewhat spoiled when the woman behind her barked out a fresh series of coughs that she actually *felt* on the back of her neck. The coughs woke, or at least disturbed, the baby at the end of the queue who expressed his or her displeasure at this turn of events by screaming uncontrollably for a full minute. Mrs Fitzgerald, meanwhile, had suddenly remembered an electrician she'd once employed who had made the dodgy plumber look like a model professional.

This is it, Holly told herself. *She can finish this one and then she'd better get out of the way.*

If anything, the old woman spent even longer on the electrician than she had on her previous topics. This was partly because she felt it necessary to go into detail about the electrical problem that had necessitated his arrival and partly because she had known his mother since childhood. This last fact led her down a historical side-alley from which she had trouble emerging. Eventually, however, she ran out of things to say. Holly held her breath. Then the chemist said, "Would she have been any relation of *David* Dunleavy's?" at which point Mrs Fitzgerald embarked on a genealogical review of the entire Dunleavy family. After thirty seconds of aunt-this and brother-in-law that, Holly's patience expired.

"Excuse me," she said, stepping forward to stand at the counter. "Sorry to interrupt. I don't mean to be rude but do you think we could get served because –"

"Excuse *me*," the chemist said, looking at her down

283

the length of his nose. "I'll be with you when I'm finished serving this lady."

Holly fought to keep her voice even. She wasn't being difficult, she told herself. She wasn't being grumpy. She wasn't being sharp *or* blunt. She was merely standing up for herself, and she was doing so with a great deal of (admittedly fake) politeness. "I'm sorry," she smiled. "It's just that our lunchtime is ticking by and we're in a bit of a hurry."

Mrs Fitzgerald had kept her eyes forward up until this point. Now she turned to give Holly the evil eye. "There's a little thing called respect for the elderly," she declared. "Have you heard of it?"

And that was that. A tipping point was reached. Holly's blood ran cold. Her smile disappeared. Her voice rose in volume and lowered in pitch.

"Oh, please. Don't play the little old lady card. Respect is a two-way street. Where's your respect for the people queueing up behind you?" She pointed dramatically. "This woman's going to cough herself inside-out if she doesn't get some Benylin or something soon."

The chemist drew himself up to his full height and put his chin in the air. "I'm on my own today, in case you hadn't noticed. Normally, there'd be two of us, but my assistant's attending her uncle's funeral. A *funeral*. I'm sorry if the man's death has inconvenienced you but –"

"OK, so now it's the funeral card. Listen: I don't *care* if you're on your own What's that got to do with it? If anything, being on your own should make you speed up, not slow down. Now, can you please put your chatting to one side for a moment and serve us? Pretty please?"

"I'll tell you what I'll do," the chemist said. "I'll invite you to take yourself out of my premises and never come back. That's what I'll do. Go on, get out. You're barred. I will not be spoken to like that under my own roof."

Holly shrugged and swivelled. "Come on, James. We're leaving. Apparently."

James didn't seem to want to catch her eye, or anyone else's for that matter. He stepped out of the queue and made his way to the door with his eyes fixed firmly on the floor. Holly followed him. Along the way, she couldn't help but trail her fingers through the dust on top of a box of hair colour. Without turning around, she brushed her fingertips together and tut-tutted. Not turning around was the key, she felt. It added a certain something to the performance. Unlike James, the woman with the cough and the girl with the baby had no problems catching her eye. She had not been surprised that they didn't back her up in the argument and she was not surprised now to see them staring at her with something like awe. It was not the first time she'd experienced such a reaction. On the street outside, she found James facing the traffic. He looked over his shoulder when she emerged and then turned to face her properly.

"Well," he said. "That was kind of embarrassing."

"Sorry," Holly said. "I couldn't help myself."

This had the advantage, at least of being true. She'd

been fully aware that she was shredding the script she had given herself for James. But she had also felt that she wasn't entirely in control of her actions. The fact that he was standing behind her, being almost audibly embarrassed, had seemed like something that had she no choice but to put aside for the time being.

"She was an old woman, Holly," he said. "You know what they're like. She probably doesn't get out much. All she wanted was a bit of conversation, a bit of attention, like I said."

"Well, I'm sorry, but I don't think that matters. You know what I'm in favour of? I'm in favour of treating old people with equal respect. Equal means equal. It doesn't mean *more*. Do you think it would have been okay to ask them to hurry it up if she had been thirty-odd and not seventy-odd?"

"Yeah, but –"

"But nothing, James. Equal respect. And anyway, it's the shopkeeper who was to blame, really. I wouldn't even have said anything to her if she hadn't gone for me first."

He shook his head. "So, you don't make any allowances, none at all, for the fact that she's old?"

"Nope."

"What if she'd been in a wheelchair?"

"Same thing. Equal –"

"You're kidding me?"

"No."

"You would start raving at someone in a *wheelchair* if they held you up?"

"I wasn't 'raving' at anyone, James, I was just making a point and, like I said, it's the shopkeeper I have a problem with in this sort of thing, not the customer."

A truck roared past. They looked at each other for a long moment. Holly was suddenly convinced that she had blown it forever. The expression on his face was not one of unbridled admiration. A sense of panic bloomed in her abdomen and crept upwards, spreading spindly fingers around her shoulders and throat. She shifted from one foot to the other.

"I still need razor blades," he said.

"No problem," Holly said. "Come on, we'll just keep going to the Spar."

James looked at his watch. "I dunno. Have we time?"

"We'll run back if we have to."

She took off, glancing at her own watch. In truth, they probably didn't have time. But she wanted another few minutes with him – a chance to make amends. After an alarmingly long pause, he caught up. They were quieter on this part of the journey, both of them, although Holly did give a fairly substantial eulogy to a tree they walked past ("It's so barky!"). When they arrived at the Spar, they found a small queue. On seeing it, James gave Holly a mock-scolding – at least she hoped it was mock – telling her that it would move quickly and that if she felt her emotions getting the better of her, she should go and wait outside. When they got to the counter, he paid for his razor blades with a Laser card and asked for cashback. The assistant was a young man of twenty-two or so. He seemed to be half-asleep at first but when he noticed

James's name, he reacted as if someone had just hooked him up to the mains.

"No way!" he screeched.

James nodded. "Heh. Yeah."

"No way!" the assistant said again. "This is your *real* name?"

"Yup."

"You didn't change it or anything?"

"Nope. Born and raised."

"Holy crap! People must give you terrible abuse the whole time, do they?"

James shook his head. "Are *you* giving me abuse?"

The assistant froze. He seemed horrified by the suggestion. "No, man, no. No way."

"People are interested, that's all. I get a bit of a slagging, obviously. No one gives me 'abuse', but everyone thinks that everyone else does." He wagged his finger. "Let this be a lesson to you, my young friend. Have a little faith in your fellow man."

"Yeah, yeah, course. Sweet." He finished the transaction with a smile on his face.

Back out on the street, Holly made a big show of wiping her brow. "Phew. For a minute there, I thought you were going to tell him my name too."

"Nah," James replied. "I have been paying attention, you know. I know you don't like to talk about it."

"I don't mind really," she said. "Sometimes I let on it bothers me more than it does."

She knew immediately that this ridiculous lie had been stillborn. It was quite obvious even before James frowned at her, looking deeply unconvinced, and said, "Hmm. If you say so."

She looked away, opened her mouth, looked back at James, closed her mouth, looked away again. Eventually, the single word "Yeah" fell from her lips. It was not the most sophisticated contribution she had ever made to a conversation but she felt relieved to have said anything at all.

"Come on," James said. "We really are late. I don't mind jogging back, but I don't want to have to sprint."

"Yeah," Holly said again. "No. Yeah, no."

Chapter 17

The razor-blade trip – as Holly came to think of it – was her last proper contact with James for quite a while. Given the way it had turned out, she couldn't help but feel that this was probably for the best.

On Wednesday of the following week she received a phone call from her mother. Mrs Christmas didn't talk for long and barely let Holly get a word in; it was more like a brief broadcast than a conversation. The gist of it was that she and Charlie were a couple now. She didn't put it that bluntly, of course; she spoke vaguely of "progress" and "new beginnings". Holly did her best to sound congratulatory but it wasn't easy. Quite apart from the fact that she didn't particularly feel that way, her mother's own tone wasn't exactly joyous. There was more than a hint of *Happy now?* about it. After she'd hung up, Holly lay on the sofa and tried to let the news bed down. It was a huge moment and she wanted to give it due attention. But all she could think about was the fact that her mother had a boyfriend and she didn't. It didn't seem fair. Although the felt considerable guilt for being so self-pitying was considerable, it was dwarfed by the self-pity itself.

Orla rang too, on Saturday. When she said that she "just wanted to check in", Holly guessed that she meant she just wanted to talk about John Lennon. And so it proved. She'd seen him a few times now and was beside herself with happiness. He was just so lovely! They always had a lovely time together, having lovely dinners or watching lovely movies. The next day he sent her lovely text messages. This flurry of lovelys brought back memories for Holly. When she'd first started going out with Dan, Mark (or was it Lizzie?) had pointed out one day that her speech was suddenly peppered with variations on the word "love". Clearly, Mark (or Lizzie) had declared with a giggle, some ancient part of her brain had already decided that she was in love and was impatiently waiting for the rest of her to catch up. Before she hung up, Orla revealed that she'd been talking to Aisling, who was off to Wexford for the weekend on a team-building course with her work colleagues. At that very moment, she was probably holding someone back in a three-legged race while complaining about the havoc that physical activity was wreaking with her nails. When the call ended, Holly flaked out on the sofa and frowned up at the ceiling, lost in fresh self-pity. How come Orla got to be so happy? It wasn't fair. A couple of minutes passed before a fresh wave of guilt washed over her. She bounded to her feet, feeling clammy and ashamed, and looked for something to scrub clean. All this resentment and jealousy – it wouldn't do. Despite her best intentions, however, the feelings lingered on into the following week.

After several days of sharing him with at least one other teacher at all times, Holly finally cornered James after close of business on the Thursday. She had dallied at the end of her last class and was thrilled to find him alone in the staff room when she stopped by to get a drink of water. He was on the phone and was not looking at all happy about it.

"Yes," he said, looking up at her and rolling his eyes. "Yes . . . Yes . . . I will . . . I *know* . . . No, I'm not snapping, I'm just say– . . . No . . . All right, then, see you tonight . . . Okay . . . Okay . . . Bye." He hung up.

Holly sat down in the armchair opposite him and took a sip of her water. "If it's any consolation," she said, "you really weren't snapping. I know snapping when I hear it and that wasn't it."

His half-smile had been conspicuous by its absence. Now it returned. Holly marvelled at the effect it had on his appearance. It was the sort of transformation that she could only achieve by spending an hour on her make-up. James could do it in a quarter of a second.

"My mum," he said. "Dad's been sick for a few days. Nothing serious. Just a viral thing. I've spoken to him a few times and he's grand. Complaining and all, but not exactly at death's door either. Mother dearest thinks I'm a terrible son because I haven't called over to see him. She hasn't said it out loud but I can tell she's just on the edge of wailing, 'While you still have the chance!'"

"She'll be singing that terrib– . . . that song at you next. 'The Living Years.'"

James lit up. "Mike and the Mechanics! That's so spooky. I had that exact same thought yesterday when she called to give out. I hate that frigging song."

"Wow."

"What?"

"Nothing. I just . . . I've never heard you saying that you hate anything before."

"Really?"

"Never. Not once."

"Oh. Well, believe me, I hate that song. Not with your sort of passion, of course. I'm not in your league."

Holly had been about to elaborate but he had thrown her off. *When it came to hating things, she was in a different league* . . . She tried for a couple of seconds but there was no way she could make that sound good in her head.

"Earth to Holly. Come in, Holly."

"Sorry. So, you're going home tonight with a bottle of Lucozade and a sympathetic look?"

"Yeah, looks like it. He'll tell me I shouldn't have bothered, I know he will."

"But you'll feel better."

"My mum will. I suppose that's the main thing."

She smiled. He smiled back. In the background, a tap dripped. Now what sort of silence was this, Holly wondered, when neither of them spoke for a few seconds. Was it comfortable or awkward? It seemed like a significant question but she had no answer.

Then James said, "I suppose life's going to get a bit more complicated for both of us any day now."

"What?" Holly squeaked.

"We're into October now. Next thing you know, people will be talking about Christmas."

Her heart stopped leaping around in her chest. *No moaning*, she told herself. *No groaning. If you can't say something nice.* "Yeah, they will. But I don't see how it complicates your life."

"It doesn't. *Quantum of Solace.*"

"Who's a what now?"

"New James Bond movie. That's what it's called. *Quantum of Solace.* It's coming out in a few weeks. The kids have started to intensify their slagging campaign already."

"Ah," Holly said. Who the hell had come up with *"Quantum of Solace"*? It sounded like a cheap perfume, something that would be sold out of a suitcase in an out-of-the-way spot. "What an interesting title!"

"You think so?"

"Interesting!" she repeated robotically. "So you're going to get a hard time?"

For a moment, Holly allowed herself to indulge in a little fantasy. James was about to make a confession. The truth was, he was just like her – the real her. He'd been pulling a fast one all along. Terrible songs by Mike and the Mechanics were just the tip of the iceberg. You name it, he loathed it and, in the privacy of his own head, tore it to tiny shreds. He was living a lie and it had to stop!

"Ah, I don't mind," he said then. "If this is all I have to complain about, things aren't so bad, are they?"

"No," she sighed.

"Anyway," he said then. "I should probably get going."

"Yeah, me too."

They got up and walked out to the car park together. When it came time to part, Holly wished James good luck with his visit home.

"Thanks," he said. "Good luck with trying not to think about Christmas."

She wasn't sure if this was an apology for raising the subject or a cheeky admission that he'd been winding her up. As she got into her car, she wished that just once, he would say something that she could read. It was so *exhausting*. She was getting sick of it. Before she had even left the school grounds, she had made a firm decision.

Mark and Lizzie were happy to see her at first. They had just finished eating and cheerfully offered her some of the leftover goulash that they'd been planning to freeze for another day. When she declined, they forced a wineglass into her hand and poured her a generous helping of the Chilean Malbec that was their new darling ("So sure of itself," said Mark; "Bold to the point of arrogance," agreed Lizzie). Everything was going swimmingly until Holly cleared her throat and said, "So . . . "

"Oh, here we go," Mark said. Lizzie held her tongue but her smile collapsed.

Suddenly, Holly didn't feel quite as welcome. In truth, she had guessed that they wouldn't be especially excited by the prospect of discussing her love life yet again. Nevertheless, she pretended to be offended, just for appearances' sake.

"What? I haven't said anything yet!"

"Yeah, but you're going to, aren't you? I can tell. James what's-his-name, right?"

"Bond."

"Whatever."

"No, seriously. That's his name."

Mark looked at Lizzie. Lizzie looked at Mark.

"Why would I lie?" Holly asked.

"James Bond?" Lizzie shrieked.

"And Holly Christmas?" her husband added in an equally piercing tone.

It would have been better, Holly thought, if they'd collapsed into laughter. Instead, they both just stared at her.

Then Mark said, "Don't be ridiculous. You can't be a couple called James Bond and Holly Christmas."

"Why not?"

He adopted the expression of someone who had just taken a swig of sour milk. "Because . . . people will take the piss."

"People already take the piss," Holly replied. "Individually, I mean. I don't suppose it would get all that much worse if we were together. And anyway" – her voice rose – "why the hell should I care what people think?"

"James Bond," Lizzie mumbled as if the news was just sinking in. "How old is this guy? Was he born in the

1950s? At least then he'd have an excuse. Because otherwise, his parents must have –"

"Look," Holly interrupted. "I don't want to get off on a whole name thing here. This is why I didn't mention it in the first place."

"How does he cope with it?" Mark asked. "Better than you, I bet."

Holly gave him a look. "*Yes*, if you must know, he copes better than I do. I told you already. he copes with everything better than I do."

"Wait a minute," Lizzie said. The sinking-in process was obviously still ongoing. "This guy's a *teacher*. They must give him hell . . ."

"He likes it," Holly said. "Or at least, he doesn't mind it. I'm telling you, nothing bothers him. Now, listen: I want to ask –"

"We've been through all this already," Mark moaned. "We told you: try being a bit more easygoing, see if –"

"I've been doing that. Or at least I've been trying too. It hasn't, uh, it hasn't always come off."

"I can just picture it."

Holly began to worry that Mark was about to experience a profound loss of patience. As subtly as she could, she shifted her attention to Lizzie, who didn't seem quite as agitated.

"I can't read the guy. Sometimes I think he's flirting and sometimes I think he's mocking me. I'm fed up with it. So I've come to a decision. I'm going to take the initiative. I'm going to ask him out."

She had dared to hope that her announcement of this

significant change in policy might be a cause for celebration. There would be a blizzard of "*Good-for-you*s" and "*Go-get-'em-girl*s" after which she would calm things down and ask for some advice on how to go about it. Instead, their response was to renew their staring. She saw that she would have to skip a stage.

"So I need some advice," she said. "How do you think I should go about it?"

"I wouldn't have a clue," Lizzie said. "I've always thought it was the man's job to do the asking."

Holly was quite sure that this was a joke, albeit a hopelessly unfunny one. "Hur," she said, non-committally.

"I'm serious," Lizzie replied. "I mean, it's up to you, obviously, but do you not think there's something a wee bit . . . undignified about it?"

"Christ!" Holly gasped. "I thought you were taking the piss. Wow . . . I'm kind of in shock here. You, of all people –"

"What? What does that mean?"

"Calm down. I'm just saying, you're not exactly old-fashioned, are you?"

Lizzie's hand automatically moved to her crown. "So I cut my hair off. Ooooh. What, you think that makes me some sort of feminist nut-job?"

"No! No. I'm surprised, that's all. I didn't think it was such a big deal for a woman to ask a man out."

"Have you ever done it before?"

"No."

Mark chipped in: "And you need advice on how to go about it?"

"Uh . . . yes."

"Well, there you go," Lizzie said. "It is a big deal."

Holly felt as if she'd been tag-teamed. And worse, she realised that they had a point. For the past few hours she'd been telling herself that while it would have been nice if James had done the asking, it would be just as easy for her to do it. She'd been kidding herself. Somewhere just beneath the surface, she had already started to panic. Now the panic bubbled right to the top.

"Shit," she breathed. "Shit, shit, shit."

"Oh, don't get all excited," Lizzie said. "How hard can it be?"

"But you don't approve! You just said so!"

"I didn't say I didn't approve, I said I thought it was undignified. But, hey, it's your dignity. If you're comfortable with throwing it overboard, then who am I to raise objections?"

"Oh. Right. Well, in that case, dignity-shmignity. So – what's my plan?"

"I got asked out for a drink once," Mark said. He nodded at Lizzie. "Not long before I met you, actually."

"Did you now?" Lizzie said. "I didn't know that."

"Well, I can hardly tell you about every single woman who finds me irresistible," he cooed. "I'd get nothing done."

"You just said it only happened once," Holly pointed out.

"Oh. Right. Yeah. So I did."

"Who was she? What did she say? How did you react?"

"Her name was Dolores. She was a barmaid in this horrible pub I used to drink in when I lived in Bray."

"Go on."

"Yeah, well, I used to chit-chat with her a bit over a pint, you know. Then one night she said that maybe we could go somewhere different some time when she was free, just the two of us."

"And you were sure this was an asking-out? It was a date she was talking about?"

"Oh, yeah. There's always a tone. At least there is any time I've asked someone out. It's unavoidable. Even if you wanted to hide it, you couldn't."

"So did you go?"

"Yeah," Lizzie added. "Did you go?" She was clearly intrigued by this glimpse into her husband's past.

Mark shook his head firmly. "I did in me hole. Dolores was the spitting image of Ian Paisley."

"Charming," Holly said. "At least tell me you admired her bravery and the two of you remained good friends?"

Another head shake. "I thought it was a bit creepy, to tell you the truth. And I never went back there again."

Holly looked to Lizzie and mouthed the word "*Help*". Lizzie responded with an impotent frown.

"If nothing else," Mark said pompously, "I hope this will be educational for you. Asking people out is *hard*."

"Seriously – you have to have something more useful to say than that."

"All right, look," he said. "There's no secret trick to this. It's not in the delivery; it doesn't matter how you say it. Actually, it doesn't even matter *what* you say. You can hire a skywriter or you can mumble and stutter your way through it while staring at your feet. At the end of the day –"

"I hate that phrase," Holly snapped. It was purely a reflex. "Sorry, sorry. Go on."

"At the end of the day, either he wants to go out with you or he doesn't. It's not something you can *debate*. You don't have to get your arguments and counter-arguments ready. If you ask him and he says no, you won't be able to convince him. There'll be no 'A-ha, but you have failed to consider X, Y and Z.' There's no need for any preparation. So stop wondering how you go about it. Just go about it."

"Hm. Yeah. Yeah, you're right. But what should –"

"And it doesn't matter what you suggest either. If Scarlett Johanssen walked in here now and asked me to take her ice-skating, do you think I'd say, 'No thanks, I don't really like skating?'"

"Oi," Lizzie said simply. She sounded like someone giving a command to a dog. Mark responded immediately.

"Of course, what I would actually say is, 'You're very nice and all, Scarlett, but you can't possibly compete with my beloved wife.'"

"Aw," Lizzie said.

To Holly's confusion, she seemed to think that he was genuinely being cute, even though she had just ordered him to be.

"The point still stands," Mark went on. "Say what you like, how you like. He'll agree or he won't. End of."

Holly felt better. She took some of her wine and

realised that every muscle in her body was tense. With an audible sigh, she relaxed all over. "Yeah. Thanks, Mark."

There was a moment of cosy silence. Then Mark said, "Mind you . . . " Irritatingly, he went no further.

Holly's muscles reclenched.

"What?"

"I have to be honest . . . "

"Go on."

"And I'm not trying to take the piss, I'm just trying –"

"Go *on*."

"Well . . . don't you think he would have asked you out himself by now if he was interested?"

"For fuck's sake," Lizzie groaned. "She said already, she can't read the guy. Don't mind him, Holly."

"Maybe she can't read him," Mark said. "But she can hear him all right, can't she? And he hasn't said anything along the lines of 'Let's go out for a drink this weekend', has he? Newsflash: men don't sit around waiting for women to do the deed. It's horrible asking, we know that. It's horrible and it's difficult and it can be completely degrading. But we always do it in the end – if we're interested."

"He could be shy," Lizzie countered. But it was obvious from the lack of passion in her voice that she had found her husband's argument convincing.

"It doesn't matter," Holly said. "I'm at tether's end. I want to know where I stand. So I'm asking him. And that's that."

"Well," Lizzie said as she got up to pour more wine, "all we can do is wish you good luck."

"Thanks," Holly said.

"Yeah," Mark said. "Good luck. Now: a toast."

The girls raised their glasses.

"I love toasts," Lizzie smiled.

Mark cleared his throat and held his own glass aloft.

"To desperation," he said.

Back in her own house, Holly had trouble settling down. She felt nervous in a way that she hadn't experienced since her Leaving Certificate days and found herself mooching from the sofa to the kettle and back in a restless, and in its own small way, exhausting loop. The decision she had made was the correct one, she was sure of that. It wasn't as if she was reconsidering her choice. But there were no two ways about it – this time tomorrow she would know for sure if James was interested. And if he wasn't, she would not only have the pain of that to contend with but also, as a sort of inverse bonus, the fact that she had found out the hard way. The embarrassing way. The humiliating way. Mark, despite his many insensitivities, had been quite correct – this was educational. All night long she winced as she recalled the various quips and slurs with which she had obliterated potential suitors in the past. From her current vantage point, it seemed obvious that very few of them – and quite possibly none of them – had enjoyed the confidence that they'd been at such pains to project. On the contrary, it was more likely that they had been sick with nerves. Uselessly, she wished that she'd been able to see then that which was so clear now – that to approach another human being with declared romantic intent was to make an open wound of yourself while handing them a packet of salt.

It was well after midnight when she finally decided to cut her losses and go to bed. She was under no illusions that she'd be able to sleep, but she thought she might as well fret under the duvet as on the sofa. Her footsteps were slow and heavy as she made her way to the kitchen to deposit her mug in the dishwasher. It needed to be emptied, she remembered, and could probably do with a . . . She stopped dead in the kitchen doorway.

Claude was sitting in the middle of the floor, looking towards the hall as if in expectation of her arrival. To his left, lying curled up with its tail wrapped around its body, was another cat. He or she was barely out of kittenhood and not more than half Claude's size. Holly didn't move for a second. How was this possible? Claude's collar contained a magnet that activated the catflap. It was feasible, she supposed, that any old magnet would open it, but the newcomer wasn't wearing a collar. After a moment, she stepped forward to get a closer look. Claude raised his head, inviting a comforting tickle, then lowered it again in disgust when it became clear that he was not going to get one. The other cat sprang to its feet – it didn't seem to have even registered Holly's arrival up to now – and ran into a corner. It was not, Holly observed, a good-looking animal. Claude's fur was uniformly smoky grey and shone like something from a shampoo commercial. The new cat was grey in places too, but it was also black and white and, in several vivid patches, bright orange. It looked as if had been put together from the off-cuts of other, more attractive cats. Holly bent her knees in a forlorn effort to make herself less threatening and took another few steps. She had anticipated that the cat would panic and leg it into another corner, but she was wrong. As she edged ever closer, it suddenly trotted forward to meet her. Then, when they were just a couple of feet apart, it lay down again and curled up into the same position it had been in when she arrived. No sooner had it done so than it got up again and walked slowly into a different corner. There it sat perfectly still, looking up at her, eyes wide, mouth half-open. Clearly, this was strange behaviour. If Claude had pulled these sorts of moves, she would have had him at the vet within the hour.

"Hello, little puss," she said, extending her hand.

The cat didn't respond at first. Then it craned its neck to give her fingertips a tentative sniff. Up close, Holly saw that it was not in good shape. It had a small cut right on top of its head which had caused the surrounding fur to matt together in bloody little Mohawk, and its left eye was weeping for no obvious reason. Most alarming of all, though, was its painful skinniness. "Are you hungry? You sure look it." She took a pouch of Kitekat from under the sink and deposited the contents in Claude's bowl. Unsurprisingly, said Claude was on it in a flash. "No, no," Holly said and scooped him up. "This one's not for you." He wriggled in her arms like a landed fish as she used her foot to move the bowl towards the other cat. Its nose started to twitch at once but it seemed to take a few seconds to recognise – or possibly to believe – that this was real food. It gave the jellied meat an experimental sniff, then a series of small licks. Finally, it fell upon it. Holly had seen Claude in ravenous form on plenty of occasions but even at his most desperate, he had never gone at it like this. The Cat of Many Colours didn't so much eat its meal as invade it. Claude's struggling became unbearable after a while and Holly dropped him to the floor. He immediately took his place beside the interloper and joined in. Holly sat down at the kitchen table, feeling a small pang of pride in her pet. He still wanted his due, granted, but he seemed perfectly willing to share. There was no growling or hissing, no puffed-up tail or flattened ears. A couple of minutes later, the food was all gone. The Cat of Many Colours spent another couple enthusiastically licking the empty bowl. While it did so, Holly got out of her chair and checked its equipment. It was a girl. Claude had long since had his reproductive capacity curtailed, so they were not – she felt silly for thinking of it in these terms – a couple. What, then? Platonic friends? They certainly didn't seem to be strangers to each other.

"Okay," she said then. "Time to go." She got up from her seat and opened the back door. Claude didn't pay the slightest bit of attention. The Cat of Many Colours looked out into the gloom but made no moves away from the bowl. "All right, now, scoot," Holly said. "Scoot. Scoot! I fed you, didn't I? Off you go now . . .

Go on . . . Go on . . ." No response. Holly went around to the cat's rear and gave it a gentle prod with her slippered toe. Frankly, she didn't want to pick it up if at all possible. It looked as if it might be providing bed and board to a great many smaller creatures, some of whom might take the opportunity to relocate. At first, the prod seemed to have an effect. The Cat of Many Colours reluctantly moved towards the doorstep, its ears swivelling, its head low to the ground. But then it stopped.

"Go on," Holly said again. "No room at the inn. Sorry. Off you go."

She gave it another little prod. It took a few steps and then stopped again. After a moment, it looked over its shoulder and gave a pathetic mewl. It was the first sound it had made. Holly didn't know whether to laugh or cry. On the one hand, it was the sound of an animal in distress and, as such, was heartbreaking. On the other, it sounded so impossibly, cartoonishly cute that it was hard to take seriously. Holly found it difficult to shake the feeling that this was something the cat had practised, possibly with Claude's help (*No, no, no! Softer! More pathetic!*). It was almost at the doorstep now. One more push should do it. "Nice try," she said, applying a third toe-prod. "But not good enough. Bye bye, now. Bye bye." This time the cat finally crossed the threshold. It turned around as soon as it had done so and repeated its plea for clemency. Holly closed her eyes and wished she could close her ears. Then she shut the door. When she turned around she half-expected to see Claude shaking his head in disappointment. But he had disappeared. She switched off the light and made her way down the hall. When she stuck her head into the front room, she found him on the sofa, already settling in, not a care in the world. So much for platonic friendship, she thought. Five minutes later, she was in bed, staring up at the ceiling, as wide-awake as she had ever been in her entire life.

It was going to be a long night.

Chapter 18

Friday morning was downright weird. Holly had only limited experience with recreational drugs but she supposed that one or more types of high felt something like this. Colours seemed brighter. Sounds seemed louder. Movements seemed exaggerated. Peter Fogarty approached her in the staff room when she arrived and for one terrible moment she thought she was going to scream. He was taller than she was, granted, but those few inches surely couldn't account for the way he seemed to loom over her like a city-destroying mutant from a Japanese movie (she felt quite convinced that everything had darkened as she fell under his immense shadow). There was no sign of James, which was probably a good thing, she decided. Given her fragile state, who knew what visions she might project onto him?

Her first classes of the day went by in a flash, largely because she talked non-stop throughout them. She was relieved when the bell rang for the mid-morning break and she got a couple of minutes in which she could try to compose herself. It was just lack of sleep, she told herself. She'd probably had no more than three hours in total and that was bound to have an effect on a person, especially when you added nervous excitement to the mix. She started for outside in the interests of getting some fresh air. Halfway along the corridor, a new fear gripped her: what if James wasn't in today? There was no way she'd be able to get through the weekend with her sanity intact. She abandoned her fresh-air plan and made her way to the staff room where she threw the door open like a cop raiding a drugs den. James was standing by the sink, sipping on a glass of water. Barry Dwyer and Julie Sullivan were there too, talking across him, both jabbering at once. He looked over to Holly and made the tiniest adjustment to his smile. Holly was sure that it meant *Help: rescue me*. She stepped across and butted in. Sure enough, Barry and Julie were discussing the history of their relationship; they should have known that such talk was pure poison to a single man. Holly made a few attempts to deflect the conversation in new directions but when the happy couple showed no interest, she was reduced to smiling sympathetically at James, who smiled sympathetically back. *Two couples*, she thought. *Before very long, we could be the school's two couples*. She felt a surge of confidence and all at once, she knew what she was going to do. When time came for them to return to class, she tugged on James's arm and suggested a lunchtime stroll.

He agreed immediately. It was a nice day and he was feeling kind of sluggish. Holly left it at that and strolled off in the direction of her next class. What, she wondered, had all the fuss been about? They would go for a walk and somewhere along the way she would ask him if he wanted to go for a drink at the weekend. And he would say yes. It all seemed so clear now, so simple.

At lunchtime Holly arrived in the staff room before James. He sat on the other side of the table from her, near the end. There was another seat immediately to his right that he could have taken. Doing so would have meant he was a little closer to being directly opposite her. She started to wonder why he hadn't sat there but quickly gave herself a mental slap across the face. The time for fretting and obsessing was over. She would have her answer within the hour. As soon as James had finished his lunch, she took her plate and cup to the dishwasher. It was difficult not to look back to see if he had followed her but she managed it. And then, just by her left shoulder, she heard him say her name. Were they going for a walk or what?

They took the same route that they'd taken the last time. For the first few minutes, they talked about their mornings. Holly, naturally, left out the bits about feeling frantic and drugged-up and restricted herself to pleasant inanities. James reported that he'd had four classes so far and that three of them had featured discussions on the new Bond movie. He was beginning to worry, in fact, about one first-year boy who seemed to be dangerously obsessed with all things 007. He had breathlessly declared his interest right at the outset when he learned his new teacher's name and James had thought nothing more of it. But there had been several occasions recently when he'd caught the lad staring at him in the manner of a humble peasant who'd been visited by a God. Frankly, he was beginning to wonder if his sense of reality was as finely honed as it could be. Holly did her best to listen and to offer coherent responses, but it wasn't easy. She was so busy rehearsing her opener – *Any exciting plans for the weekend?* – that the words seemed to be the only ones that she had access to. She felt incapable of forming a sentence that didn't use them. When they came to the chemist, Holly pretended to need shampoo and greatly enjoyed James's reaction when she made a move for the door; it was a special treat when he took her wrist to halt her progress.

Shortly afterwards, James said that they should probably head back. It had been nice to get a bit of fresh air but he had a couple of phone calls to make before the first class of the afternoon. So they turned around. They had taken no more than a few steps in silence before Holly started to panic that they might walk the whole way back without saying another thing. It was hardly a romantic atmosphere. Her mind spun. There had to be something she could say. Jesus, what did they usually talk about? And then the words just fell out of her mouth.

"Any exciting plans for the weekend?"

312

She almost slapped a hand over her gob. It was too soon! She was supposed to have carefully picked her moment! But it was out there now. There was no time for analysis. The trick was not to panic, to segue easily and naturally into her follow-up – the main event. And then she noticed that James was taking a long time to respond. She moistened her lips with her tongue.

"James?"

"Yeah . . . uh . . . actually, I'm going to be seeing Aisling."

A great hammer swung into Holly's chest. It felt as if every ounce of oxygen in her lungs was expelled at once. She only just stopped herself from doubling over. *Say something quickly*, a Sergeant Major in her head commanded.

"Really?"

James scratched the back of his head. He was still walking at his normal pace but Holly was suddenly finding it tough to keep up. "Yeah. We, uh, got together a while back but we haven't managed to see much of each other since."

"The play?" she said through barely parted lips.

"That's right, yeah. That was the start of it. Seemed to be something in the air that night, eh? Orla and John, me and Aisling . . ."

Holly forced a nod. Her body was seizing up. Every movement required conscious effort. "Hm."

"Look," James said and rubbed his forehead. "You're probably wondering why we didn't mention it."

"Hm."

"The thing is . . . Shite, this is going to sound weird, but I'm just gonna . . . The thing is, we didn't want to say anything for a few weeks, just in case it turned out to be nothing. Aisling said there was no point in upsetting you –"

"Why would I be upset?" Holly said. Then she thought, *If he says, "Because you obviously like me," I'm jumping into the traffic.*

James frowned. "Aisling has this idea that you might feel a bit . . . left out. Because everyone around you is coupling up. Us, Orla and John. Your mum, even."

The laugh that burst forth from Holly was bitter and brittle. She realised as much when she heard it and issued a second, fabricated version that sounded a little warmer.

"I'm well used to being the single one, James," she said. "There's no need to worry on that score." Now that she had faked nonchalance almost by accident, she set about reinforcing the image. *Light and easy*, the Sergeant Major barked. *Step to it.* "So you've been out a few times then?"

"Yeah, just the usual, you know. Drinks, dinner. We're going to spend the day together tomorrow. See if we can stomach each other for more than a few hours."

Holly took a deep breath as subtly as she could and forced a smile. "I'm sure you'll manage. Aisling's pretty easy to be around."

"Oh yeah. Tell you the truth, I can't believe my luck."

314

Her smile hardened. "You can't believe your luck or you can't believe her looks?"

He smiled back. "Bit of both."

Holly could tell that he was relieved to see that this was going well. It was entirely to her advantage, she knew, that it should continue to do so. "Funny how things work out, isn't it?" she said. It was already becoming easier to fake a positive reaction. Every word she uttered made it easier still. "You started out trying to do a good deed for John and you ended up doing one for yourself."

"Well, you're the lynchpin here, don't forget. You're the one we all have in common."

"Yay for me."

"I'm serious. What do they call it? A . . . social hub? You're a social hub, Holly. You should be proud."

This statement was a little patronising, but she decided to ignore that. Nothing good could come from her getting angry. They spent the rest of the walk back to school discussing options for James and Aisling's day out. Holly presented a brief argument for the National Gallery, citing the wonders it had done for her mother and Charlie. James wasn't sure. He liked the idea of having something outside themselves that they could talk about, but he thought that the zoo might be a better idea. They went back and forth on it with neither one fully convincing the other – largely because one of them wasn't really trying – until they arrived at the front entrance. Holly had frankly astounded herself with her performance. By the time they said goodbye, the look of relief on James's face had given way to excitement. He had a new girlfriend. They were about to step things up a gear. And the only person who might possibly have a problem with it had been dealt with. As he skipped away to make his phone calls, she wished him good luck with the zoo or gallery or whatever, just in case she didn't see him again. He thanked her as he disappeared around the corner. Then she stepped outside again and reached for her own phone. She'd done a great job of keeping reality at bay so far, but it was scrabbling at the door and rattling the windows. Any minute now, it would break through. The call had to be made, so it might as well be now while she was still in the zone.

"Hi, Aisling," she said when the call was picked up.

"Ah, Miss Christmas. How's tricks?"

"Grand. Listen: I've just been talking to James. About you."

"Oh."

"Yeah, *oh*. What's with all the secrecy?"

Aisling didn't answer right away. Holly used the time to straighten her back and redo her fake smile.

"I just . . . " Aisling began. "I don't know, I just didn't want you to feel . . . left out. I know you're . . . sensitive about all that . . . being single . . . stuff."

"I'm not made of glass," Holly said. Her voice didn't sound as cheerful now. The façade was beginning to crumble.

"I know, I know. It was silly. But it was just a casual

thing, with us, to begin with. There was no point taking the risk that we might annoy you for no good reason. Tell you the truth, we had half a plan to try to get you hooked up with someone before we told you."

"I might have been up for that," Holly lied.

"Yeah. But we couldn't think of anybody . . . suitable."

Holly closed her eyes. "Right."

"It's weird though, isn't it? We try to get Orla fixed up and wind up getting a twofer."

"Yeah. Weird." *One last big push*, she thought. "Anyway: I better get back to it. Just so you know, I'm chuffed for the pair of you. Of course I am. And for Orla and John too. Why wouldn't I be? There was no need to keep it to yourselves."

"Aw. Thanks, Holly. You're a star."

"Okay then. I'm away."

"All right. See ya. Thanks for the call."

Holly hung up and put her phone away. She didn't have a class straight away. That was good. She re-entered the building and turned down the first corridor. *Just put one foot in front of the other*, she told herself. *That's all there is to it. Left, right, left, right.* Faces floated past her as she walked. Boys, scurrying to beat the bell, Greg Tynan and Nuala Fanning, heads almost touching as they spoke in low whispers about something or other. Holly felt sure that she was going to bump into Eleanor Duffy but she was spared that, at least. When she emerged on the other side of the main building, a first-year boy – she didn't know his name – ran smack

317

into her, head-butting her breasts. He looked up at her in horror and seemed unable to believe his luck when she just shook her head at him and walked on. The apology that he delivered to her back seemed genuine.

The school's gym was a separate building, set some distance back from its parent. Holly had always hated the sight of it. There was no reason for it to be pretty, she knew, but at the same time, there really didn't seem to be any excuse for it to be quite this bland. It looked as if it had been drawn by a child – two straight lines for walls, two angled lines for a roof. She approached it slowly; it was quite likely that it would be in use by some PE class. But there was no one around. She made her way down the side and around to the rear. "The back of the gym" was the Wild West in school folklore. It was the place where fights happened, the place where cigarettes were smoked. And now it was the place where Holly Christmas came to sit on the grass and cry.

In the middle of the night, while staring at her bedroom ceiling, she had tried to imagine how she would feel if James turned her down. The best she could hope for, she'd concluded, was for him to say that he just didn't fancy her. There was very little she could do about her looks, after all, and besides, she had never been particularly insecure on that front. She wasn't exactly stunning, she knew that. But she didn't frighten children in the streets either. It would be terrible but manageable. The worst possible outcome was that he would say no and then go on to explain that, despite her recent efforts, she was just too much of a smart-arse, too sarcastic, too blah blah blah. So now what? She was in no man's land. He had rejected her by default and she would never know why. It was going to drive her mad. Was it too late, she wondered through her tears, to ask him now? As soon as this thought had crystallised, she twisted her body in disgust. How the hell would that work? *Hey, James, you know the way you never asked me out? Why was that, exactly?*

It was starting already. She was losing her marbles.

Chapter 19

The weekend barely existed for Holly. She didn't leave the house at all and spoke only once on the phone. That call was from her mother. It seemed to serve no purpose other than to report the news that she and Charlie were still together. Holly's monosyllabic replies (she was sorry she'd picked up) led to the obvious question: was she all right?

"I'm fine," she said. "I haven't been sleeping very well. I'm tired, that's all."

There was just one other call at the weekend – from Aisling. Holly ignored it. The recorded message spoke of a lovely day out at the zoo. Over the course of the following week, she wandered around like a ghost, interacting with nothing and no one. The only time she spoke voluntarily was when she was teaching and even then, she said as little as possible. People noticed, of course. Was she all right, they asked, again and again and again? Holly brushed them all aside.

"I'm fine," she said. "I haven't been sleeping very well. I'm tired, that's all."

James was one of those who made enquiries. When he asked what was up, Holly made a special effort. Just between them, she said, she was suddenly having something of a career crisis. Teaching seemed like a bit of a chore these days. Nothing to worry about. It would pass. James seemed to buy it. He offered some kind words and left it at that. Through a combination of shrewd tactics and luck, Holly managed to avoid Eleanor Duffy for quite a while. Last thing on Friday, however, just as she was struggling to believe that a whole week had floated by since D-Day, she came around the corner by the staff room and ran straight into the encounter that she'd been dreading. Holly was not at all surprised to learn that Eleanor had noticed her bad humour – she'd been able to avoid a private conversation, but she hadn't been able to avoid contact altogether. They went through the routine. Eleanor didn't seem to find the tiredness excuse as convincing as everyone else had done, but she didn't press the issue. Then she asked if there was any news on the James front. Without hesitation, Holly reported that there wasn't and there wasn't likely to be, either. Apparently, he was going out with one of her oldest friends. Had been for a while. They seemed very happy together. As Eleanor paled, Holly ran through some lines about being fine with it and then – either daringly or ridiculously; she wasn't sure – went back to lying about how knackered she was and how keen to get home. By the time Eleanor had stopped wringing her hands and started talking again, Holly was already moving away and wishing her a pleasant weekend.

Just after lunch on Saturday, Holly's mother called. Like its predecessor, the call seemed to have but one function: to verify that she was still seeing Charlie. It was only after they'd hung up that Holly allocated any of her beleaguered mental resources to it. That tone had been there again too – *Happy now?* What was all that about? It was something to worry about, almost certainly, but that worry would have to wait for another day, possibly even another month. She simply didn't have the energy right now. The phone rang twice more that day. Once call was from Aisling, the other from Orla. For fear of giving the game away, Holly answered Aisling's. When her mood was questioned, she was careful to mirror the reply she'd given to James. Just between them, she said, she was having something of a career crisis. Teaching seemed like a bit of a chore these days. Nothing to worry about. It would pass. Aisling said that, yeah, she'd heard as much. It should have come as no surprise, of course, but somehow Holly was taken aback by the realisation that she had been a topic of discussion between the happy couple. She found it impossible not to picture the scene: the two of them snuggled up together, Aisling holding forth: *Pay no attention. Holly's always been the dark'n'moody type. That's why she can't keep a man for more than ten minutes.* She made an excuse and got off the phone before her voice betrayed her distress. As for Orla's call, she simply ignored that. The recorded message was cheerful to the point of parody.

On Sunday night, while Holly was standing in the kitchen, waiting for the kettle to boil, Claude poked his head through the catflap. He paused, half in and half out, and looked up at her. Then he stepped inside. The flap swung back behind him but didn't close. Holly narrowed her eyes. Before she even had time to think about what might be blocking it, it started to open again. And slowly, tentatively, the Cat of Many Colours poured in. Holly's first reaction was to marvel at the ingenuity. So that was how she was gaining access – she was *tail-gating*. Her appreciation of this clever stratagem was short-lived, however. When the two of them sat in front of her, looked up and cried in perfect unison, she was overcome by a feeling of resignation. She had acquired another cat. There was no point in complaining or trying to find a way around it. It was a sign from God. She was indeed destined to be a little old cat lady and would be alone forever. The knowledge that she didn't believe in signs or God, much less signs *from* God was of no comfort. Quite the reverse, in fact – it seemed to reinforce her conviction that, on top of everything else, she was losing her grip on reality. The circular nature of this notion – the sign from God was all the more awful because she didn't believe in signs from God – made her head swim.

She stared down at the cats for a while, feeling utterly paralysed. They stared back. The Cat of Many Colours looked a bit more healthy than she had done on her first visit. Compared to Claude, she was still a ragged little tumbleweed of a creature, but she didn't seem quite as skinny now and her bloody Mohawk had gone. The staring competition ended when Claude padded forward to rub himself against Holly's lower leg. She snapped out of it and got a couple of food pouches from under the sink. Once their contents had been deposited in the bowl, the cats attacked them from opposite angles, their heads side by side, their ears twitching as they touched. Holly made her cup of tea and, having no better idea what to do with herself, sat down at the kitchen table to watch them eat. The Cat of Many Colours would have to be spayed. And she would need her own magnetic collar. It might be best to get a batch of collars, in fact. For all Holly knew, God might be planning on sending her a few more signs, just to make sure that she really got the message.

The school week that followed was much like its predecessor. Holly was there, but not there. She spoke when it was strictly necessary, but otherwise stayed mute. No one, not even Eleanor, asked her if she was feeling okay. It took a couple of days for her to realise that this was not a good thing. They weren't avoiding the question because she'd already told them she was feeling tired; they were avoiding the question because it had become obvious that she'd been lying and they didn't want to delve any further. When she got home on Friday evening, she realised that she couldn't remember having a single conversation with anyone all week. It was not healthy, she knew, that she sincerely hoped she wouldn't have any over the weekend either.

At around eight o'clock, just as she was finishing dinner (a boil-in-the-bag beef curry), the phone rang. It was Orla. Holly bit her lip. It would be poor form to ignore two calls in a row. On the other hand, what were the chances of her sitting through another sermon about John without saying something massively inappropriate? In the end, she picked up out of simple guilt. The guilt deepened when Orla made no mention of her new boyfriend but concentrated instead on Holly. She'd been very quiet lately. Aisling said so too. Was anything wrong?

"I'm all right," she said. "Just having a bit of a career crisis these days. Nothing serious. Sometimes I feel a bit –"

"I don't believe you."

"Sorry."

"You heard me. I have a theory of my own. Do you want to hear it?"

"Would it matter if I said no?"

"I think you're pissed off because everyone around you is coupling up."

"Is that right."

"Yep. Do you not think it's weird that we haven't even had a gossip about Aisling and James getting together?"

This was dangerous territory. Holly moved quickly. "It's nothing to do with my love life, or lack of one. I'm delighted for Aisling and James. I'm delighted for you and John. I'm delighted for my mother and Charlie. And I'm delighted for Claude, even if they are just good friends."

She hoped that this last statement would generate a follow-up question and thus divert the conversation. But Orla was undeterred – and unconvinced.

"Holly, I know what it's like to be lonely and think that there's no one special for you. But you can't just give up. You have to put yourself out there, stay open to possibilities."

Now this, Holly thought, was really something. Orla had only had a boyfriend for ten minutes herself and now she was giving advice? And she hadn't "put herself" anywhere. She'd been set up. Even then, her initial reaction had been to run away to drink alone in the nearest pub. Although she was sorely tempted to say all of this and more, Holly ultimately decided that it would be a mistake to raise the temperature.

"For the last time, I'm just tired," she said. "I mean – it's just work."

"Okay then," Orla sighed. "Do you want to talk about it?"

"No," she said. "Not really."

There was a long silence. Then Orla said, "We're going out for dinner tomorrow night, myself and Aisling and the two boys. Nothing fancy. Pizza and a few glasses of wine. Why don't you come along?"

Although she tried hard, Holly was unable to prevent herself from forming a mental picture of the scene. Her skin crawled. Sooner or later, she would have to face them all, of course. But if she had any say in the matter, it would definitely be later.

"Thanks, Orla. But no thanks."

"Fine," Orla said somewhat angrily. "Suit yourself. Give me a ring any time if you want to talk about it. Your school problems, I mean."

Holly thanks her, mumbled some promises about getting back into society soon and then got off the phone as quickly as possible.

She would be discussed over pizza the following night, there was no doubt about that. What would they say, she wondered? Her career-crisis story had probably held water for a couple of days but it was obviously past its sell-by date now. She could just about stomach the idea of them talking about her being miserably single. Her real fear was that one of them would hit on the idea that she had wanted James for herself. All she could do, she supposed, was hope that they wouldn't.

After another half hour of staring at the TV without even registering what she was watching, she began to contemplate going next door. She had almost gone several times in recent days but had always stopped herself. Why should *she* go to see *them*? They knew she'd been about to ask James out. If they cared, wouldn't they already have come knocking to get the latest? She started down that mental path again now, but the frenzy of righteous indignation ended when she reminded herself with a sigh that there was no point in grumbling; Mark and Lizzie simply didn't do visits. They'd been in her house precisely once, not long after she'd moved in, and only came then because she'd literally begged them to judge some paint samples she'd daubed on the kitchen wall.

Mark and Lizzie greeted her in sombre tones. They had of course guessed that it had all gone wrong and had assumed that she would talk to them when she was good and ready. Over the course of two large glasses of wine – they didn't offer any opinions on it, which spoke of their solemnity, she felt – Holly gave them the headlines. They listened attentively and made appropriately sympathetic noises. When she told them about the Cat of Many Colours, she thought she saw Mark stifling a giggle, but was gratified to see that Lizzie, at least, maintained a look of concern.

"The worst part," she said, "is that I don't know where I stand with the stupid positivity experiment. The night I started trying it was the night he took up with Aisling. He wasn't paying the remotest bit of attention to me all along. Not that I was any good at it anyway. I tried, I really did, but it wasn't easy. So what am I going to do now? Should I try it again on some other poor bastard? Maybe try . . . harder?"

And then she began to ramble. She knew that she was doing it, looping and backtracking, repeating the same points over and over again, but she didn't seem able to stop herself. It was a consequence, she supposed, of having been essentially dumb for a fortnight. Her meandering rant had been going on for some time when Lizzie butted in. There was something about the manner of her interruption – the raised finger, the deep inhalation – that made Holly instantly nervous. She braced herself.

"I want to ask you something," Lizzy said, after a dramatic pause. "Are you really sure that you fancied James in the first place?"

"What? What's that sup–"

"The reason I'm asking is that all your current complaints are exactly the same ones you had when Kevin dumped you. Is it your own fault that you're single, would being a bit more happy-clappy make any difference, cat lady this, doomed to be alone that, yada yada. There's nothing in there about James himself."

Mark nodded slowly. "Yeah. Yeah, that's right. You've never gone all soppy over his manly jaw or thick, wavy hair or piercing blue eyes or whatever. The only time you ever complimented him, actually, was to say that he was, what was it, 'intriguing' because he was so different from you."

Lizzie clapped her hands together and turned to face him. "*Yes*. That's it. She was never really attracted to this James in the normal sense. She just picked on him because he was so unlike her, so chirpy and cheerful, stupid name and all. He was a challenge, that was the point. She isn't sorry that she hasn't acquired him as a boyfriend; she's sorry that she still hasn't found out if the problem is her personality."

She clapped again. This time she seemed to be applauding herself.

Holly fell back into her chair, cradling her empty glass as if it was a favourite cuddly toy. She felt as if some tiny tornado was laying waste to her mind, up-ending and uprooting as it went. As the seconds ticked by, the sensation grew so strong as to be mildly nauseating.

When Mark rose from his seat to pour more wine for everyone, Holly avoided his eye. She sipped from her glass for a moment and then finally mumbled a response.

"Bullshit," she said. "Of course I fancied him. Fancy him. I know I'm not exactly on top of my game these days but I'm not *crazy*."

Mark and Lizzie failed to reply at first. Then Mark said, "There is some good news. Now that you know the thing with you and James was a figment of your imagination, you don't have to avoid him and Aisling any more."

Holly gaped at him. "*That's* your idea of good news? I – I have to go."

She was up and moving before they could even ask her to reconsider.

Back in her own house, she found Claude and the Cat of Many Colours lying at either end of the sofa, apparently waiting for her. She wasn't in the least surprised. It seemed like a perfectly logical next step in her downward spiral. She sat down between them and gave them each an absent-minded tickle. Claude leaned into his straight away. The Cat of Many Colours was more hesitant at first but soon got the idea. She was making herself at home now. Settling in.

Over the course of the next couple of hours, Holly moved only to pet the cats. Around about the time when her hand began to go numb – she looked down at one point and realised that she was stroking a cushion – an idea occurred to her. Although she found it interesting at first, she soon pushed it away on the grounds that it was utter insanity. But it wouldn't stay pushed away. The harder she pushed, in fact, the more forcefully it returned; she felt as if she was slamming a tennis ball against the side of a house. After a while, she surrendered and started to give the idea serious thought. Somewhere along the way, it started to sound less insane. Risky, certainly. But not insane. By the time she got up to go to bed, it didn't even feel all that risky any more. The word for it, she decided, was . . . bold. Yes. She would be bold. Tomorrow was as good a day as any. All she needed was a hammer.

Chapter 20

It was just after twelve thirty on Saturday afternoon when Holly pulled in at her destination. She yanked the handbrake and took a moment to compose herself.

Despite the previous night's excesses, she was feeling remarkably clear-headed. It was the sort of clarity, she imagined, that assassins felt as they settled in on the rooftop and adjusted their sights. She was wearing a pair of khaki-coloured trousers and a pale blue shirt. Both items had been dragged from the very back of her wardrobe where they had languished unattended since the day of their purchase. She had a sneaking suspicion that she'd bought them both at the same time during one of the anything-but-black mini sprees that Aisling occasionally harrassed her into. Holly had never ever read very much into her fashion choices; she just liked black, that was all – dark grey at a push. It was unfortunate because it opened the door to a lot of lame jokes, but it wasn't significant. Anyone who thought otherwise had a child's grasp of psychology. And yet, she had given the matter a lot of thought this morning. She'd often heard actors saying how they didn't feel that they were really getting to grips with a new character until they tried on the beard or the crown or the spacesuit. A similar notion had run through her head while she was getting ready. She was under no illusions that dressing differently would influence the outcome – but she hoped that it would help her give a better performance. The only real down-side (apart from the fact that she felt distinctly odd) was that she was half-freezing. She would have worn a jacket or cardigan, but she found that she didn't own any that weren't black. After she stepped out of the car and closed the door behind her, she paused and gave herself another chance to change her mind. She didn't take it.

Inside, she found that the place was pretty much as she remembered it. There were a lot more plants than there had been before and the walls were a different colour, but the basic layout was the same. She approached the counter and waited for the attendant to get off the phone. "Sorry about that," he said when the call finally ended. "What can I do for you?"

"Hi," she said. "It's nothing too serious. I just need a new wing mirror. I went out to the car this morning and someone had smashed one off."

He shook his head. "Scumbags. They're everywhere, I swear to God. Drunk, no doubt, or worse."

Holly shrugged. "High jinks. We were all young and stupid once."

"Young and stupid, maybe – violent scumbags, no. Anyway: make and model?"

"Oh-six Yaris."

"Driver's side, pass–"

"Driver's side. It wasn't electric, if that makes any difference. Which I suppose it would."

He made a note on his clipboard. "Wouldn't be all that easy to get a mirror off. They must have hit it some whack. Wonder what they used."

"God knows," Holly said, studiously avoiding his eye. He was quite right. It hadn't been easy to get the mirror off. By the time she finally managed it, she'd lost track of how many times she'd either glanced the hammer off it or missed altogether. Four o'clock in the morning. She'd set her alarm specially.

"This is going to take a day or two, you know. We'll have to get one in."

"Yeah," she said. "I guessed as much."

"So, do you want to leave it with us now or come back on Monday? You might as well come back, to be honest. It's just going to be sitting here until the part arrives. Mind you, if anybody asks, I didn't say that. If anybody asks, I told you that you can't go driving around with no driver's side mirror."

"Got it," Holly smiled. "Eh . . . listen. I don't suppose Dan's around, is he?"

"Dan? Yeah. He's up in his office. Will I give him a shout for you?"

This really was the end of the line. Her very last

chance to back out. "Yeah," she said. "If you wouldn't mind. I'm an old pal of his."

"Oh, right. I'll tell him you're here. What's the name?"

"Holly. Holly Christmas."

He gave her the look. *Are you joking or what?* "Really?"

"I know," she said. "If you have any jokes, feel free to let me have 'em. I've heard a good few at this stage, but you never know, you might have something original up your sleeve."

"I'll have a think about it while you're filling this in," he said and handed her his clipboard. "Jesus . . . Holly Christmas. You must be driven mad."

·"I really don't mind," she said as she scribbled. "I mean, you can't have a name like mine and not expect to get a few cracks thrown your way."

"I suppose not. It gets earlier every year, doesn't it, Christmas? Sure lookit, we have a few cards already."

He pointed behind him. There were indeed three Christmas cards on the shelf. All three had snowmen on them. This, Holly realised, was a serious test. It was the middle of October. The leaves were still falling. She gathered her strength together and said, "Oh well. It's nice to get the atmosphere going early."

"If you say so. Right, I'll get himself. Back in a minute."

He disappeared through a door behind him. Holly waited for a sense of panic to rise up inside her. None did. She was being bold. And it was going well. It was

335

good to have got some practice in on someone else first. A warm-up, as such. No more than thirty seconds after he'd left, the attendant returned. He held the door open behind him and out stepped Dan.

She beamed at him and extended her hand. He took it and gently squeezed.

"Holly," he said.

"Hi, Dan. It's been a while."

He nodded and smiled. "It sure has. So – car trouble?"

There was no sense of awkwardness in his voice; there was barely even any surprise. It was just as Holly had expected. The guy had always been essentially unembarrassable. The last time they'd spoken, he'd broken her heart. Yet, here he was, straight into the car talk.

"Yeah. I was just telling your colleague there, someone took my wing mirror off last night."

Dan nodded again. She could practically see the question forming on his lips. *And there were no other garages you could have gone to?* She sincerely hoped he wouldn't give it voice. Despite giving the matter a great deal of thought, she had failed to come up with a plausible answer.

"Will we take a look?" he said.

There was nothing to look at, of course. But Holly understood that he didn't want to talk to her in front of anyone else, just in case it all went weird. "Sure," she said and led the way outside. "Lovely day, isn't it?" she trilled as the door closed behind them.

"Uh, yeah, not bad."

"So. Your dad finally let you out from behind the front desk?"

"He retired, actually. I'm running the place now, if you can believe it."

This was news indeed. The business was Dan's father's. He had built it up from nothing and had always maintained that his son would take the reins from his cold, dead hands. It had been a major bone of contention, Holly recalled.

"Wow," she said. "Congratulations. He isn't ill or anything, is he?"

"No, nothing like that. He just woke up one day and decided he wanted out. Did a lot of talking about seeing the world, but he's hardly left the house, as far as I can see. About a year ago, this was."

"Well, good for you."

"Yeah. Cheers. I'm enjoying myself." They had reached the car now. Dan ran his fingers over the jagged wound where the mirror had been attached. "I'm surprised I didn't hear the screams from here," he said.

Holly played dumb even though she knew fine well what he meant. "What screams?"

"You. I'm sure you had a fit when you saw it."

"Nah, not really. I mean, I wasn't exactly pleased but sure what can you do? No point in getting upset about these things."

He turned to face her and tilted his head to one side. "Wow. Have you taken up meditation or something?"

Would it be overdoing things to fake ignorance again? She decided not. "Sorry? Meditation?"

"Or found religion? The Holly Christmas I knew would have gone absolutely apeshit at the sight of this."

"Oh. I see. No, no meditation. No religion either. I suppose I was a bit of a ranter and raver back then, wasn't I?"

"Well . . . "

"I don't mind if you agree, Dan. People are always reminding me of the way I used to be in the bad old days."

"They're the 'bad old days' now?"

"You know what I mean."

He rolled his head about on his shoulder, neither nodding nor shaking. "Still teaching?"

"Yeah, still at it."

"As much fun as ever?"

"It's great, yeah. Can't complain."

"Oh . . . I was joking."

"What? When?"

"When I said, 'As much fun as ever.' You used to give out shite about it all the time."

"Did I? I suppose I probably did. But I used to give out about a lot of things, people tell me."

"Holly, are you sure you haven't had a bang on the head or something?"

She fake-laughed, badly. "Ha! Ha! People are always tell–"

"There you go again. What's all this about 'people'

telling you stuff? You sound like you've lost your memory."

Oops – she had gone too far. It was time to apply the brakes. "Ha! Ha! My memory's fine, thanks. So, are you still living in Ranelagh?"

He took a moment to respond. "Yeah. Same old place. Better furniture now, that's about all."

"Aw, don't tell me you got rid of the orange sofa?"

"I did, yeah. Sorry. It served me well but I had to put it out of its misery. Poor old thing was falling apart. What about you? Still in Portobello?"

"Yup. And I still have the same old furniture too. No fancy promotions for me."

"And how's Aisling and, uh . . . "

"Orla. They're fine."

"Tell them I was asking for them, will you? Especially Aisling."

When they were a couple, Holly had let it slip – quite deliberately – that Aisling had a crush on him. It had been a running joke between them. One day, he was going to run off with her, and so on. It hadn't seemed quite as funny after they'd broken up and it didn't seem particularly funny now.

Holly swallowed the indignation that was creeping up in her and went with the first banality that occurred to her. "I will. They'll be delighted to hear that you're doing so well. How are Tommy and Olly and Nutter and the boys?"

"Same as ever. You know yourself."

"Yeah. Tell them I said hello."

"Even Nutter?" Dan asked.

"Of course."

"Seriously. I'm getting worried now. You *hated* Nutter."

This was true. Nutter was so-called by Dan's crowd because he was "a character" who was "liable to do anything". As soon as she'd laid eyes on him, Holly had pegged him as a cretinous boor who made up for his lack of genuine wit by shouting a lot and falling off things while drunk. He was the only one of Dan's friends who had ever slagged her off about her name. She had greatly enjoyed taking lumps out of him when he did.

"We didn't get on at first, maybe," she said.

"You didn't get on at all, ever," Dan corrected. "But I'll pass on your greeting."

They looked at each for a moment and then both looked away. Holly's mouth went dry. It was all going wrong. The plan had been to engage him in polite conversation, over the course of which he would slowly come to realise that she was a different person now. After they'd spent a while singing a few of the old songs, she would suggest that they go out for a drink some time, just to catch up properly. But she'd overdone it. Instead of letting him come to his own conclusions, she had dragged him there by the scruff of his neck. Now the conversation was running out of steam and all she'd managed to do, apparently, was mildly freak him out. She shifted her weight onto one hip and searched desperately for something useful to add. Then Dan said,

"So, what about your, uh . . . personal life? Anything wild happening there?"

Her mouth opened and closed. *Holy shit.* Why would he ask her that if he didn't have a follow-up in mind? "Not a thing. I'm profoundly single." She swallowed. "You?"

"Engaged, would you believe. Big day's in April next year."

"Congratulations to you both," someone said. A moment later Holly realised that it had been her. "That's great. That's really great. So great. Great."

"Yeah, cheers. Christ, there's an awful lot of organising to be done. You wouldn't believe it. Mind you, I get to stay out of most of it. Polly's the one under stress."

"*Polly?*"

"Yeah, that's her name. I know, it's weird. From Holly to Polly."

After a long moment, Holly said, "Wait, so this is the girl you dumped me for?"

He winced. "Uh . . . yeah. Yeah it is, actually."

For reasons that she couldn't immediately fathom, that made it a lot worse. *OK*, she told herself as her heart slammed against her ribcage. *Keep calm. All you can do now is back away as gracefully as possible.*

"Right. Okay. Right. Well, congratulations to you both."

"Yeah, you said that already."

Just like that, she snapped. There was no preamble,

no building up of pressure. One moment she was concentrating hard on her façade and the next she was on her toes and hissing at him. "Oh, excuse fucking me! I *do* apologise! How can you ever forgive me!"

Dan leaned back – in shock, Holly supposed, although the look on his face suggested that he might also be anticipating a punch. Then he folded his arms and stood a little taller, "I'm sorry, Holly. I shouldn't have –"

"Dumped me over the phone on fucking Valentine's Day?"

He stared at her for several seconds. "I was going to say that I shouldn't have brought up the subject of relationships. I thought we were swapping news. But yes, now you mention it, ending it on Valentine's Day was a shitty move and I apologise. I've thought about it a lot since and I am truly sorry. I was just so excited to have met someone who I knew, right away, was my future wife."

"The phone!" she repeated hotly. "Over the fucking phone!"

She could only imagine how bizarre her transformation must have seemed. But it was too late to row back now.

"Yeah," Dan said in a harsher tone. "Yeah, this is more like the Holly Christmas I remember. Shouting and swearing and going purple in the face. Is this why you came here? To have a go at me, what, nearly three years later?"

Holly huffed and puffed for a moment. She felt sick

and dizzy and wanted nothing more from life than to be somewhere else, anywhere else. "I'm going," she said. "I have to go."

"You could at least pretend to be happy for me," he said. "Despite everything. You could at least . . . " His eyes rolled closed, then snapped open. "Oh my God. I've just got it. Holly . . . Did you come here to try to get me back?"

"What? Don't be r–"

"You did, didn't you? Jesus. That's what all the amnesia shit was about. You came here letting on you'd changed so –"

"I have to go," she said again and pushed past him. He dropped his arms to his sides and stood motionless as she fumbled with her keys. She tried not to look out of the window as she started the car but she couldn't help herself. The expression on his face was one of sympathy. She took another glance back in the rear-view mirror as she sped away. Now he was shaking his head in disbelief.

When she made it back home, Holly could think of nothing better to do than climb into bed and pretend that she'd never been born. She drifted in and out of sleep for a few hours but the experience was the polar opposite of rest; the longer she lay there, the more taut and exhausted she felt. It didn't seem possible that the plan – she physically flinched to think of that word – could have gone any worse. It hadn't gone badly. It had been a complete catastrophe. There were earthquakes that had greater upsides. When she finally gave up on bed, she had a scalding shower and was not at all surprised to find that it didn't make her feel any less grubby. Downstairs she found the Cat of Many Colours asleep on the couch. There was no sign of Claude. This could mean only one thing; he had taken to letting his pal inside before going off about his business. The Cat of Many Colours woke up while Holly was standing there staring down at her. She looked up, yawned and slowly blinked. There was no doubt about it – she was feeling right at home now.

After making herself a cup of tea – she hadn't eaten so far today, and didn't anticipate doing so any time soon – Holly joined her new pet on the couch. She sat there motionless for quite a while. Shortly after four thirty, her mobile rang. It was her mother.

"What's wrong?" Holly said instead of hello. She had realised immediately that all was not well.

"What makes you think there's something wrong?" her mum asked.

"I can tell. You don't sound right. What is it? And where are you? I hear people."

"I'm in town. In the Gresham."

"The hotel?"

"Is there any other Gresham?"

"What are you doing there?"

There was a pause. "I came in to meet Charlie. Me and him . . ." Another pause. This one was longer. When she spoke again, Mrs Christmas seemed to have a frog in her throat. "It's all over with."

"What? Why? Who –"

"It was my idea. I just . . . "

Holly heard what sounded like muted sniffling. "Mum? Mum, are you there?"

"Yes. Sorry. Don't mind me, I'm a bit upset."

"Stay where you are. I'll come in."

"No, Holly, there's no need, I'm grand. And anyway I'm going up to the hospital to see Lillian. She was taken in overnight."

"Mum, I'm coming in." She expected further objections and when none were forthcoming, she knew that she had said the right thing. "Sit tight. I'll be as quick as I can."

"All right. Okay. I'm in the front bit, you can't miss me."

"I'm on my way."

Holly had one of those rare trips into town in which every light was green and every bus pulled in just as she was about to get stuck behind it. She parked in the Jervis Street car park and made her way up to the Gresham in a manner that was more jog than walk. As she had promised, Mrs Christmas was sitting in an unmissable spot in the lobby. There was a tea setting for one on the low table in front of her. Holly guessed that she'd been there for so long that a member of staff had long since removed all traces of her former companion.

"Hi, Mum," she said and planted a kiss.

"Thanks for coming in, love. There was no need, I'm fine."

Holly took a seat. "No, you're not. Look at the cut of you." She was trying to lighten the tone and was pleased to see her mother make an attempt at a smile. Nevertheless, she had half-meant it. Mrs Christmas had the washed-out and slightly crumpled look of a woman who had recently shed tears. Holly pictured her hiding herself away in a toilet stall, trying to cry quietly, and felt weak with pity.

"Thanks. I knew I could rely on you to say the right thing."

"So, tell me. What happened?"

Her mum folded her hands on her lap and then suddenly raised one.

A passing waitress stopped and smiled. "Madam. What can I get you? More tea?"

"Just water for me, I'm all tea'd out. Fizzy water. I mean, oh, eh . . . "

"Sparkling water for yourself," the waitress said. "And . . . ?"

"Coffee for me, please," Holly said.

The waitress nodded and left.

"Go on, Mum. What happened?"

She folded her hands again and breathed deeply for a moment. "I don't know, I just didn't . . . I didn't . . . like him."

If her own emotional state had been less bleak, Holly was sure that she would have laughed out loud. She had expected to spend quite a bit of time painting her mother into a corner where she would have no choice but to give a straight answer.

"Well, that's pretty clear," she said. "If you didn't like him, then that's that."

"Hm."

"What did you say? I presume you didn't say, 'I don't like you'. . . Did you?"

Mrs Christmas shook her head sadly. "I hadn't a clue what to tell him. I think he knew something was up when I asked him to come in and meet me. Because that was a first. It was always him that did the organising."

"Yeah."

"So he showed up anyway, sat right where you're sitting and we had a bit of a chat for a while, about nothing, really. He knew something was up. I know he did. I could see it in him. Then he flat-out asked me. I didn't know how else to say it, so I just told him the truth. Told him I wasn't happy being . . . with him. That I felt better in myself when I was on my own."

"And how did he take it?"

"Not well."

"Oh."

"He didn't get angry or anything but he was badly, I don't know . . . disappointed. He turned into a wee boy, all huffy and puffy. He hung around for ages too. I thought maybe he'd get up and leave straight away, but no."

"So how did you part?"

"With a handshake. All very formal."

She'd been doing well up until this point, Holly thought, but now her eyes moistened. "Come on, Mum. Don't upset yourself."

Mrs Christmas reached for a well-used hankie that she'd stuffed away down the side of her chair and dabbed at her eyes. Then she suddenly dropped it and looked up. "Nothing happened. I want you to know that. Nothing . . . sexy."

"Okay, Mum. Okay."

"That's something. At least that's something. Isn't it? I mean, things could be worse, couldn't they?"

Holly couldn't help but glance around. No one had noticed the tears yet but it seemed inevitable that they soon would.

"Please, Mum –"

"Remember that conversation we had when I said I was worried about breaking my record or however it was that I put it?"

"Yes."

"And you had an example, giving up cigarettes and then having just the one?"

"I remember."

"Well, that's exactly it, that's exactly the way I feel. Just the very thing I was most worried about – that's what's come to pass."

"Oh, Mum . . ."

"I feel like I've been unfaithful."

"You haven't, of course you haven't. You can't –"

"To his memory, Holly. To his *memory*. I've ruined

348

something and I can never un-ruin it. Oh God, I feel like I'm going to faint or something."

"Did –"

"I think it's worse because there was nothing to it. Maybe if it had been some grand love affair I wouldn't feel as bad. But to mess everything up for a few nights out with *Charlie* . . ."

On her way into town, Holly had concluded that her mother's return to single status was undoubtedly a good thing. She'd be a little bit upset, obviously, but facts had to be faced; Charlie had dickish tendencies and would have been no good for her in the long run. Two unpleasant notions struck her now. The first was that she had underestimated how much damage her mum had sustained. The second was even more disturbing: this whole mess was her fault. She had been given multiple chances to stop the relationship before it even started and then, once it had, to put a dampener on it. But she'd taken none of them. Her mother's heart had never been in it, clearly. If she'd said the right thing at the right time, she could have saved her all this grief. As these thoughts whirled in her head, her breathing became increasingly erratic. And then she realised that she too was starting to cry. Just as she picked up her handbag in the hope of finding a hankie of her own, their waitress returned with their drinks. She did a very good job of pretending not to notice anything out of the ordinary and was gone before either of them could even scrape together a thank-you.

"What's wrong?" Mrs Christmas croaked. "What are you getting upset about?"

"It's all down to me," Holly croaked back. "You would never have got into this if I hadn't pushed you."

"Don't say that."

"No, it's the truth. I know it is. You even rang me a couple of times to point out that you and him were still together, like it was for my benefit. I knew that was weird, I *knew* it. You were only doing it for me . . ."

"I wasn't doing it *for* you."

This was a less than full-throated denial of her central point, Holly thought. She covered her eyes with the ragged tissue she had found in her bag, like a child trying to blot out a difficult reality. "*Because* of me, then. You wouldn't have gone ahead with it if I hadn't stuck my nose in."

"You didn't stick your nose anywhere, Holly. I asked you for your advice."

"I thought I was doing the right thing. I thought you were lonely."

"I was lonely. I *am* lonely. Sometimes. Sure I told you that myself."

Mrs Christmas had regained her composure now. Holly got her own tears under control and sniffed herself back to relative normality.

"I'm sorry," she said. "I'm sorry I encouraged you. Especially considering . . ." She trailed off, having realised that she'd started out on an undesirable path. But her mother guessed where she'd been going.

"You never really liked him, did you?" she asked.

"I wouldn't say that, I –"

"Holly."

"Well. I had my doubts about him."

"Hm. That's not what you said when I asked, is it?"

"I'll make it up to you," Holly said. "I promise. We'll . . . we'll go to the Christmas Convention of Christmases."

"Oh, come on. You're not thinking straight."

"I mean it. Just say the word. I know you wanted to go."

"We'll talk about it some other time when you're feeling more like yourself."

Holly reached for her coffee and took a sip. How could the day get any worse, she wondered? A nice roof collapse, maybe? An outbreak of Ebola?

"I mean it," she repeated. "I'll do it." Her frown deepened. She'd sounded like a bank robber holding a gun to a cashier's head. It was not the tone she was after.

"I believe you."

Holly felt sure that there must be something else she could say, something comforting, something reassuring. But she drew a blank. She reached for her coffee again and her mother took a little water. A painful silence ensued. Then Mrs Christmas put down her glass.

"I'm sorry, Holly," she said, "but I really have to go."

"Oh. But I've only just . . . Oh. Okay."

"Lillian. I did say as much on the phone. Visiting starts at six. I want to get in and out quickly in case that nephew of hers shows up."

"How is she?"

"I don't think she's in danger or anything. Lung trouble, the ambulance guy said. Might be pneumonia."

Holly shook her head. "Come on then, I'll drive you. What hospital?"

"St James's. But it's all right, I'll get a taxi outside."

"No, I'll –"

"It's okay, really. I'd rather, y'know . . . be on my own for a bit."

Holly had been halfway out of her seat. She sat down again – heavily. "You don't want me around. You're mad at me. Of course you are. I understand."

Mrs Christmas sighed as she got to her feet. "I'm not mad at you. I'm mad at me. But next time, please tell me the truth when I ask your opinion. What am I saying – there's not going to be a next time."

"Okay."

They looked at each other. Then Mrs Christmas opened her bag. "Here, I nearly forgot to leave money."

"Don't worry about it," Holly said. "I'll get it." She expected an argument. But there was none.

"All right then," her mother said. "I'll see you soon."

"Tell Lillian I was asking for her."

"I will, yes. Bye now."

She took off. Holly sank a little lower into her seat. Just then, their waitress happened by again. Holly caught her eye.

"Excuse me."

"Yes. What I get you?"

352

"I'll have a white wine, please."

"Certainly. Dry or –"

"Anything. Anything at all."

Three quarters of an hour later, as she ordered her third glass of wine, Holly was still telling herself that she could be fully sober before the car park closed for the night. All she had to do was take a long walk or go to the cinema or something. It was nonsense, of course – the feeble rationalisation of the casual drunk driver, a species that she had spent several hours of her life complaining about. She knew as much even as she formed the thought. It wasn't until a little while later, when she was paying the bill, that she finally accepted that she wouldn't be driving anywhere tonight. The waitress had been a model of discretion, given that she had borne witness to simultaneous crying jags sandwiched between tea and wine binges. Her smile had never faltered and her eyes had never rolled. It wasn't her fault that Holly felt embarrassed to the point where she felt that she had to leave. The least she could do, she thought, was bequeath a substantial tip.

Outside on O'Connell Street, she drifted south towards the river with no real destination in mind, just a vague ambition to walk along the quays. She was doing so when it occurred to her that she hadn't been in the Morrison Hotel for quite a while. It had been one of their regular haunts for a period, largely because Aisling had fancied someone who practically lived in its bar. Why not call in, she asked herself? Not for anything in particular – just to see if the place had changed. She was halfway through her second glass of wine before she allowed herself to admit that obtaining same had been her sole motivation for the visit. It was still early and there weren't many other customers. One of the few was a slim and fit-looking middle-aged man. He sported cool rimless glasses and a chunky, militaristic watch. His hair was silver and closely cropped. His clothes were casual but obviously expensive. His tan was deep and apparently natural. He was certainly attractive, she thought, but there was something oddly reptilian about him. Or maybe the word was "predatory". On the third occasion when she caught him looking in her direction, she had a strong premonition that he was about to come over or – ugh – send her a drink. She downed her wine and legged it.

Out on the quays again, she crossed the bridge into Temple Bar and this time she didn't bother kidding herself. She went into the first pub she passed and, on a whim, took a barstool right by the taps (it seemed appropriate somehow – miserable drunks didn't bother with the comfy chairs, did they?). This place was busier than the Morrison but not by much. If it hadn't been for the tourists who didn't know any better, it too would have been almost empty. The barman was a slightly tubby guy in his early twenties. He grunted at her when she asked for a white wine and then, having delivered it, retreated to his base at the other end of the bar where he re-buried himself in a tabloid. Sitting on a bar stool, it turned out, was both uncomfortable and boring; there was nothing to look at. Holly finished her drink quickly and caught the barman's attention again. Her plan was to relocate to a proper seat from which she could at least observe the tourists.

The barman finished the paragraph he was reading before he dragged himself in her direction. When he was still some distance away he told her to cheer up because it might never happen.

Just like that, she burst into tears. The barman recoiled and then seemed to physically shrink. She wanted to tell him that, ordinarily, she wasn't one of life's criers and that he had caught her on a particularly bad day. In addition, she wanted to tell him to mind his own damn business or at least be more careful about the way he spoke to people. Neither sentiment made it past her sobs. And then, just to add to the strangeness of the moment, her phone started to dance around on the bar. She grabbed it and her bag, slipped off her stool and ran outside, breathing in great gulps as she went.

There was a text message from Orla: **He u change ur mind about dinner**, it read, **we be in white knight for drinks first @ 745.** She checked the time. It was half past seven. Orla had probably texted from a taxi. That seemed to suggest that this was a courtesy rather than a serious attempt to get her to come along. Nevertheless, she was surprised to find that she wanted to go, for drinks if not for dinner. The novelty of boozing alone had worn off fast. And besides, she had things she wanted to say. She took a moment to get herself together and set off for Wicklow Street.

Temple Bar was getting busier now and the volume of human traffic coupled with her substantial level of inebriation made her feel quite dizzy. It would be a good idea, she decided, to finally get something to eat. The thought of fast food made her feel even more queasy, so she settled for a Londis ham sandwich with a bag of cheese'n'onion as a sort of half-assed dessert. As she crossed Dame Street, she suddenly saw herself as everyone around her surely did – a drunken woman stumbling along shovelling crisps into her gob. She had thought that her self-image couldn't possibly deteriorate, but here was proof that it could. It seemed to take an age to reach White Knight. As she trudged along, she was reminded of those dreams where no matter how quickly you run, you never get anywhere. When she finally arrived, she was briefly alarmed to see that the bouncer on duty was a very serious-looking individual. She made a point of avoiding his eye and concentrated hard on her gait as she passed him.

This was Holly's first visit to White Knight; it had only been open for a matter of months. As soon as she stepped inside, she knew that it had been Aisling's choice. The décor was coolly minimalistic, the clientele young and fashionable. If she hadn't been quite as drunk, she supposed that she would have felt decrepit and dowdy. She saw the others almost immediately. They had a horseshoe-shaped sofa to themselves on a sort of dais on the far side of the room and seemed to be having a grand old time. She started off towards them and then realised, to her shock and shame, that she wanted the fortification of yet another drink first. The bar was busy and it took her a couple of minutes to get her hands on a fresh glass of wine. After she'd downed about half of it, she headed off towards the dais, keeping a careful lookout for treacherous steps. Orla spotted her as she crossed the floor and waved with wild enthusiasm. Holly pretended not to see her; she wasn't sure why. All eyes were on her when she arrived. She gave a general wave of hello and took a seat.

"You made it after all," Orla said. "Great."

Holly nodded.

"Are you coming for dinner too?" Aisling asked. "Because we should ring ahead and get another place set."

Holly shook her head.

"Are you all right?" James asked. "You look a bit . . . Are you all right?"

She nodded. Then she shook her head. Then she drew a breath. "I . . . "

The others leaned in a bit.

"I'm doomed to die alone surrounded by cats."

No one said anything for a moment.

Then Orla asked, "Are you drunk?"

"Oh yes," Holly said. "Yes, indeed. Yup."

"What happened?" Aisling said.

"I started drinking and then I kept on drinking and the next thing I knew, I was drunk."

"I mean –"

"I know what you meant. See? That was me being funny. I do that sort of thing a lot. But people don't seem to like it. So I'm all on my own-io. And I've got a new cat. You can see where this is going." She made a dismissive gesture that cost her some of her wine. "Oops."

Aisling tried again. "Start at the start. Did something happen *today*?"

"Ah, today," Holly said. "Good old today. Well, I kicked it off nice and early. Four o'clock in the morning. I took a hammer to the wing mirror on the car, just so I'd have an excuse to go and see Dan."

"*Dan?*" Aisling and Orla screeched together.

"Who's Dan?" John asked. Everyone looked at him. He seemed surprised by his contribution himself.

"Dan is her ex," Orla told him. "From a few years ago."

"That's him," Holly said, mock-cheerfully. "He dumped me because I wasn't uppy-beaty enough. Too sharp, too blunt, too sarcastic, all that. You know, the usual."

"What have wing mirrors got to do with it?" James asked.

"Dan works in a garage," Aisling explained.

"No, no, no," Holly said. "Dan *runs* a garage now. He's moving up in the world. And guess what? He's getting married. Isn't that super-duper?"

There was a moment of silence in which Aisling and Orla exchanged a long look.

358

"I don't get it," Aisling said then. "I don't get why you would want to see him."

Holly took a swig of wine. "Why, to win him back, of course! Yeah, I know – a brilliant, brilliant plan. Yay for me."

All four of them stared at their laps.

"Wait, it gets better," she continued. "After that I went into town to meet my mother. Turns out I've cocked up her life too. James. Oi. James. I said, I've cocked up her life too. Followed your advice to a tee. Held back. Let on I was all in favour of her going out with your man. Now it's all over and she thinks she's ruined my father's memory. So cheers!"

"Hang on," Aisling said. "What's all this about? Why are you having a go at him?"

Holly ignored the question and kept her gaze on James. "Fucking advice. Fucking people sticking their noses in. You told me to hold my tongue around Charlie. And my neighbours told me to hold my tongue around you, if I wanted to stand any chance with you. Look how well it all worked out! Eleanor Duffy was another one. She said you liked me. She was dead sure of it. Ha!"

Aisling's jaw hung open. She looked at James, who furrowed his brow at her, and then back to Holly. "What the fuck, Holly? Stand a chance with him? What are you talking about?"

"Don't get all excited," Holly said. "He never even noticed I liked him, let alone anything else. I tried it on Dan too, by the way. Being all jolly and chirpy or whatever the fuck it is that men like. Tried *really* hard. Oh, and wait'll you hear this – I even made sure I wasn't wearing anything black because you know how that gets on everybody's nerves. Pathetic, isn't it? Still, I'm back in uniform now, as you can see." She finished her wine with a flourish. "I'm going to the bar. Would anyone like another drinkie?"

"Just sit there," Aisling snapped. "What are you saying here? You've had a thing for James all along, is that it?"

"I don't know," Holly slurred. "Probably not, actually. Doesn't make any difference now, does it?" Four pairs of eyes stared at her. "All right, then," she said as she rose unsteadily to her feet. "To the bar!" The room spun. She sat down again. "Maybe someone would like to go for me? John? Would you be a gent?"

He sat forward a little as if he meant to get up, then froze. Orla put her hand on his arm as if to make sure he stayed that way.

"I think you've had enough," she said to Holly.

"But I'm getting so good at it," Holly moaned. "Practice makes perfect. Yes, it does. By the way, has anybody got an old moggy they're trying to get rid of because I'm taking them in, apparently. Which is handy. I don't have to go looking for cats to complete my image, oh no. *They* come looking for *me*. Works out great."

No one said a word or moved a muscle for a few seconds. And then James stood up. He looked exceedingly angry.

"Come on," he barked at Holly. "You're coming with me."

Before she had time to react, he had come round to her side of the table and taken her by the arm. Next thing she knew she was on her feet and moving. She was halfway across the floor before she realised that she wasn't doing so voluntarily.

"What the fuck?" she squeaked. "My bag!"

"I've got your bag."

"Let go of me. I'm staying."

"Wrong. You're leaving."

"Let go!"

"No."

"Help! Kidnap! I'm being kidnap! Kidnapped!"

"Shut up."

They were at the door now. He pushed her through it and followed right behind. She turned to face him, teeth bared. He took her by the wrist and dragged off to the side, out of the bouncer's earshot. Then he folded his arms and stared at her. She stared back.

"Bastard," she hissed, snatching her bag from him.

"Holly," he said steadily. "It's kick-in-the-hole time."

"What?"

"You. It seems you need a good kick in the hole. And I'm going to give it to you."

"Excuse me –"

"Shut up. You made a complete fool of yourself in there. And you didn't just embarrass yourself, you embarrassed the rest of us too. What the hell's the matter with you? What were you babbling about – dying alone with a cat? *What?*"

"Cats," she corrected. "Dying alone with cats. Surrounded by them. All miserable and angry. It's going to happen, I know it is."

"This is about you not having a boyfriend, is that it?"

She threw her arms in the air. "Yes, *genius*, this is about me not having a boyfriend."

"And you think you're going to get one by pretending not to be so grumpy and sarcastic all the time? Did I pick that up right?"

"I don't know what I think, okay? I'm fucking confused!" Her head drooped.

"And I was a candidate?" James continued. "You thought maybe . . . you and me . . ."

She shrugged. "Maybe."

"Wait, let me get this straight. All those times you and I were together, that was you doing your best to be positive and easy-going?"

"Yeah."

"Wow . . ."

"Shut up. It was hard."

"Let me clear this up for you, Holly. There's no way on Earth it would ever have worked out between you and me. You know why? Because you're so bloody grumpy and sarcastic all the time."

She looked up in horror, certain at first that she had misheard him. "What –"

"Not my type. No way. You're not my type at all."

"Are you try–"

"And the idea that maybe it would have worked out

362

if you'd tried being different? Come on. Do you really need me to point out what a colossal load of crap that is? What, every single minute we were together, you were going to be putting on a show? Biting your tongue every time someone got on your nerves or said something stupid? Pretending to like things you hated?"

She swayed back and forth. "I never said I thought it was a good idea."

"But you gave it a go. And then again with this Dan fella?"

"I was *desperate*, all right? I know you're supposed to 'be yourself', all right, I know that, I knew it all along, I'm not *stupid*. But it's bloody hard when, year after year, it doesn't fucking work."

"Well, guess what? It might be another few years before it works. It might be ten. It might be twenty."

"Jesus Christ. You're a great help, you are. Thanks. Thanks a million."

"Shut up."

"I –"

"Shut up. Or it might work next weekend. You never know. But it'll work eventually. You know why? Because the thing that makes you a tough sell to most people is the very thing that someone out there will go nuts over. Take my word for it."

"Hmph. That's very nice and all but you don't know that for sure. There's no way –"

"Holly, I said you're not for me, girlfriend-wise. But I like you. I've always liked you. Eleanor was half-right, at least. I like the dark sense of humour and the pushiness and all the rest of it. I don't want to go out with it, but I like it in a friend. The only trait I've ever seen you display that I didn't like is the one you're displaying tonight. And that's self-pity. Are you listening to yourself? You're *drowning* in it. Drop it. Drop it right now, or I swear to God, every man you meet will run a mile."

They looked at each other for a long time. As the staring match continued, Holly felt herself beginning to cool. Her stance softened. Her jaw unclenched. Her breathing slowed. And finally she drew her eyes away.

"All right, granted, all right, maybe I am feeling a wee bit sorry for myself."

"Yes. You are."

"And maybe I've been doing too much thinking lately".

"Sounds like it."

"Over-alan – over-alan – over-anan-alysing. Or whatever."

"Yes. Clearly."

She started a new staring match with the ground. It went on for even longer than its predecessor. James was apparently content to let it run.

"I want to clear something up," she said after a while. "I'm not sure I ever really fancied you. I might just have been intrigued because you're like reverse-world me. Okay?"

"Understood."

"We're clear on that?"

364

"Perfectly."

"So there's no need for any awkwardness or anything."

"Got it."

"I'm happy for you and Aisling. All things considered."

"Grand. Anything else?"

She thought it over. "Uh . . . no."

"Right. Come on. I'm putting you in a taxi."

"I'll be all right on my own."

"I'm not taking any chances. There are pubs along the way."

"Huh. I'm never drinking again, believe me."

They started walking down towards College Green; neither of them said anything along the way. Holly was already beginning to feel a deep sense of mortification. She could only imagine how bad it would be in the morning. It was some consolation, she supposed, that the queue at the taxi rank was short. Despite her protestations, James stayed with her as she shuffled forward in it. When she made it to the front, he waited until a car pulled up before giving his parting shot.

"Your mother will be fine," he said. "Mark my words."

She opened the taxi door "So, we're all right now, are we, me and you? I mean, we're, what . . . friends?"

He shrugged. And then his half-smile returned. "I don't see why not."

She paused, halfway in and halfway out of the car. Then she nodded and got in.

Holly's taxi driver was an alarmingly old-looking man. He could see that she was the worse for wear in more than one sense and made polite enquiries about her state of mind. When she assured him that she was fine, he dropped the subject and embarked on a long summation of his recent holiday in Italy. Even if she'd wanted to pay attention – which she didn't – Holly doubted that she would have been able to. Chief among the many emotions coursing through her was shame, obviously, but she was surprised to find that there was something else in there. It felt like the bass line from a song – not the first thing you might notice but persistent and conspicuous once you did. That emotion was relief. She was concentrating so hard on trying to get her thoughts straight that the journey went by in a flash. The first time she looked out the window to check where they were, she saw that they were passing her local shop. All at once, she was overcome by a craving for chip butties. It was the drink talking, she knew, but she rationalised it by telling herself that tomorrow's hangover would undoubtedly be worse if she went to bed having eaten nothing all day but a sandwich and a bag of crisps. She asked the driver to pull in and paid him what she owed.

The shop was shockingly busy. Holly supposed at first that her fellow customers were all in the same boat as she was, drunk and desperate for munchies on the way home. Then she remembered that it was not yet nine o'clock. She stood up a little straighter and made a note not to breathe into anybody's face. It said a great deal, she supposed, that the preparation of oven-ready chips felt like too much of a challenge. She plumped instead for the microwavable variety and felt pleased with herself for not adding microwavable sausages to the mix. There were seven or eight people in the queue in front of her and each of them, it seemed, was trying to pay with a third-party cheque. By the time Holly made it to the counter, her embarrassment over the poverty of her culinary choice had been swept away by her growing hunger. She nodded her head defiantly when the assistant asked if that was all she was buying and strode away holding the little cardboard box in what she liked to think was a casual, devil-may-care sort of fashion. When she stepped out onto the street, the fresh air seemed a little fresher than it had previously. She paused for a moment and waited for her head to stop spinning. *Never again*, she reminded herself. *Absolutely never again.*

And then she caught something out of the corner of her eye. She snapped her head to the right. The shop window was festooned with flyers advertising this and that – yoga classes, English lessons, decorating services. Right in the middle was one labelled MISSING CAT. The pictured animal was the Cat of Many Colours. She was wearing a collar in the photo, granted, and she looked a good deal sturdier, but it was her all right. There was no doubt about it. Holly stepped closer and foraged for details. She was "a much-loved pet", apparently, who hadn't been seen for several weeks. Her real name was Combo. Someone called Sam was offering a reward for her return. There was a phone number and an address. *Combo* . . . Holly liked that. She wished she'd thought of it herself. Sam hadn't gone far to post the flyer; he or she lived in the street that ran down the side of the shop. Holly gave it some thought. On the one hand, this Sam person was probably frantic. On the other hand, they'd already been frantic for several weeks. One more night wasn't going to kill them. Then there were the chip butties to consider. She paused, biting her lip. Chip butties didn't seem like a good enough reason to go straight home. She *was* drunk, of course. No one liked having a drunk showing up on their doorstep on a Saturday night, even if they did bring good news. And besides, it might be nice to have Combo's company for a night knowing that it wouldn't be permanent. She could sit on the sofa and give her a little tickle, safe in the knowledge that she was no longer a harbinger of doom. Yeah. Tomorrow would do fine. She headed for home.

Epilogue

Simon Christmas tapped the microphone and then bellowed into it. "ONE-TWO, oops, sorry. One-two? Hello? Yes? Hello? You can all hear me all right, can you?"

The crowd, as they had frequently been reminded, was forty-four strong. Forty-three of them yelled back that they could hear him loud and clear.

"Good then!" Simon declared. He adjusted his paper hat with his free hand and somehow managed to make it look even more ridiculous. "Well. Where do I begin? I have to hold my hand up and say that in all honesty, no word of a lie, may God strike me down, hand on heart, this has been one of the best days of my life."

His voice had cracked towards the end of this statement. There was a small smattering of applause.

"Oh God," Holly said. "He's going to cry. Sweet Jesus, no." She tried to pull her paper hat down over her eyes but stopped when it started to split. There was no point in destroying the thing. Earlier in the evening, she had "accidentally" ruined three others. Replacements had been found and planted on her head within seconds. Apparently there was an inexhaustible supply. Resistance was futile. Her mother was sitting on her right.

"Shhh," she said. "I want to hear this."

"It's hard to know which bit I enjoyed the best," Simon continued. "Meeting you all for the first time was a great joy, of course, and one that I know I will never forget. But even better than that – and I know, I know, it's only been a few hours – even better than that was getting to know you. I already feel like I've made some friends for life."

"Huh," Holly said. "He spent most of his time on *me*." She was exaggerating but not by much. Simon's delight at meeting someone with what he called a "doubly festive" name had been something to behold. There had been moments when she had feared for his health.

"Quiet, *please*," her mother begged.

"To meet Christmases from all over the world has been every bit as special as I always hoped it would be," Simon said. He adjusted his hat again. It was bright yellow. Holly's was pink. "Canada, Australia, America, Wales. We have representatives, as the old proverb goes, from every corner of the world."

"That's not a proverb," Holly hissed through her teeth.

"We even have a last-minute South African!"

A small cheer went up from those who were seated with the man in question. He got to his feet and raised his glass. "Thenks!" he cried. "Thenk you for the welcome!"

"South Africa!" Simon marvelled. "Imagine! The jewel of the . . . the jewel of the . . . South Africa!"

Holly tried to position her hands so that they would cover both her eyes and her ears. Mrs Christmas slapped them down again.

"And, of course, how could I forget, I hope you've all met my new best friend among you. Where are you, dear? There she is! Stand up, would you, please? Ladies and gentlemen – how special is this? Holly! Christmas! That's right, you heard me – Holly! *Holly!*"

There was more applause, this time accompanied by cheers and a few whistles.

Holly's mum elbowed her in the ribs. "Get up. Please. Don't just sit there. It won't kill you. Please. Give them a wave."

"Fuck me," Holly said and got to her feet. She waved to both sides of the room and dropped into her seat again.

"If I ever have a daughter . . ." Simon said. He was becoming emotional again.

Holly dared to hope that he would be unable to continue, but no, he soon recovered. "All right then. I don't want to go on for too long because I don't know about you, but I smell turkey and the sooner I sit down, the sooner we can all get tucked in. Am I right? And

371

besides, this isn't my proper speech – that comes at the end of the night. This is just a warm-up."

Holly experienced a brief strangling sensation. "Gaggghhh," she said.

"I just want to remind you all that you don't have to go easy on the crackers, you can pull away. More will be put out after every course. Oh yes, I've thought of everything. I also want to let you know that we're going to go round the tables after dessert to give everybody a chance to relate their favourite Christmas anecdote, so get thinking. It can be anything – the time you received that one special gift as a child, a lovely story about a Christmas reunion, anything at all. So long as it features our favourite time of the year, that's good enough. All right then. Without further ado, let's bring on the soup! I don't want to ruin the surprise but if you're a fan of vegetable, your luck's in!"

He switched off the microphone and dropped it to the table. Then he raised his arms above his head in a V as if he'd just scored in the cup final. There was yet more applause.

"An anecdote?" Holly gasped. "A fucking anecdote? Someone kill me now. Please. Make it quick."

"You'll be fine," said the man to her left.

Holly dabbed at her brow. "I knew it would be bad. I mean, I *knew* it would be bad. But this . . . this is . . ." Words failed her.

"Well, I'm having fun anyway. And I can't wait to hear your anecdote. I'm sure it'll be . . . jolly. I might record it on my phone. You know, so I can enjoy it again and again and again and again." He dissolved into laughter.

"Arsehole." She turned to face him.

He laughed all the harder.

Despite herself, she smiled. "Thanks for coming," she said. "I mean it."

"Wouldn't have missed it for the world. This is epic entertainment. Epic."

"I'd be even worse if you weren't here."

"I can only imagine."

She leaned across and kissed him. "I'm being serious. Thank you."

"You're welcome," said Sam.

The End

If you enjoyed *Little Black Everything*
try *The Bright Side* also published by Poolbeg

Here's a sneak preview of Chapter One

The
Bright
Side

ALEX COLEMAN

POOLBEG

Chapter 1

It was a Friday the 13th, the day I caught Gerry having sex with our next-door neighbour. Not that I ever thought the two things were connected. I'd always hated all that superstitious malarkey. A broken mirror didn't mean seven years bad luck in my book – it meant a trip to the mirror shop. Still, there was no denying that I'd been having a really brutal 13th, even before I caught the pair of them puffing and panting over the back of my good sofa like a couple of knackered greyhounds. I slept in, for a start, and that always got on my nerves (no matter how often it happened). Skipping breakfast didn't bother me so much, but I really resented having to rush my shower. A rushed shower, in my opinion, was worse than none at all. You got all the hassle of getting wet but none of the benefits. It wasn't much different to getting caught in the rain. And this was a real in-and-out job: the first drops of water had barely hit the floor before I was back in the bedroom, swearing under my breath and rooting through my underwear drawer. Gerry was gently snuffling in his sleep, as usual (he was very rarely out of bed before me, even when I wasn't up on time). When we first got married, I found his snuffling seriously cute. He used to say that I'd soon change my tune about that one. But he was wrong. It always stayed cute to me, even after twenty-one years.

My day didn't improve a whole pile when I finally made it across to First Premier in Santry. When I'd started working there, about three years previously, I'd foolishly pointed out to my manager, Jenny, that "first" and "premier" meant the same thing. She'd fixed me with one of her non-smile smiles and said, "Do you really think we don't know that here at First Premier?" I discovered later that Jenny elbowed the phrase "here at First Premier" into approximately fifty per cent of her conversations. My job title was "Data Entry Operative". I liked the "Operative" part. It made me sound like a glamorous spy. It was the "Data Entry" bit I had trouble with, both as a title and, sadly, as an everyday activity. That morning, as I came through the door of our humongous open-plan office, afraid to look at my watch but knowing it was getting on for ten, I just knew that Jenny was lying in wait for me like a badly permed leopard. Sure enough, I wasn't even halfway to my desk – my workstation, rather – before she pounced.

Good afternoon, I thought.

"Good afternoon," said Jenny. This was her standard greeting for latecomers. It was so obvious and childish and unfunny that it always made me want to cry, even when it wasn't being directed at me.

"Hello, Jenny," I said, trying my best to smile. "I'm a bit late."

She gazed back at me with the cold, unblinking eyes of a doll. "I hope everything's all right at home," she cooed then, doing a sympathetic head-tilt.

I resumed walking. Jenny followed half a pace behind, like one of those small, annoying dogs that goes *Yip* instead of *Woof*.

"Everything's fine at home," I said. "Alarm clock let me down, that's all. Dead battery or something."

"Hmmm," Jenny said.

There was something about the way she said it, some vague hint of menace, that made me stop and turn to face her.

"It won't happen again," I lied.

Jenny frowned. "The thing is, Jackie, you've said that before."

She had a point there. I'd said it many, many times before, some of them, if memory served, in the past couple of days. There didn't seem to be any point in adding that being late annoyed me as much as it did her and that I dearly wished it wouldn't happen so often. I decided instead to try the light-hearted approach. Nothing in my experience of Jenny told me she would appreciate the effort, but I gave it a whirl anyway.

"I know I've said that before," I told her with what I hoped was a loveable grin, "but this time, I really, really mean it." I held up my right hand with fingers crossed and when Jenny failed to respond, I held the left up too.

Her brow creased and uncreased. "You're aware, no doubt, of the new tardiness policy we've implemented here at First Premier?"

I half-remembered seeing an e-mail with some of those words in it. It had caused a bit of a fuss about a week or two previously. I hadn't read the thing properly and hadn't participated in the fuss. "Of course."

"Well then, you'll know all about the points system."

I drew a blank at that one. "Points system. Sure."

"Well, Jackie, I'm afraid that today's nine-fifty-seven coupled with Wednesday's nine-oh-eight, Tuesday's nine-twelve and last Thursday's nine-twenty-one puts you over the top for this month *already*. And it's only –"

"The 13th," I sighed. "It's Friday the 13th."

"Unlucky for some," Jenny said with what looked, for a change, like a genuine smile. "So you'll do it?"

I hadn't a clue what "it" was, but I knew I'd find the answer in the e-mail. "Looks like I'll have to, doesn't it?" I said.

Jenny nodded. "It's policy."

I turned and left her, hoping to God that I was merely imagining the bright bolts of pain that had started to flash along the right side of my head.

I started getting "my headaches" – I always called

them that as they seemed very personal – when the kids were entering their teens. We used to joke, on the days when I felt like joking about it, that it must have had something to do with all the stereos in the house suddenly getting cranked up. But really, I had no idea what the cause might be. I didn't get them very often – four, maybe five times a year. That was plenty. Nothing seemed to provoke them – nothing that I could identify anyway. They always started the same way, with brief, shooting pains that were gone before I could even wince. Some time after that – it could be minutes, it could be hours – the party really got going; the pains returned, and this time they stayed. There were lots of suitable analogies; I usually plumped for something with white-hot six-inch nails.

As soon as I got settled in at my desk, Veronica, who sat directly opposite me, peeped over the partition and gave me an update on her battle with the kids who gathered on her front wall every night to smoke cigarettes. There had been an escalation, by all accounts. One of the kids, a girl of no more than twelve, had called Veronica a "frigid old bitch" (it was the "old" part that really hurt, apparently). Veronica had responded with something about children who dressed like little prostitutes and feared she had gone too far.

I tried to seem interested, but my mind kept wandering back to Jenny. It occurred to me that she'd had my tardiness details on the tip of her tongue. That meant that she'd looked them up in some sort of file, no doubt hoping that I'd be late, as opposed to absent, so she'd able to throw them at me. She'd even *memorised* them. I grabbed the edges of my desk and tried to think pleasant thoughts. Cute little puppies, gently babbling brooks, the last five minutes of *An Officer and a Gentleman* . . . I was still gripping hard and muttering darkly to myself when Eddie Hand appeared by my side.

Eddie sat at the end of our little section, facing Veronica and me. He was a forty-something bachelor who wore the same navy-blue woollen tie quite literally every day, even though he could have showed up in an Iron Maiden T-shirt for all First Premier cared. In summer he wore his tie over a short-sleeved shirt. In winter he wore it under a V-necked jumper. Every couple of days or so, I vowed to ask him why he was devoted to that one item of clothing. I never followed through, partly because I was afraid he would tell me that it had been a present from his childhood sweetheart who had died in a tragic boating accident (or something), and partly because I didn't want him to think that I was interested in being his friend. Eddie wasn't exactly the type who set the room on fire when he walked in – not unless he accidentally knocked over a candle while creeping round the edge of the group, looking for a place to hide. I wasn't proud of the attitude I had towards him. Certainly not. But I rationalised it by telling myself that most people probably had someone like that in their lives, a colleague, a neighbour, a familiar face on the bus.

Someone they suspected to be a little bit sad, a little bit lonely. Someone they could possibly cheer up quite a bit, if only they'd take the time. But they didn't, and I didn't, for fear that the lonely person might start appearing on the doorstep, suggesting nights out or, worse, weekends away. Best to just smile politely and shimmy past them, that's what we all told ourselves. I smiled politely at Eddie when he showed up that morning and if I hadn't been sitting down, I would have shimmied past as well.

"Hello," he said. "Are you okay?"

I gave him a smile every bit as fake as the one Jenny had worn earlier. "I'm fine, why?"

He shrugged and cast his eyes to the right. "I dunno. You seem a bit . . . you know . . ." He pointed with his head. "Your knuckles are all white."

I loosened my grip on the desk and went into my drawer for headache tablets. "I'm okay, Eddie, really. Just a bit tense, that's all."

He nodded. "Is it because of your hair?"

On the Monday of that week I'd shown up in wicked humour on account of a weekend haircut that had gone seriously awry. My usual girl had called in sick at the last minute, but rather than make a new appointment, I'd gone ahead with another stylist. I should have known better. The replacement stank of last night's booze and seemed to be having trouble forming proper sentences ("Have you been to holiday this year, have you?" she asked me at one point). She was still drunk, I was absolutely sure of it. Long story short, I wound up with a hairstyle like Stephen Fry's. It had annoyed me for a few days, naturally, but I had more or less forgotten about it until that moment.

"No, Eddie," I said, "it's nothing to do with my hair." I wasn't at all disturbed by his contribution. He wasn't trying to be malicious or even amusing. He could see that I was upset and he knew that I'd been unhappy about my hair. He'd put the two together, that was all. He was really *asking*.

"Okay," Eddie said and smiled for a fraction of a second. He tore off then, as if frightened by a loud noise.

I watched his back as he made his way to the photocopier, wondering if that was the longest conversation he'd had all morning. Then I told myself that I was inventing a sob story where one didn't necessarily exist. For all I knew, Eddie spent his evenings sipping champagne in fancy restaurants with a succession of sex-addicted lingerie models. When I turned back to face my computer, Veronica was half-standing again and making kissy faces. It was her firm conviction that Eddie fancied me. She seemed to have based this theory on nothing but the fact that once in a blue moon, the previous incident being a prime example, he spoke to me without my speaking to him first. He didn't do that with anyone else, not according to Veronica at any rate.

"*Eddie and Jackie up a tree!*" she chanted. "*K-I-S-S-I–*"

I threw the cap of a yellow highlighter at her and was pleased to see it bounce off her forehead and land in her coffee.

If I hadn't found the e-mail straight away, I might have given up and turned to the eight-inch-high pile of data that was teetering by my left elbow, waiting to be entered. My stress level would still have gone up, no doubt, but it wouldn't have instantly doubled the way it did when I got a look at the e-mail. The gist of the thing was this: tardiness had become a serious problem for First Premier and was affecting its ability to meet targets, going forward (as opposed to backwards or sideways). Management weren't callous, unfeeling monsters – as if – and could forgive an occasional five-minute slip-up here and there. However! Persistent offenders could no longer expect to get away scot-free. The new system (they called it a system four times) was points-based. If you arrived for work five to ten minutes late, you got a single point. Ten to fifteen minutes late, got you five of them. Fifteen to thirty, you got ten. Half an hour plus, you got twenty. Anyone who scored more than thirty points in a month had to do a forfeit. At that point the e-mail stopped being irritating and started being excruciating. In a breezy, matey I-Can't-Believe-We-Get-Paid-To-Work-Here! tone, it revealed that transgressors would be obliged to wear a special tardiness hat for one whole working day. Anyone who refused to play along would be excluded from all social club activities until they did what had been asked of them. They would also be named and shamed as a "spoilsport". There was a photo attached to the e-mail. It showed a dunce's cap with a letter T where the D should have been. When I finished reading, all I felt was relief. I didn't give two hoots, one hoot even, about the social club; if I really wanted to go to a pub quiz or karaoke night, I was sure I'd be able to organise it myself. And, I thought, they could name me every day until 2050, I'd still never be shamed. This meant that I could ignore the entire policy, hat and all. The relief didn't last long though. It was swept away almost immediately by bitter, jagged anger. Why hadn't they just declared that employees who were consistently late would be chucked out of the social club? Or fired, for that matter? Why bother with all the nonsense in between? Why did it have to be "fun"? It was Fancy Dress Friday all over again. That was a one-off event that had brightened all our lives a few months previously (it wasn't supposed to be a one-off; it just worked out that way). I didn't know how it had gone company-wide, but in Data Entry there were precisely three takers, out of a possible thirty-something. Jenny came as Wonder Woman and a bloke called Terry came as a vampire. They looked ridiculous, of course, mooching from their desks to the water cooler and back, but at least they had hired proper costumes. The third participant was Eddie. He came as a Roman gladiator in a bunch of kit he'd made himself out of cardboard, tinfoil and other cardboard. Not once, all day long, did he remove his helmet. It had taken him several hours to perfect, he said, and he was determined to get good wear out of it.

"Did you read this rubbish about the tardiness hat?" I called out to Veronica.

She looked up from her keyboard. I could see the top half of her head over the partition. The top half of her head looked surprised.

"Yeah," she said. "I saw it a fortnight ago with the rest of the company. Did you hear about John Lennon? Shot dead!"

I ignored the last part and went back to fuming. It was just about then that the first six-inch nail was driven into my skull. I had no sooner registered the news that my day was going from bad to much, much worse when my mobile phone jangled in my handbag. The caller was Robert, my eldest (by twelve minutes). I couldn't remember the last time he had called me and said something I wanted to hear. The smart thing to do, I told myself, would be to ignore it and get back to my impending headache. But it's never easy to ignore your own flesh and blood. And so, like an eejit, I answered the damn thing.